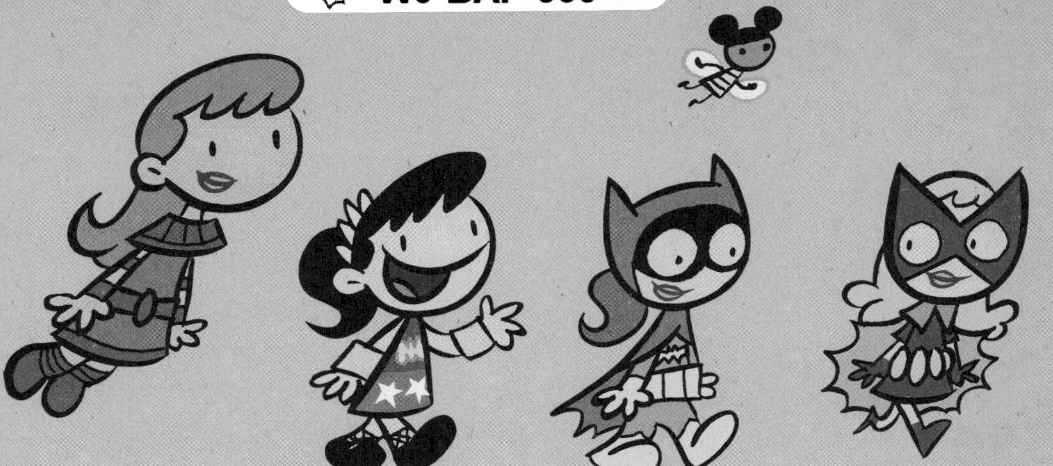

tiny titans
FIELD TRIPPIN'

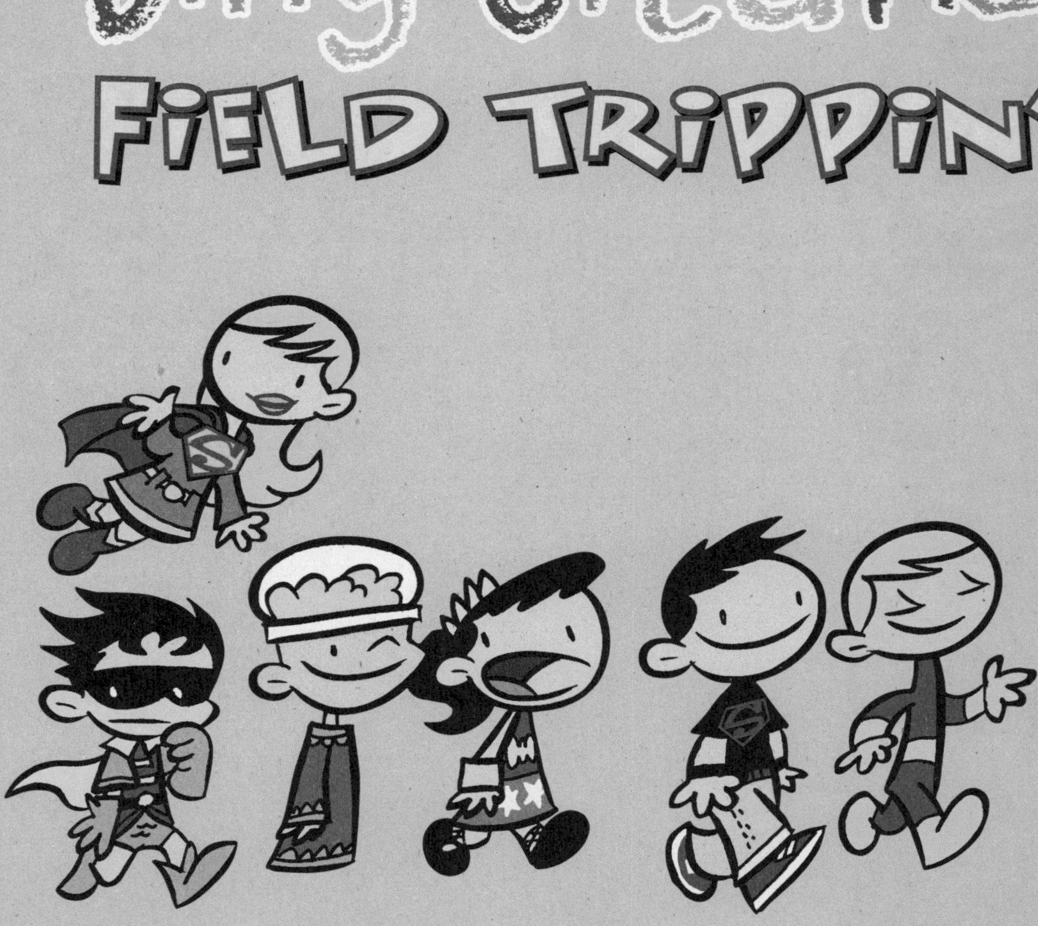

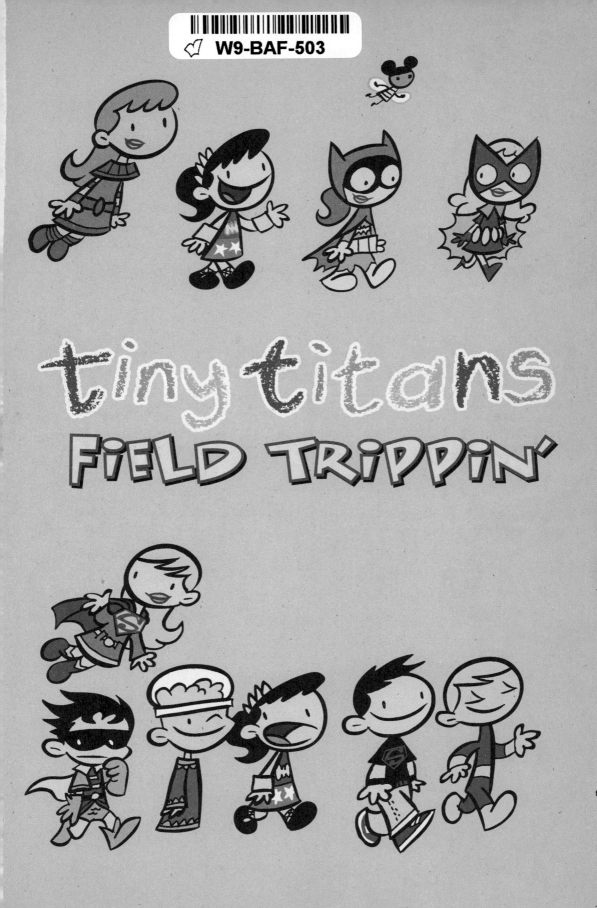

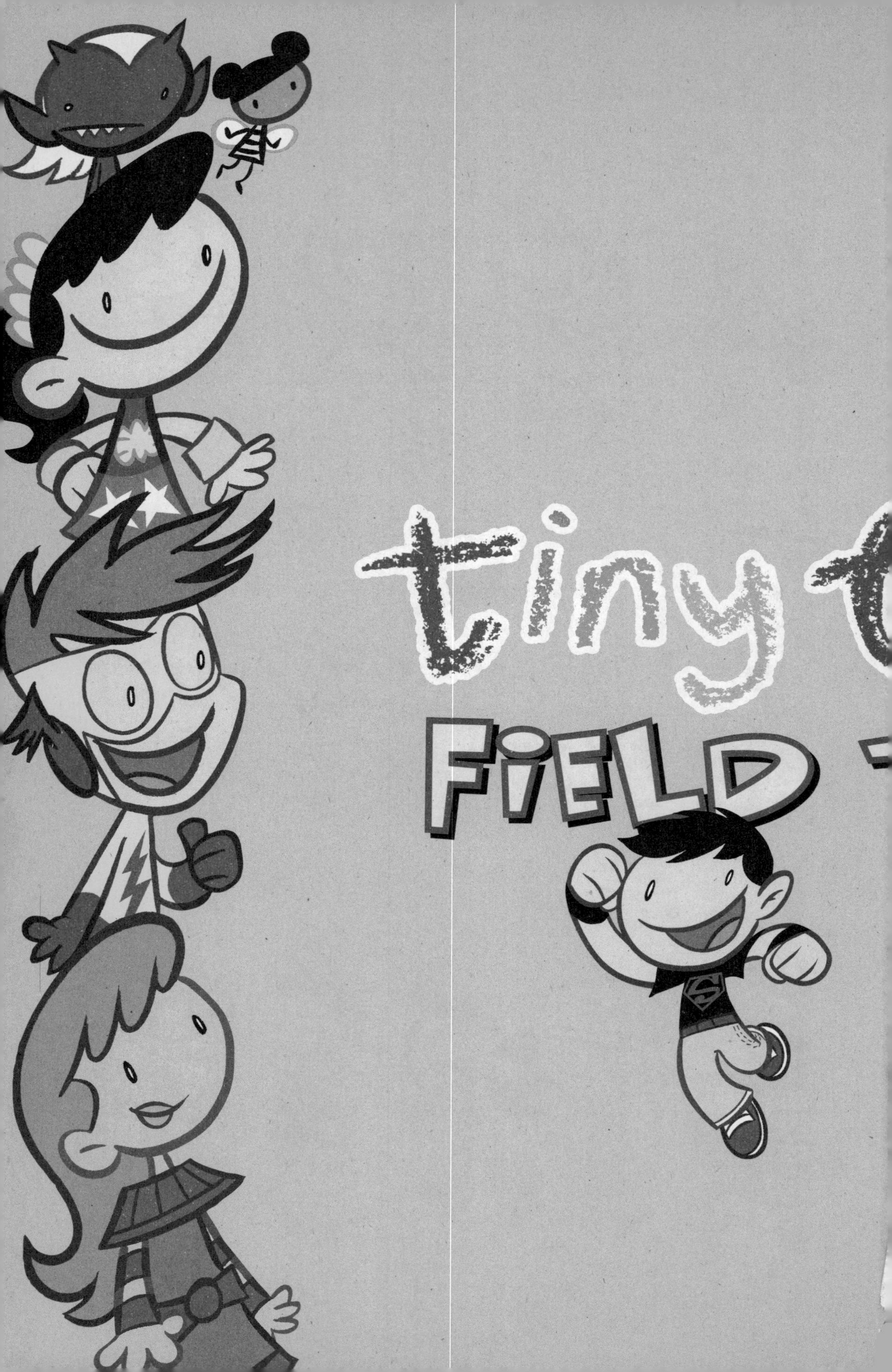
tiny
FIELD

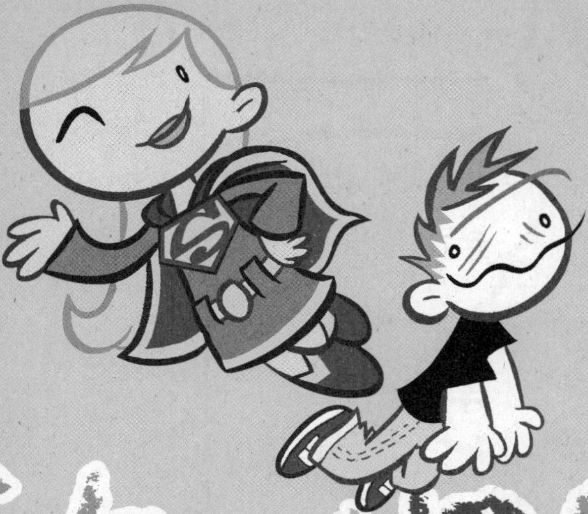

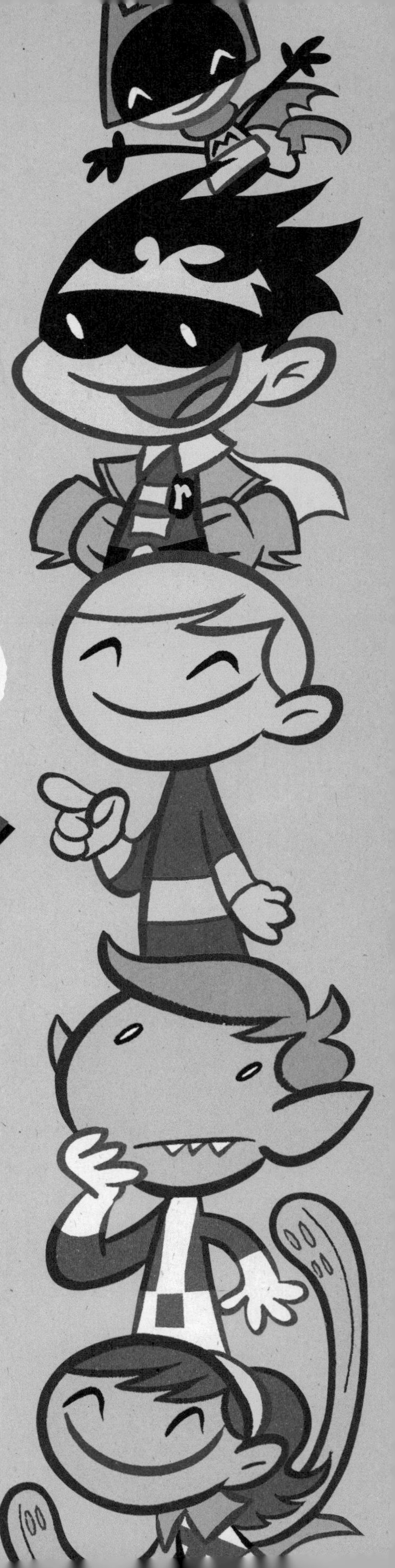

itans

'RiPPiN'

Art Baltazar & Franco
Writers

Art Baltazar
Artist & Letterer

Elisabeth V. Gehrlein Kristy Quinn Chynna Clugston-Flores Editors-original series
Bob Harras Group Editor-Collected Editions
Robbin Brosterman Design Director-Books

DC COMICS
Diane Nelson President
Dan DiDio and **Jim Lee** Co-Publishers
Geoff Johns Chief Creative Officer
Patrick Caldon EVP-Finance and Administration
John Rood EVP-Sales, Marketing and Business Development
Amy Genkins SVP-Business and Legal Affairs
Steve Rotterdam SVP-Sales and Marketing
John Cunningham VP-Marketing
Terri Cunningham VP-Managing Editor
Alison Gill VP-Manufacturing
David Hyde VP-Publicity
Sue Pohja VP-Book Trade Sales
Alysse Soll VP-Advertising and Custom Publishing
Bob Wayne VP-Sales
Mark Chiarello Art Director

TINY TITANS: FIELD TRIPPIN'
Published by DC Comics. Cover and compilation Copyright © 2011 DC Comics.
All Rights Reserved.

Originally published in single magazine form in TINY TITANS 26-32.
Copyright © 2010 DC Comics. All Rights Reserved. All characters, their distinctive
likenesses and related elements featured in this publication are trademarks of
DC Comics. The stories, characters and incidents featured in this publication are
entirely fictional. DC Comics does not read or accept unsolicited submissions of
ideas, stories or artwork.

DC Comics, 1700 Broadway, New York, NY 10019
A Warner Bros. Entertainment Company
Printed by Quad/Graphics, Dubuque, IA, USA. 4/1/11. First Printing.
ISBN: 978-1-4012-3173-6

SUSTAINABLE
FORESTRY
INITIATIVE
Certified Fiber Sourcing
www.sfiprogram.org
Fiber used in this product line meets the
sourcing requirements of the SFI program.
www.sfiprogram.org SGS-SFICOC-0130

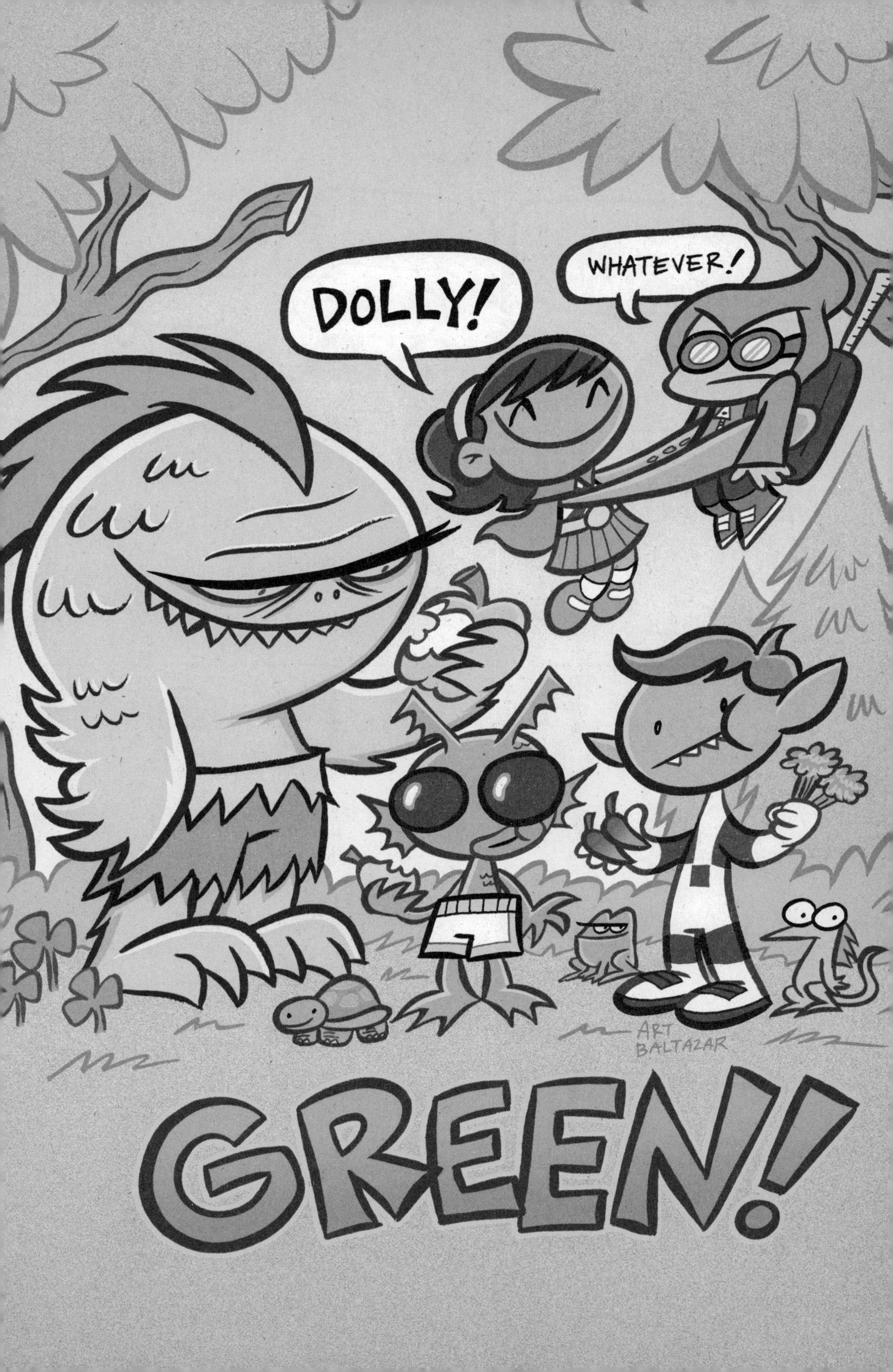
DOLLY!
WHATEVER!
ART BALTAZAR
GREEN!

tiny titans

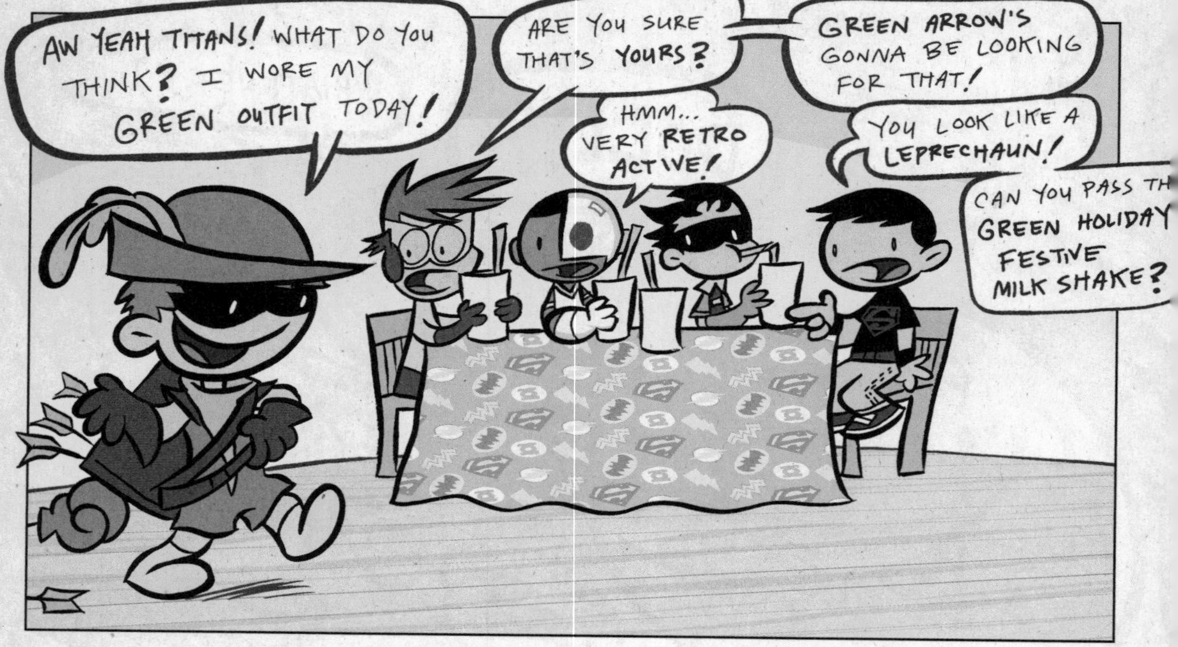
AW YEAH TITANS! WHAT DO YOU THINK? I WORE MY GREEN OUTFIT TODAY!
ARE YOU SURE THAT'S YOURS?
HMM... VERY RETRO ACTIVE!
GREEN ARROW'S GONNA BE LOOKING FOR THAT!
YOU LOOK LIKE A LEPRECHAUN!
CAN YOU PASS TH GREEN HOLIDAY FESTIVE MILK SHAKE?

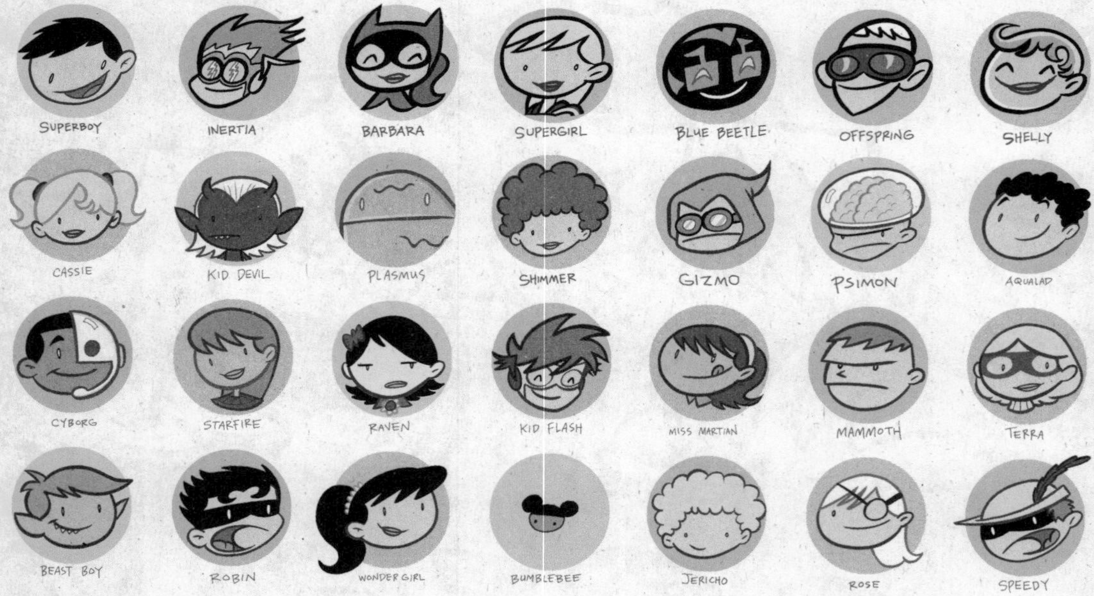
SUPERBOY
INERTIA
BARBARA
SUPERGIRL
BLUE BEETLE
OFFSPRING
SHELLY
CASSIE
KID DEVIL
PLASMUS
SHIMMER
GIZMO
PSIMON
AQUALAD
CYBORG
STARFIRE
RAVEN
KID FLASH
MISS MARTIAN
MAMMOTH
TERRA
BEAST BOY
ROBIN
WONDER GIRL
BUMBLEBEE
JERICHO
ROSE
SPEEDY

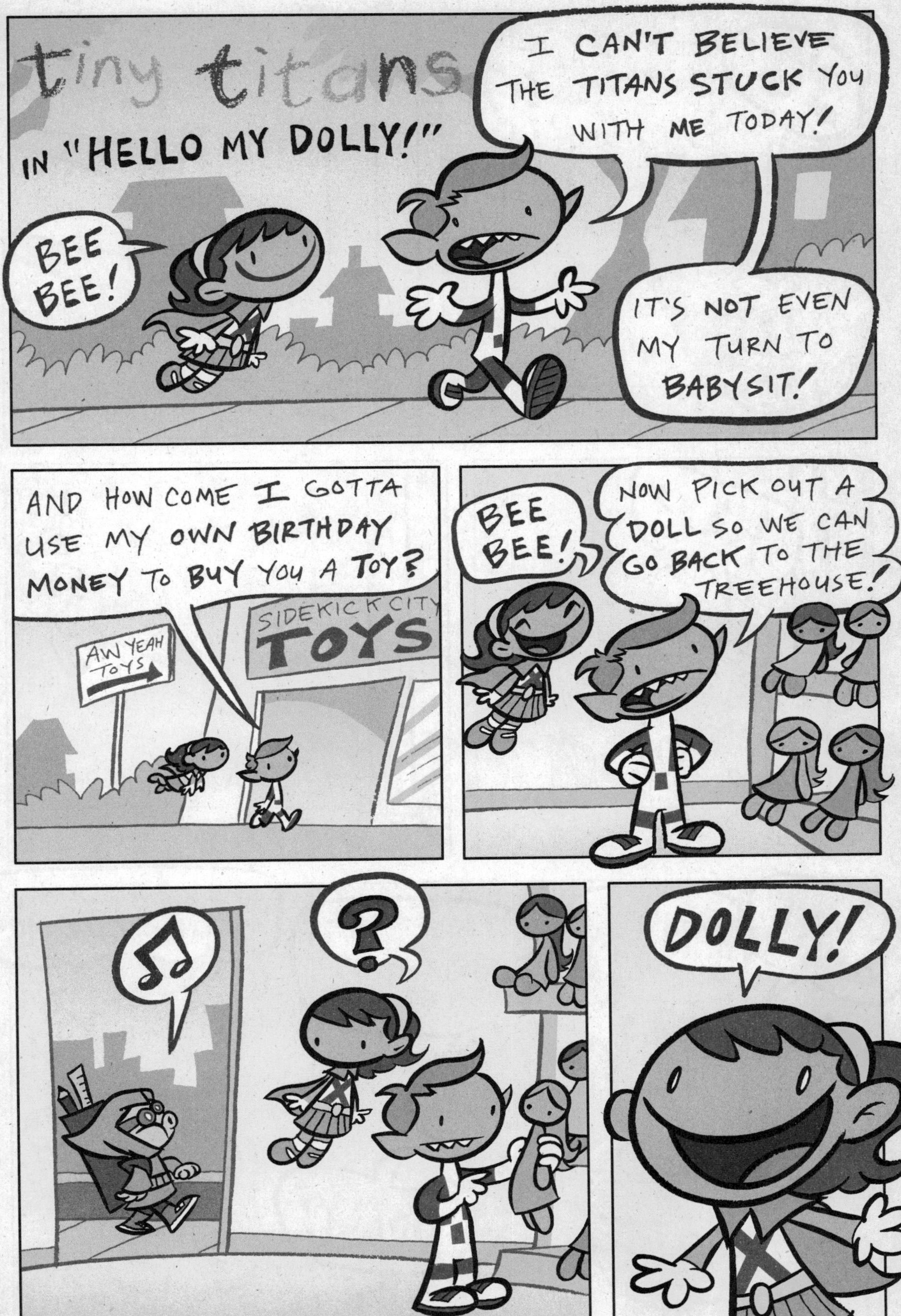
tiny titans
IN "HELLO MY DOLLY!"
I CAN'T BELIEVE THE TITANS STUCK YOU WITH ME TODAY!
IT'S NOT EVEN MY TURN TO BABYSIT!
BEE BEE!
AND HOW COME I GOTTA USE MY OWN BIRTHDAY MONEY TO BUY YOU A TOY?
SIDEKICK CITY TOYS
AW YEAH TOYS
BEE BEE!
NOW PICK OUT A DOLL SO WE CAN GO BACK TO THE TREEHOUSE!
?
DOLLY!

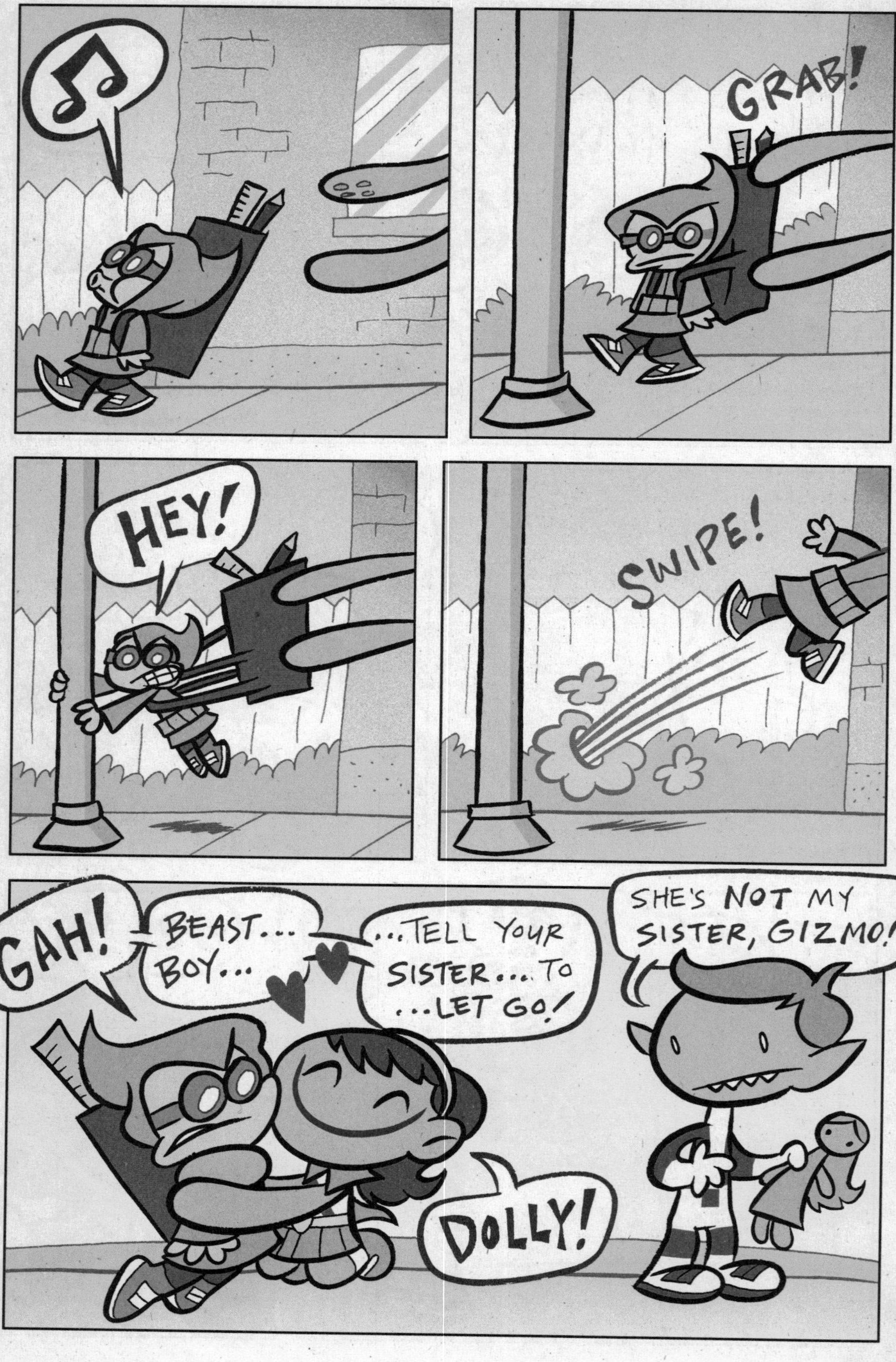
♫
GRAB!
HEY!
SWIPE!
GAH!
BEAST... BOY...
...TELL YOUR SISTER... TO ...LET GO!
SHE'S NOT MY SISTER, GIZMO!
DOLLY!

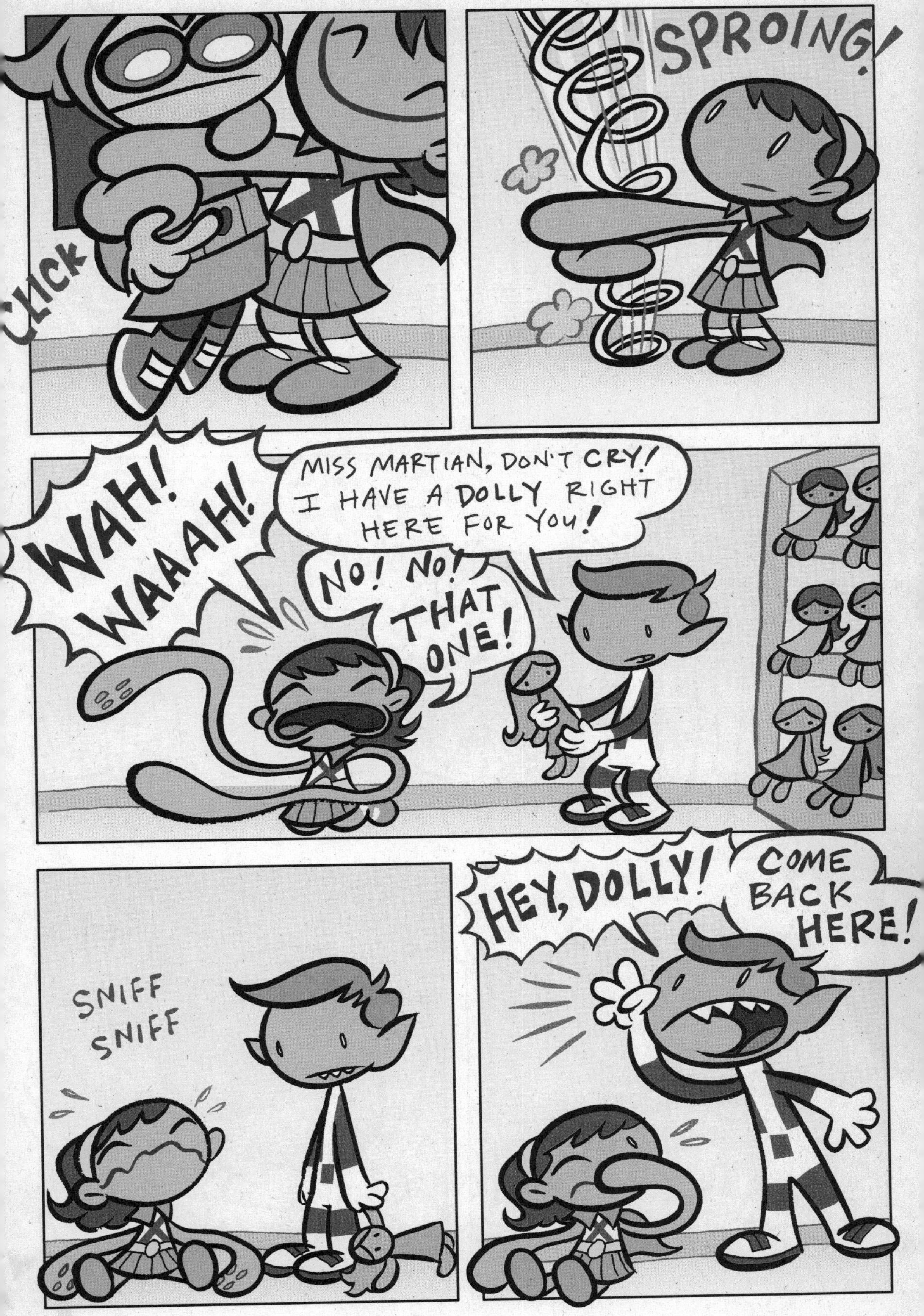
CLICK
SPROING!
WAH! WAAAH!
MISS MARTIAN, DON'T CRY! I HAVE A DOLLY RIGHT HERE FOR YOU!
NO! NO! THAT ONE!
SNIFF SNIFF
HEY, DOLLY!
COME BACK HERE!

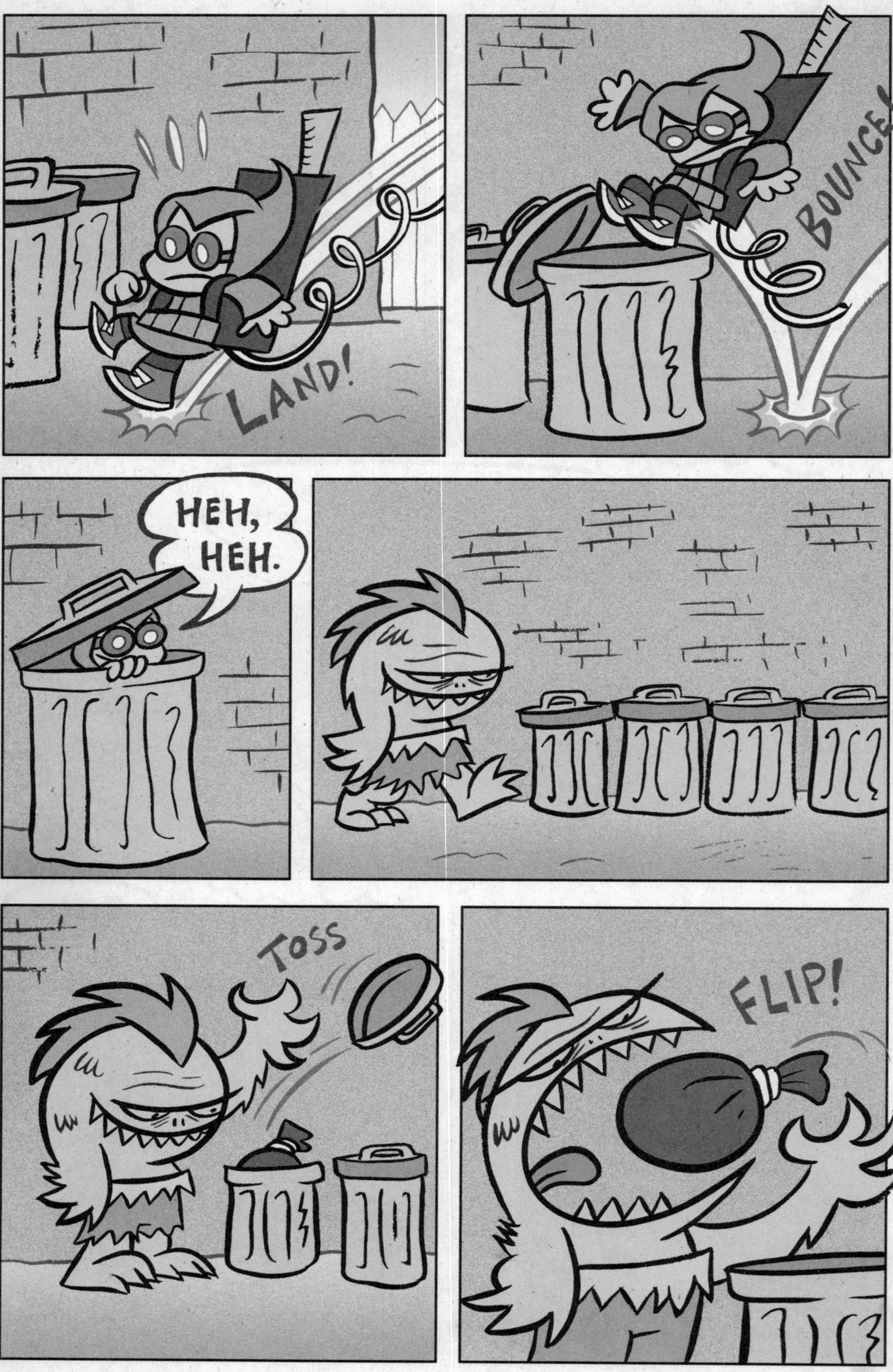
LAND!
BOUNCE!
HEH, HEH.
TOSS
FLIP!

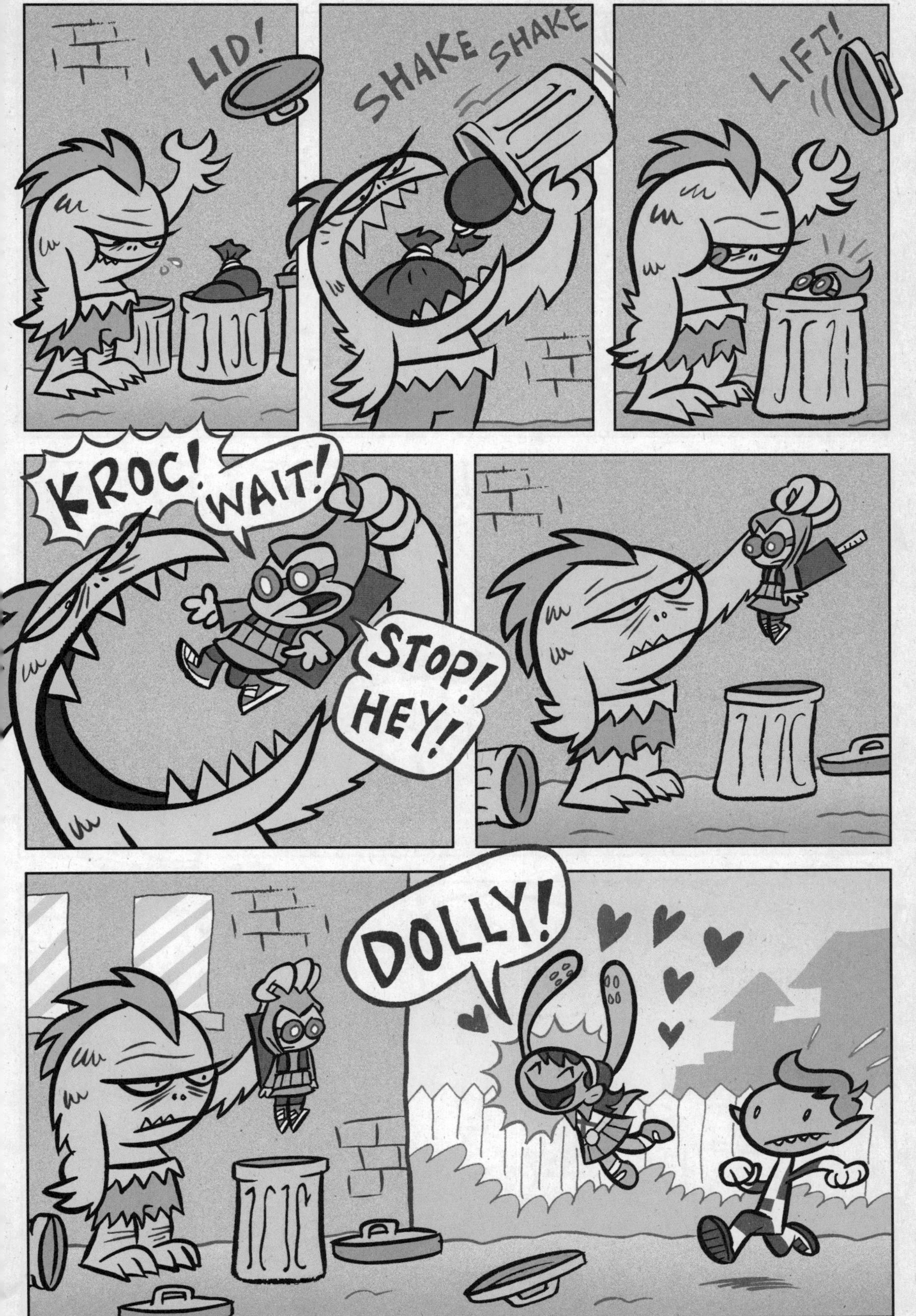
LID!
SHAKE SHAKE
LIFT!
KROC!
WAIT!
STOP! HEY!
DOLLY!

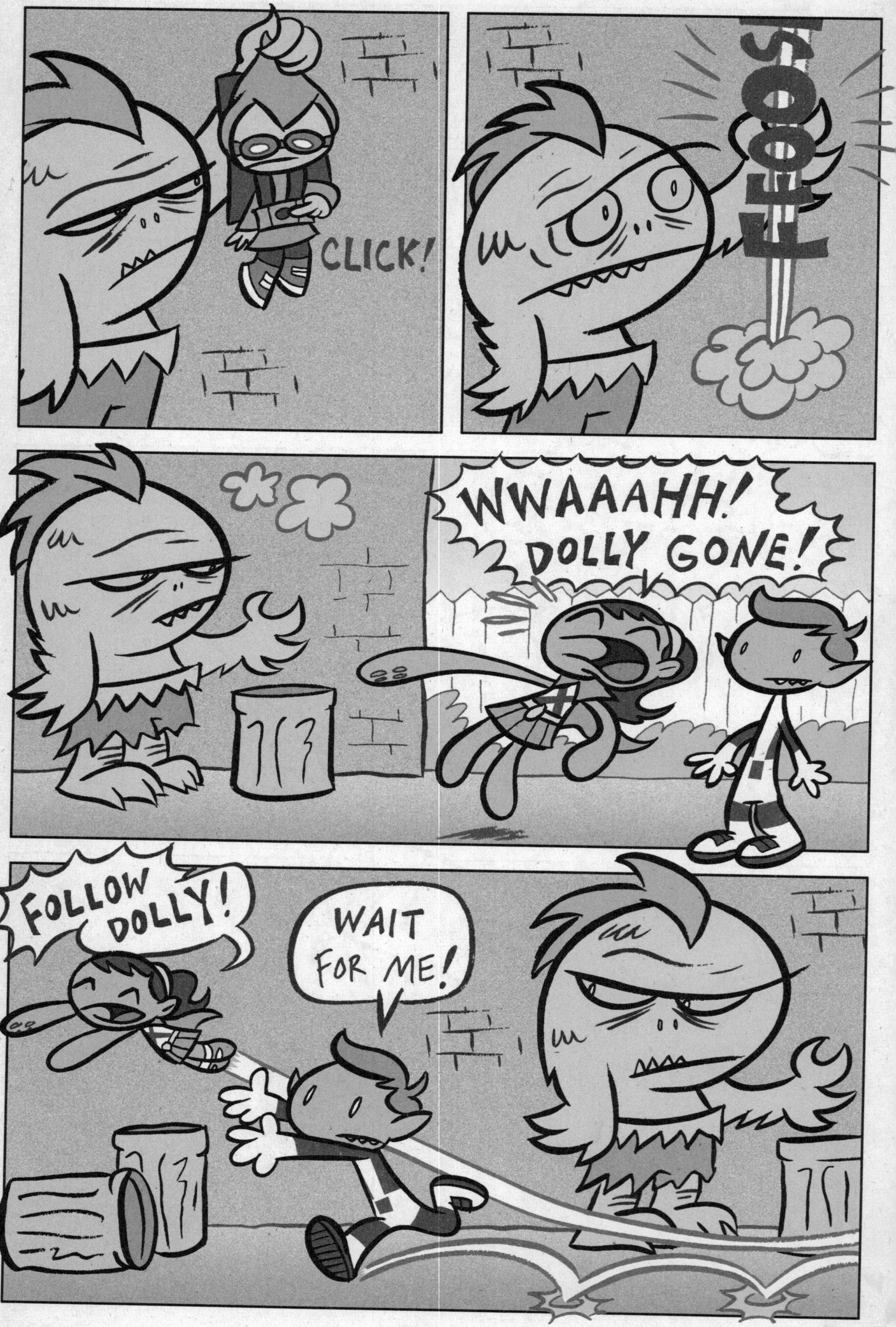
CLICK!
FOOSH
WWAAAHH! DOLLY GONE!
FOLLOW DOLLY!
WAIT FOR ME!

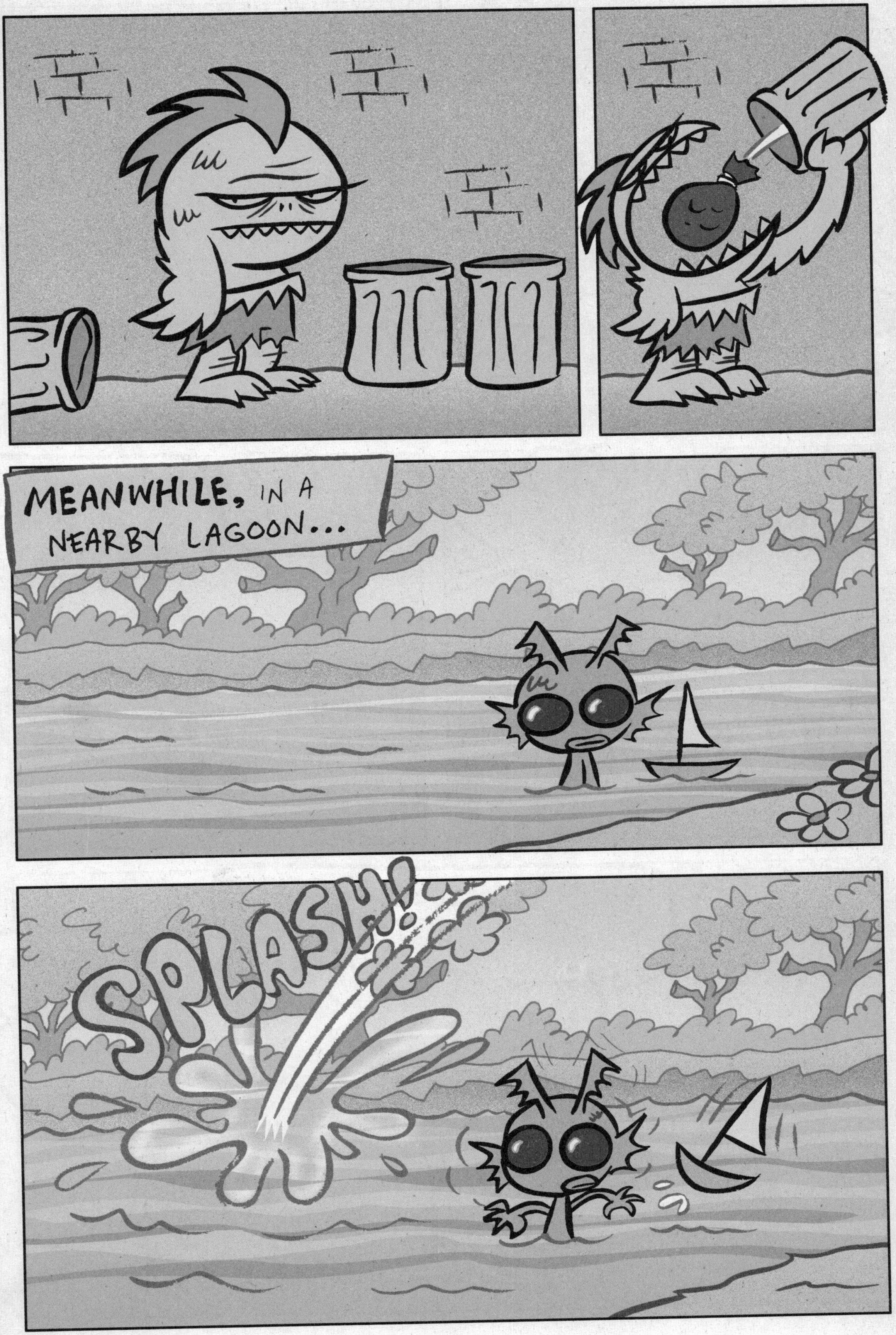
MEANWHILE, IN A NEARBY LAGOON...
SPLASH!

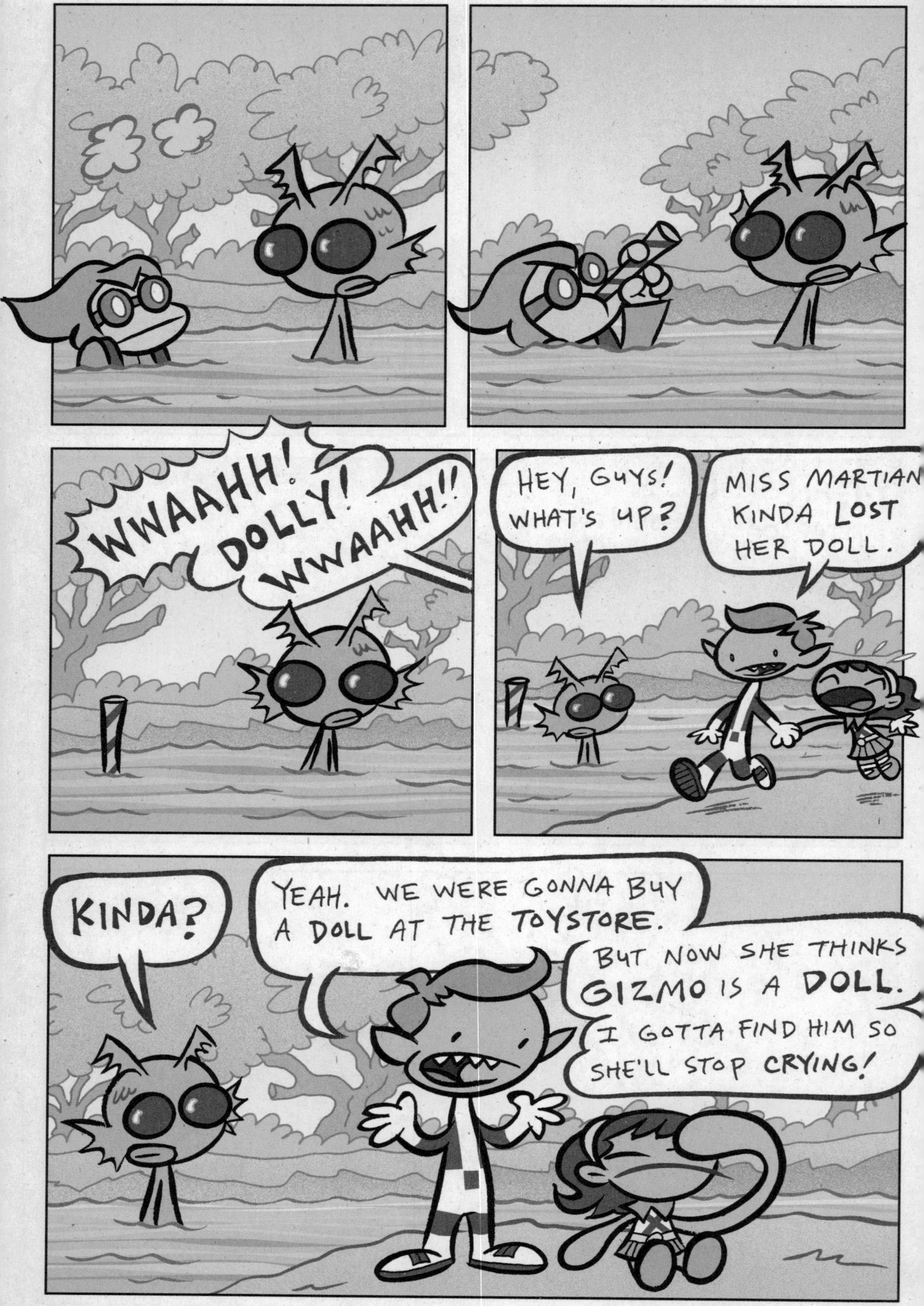
WWAAHH! DOLLY! WWAAHH!!
HEY, GUYS! WHAT'S UP?
MISS MARTIAN KINDA LOST HER DOLL.
KINDA?
YEAH. WE WERE GONNA BUY A DOLL AT THE TOYSTORE.
BUT NOW SHE THINKS GIZMO IS A DOLL.
I GOTTA FIND HIM SO SHE'LL STOP CRYING!

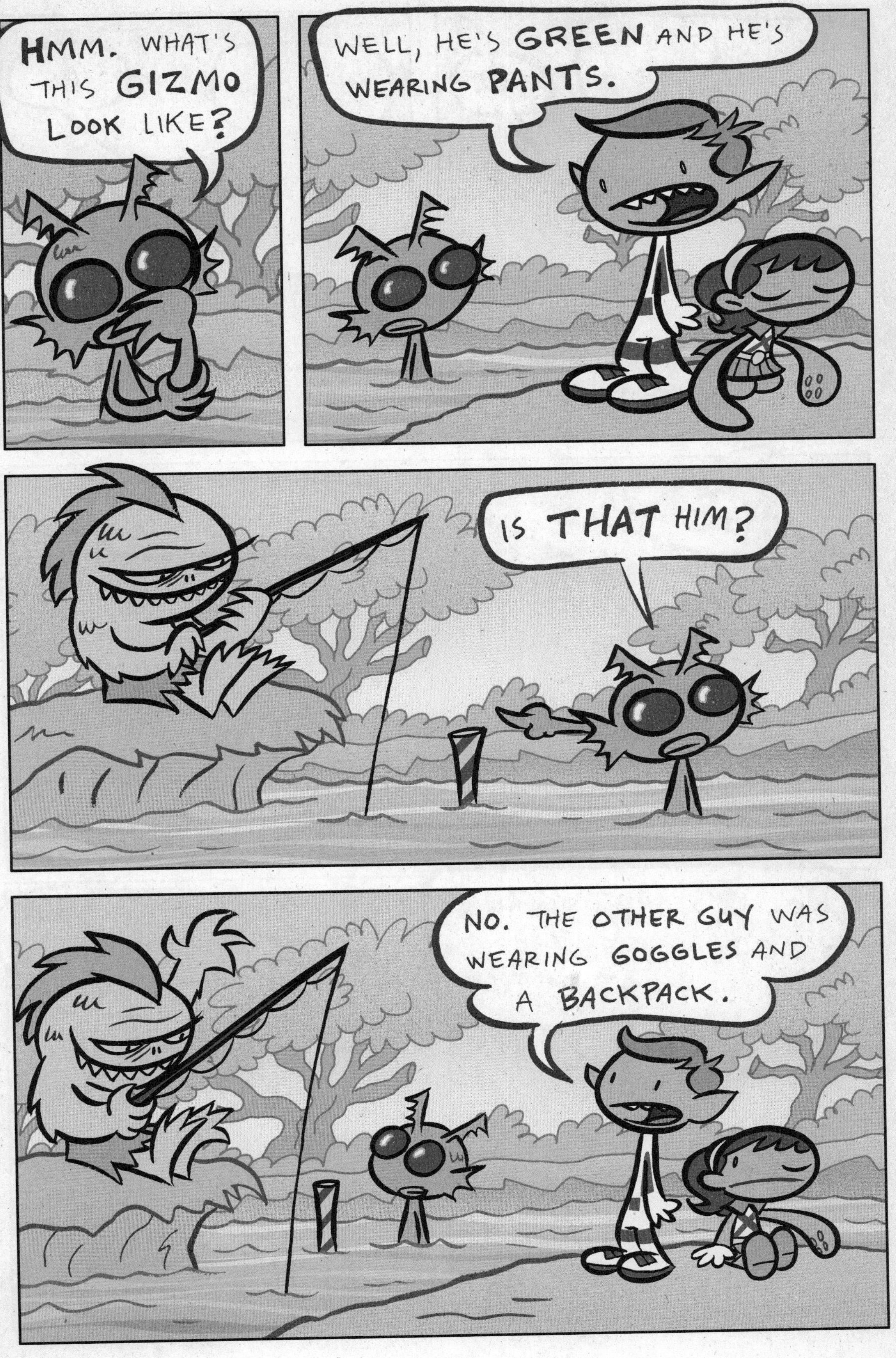
HMM. WHAT'S THIS GIZMO LOOK LIKE?
WELL, HE'S GREEN AND HE'S WEARING PANTS.
IS THAT HIM?
NO. THE OTHER GUY WAS WEARING GOGGLES AND A BACKPACK.

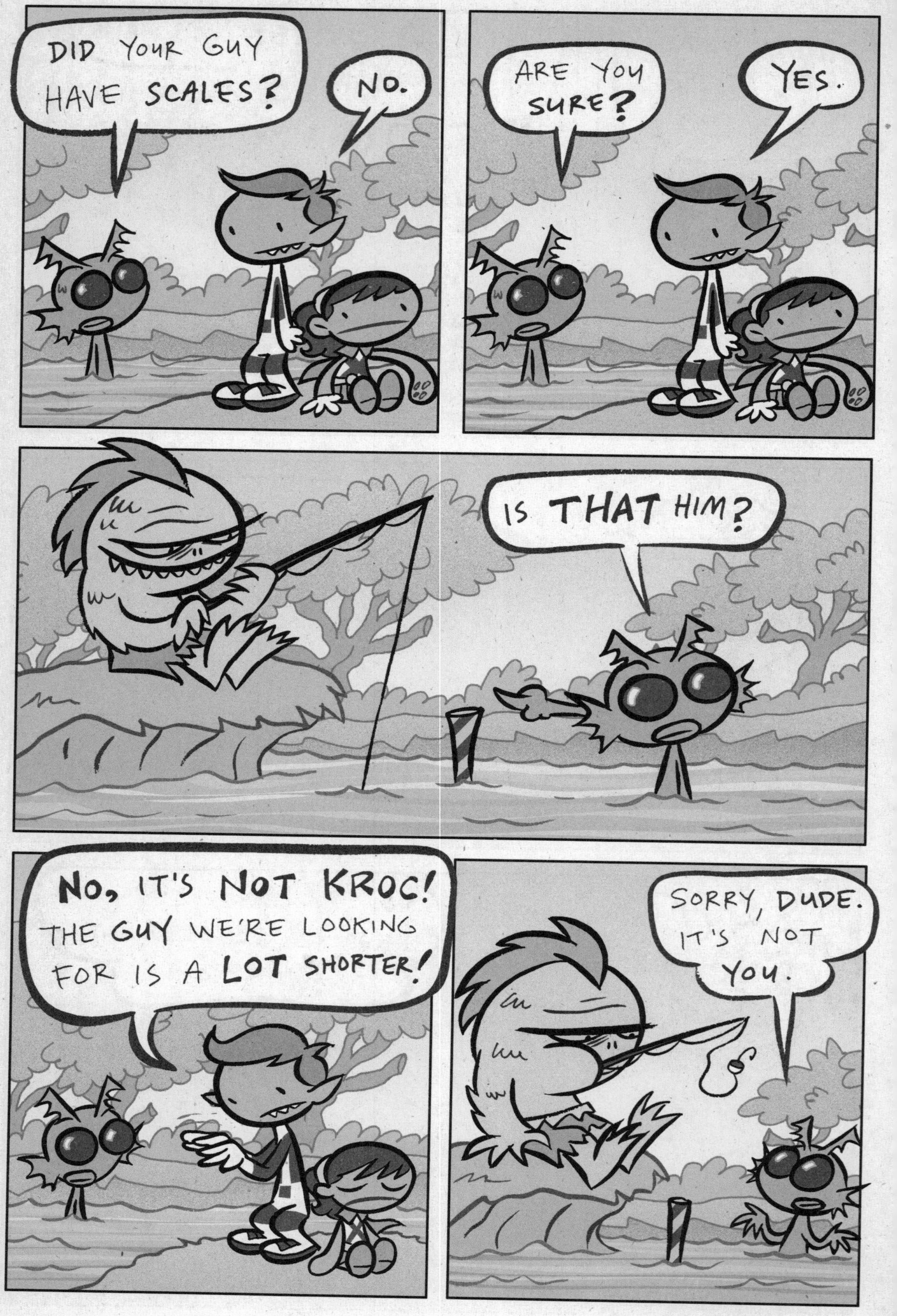
DID YOUR GUY HAVE SCALES?
NO.
ARE YOU SURE?
YES.
IS THAT HIM?
NO, IT'S NOT KROC! THE GUY WE'RE LOOKING FOR IS A LOT SHORTER!
SORRY, DUDE. IT'S NOT YOU.

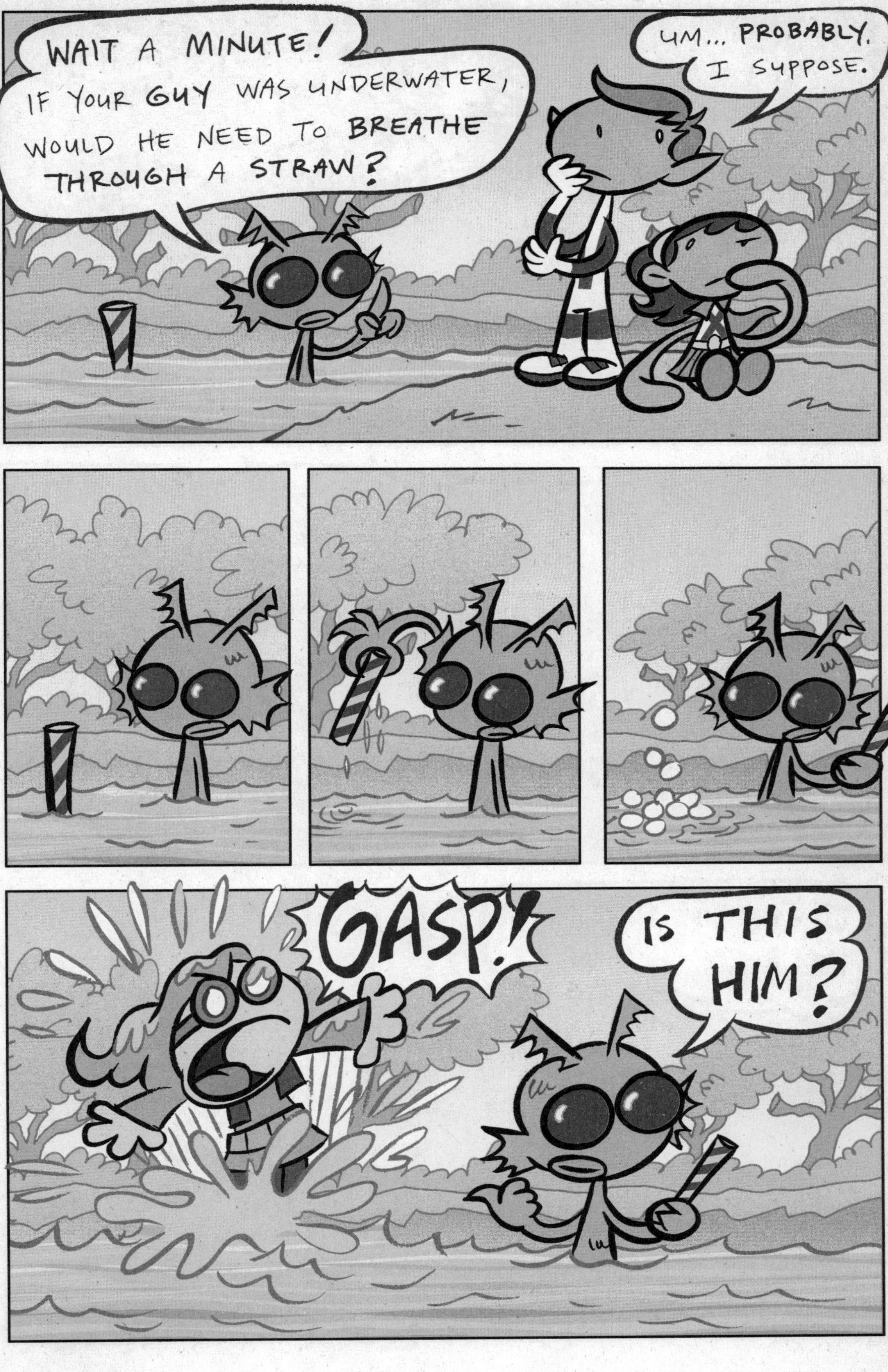
WAIT A MINUTE! IF YOUR GUY WAS UNDERWATER, WOULD HE NEED TO BREATHE THROUGH A STRAW?
UM... PROBABLY. I SUPPOSE.
GASP!
IS THIS HIM?

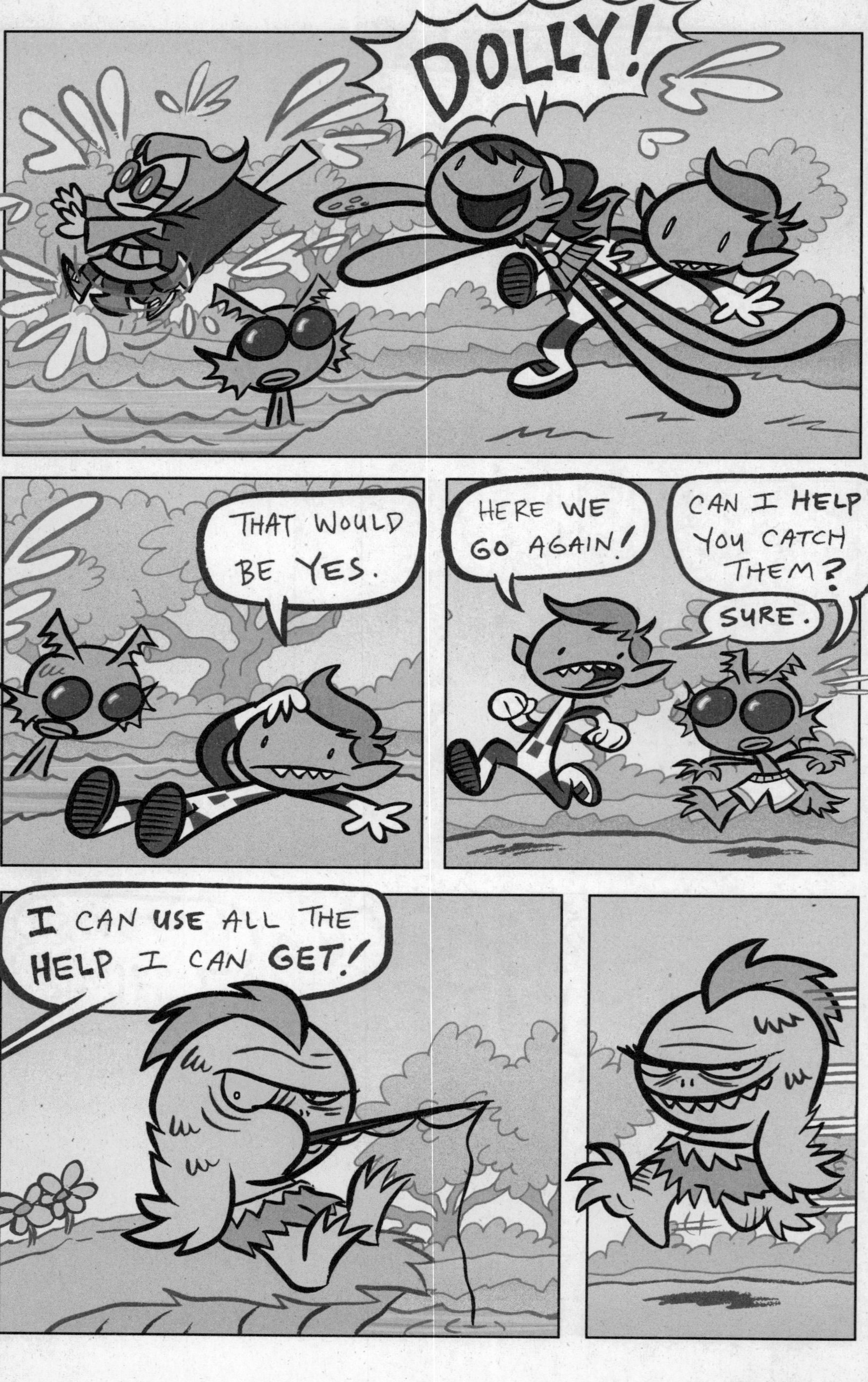
DOLLY!
THAT WOULD BE YES.
HERE WE GO AGAIN!
CAN I HELP YOU CATCH THEM?
SURE.
I CAN USE ALL THE HELP I CAN GET!

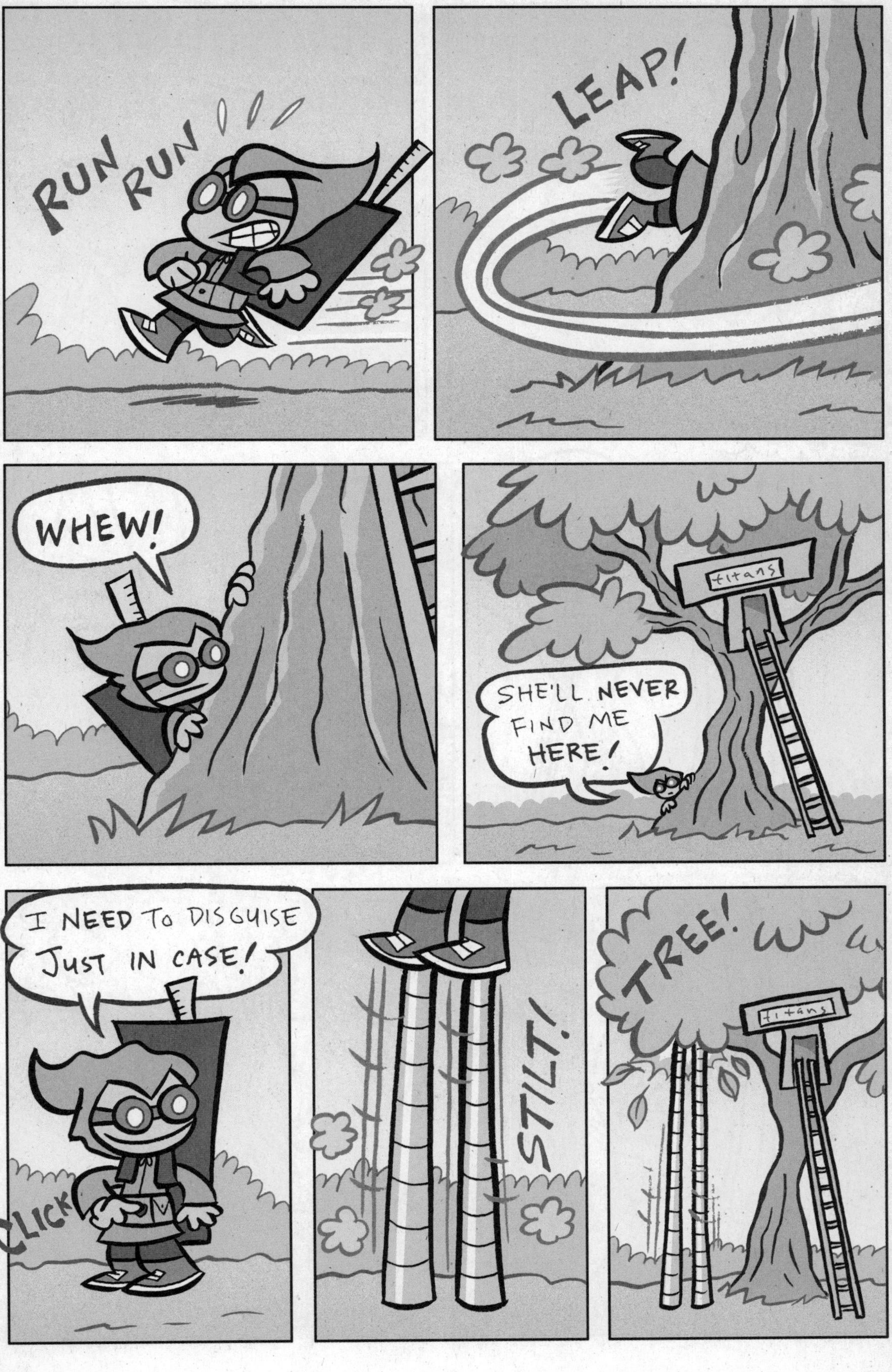
RUN RUN
LEAP!
WHEW!
SHE'LL NEVER FIND ME HERE!
titans
I NEED TO DISGUISE JUST IN CASE!
CLICK
STILT!
TREE!
titans

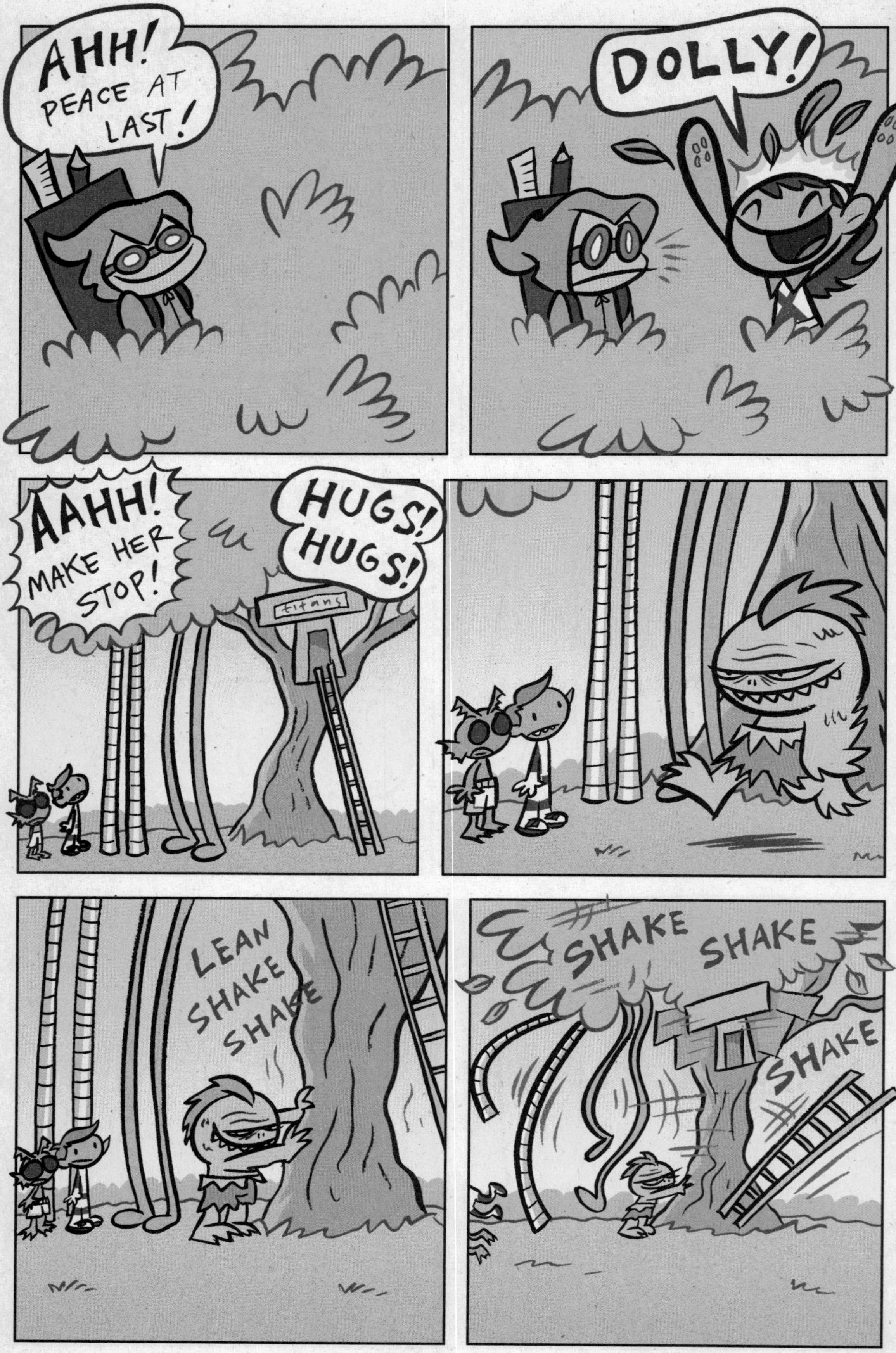
AHH! PEACE AT LAST!
DOLLY!
AAHH! MAKE HER STOP!
HUGS! HUGS!
titans
LEAN
SHAKE
SHAKE
SHAKE
SHAKE
SHAKE

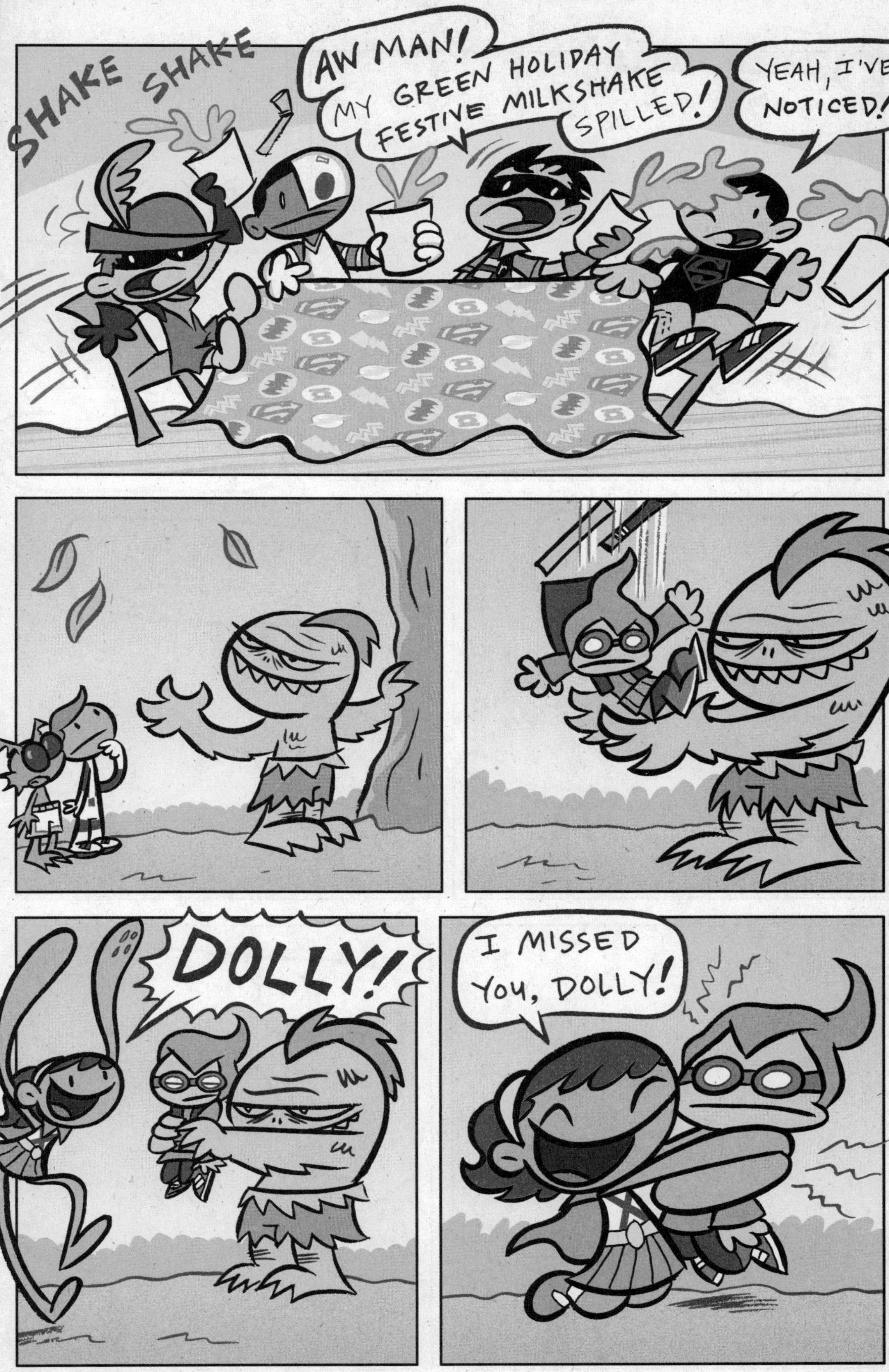
SHAKE SHAKE
AW MAN! MY GREEN HOLIDAY FESTIVE MILKSHAKE SPILLED!
YEAH, I'VE NOTICED!
DOLLY!
I MISSED YOU, DOLLY!

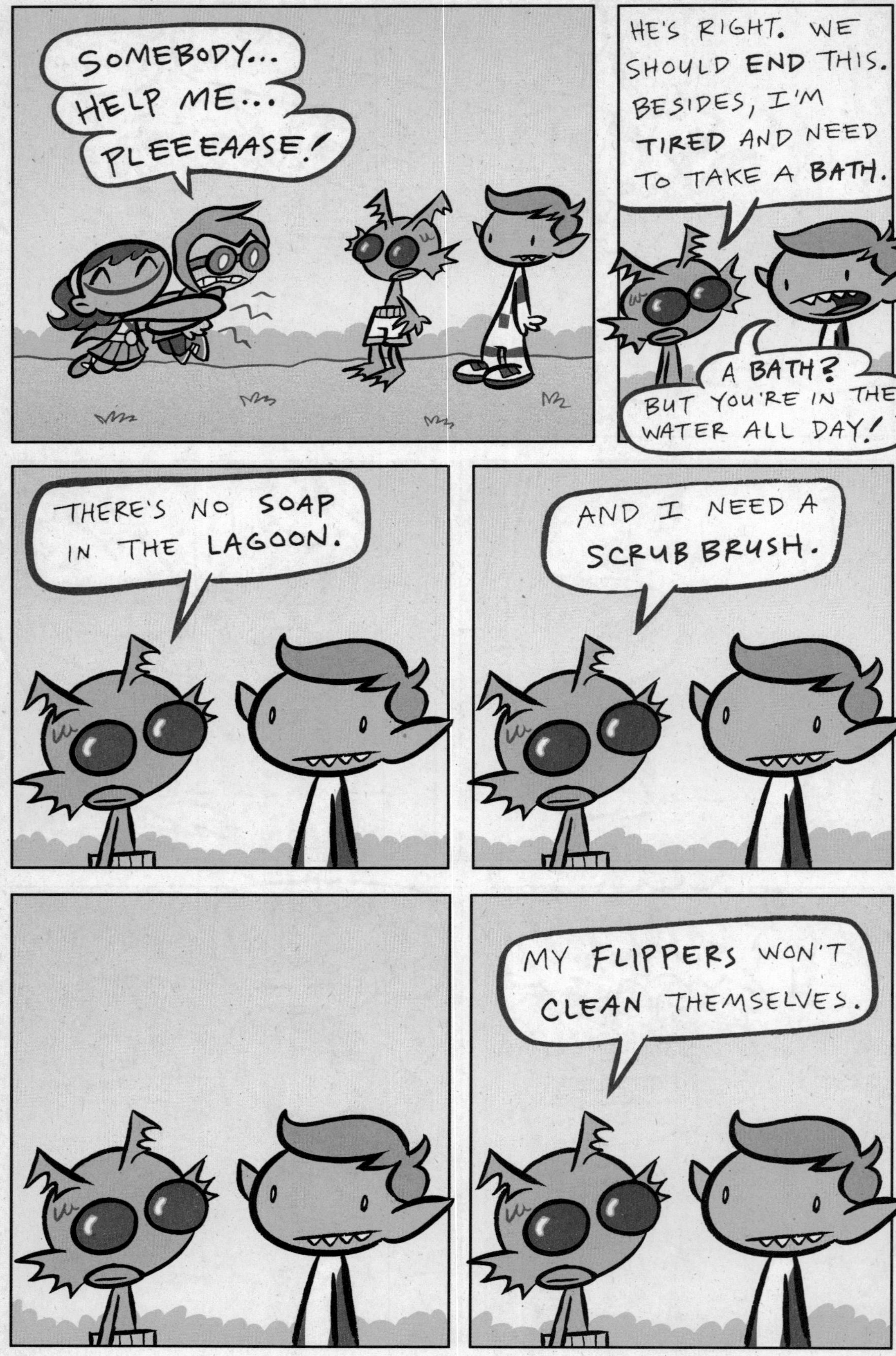
SOMEBODY... HELP ME... PLEEEAAASE!
HE'S RIGHT. WE SHOULD END THIS. BESIDES, I'M TIRED AND NEED TO TAKE A BATH.
A BATH? BUT YOU'RE IN THE WATER ALL DAY!
THERE'S NO SOAP IN THE LAGOON.
AND I NEED A SCRUB BRUSH.
MY FLIPPERS WON'T CLEAN THEMSELVES.

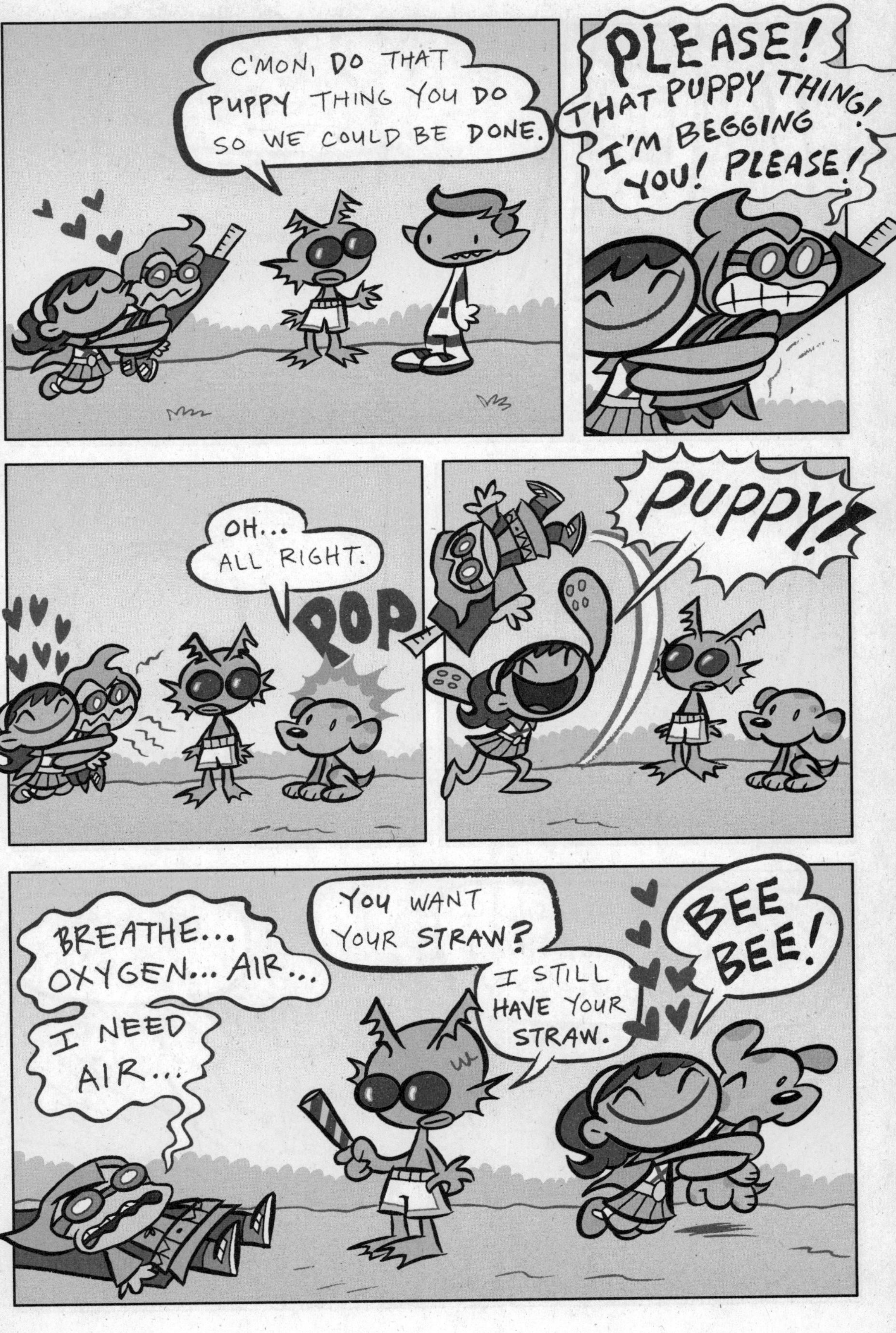

C'MON, DO THAT PUPPY THING YOU DO SO WE COULD BE DONE.
PLEASE! THAT PUPPY THING! I'M BEGGING YOU! PLEASE!
OH... ALL RIGHT.
POP
PUPPY!
BREATHE... OXYGEN... AIR...
I NEED AIR...
YOU WANT YOUR STRAW?
I STILL HAVE YOUR STRAW.
BEE BEE!

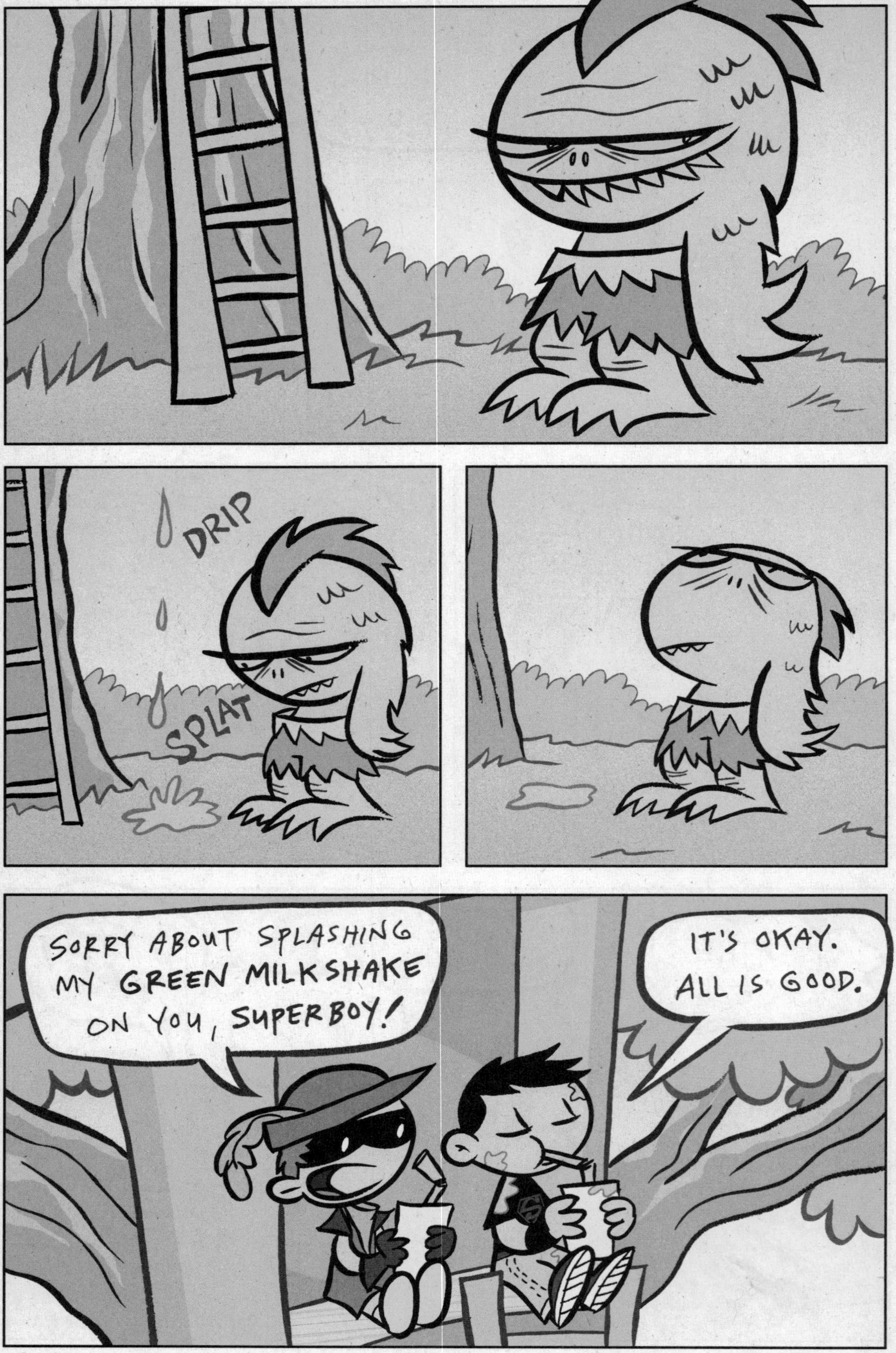
DRIP
SPLAT
SORRY ABOUT SPLASHING MY GREEN MILKSHAKE ON YOU, SUPERBOY!
IT'S OKAY. ALL IS GOOD.

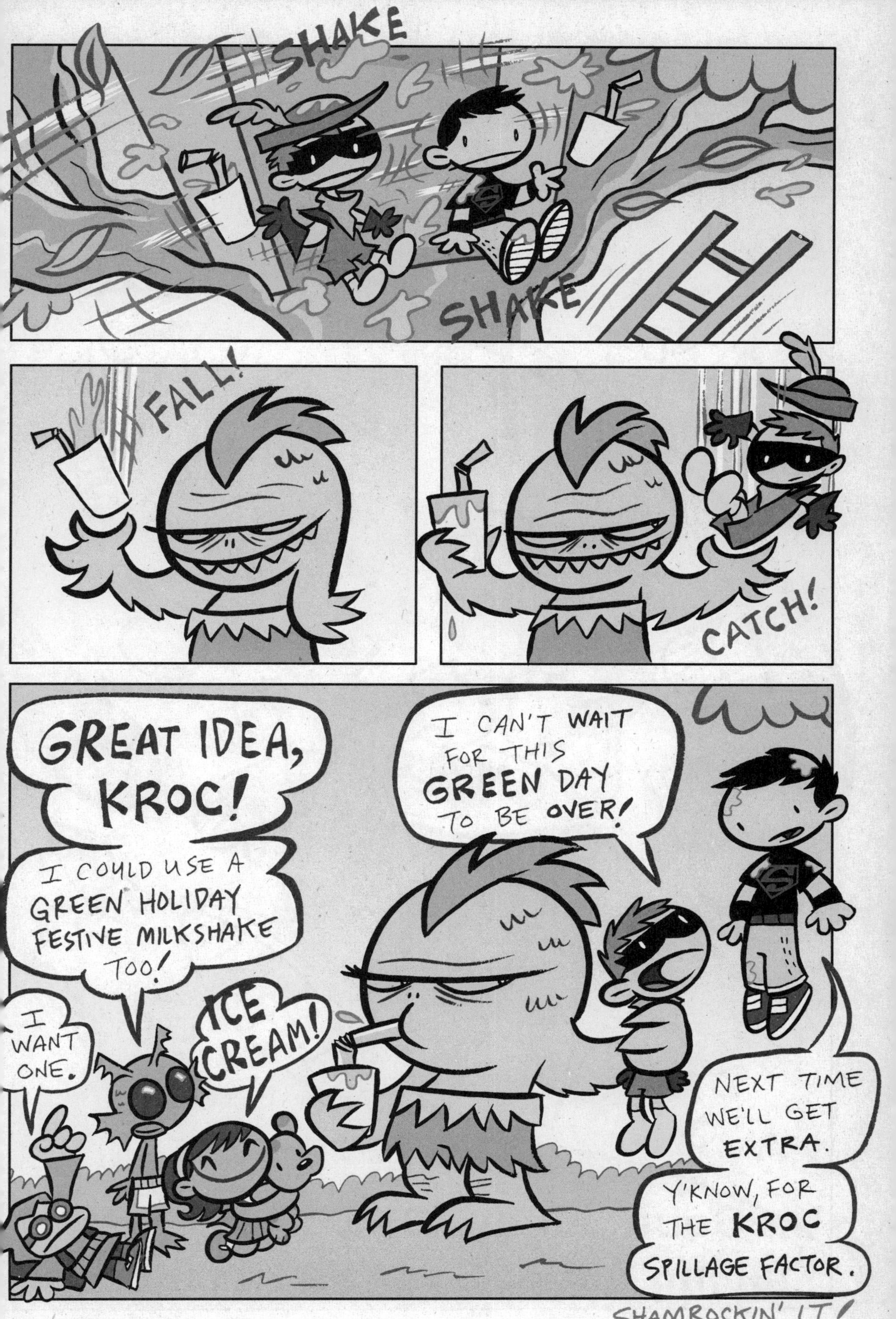
SHAKE
SHAKE
FALL!
CATCH!
GREAT IDEA, KROC!
I COULD USE A GREEN HOLIDAY FESTIVE MILKSHAKE TOO!
I CAN'T WAIT FOR THIS GREEN DAY TO BE OVER!
I WANT ONE.
ICE CREAM!
NEXT TIME WE'LL GET EXTRA.
Y'KNOW, FOR THE KROC SPILLAGE FACTOR.
SHAMROCKIN' IT!

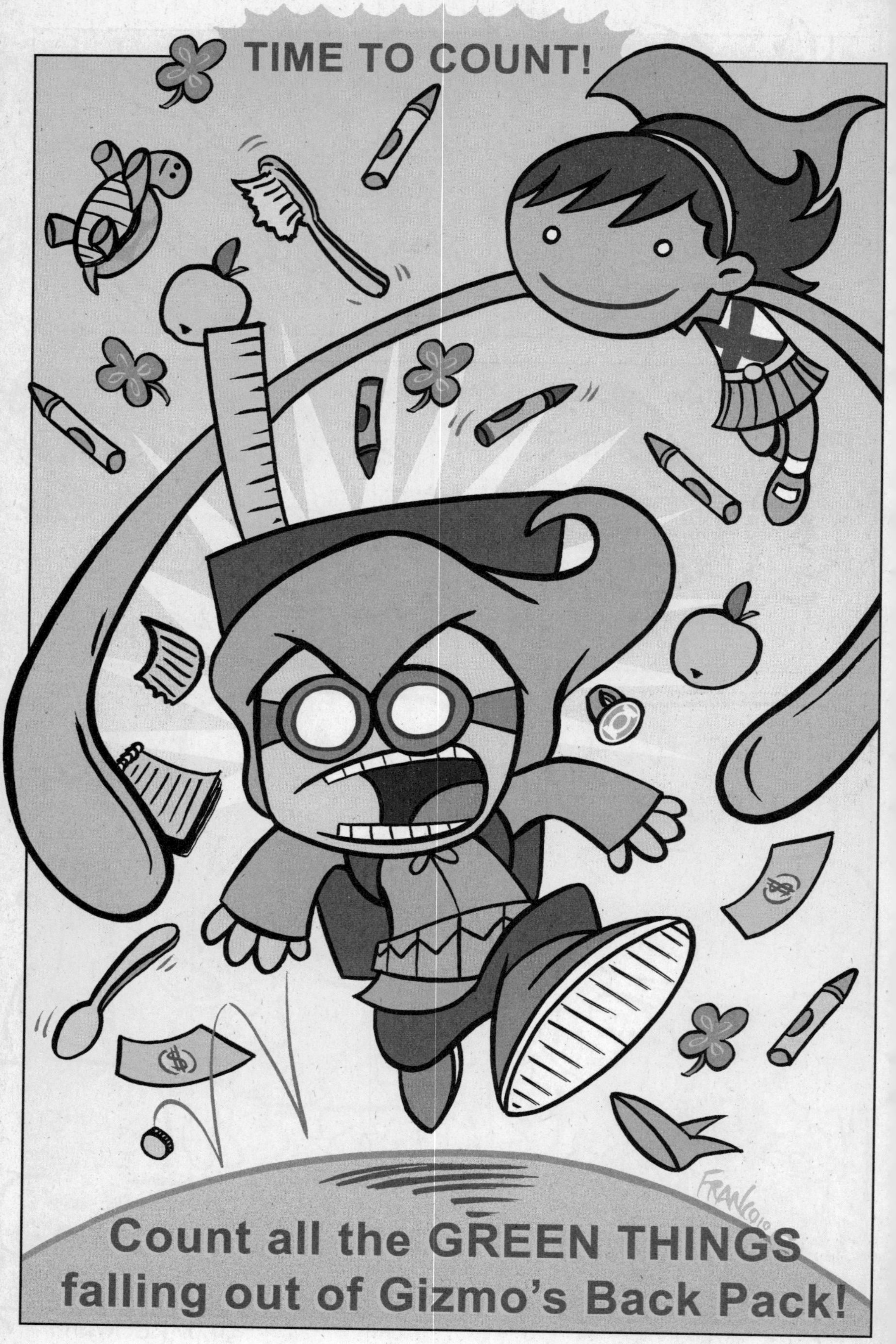

TIME TO COUNT!
FRANCO10
Count all the GREEN THINGS
falling out of Gizmo's Back Pack!

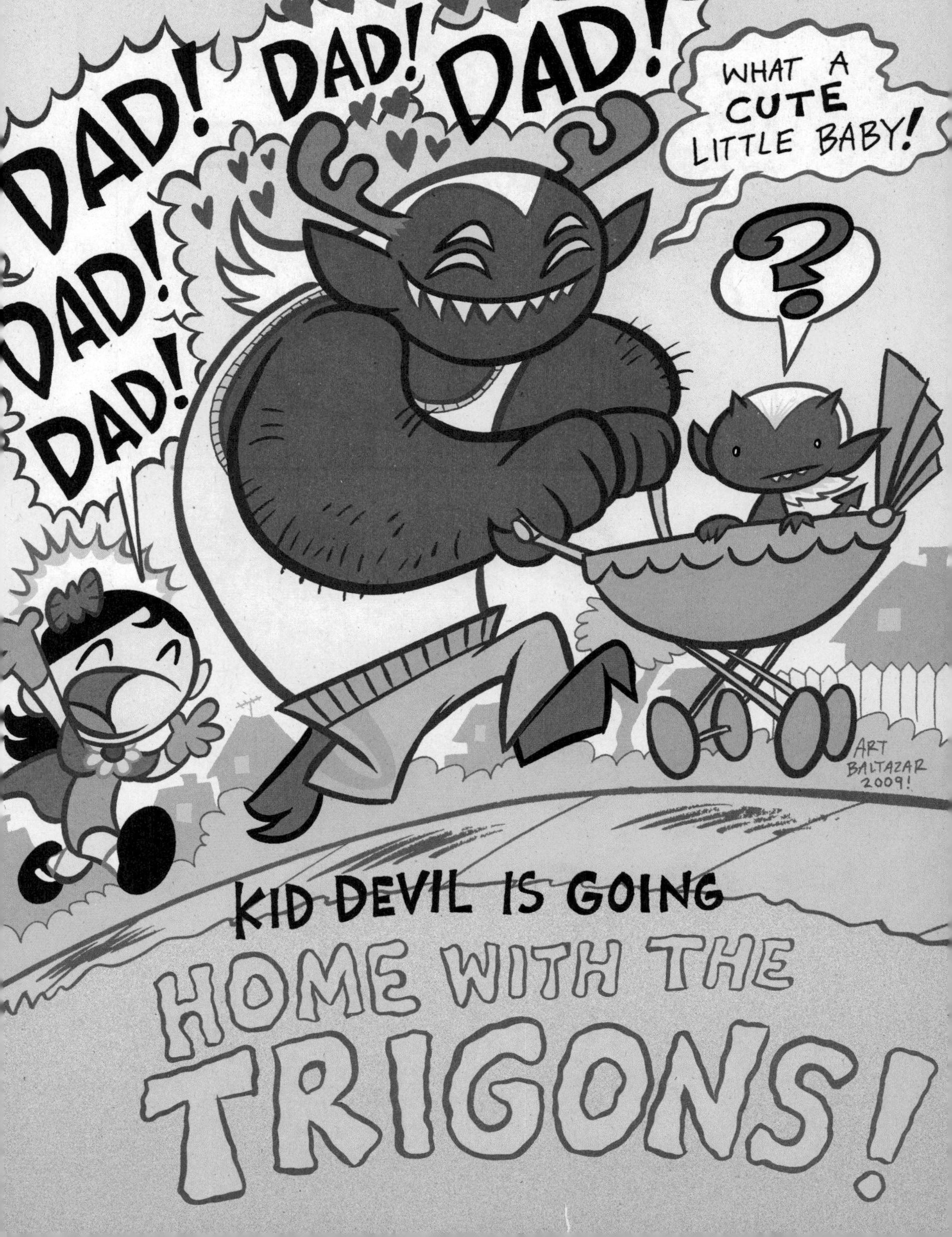
DAD! DAD! DAD! DAD! DAD! DAD!
WHAT A CUTE LITTLE BABY!
?
ART BALTAZAR 2009!
KID DEVIL IS GOING HOME WITH THE TRIGONS!

tiny titans

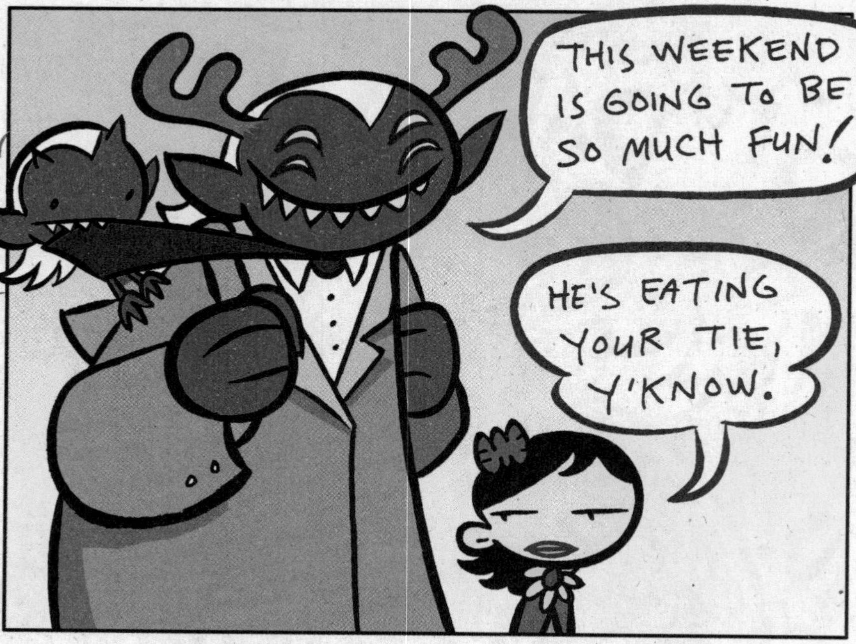
THIS WEEKEND IS GOING TO BE SO MUCH FUN!
HE'S EATING YOUR TIE, Y'KNOW.

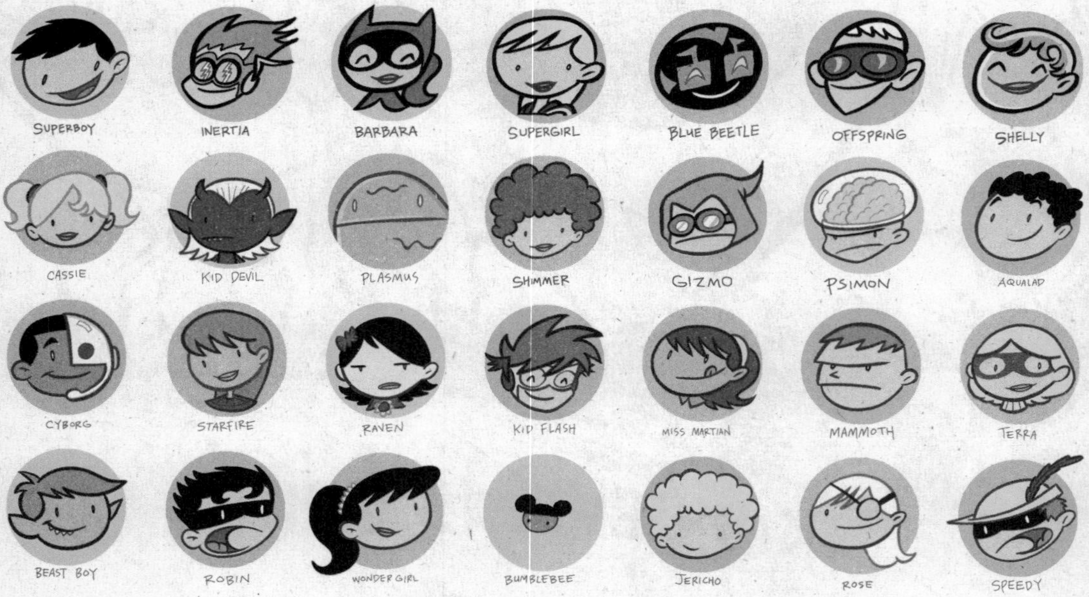
SUPERBOY
INERTIA
BARBARA
SUPERGIRL
BLUE BEETLE
OFFSPRING
SHELLY
CASSIE
KID DEVIL
PLASMUS
SHIMMER
GIZMO
PSIMON
AQUALAD
CYBORG
STARFIRE
RAVEN
KID FLASH
MISS MARTIAN
MAMMOTH
TERRA
BEAST BOY
ROBIN
WONDER GIRL
BUMBLEBEE
JERICHO
ROSE
SPEEDY

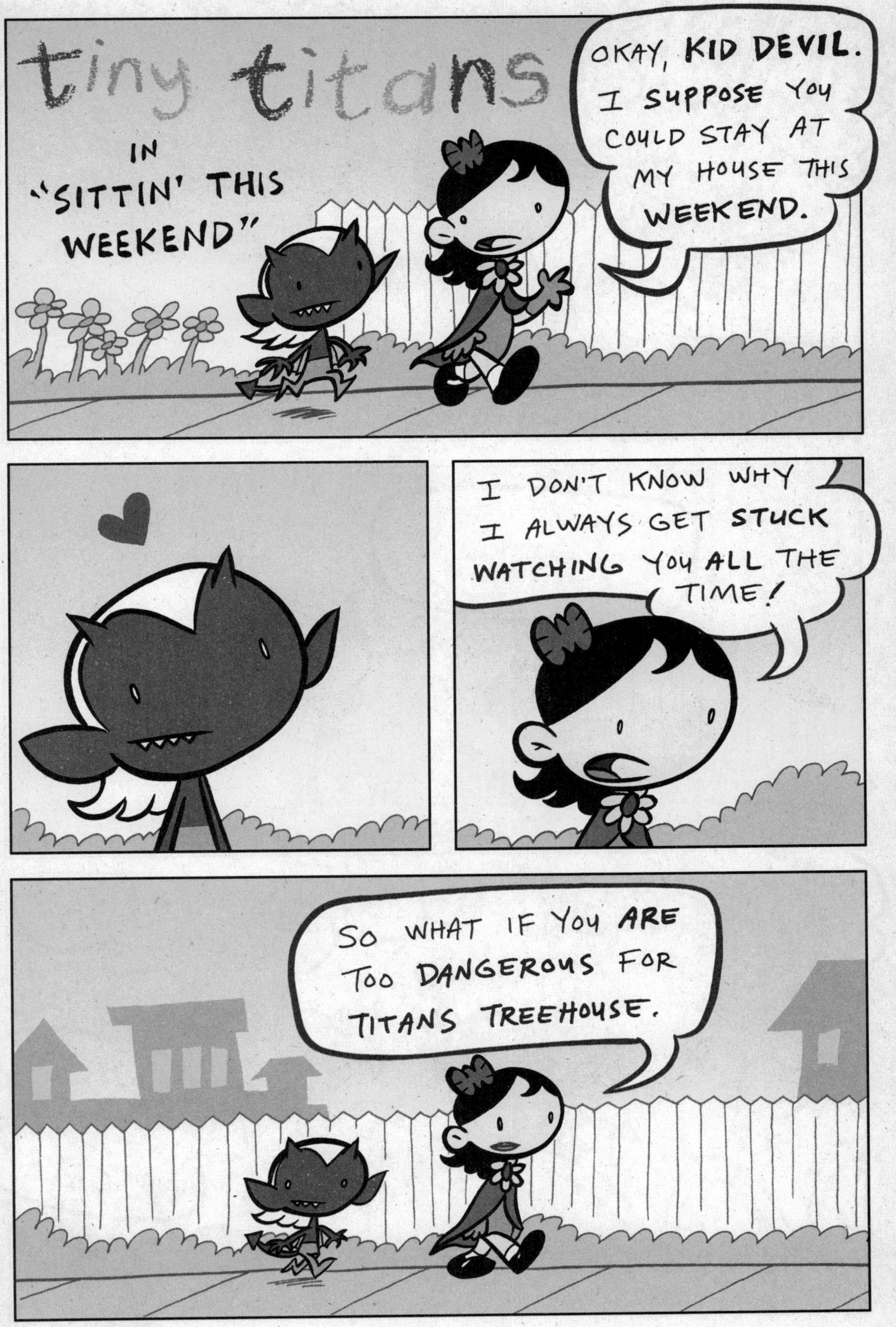
tiny titans
IN "SITTIN' THIS WEEKEND"
OKAY, KID DEVIL. I SUPPOSE YOU COULD STAY AT MY HOUSE THIS WEEKEND.
I DON'T KNOW WHY I ALWAYS GET STUCK WATCHING YOU ALL THE TIME!
SO WHAT IF YOU ARE TOO DANGEROUS FOR TITANS TREEHOUSE.

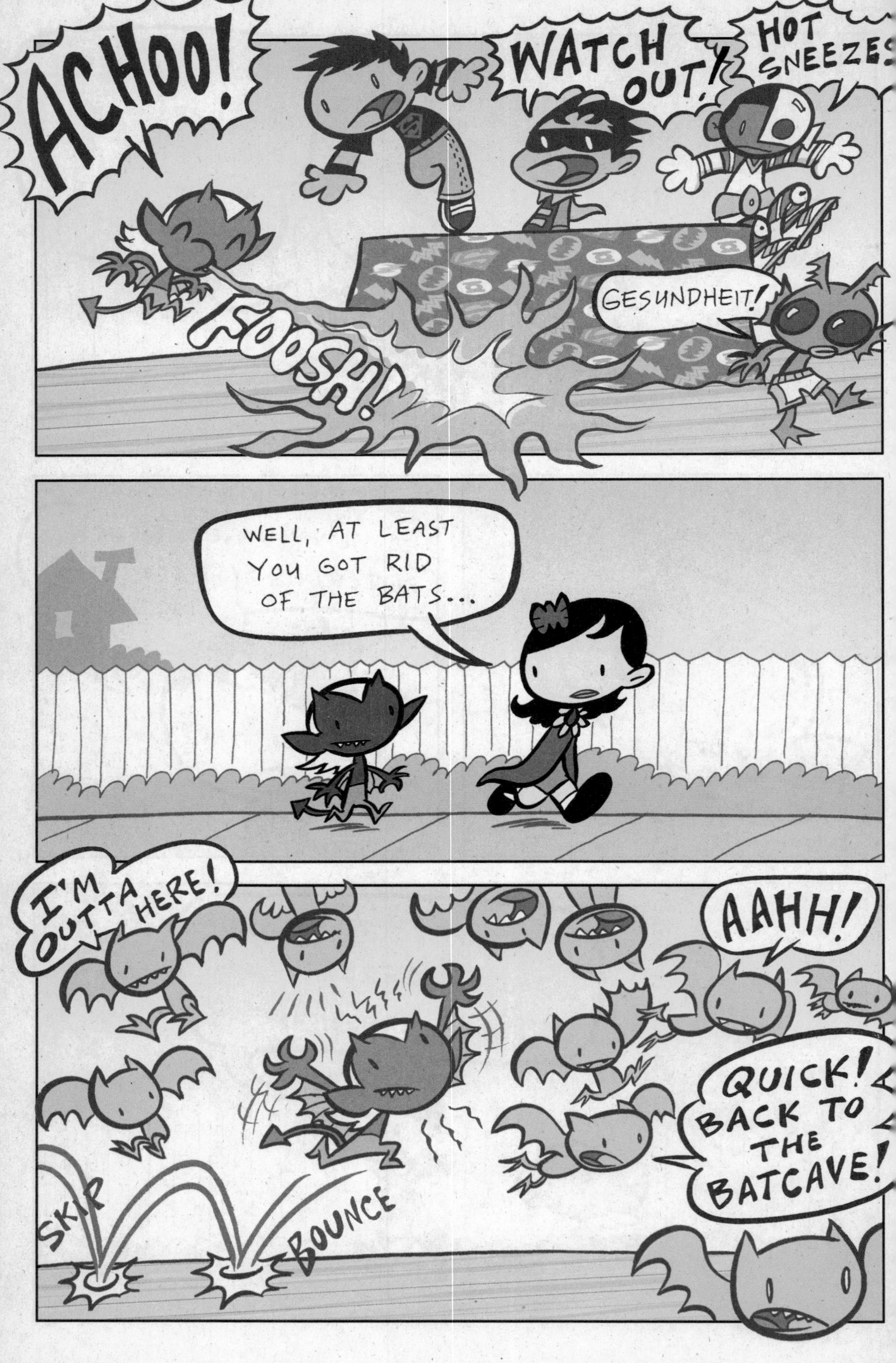
ACHOO!
WATCH OUT!
HOT SNEEZES!
FOOSH!
GESUNDHEIT!
WELL, AT LEAST YOU GOT RID OF THE BATS...
I'M OUTTA HERE!
AAHH!
QUICK! BACK TO THE BATCAVE!
SKIP
BOUNCE

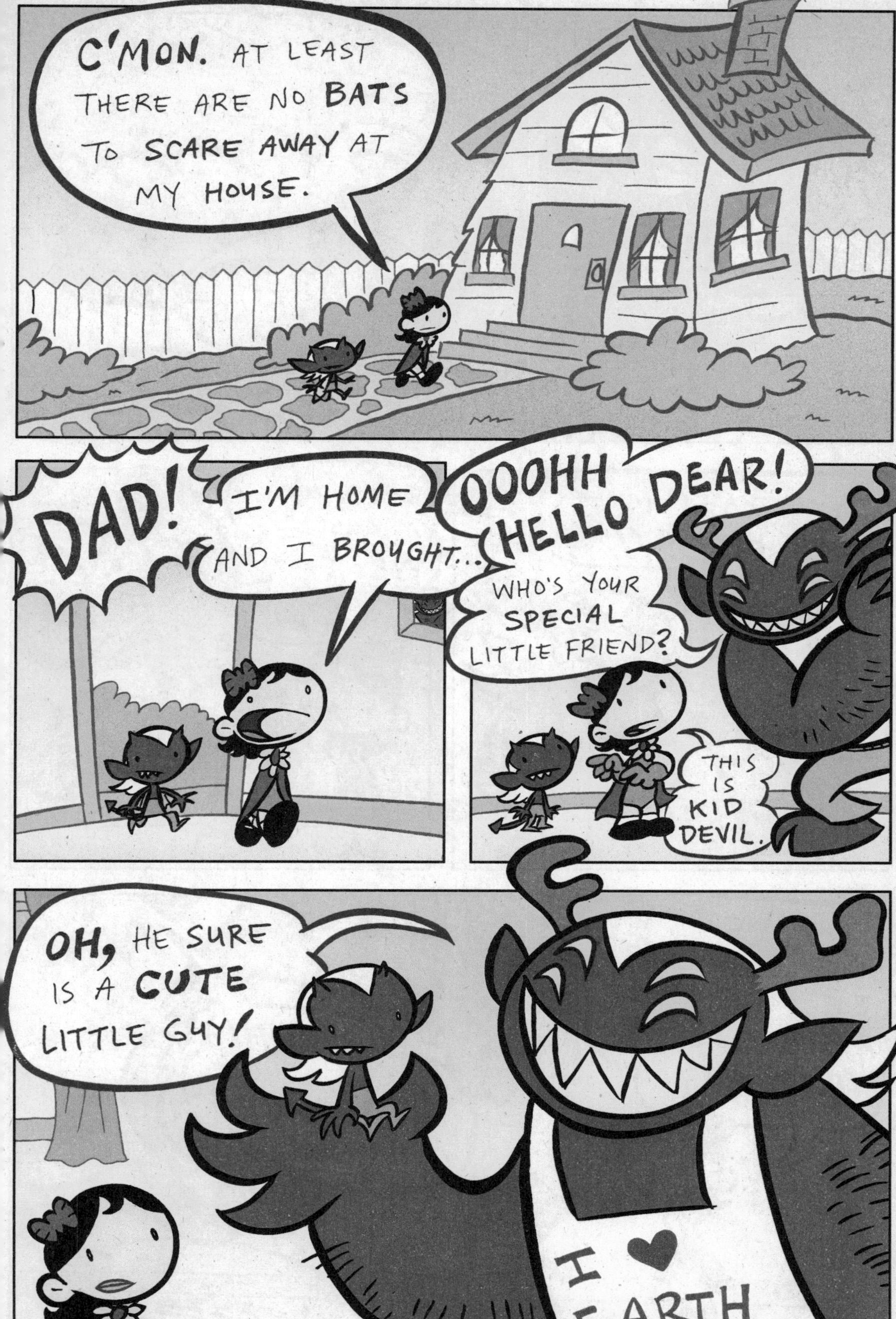
C'MON. AT LEAST THERE ARE NO BATS TO SCARE AWAY AT MY HOUSE.
DAD!
I'M HOME AND I BROUGHT...
OOOHH HELLO DEAR!
WHO'S YOUR SPECIAL LITTLE FRIEND?
THIS IS KID DEVIL.
OH, HE SURE IS A CUTE LITTLE GUY!
I ♥ EARTH

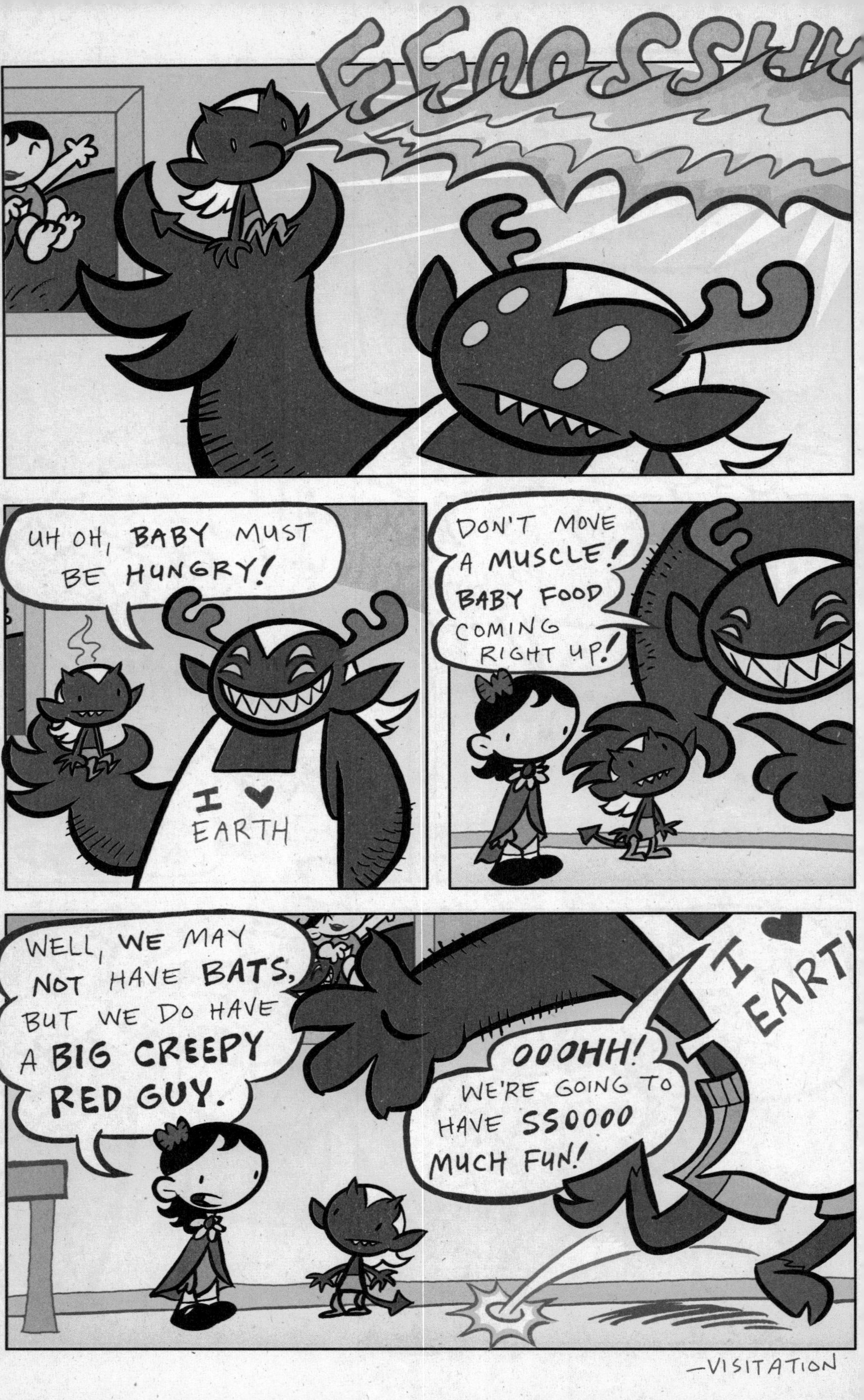
GGAAOSSHHH
UH OH, BABY MUST BE HUNGRY!
I ♥ EARTH
DON'T MOVE A MUSCLE! BABY FOOD COMING RIGHT UP!
WELL, WE MAY NOT HAVE BATS, BUT WE DO HAVE A BIG CREEPY RED GUY.
OOOHH! WE'RE GOING TO HAVE SSOOOO MUCH FUN!
—VISITATION

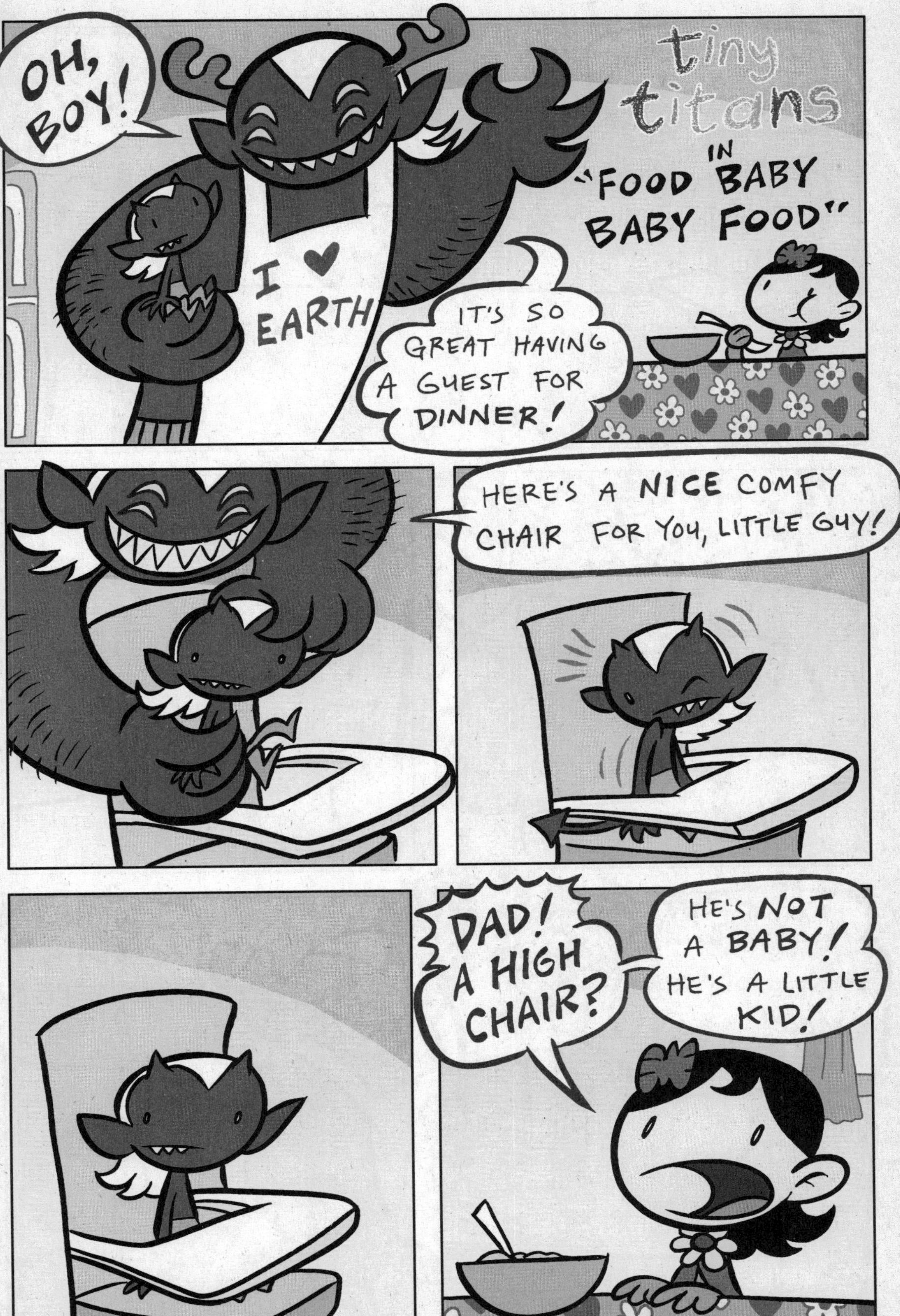
tiny titans
IN "FOOD BABY BABY FOOD"
OH, BOY!
I ♥ EARTH
IT'S SO GREAT HAVING A GUEST FOR DINNER!
HERE'S A NICE COMFY CHAIR FOR YOU, LITTLE GUY!
DAD! A HIGH CHAIR?
HE'S NOT A BABY! HE'S A LITTLE KID!

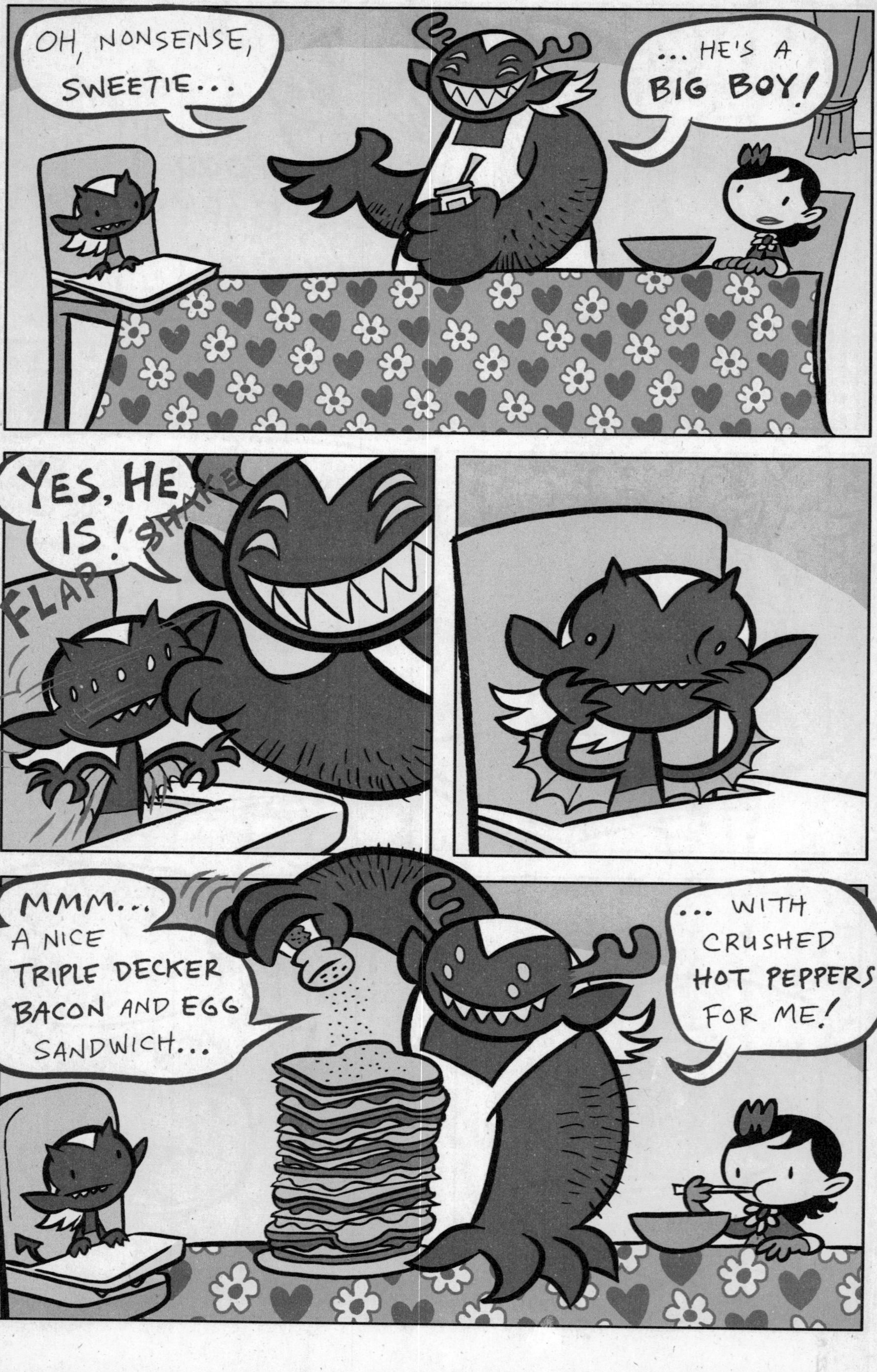
OH, NONSENSE, SWEETIE...
... HE'S A BIG BOY!
YES, HE IS!
SHAKE
FLAP
MMM... A NICE TRIPLE DECKER BACON AND EGG SANDWICH...
... WITH CRUSHED HOT PEPPERS FOR ME!

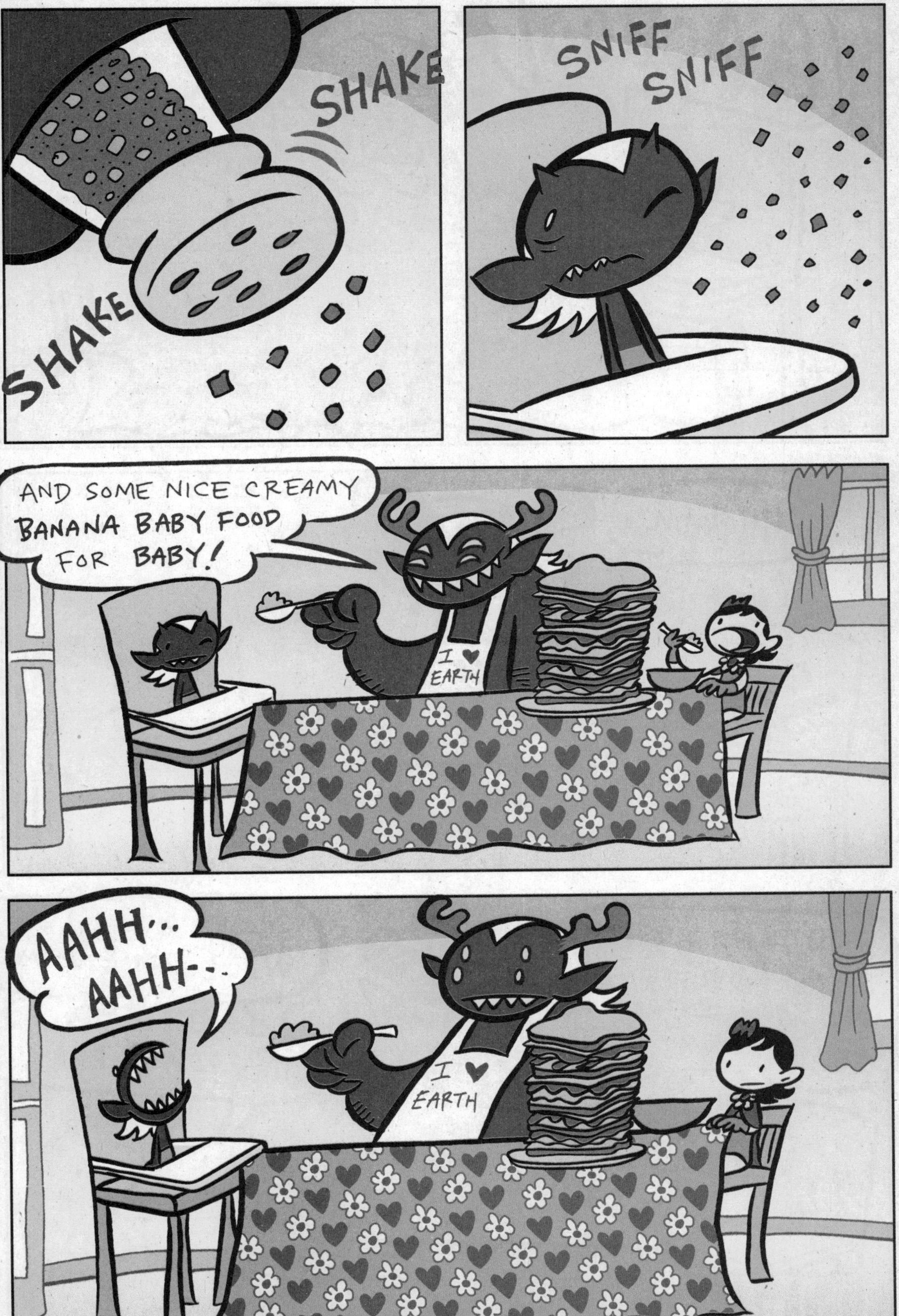
SHAKE
SHAKE
SNIFF
SNIFF
AND SOME NICE CREAMY BANANA BABY FOOD FOR BABY!
I ♥ EARTH
AAHH... AAHH---
I ♥ EARTH

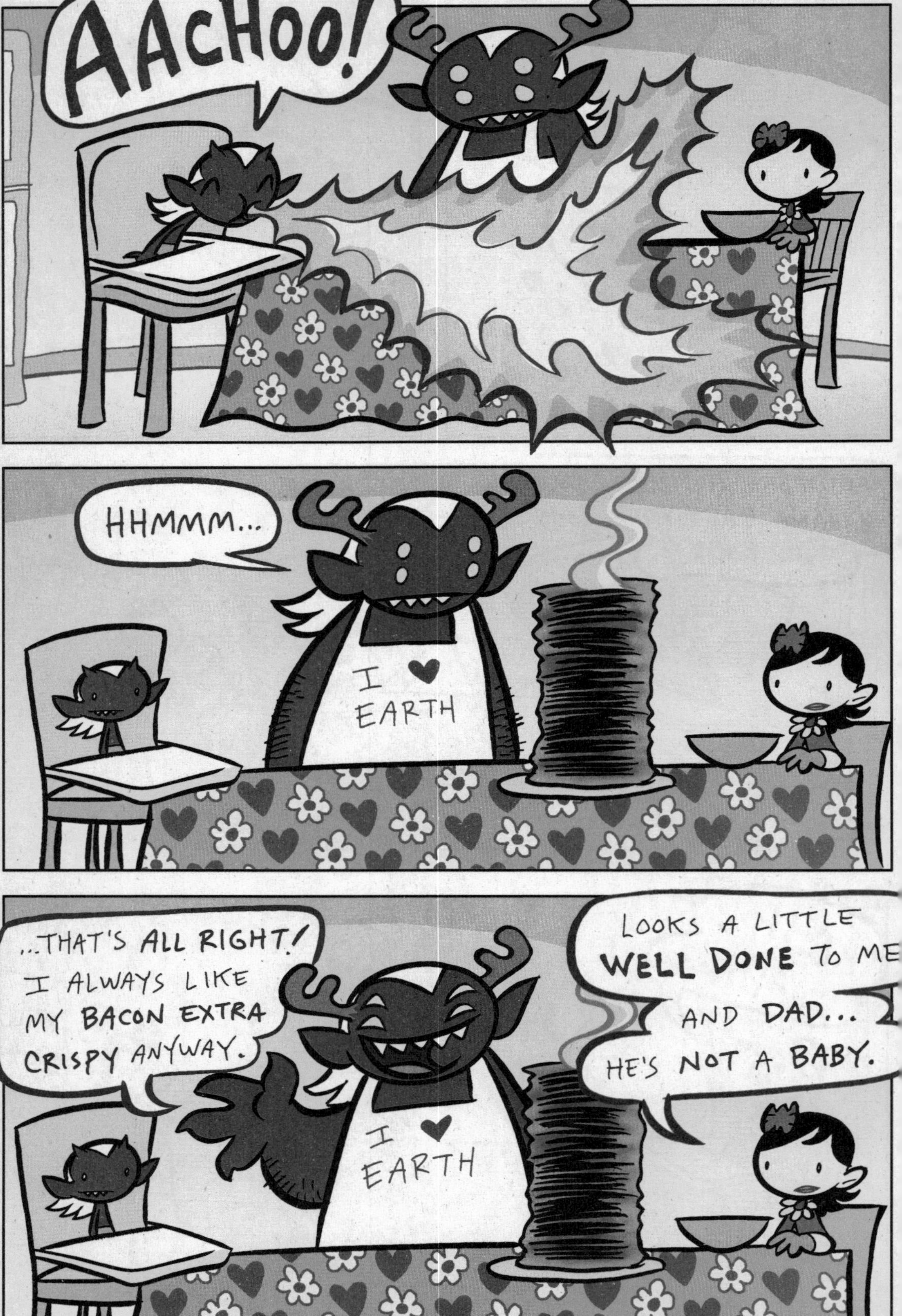
AACHOO!
HHMMM...
I ♥ EARTH
...THAT'S ALL RIGHT! I ALWAYS LIKE MY BACON EXTRA CRISPY ANYWAY.
LOOKS A LITTLE WELL DONE TO ME
AND DAD... HE'S NOT A BABY.
I ♥ EARTH

-COOKING.

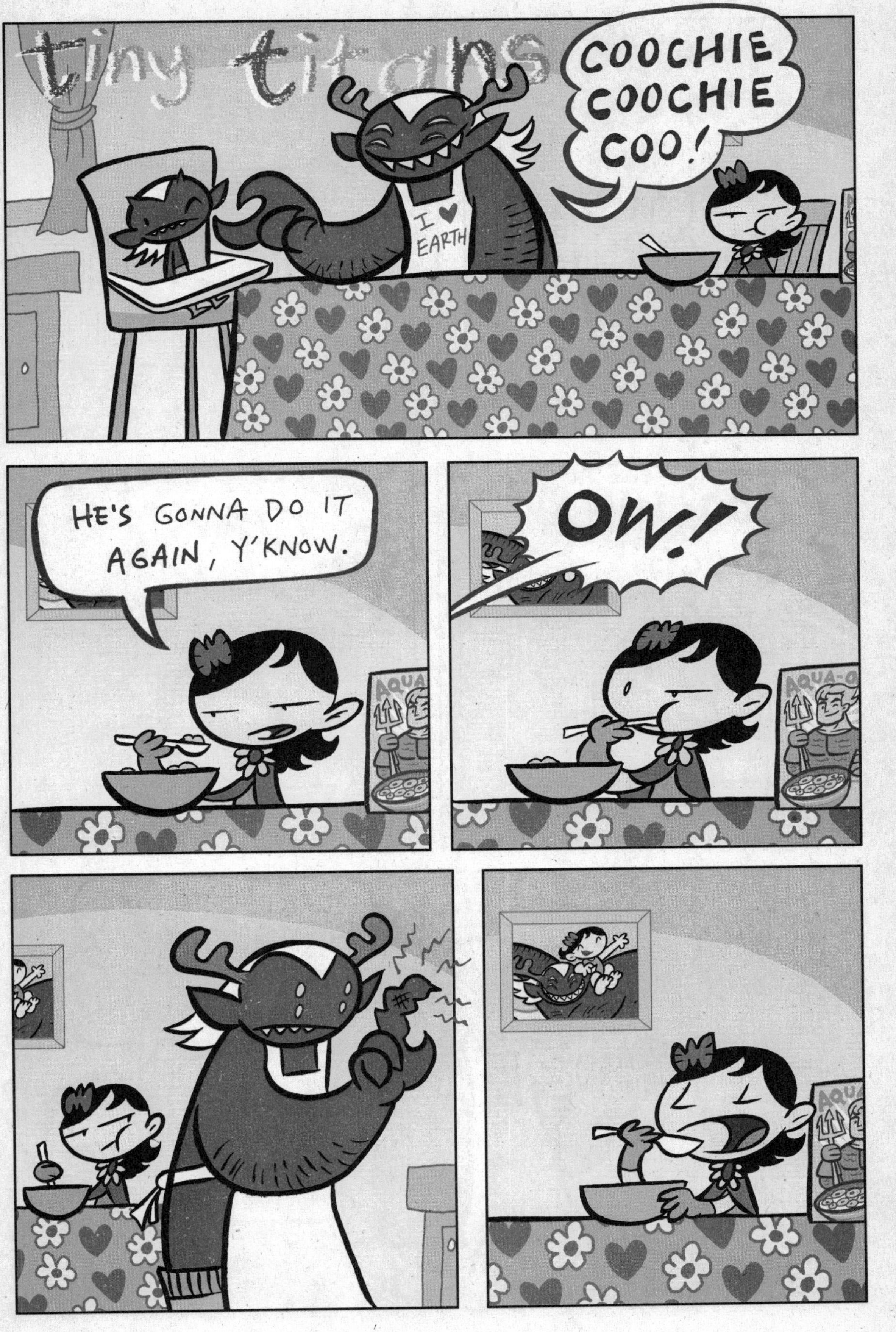
tiny titans
COOCHIE COOCHIE COO!
I ♥ EARTH
HE'S GONNA DO IT AGAIN, Y'KNOW.
AQUA-
OW!
AQUA-O

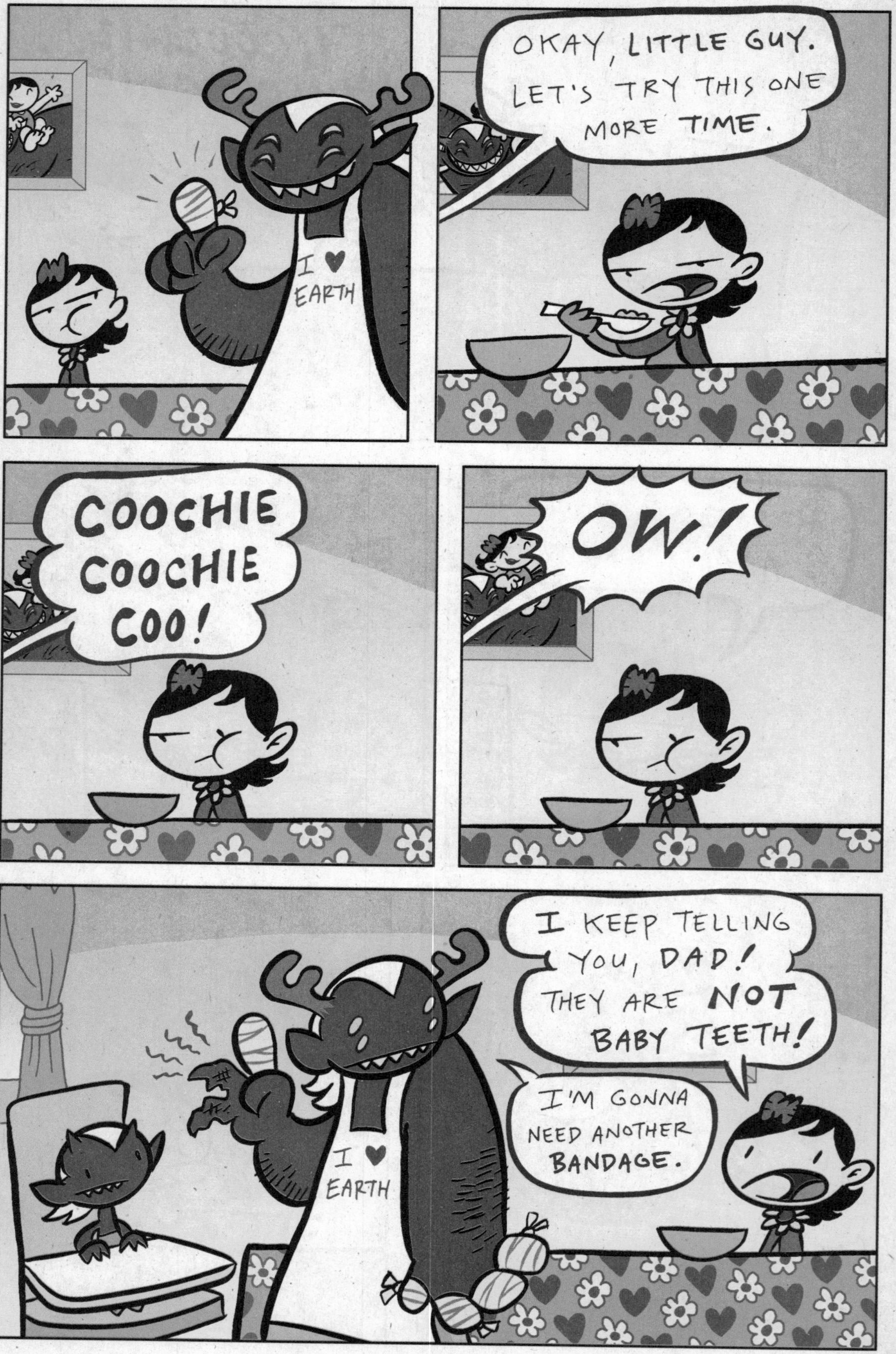
I ♥ EARTH
OKAY, LITTLE GUY. LET'S TRY THIS ONE MORE TIME.
COOCHIE COOCHIE COO!
OW!
I ♥ EARTH
I KEEP TELLING YOU, DAD! THEY ARE NOT BABY TEETH!
I'M GONNA NEED ANOTHER BANDAGE.

—BITE.

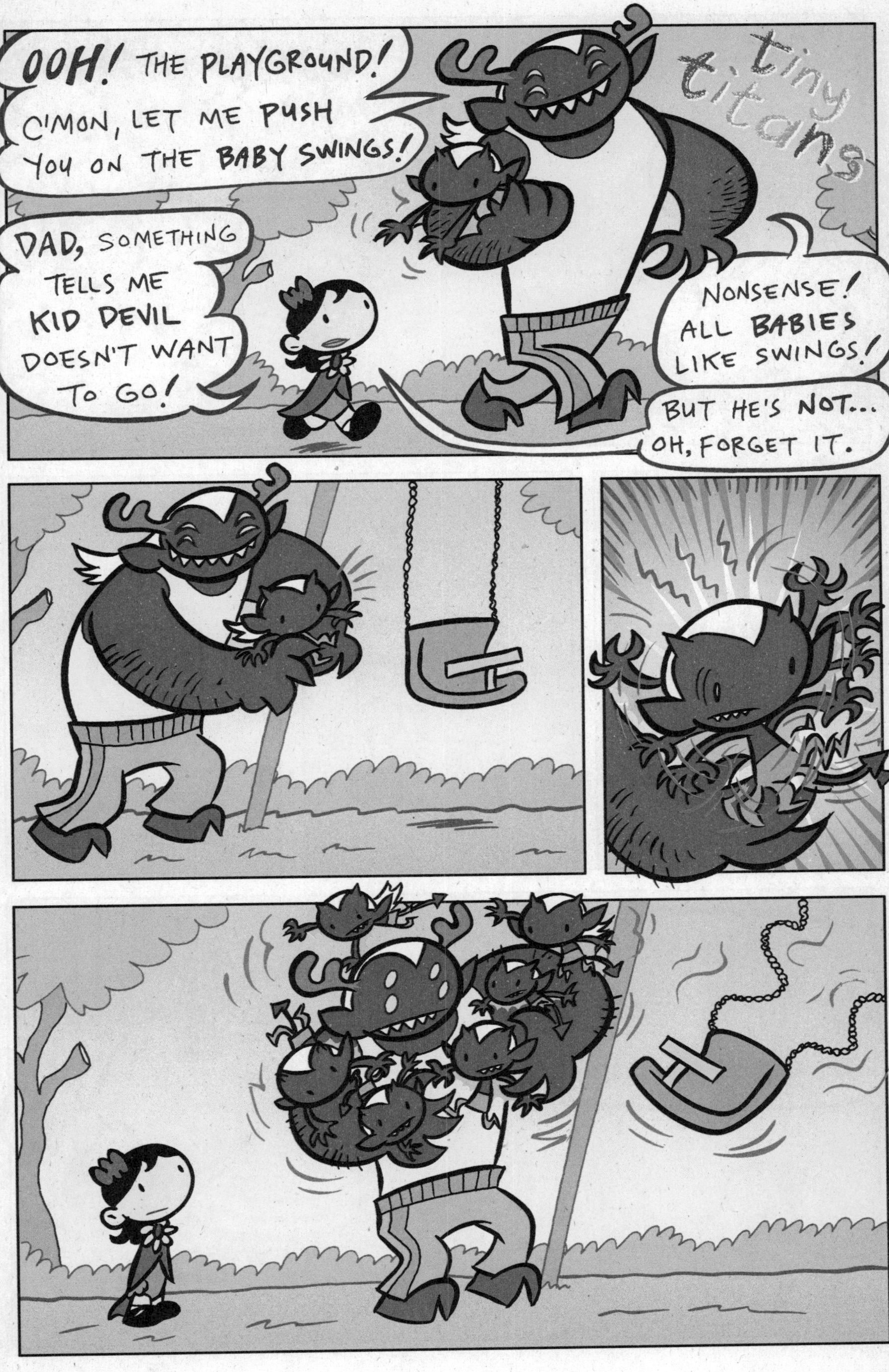
tiny titans
OOH! THE PLAYGROUND! C'MON, LET ME PUSH YOU ON THE BABY SWINGS!
DAD, SOMETHING TELLS ME KID DEVIL DOESN'T WANT TO GO!
NONSENSE! ALL BABIES LIKE SWINGS!
BUT HE'S NOT... OH, FORGET IT.

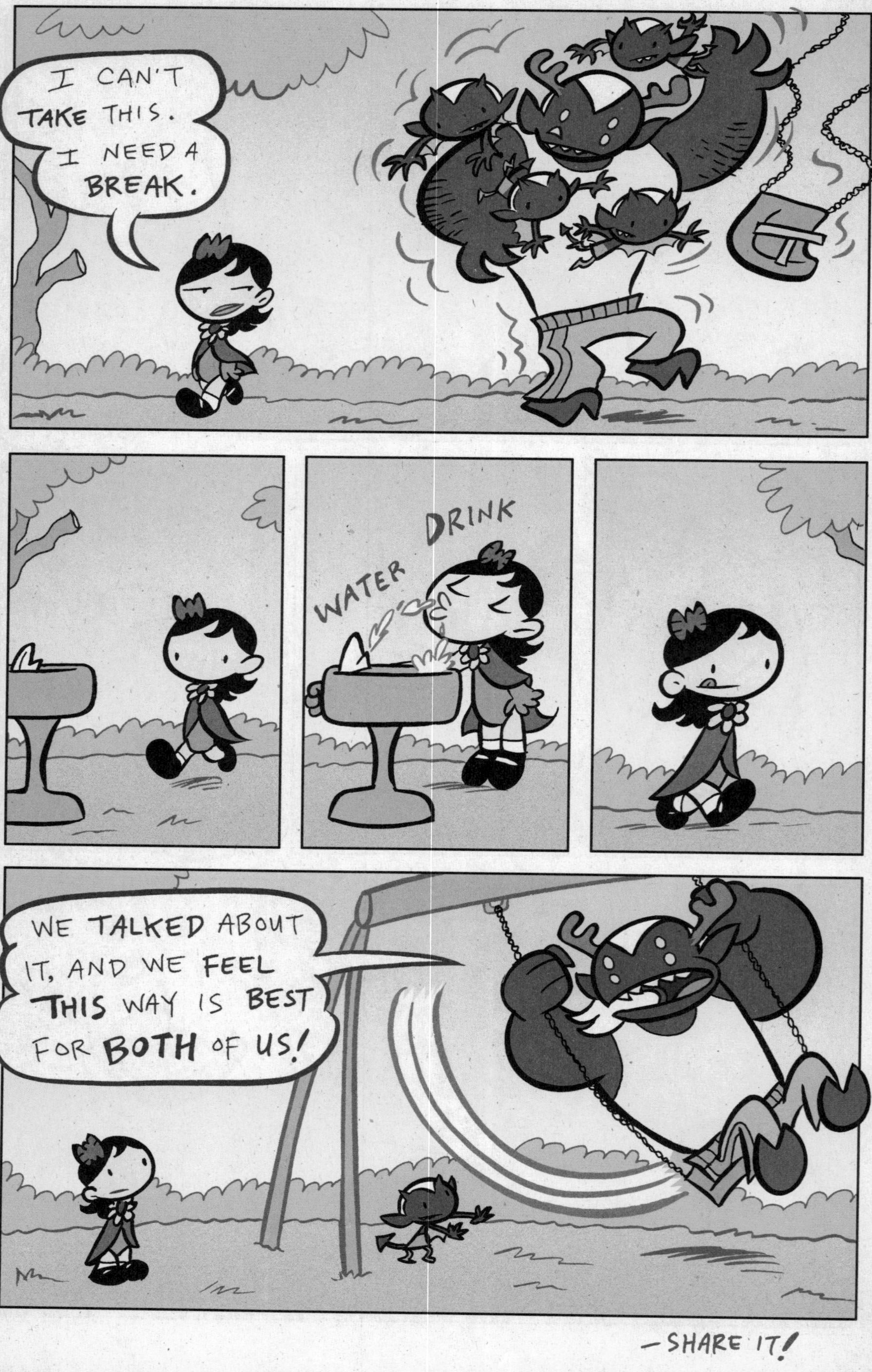
I CAN'T TAKE THIS. I NEED A BREAK.
DRINK
WATER
WE TALKED ABOUT IT, AND WE FEEL THIS WAY IS BEST FOR BOTH OF US!

— SHARE IT!

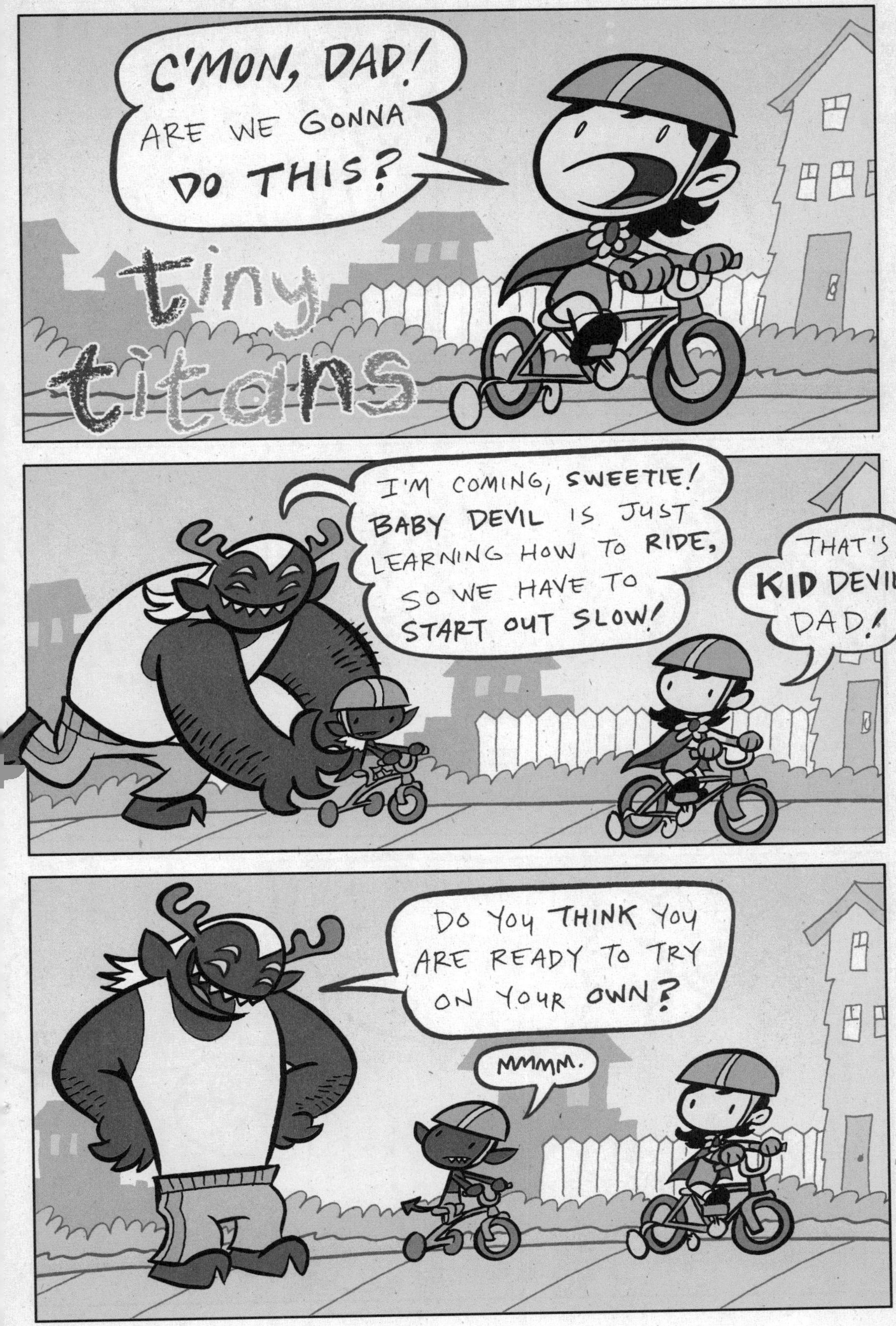
C'MON, DAD! ARE WE GONNA DO THIS?
tiny titans
I'M COMING, SWEETIE! BABY DEVIL IS JUST LEARNING HOW TO RIDE, SO WE HAVE TO START OUT SLOW!
THAT'S KID DEVIL, DAD!
DO YOU THINK YOU ARE READY TO TRY ON YOUR OWN?
MMMM.

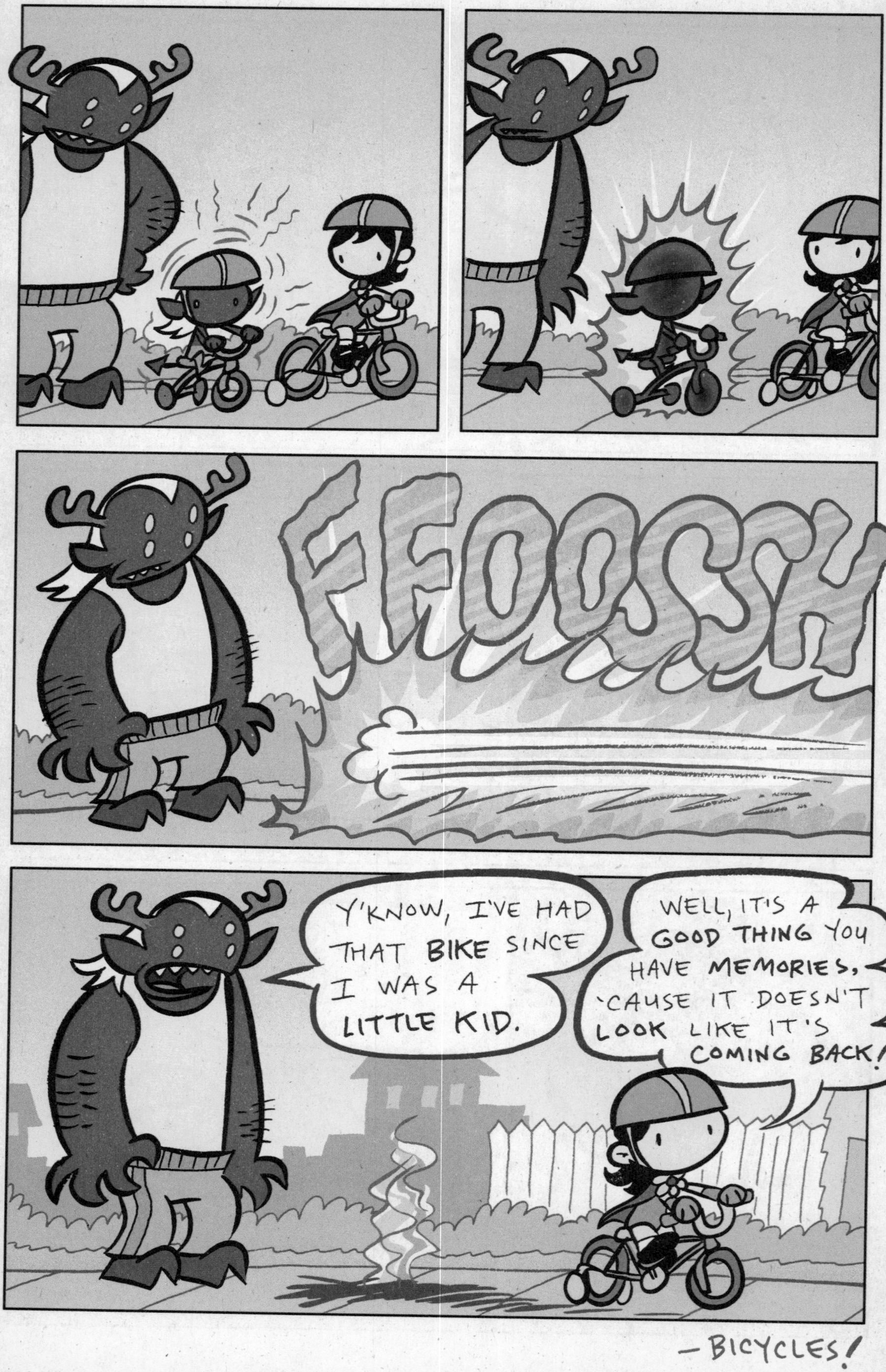
FFOOSSH
Y'KNOW, I'VE HAD THAT BIKE SINCE I WAS A LITTLE KID.
WELL, IT'S A GOOD THING YOU HAVE MEMORIES, 'CAUSE IT DOESN'T LOOK LIKE IT'S COMING BACK!

—BICYCLES!

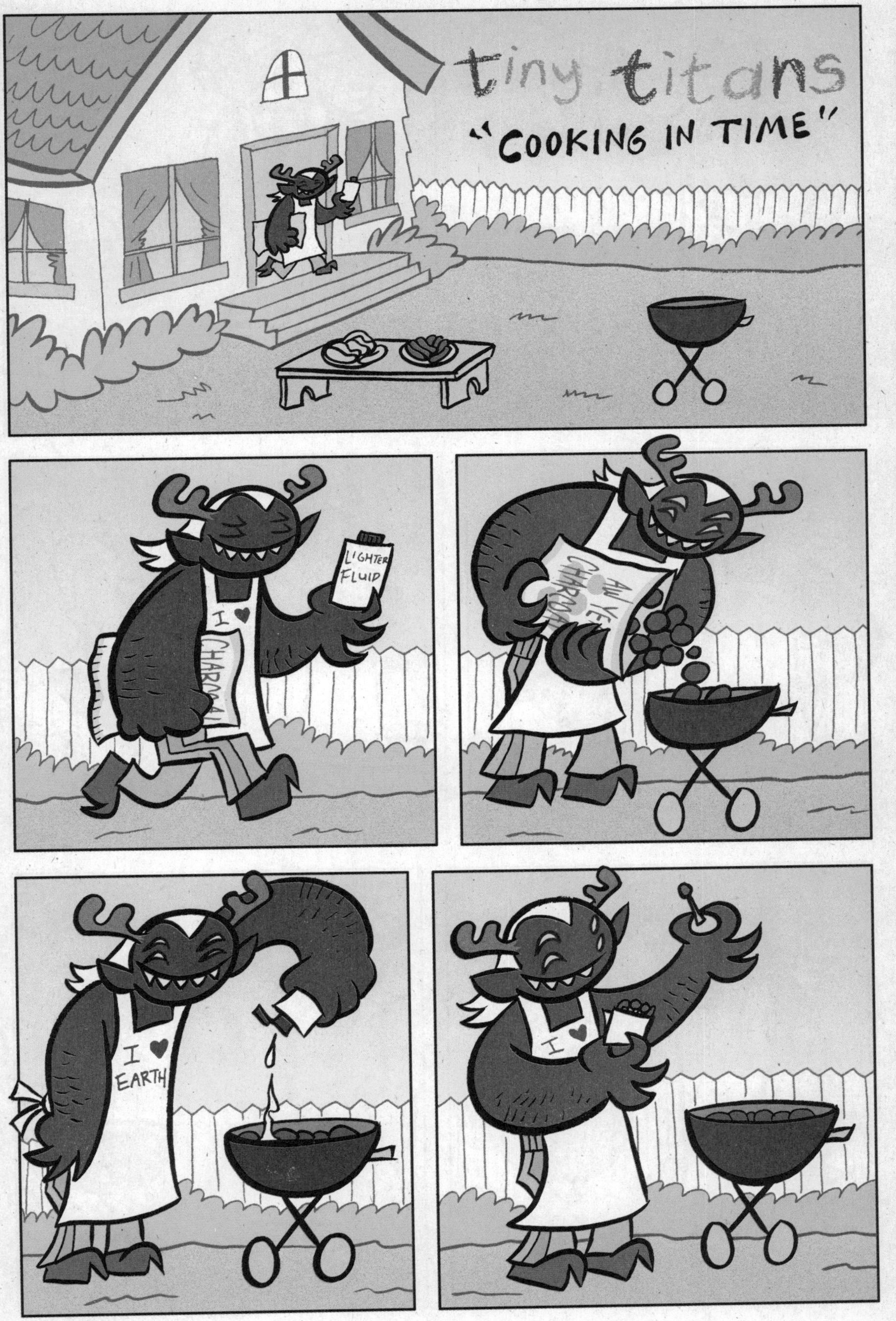
tiny titans
"COOKING IN TIME"
LIGHTER FLUID
I ♥
I ♥ EARTH
I ♥

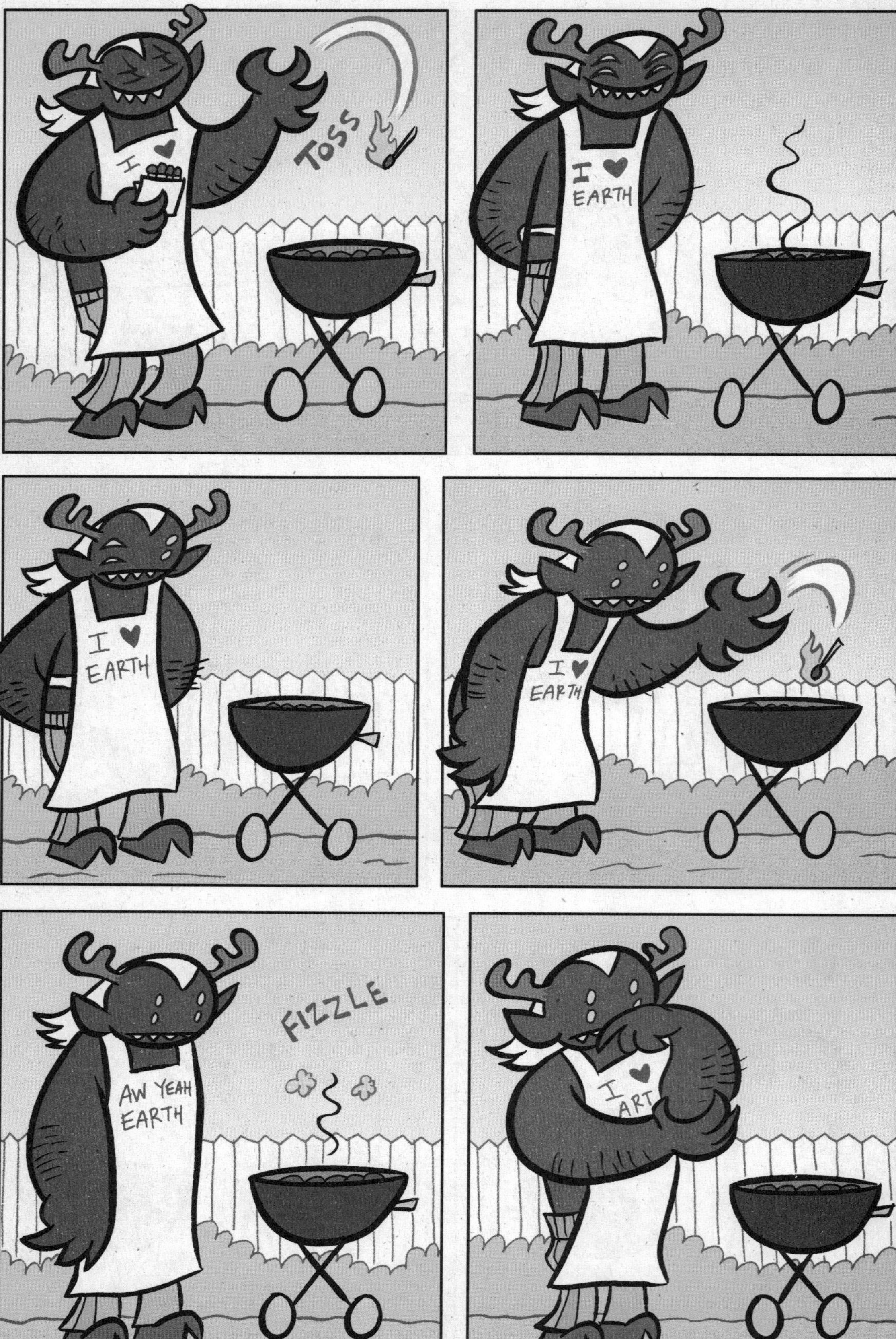
TOSS
I ♥
I ♥
EARTH
I ♥
EARTH
I ♥
EARTH
FIZZLE
AW YEAH
EARTH
I ♥
ART

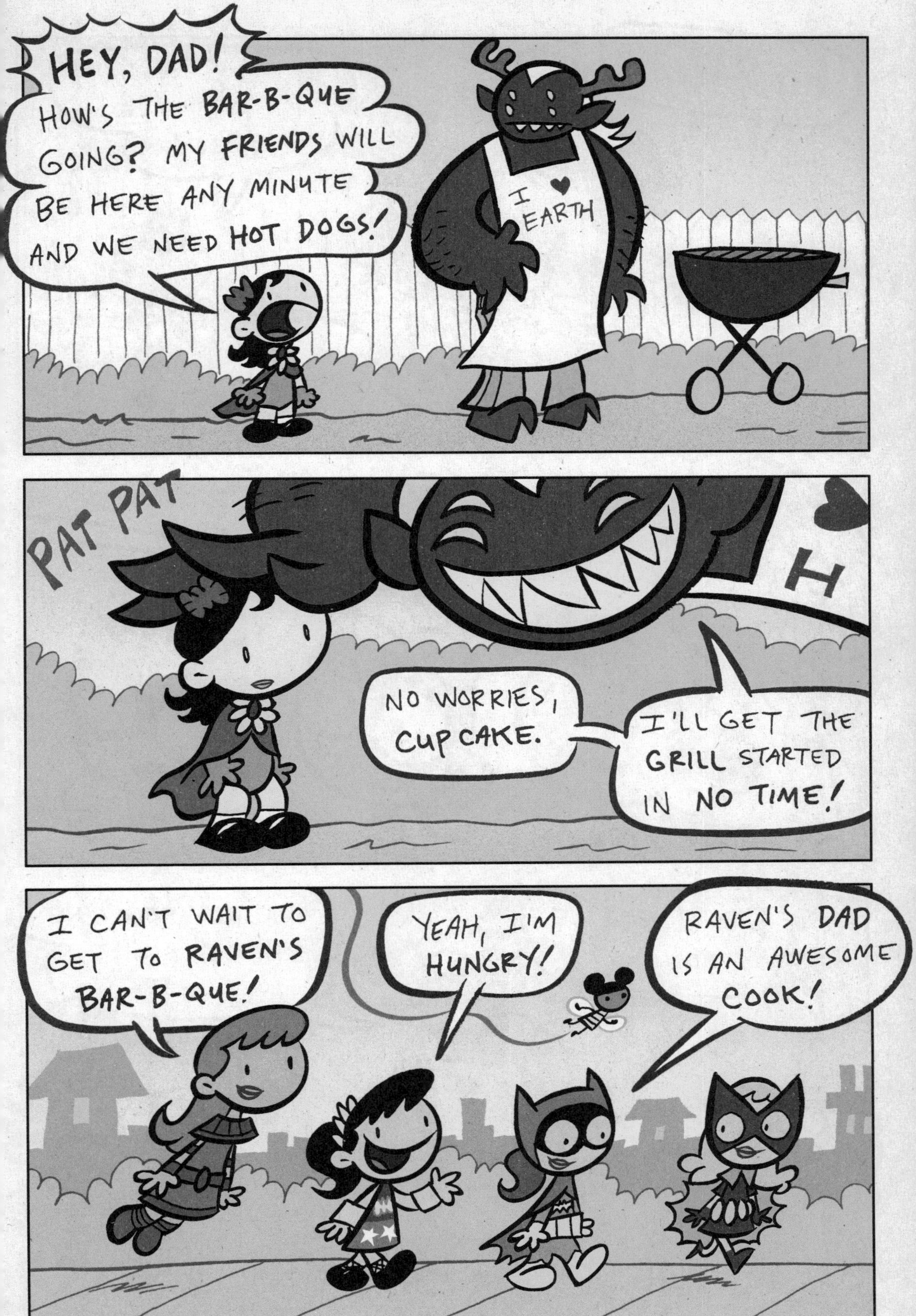

HEY, DAD!
HOW'S THE BAR-B-QUE GOING?
MY FRIENDS WILL BE HERE ANY MINUTE AND WE NEED HOT DOGS!
I ♥ EARTH
PAT PAT
NO WORRIES, CUPCAKE.
I'LL GET THE GRILL STARTED IN NO TIME!
I CAN'T WAIT TO GET TO RAVEN'S BAR-B-QUE!
YEAH, I'M HUNGRY!
RAVEN'S DAD IS AN AWESOME COOK!

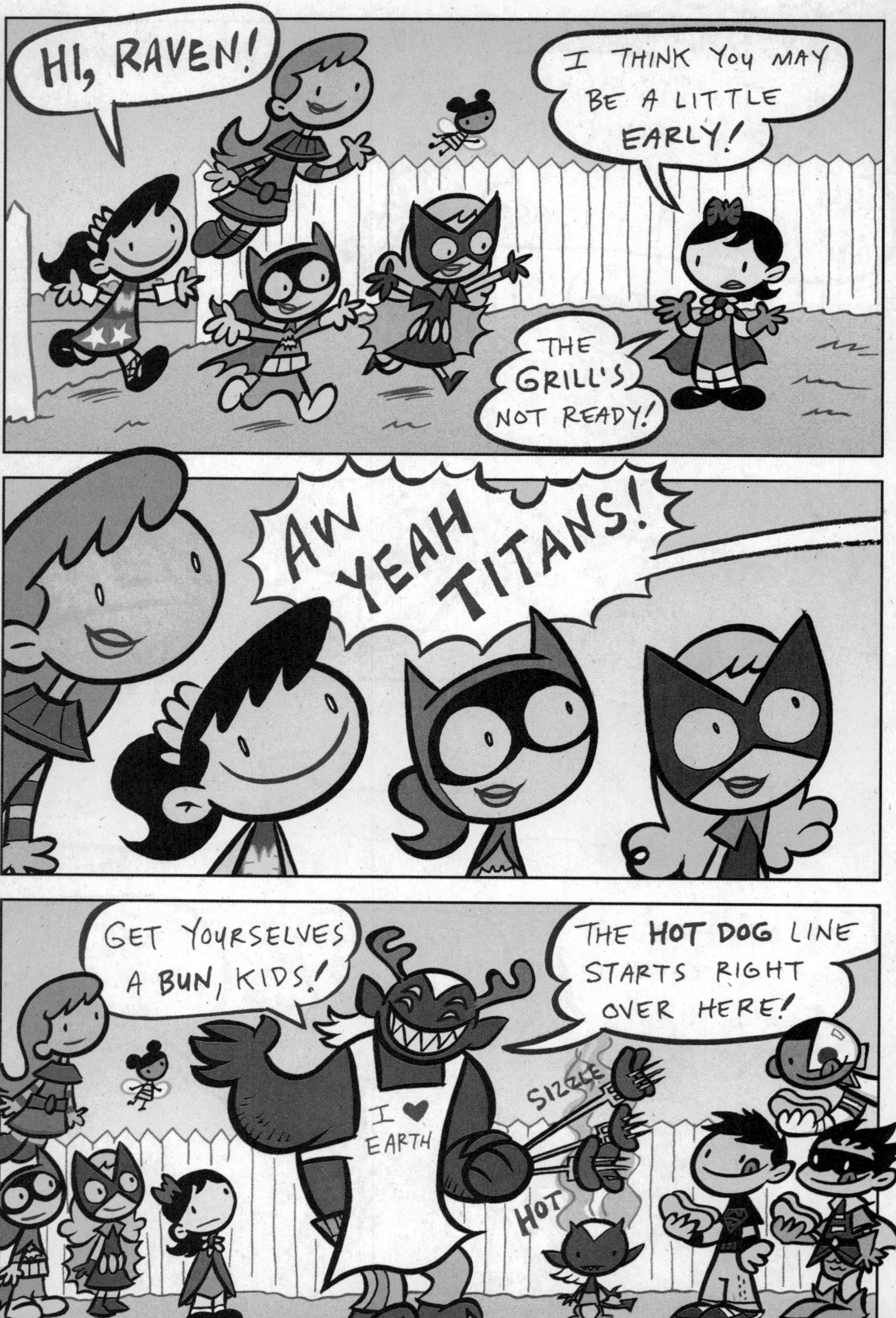
HI, RAVEN!
I THINK YOU MAY BE A LITTLE EARLY!
THE GRILL'S NOT READY!
AW YEAH TITANS!
GET YOURSELVES A BUN, KIDS!
THE HOT DOG LINE STARTS RIGHT OVER HERE!
I ♥ EARTH
SIZZLE
HOT

-HUNGRY?

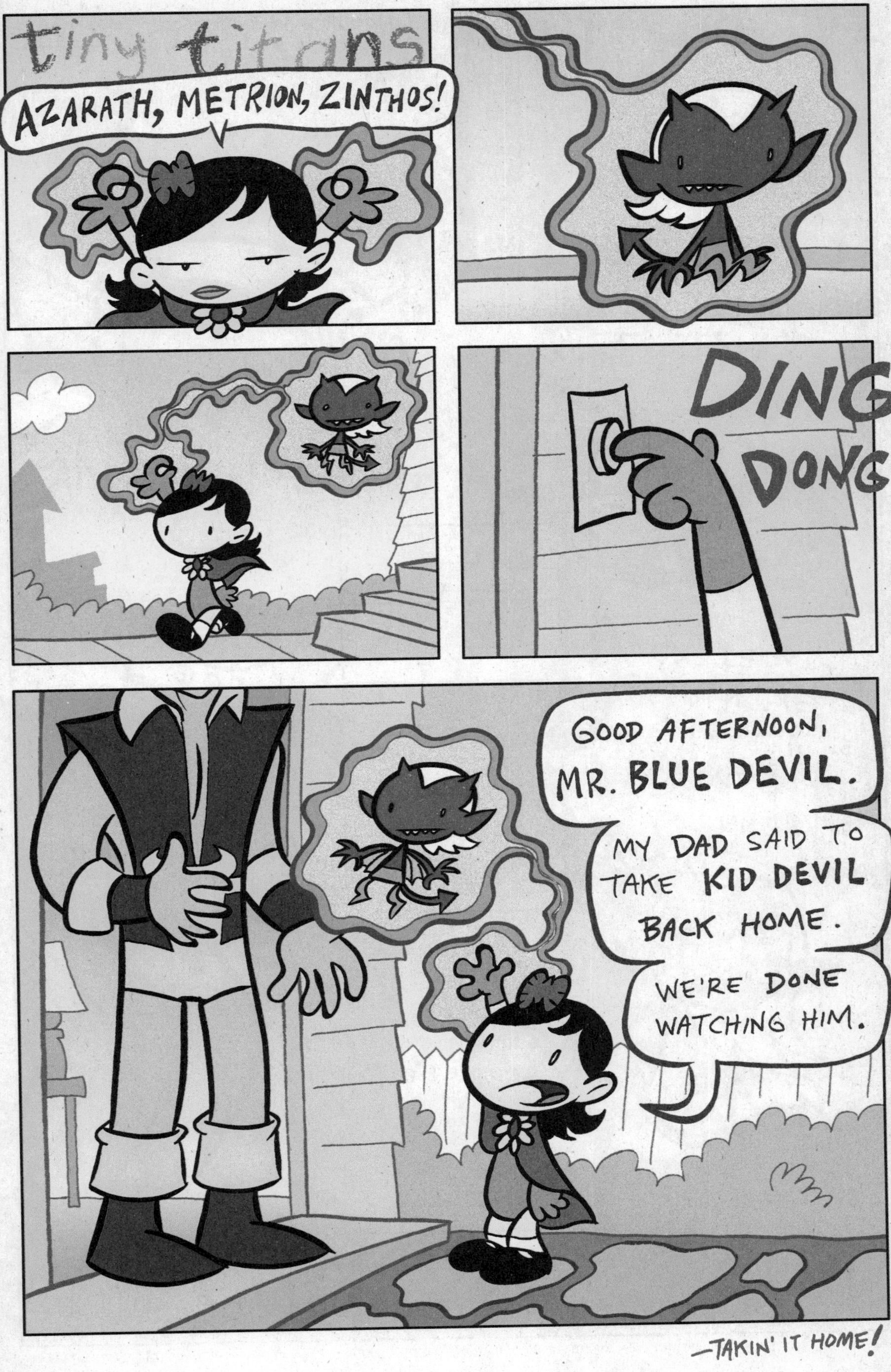
tiny titans
AZARATH, METRION, ZINTHOS!
DING
DONG
GOOD AFTERNOON, MR. BLUE DEVIL.
MY DAD SAID TO TAKE KID DEVIL BACK HOME.
WE'RE DONE WATCHING HIM.
—TAKIN' IT HOME!

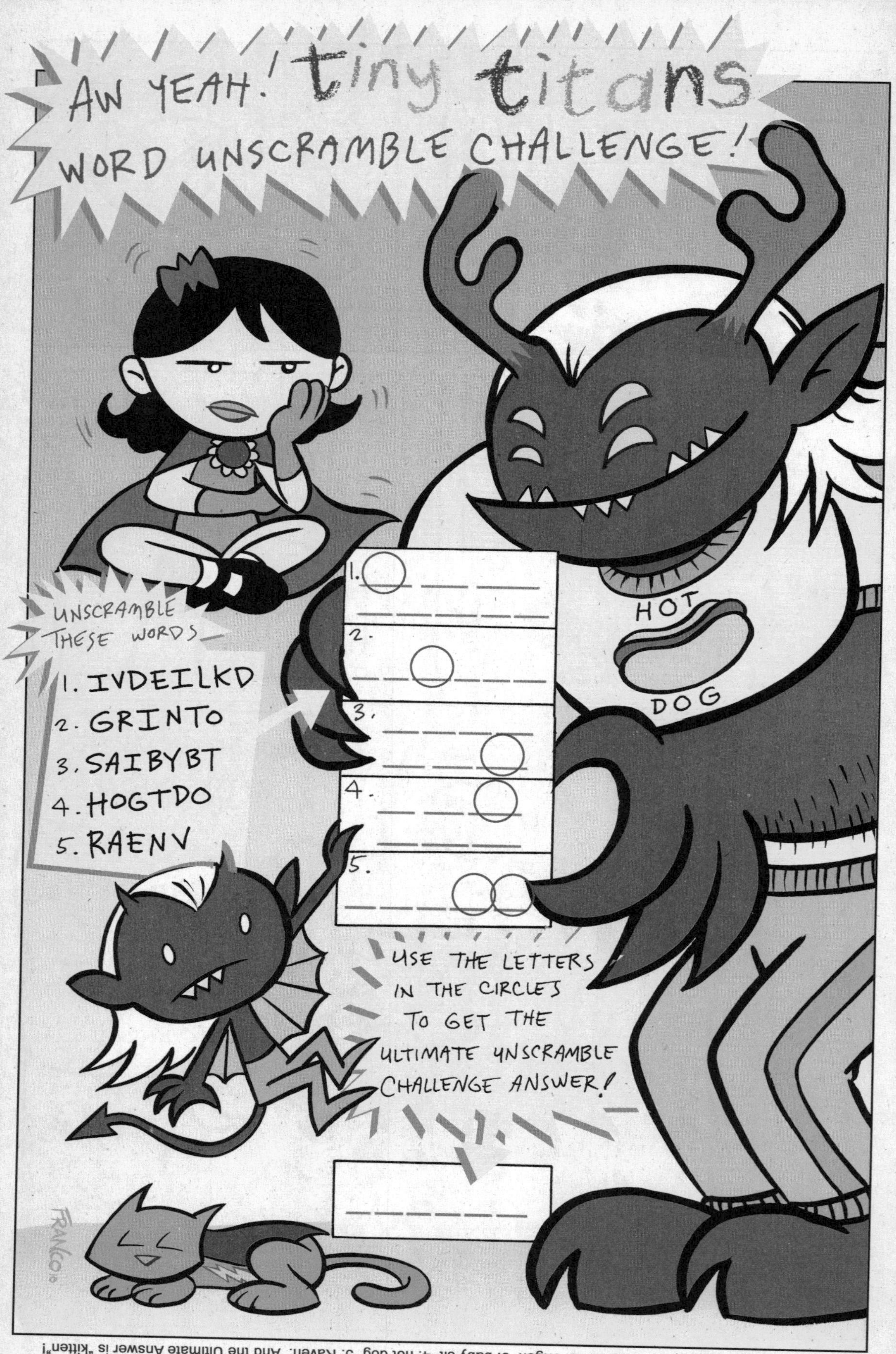

AW YEAH! tiny titans
WORD UNSCRAMBLE CHALLENGE!
UNSCRAMBLE THESE WORDS
1. IVDEILKD
2. GRINTO
3. SAIBYBT
4. HOGTDO
5. RAENV
1.
2.
3.
4.
5.
HOT DOG
USE THE LETTERS IN THE CIRCLES TO GET THE ULTIMATE UNSCRAMBLE CHALLENGE ANSWER!
FRANCO

Secret Answers! (Ssshhh...) 1. Kid Devil 2. Trigon 3. baby sit 4. hot dog 5. Raven. And the Ultimate Answer is "kitten"!

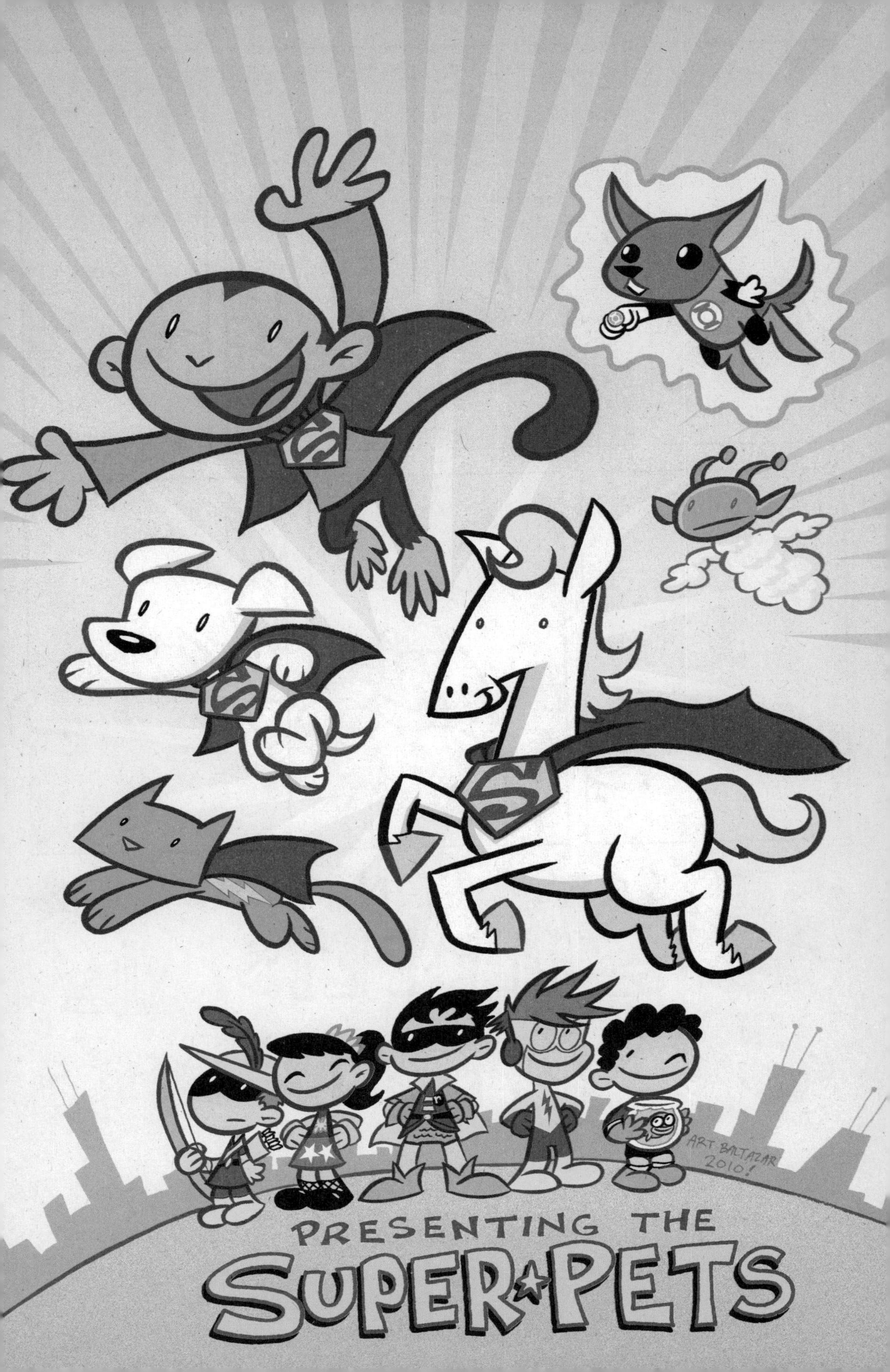
ART BALTAZAR 2010!
PRESENTING THE
SUPER★PETS

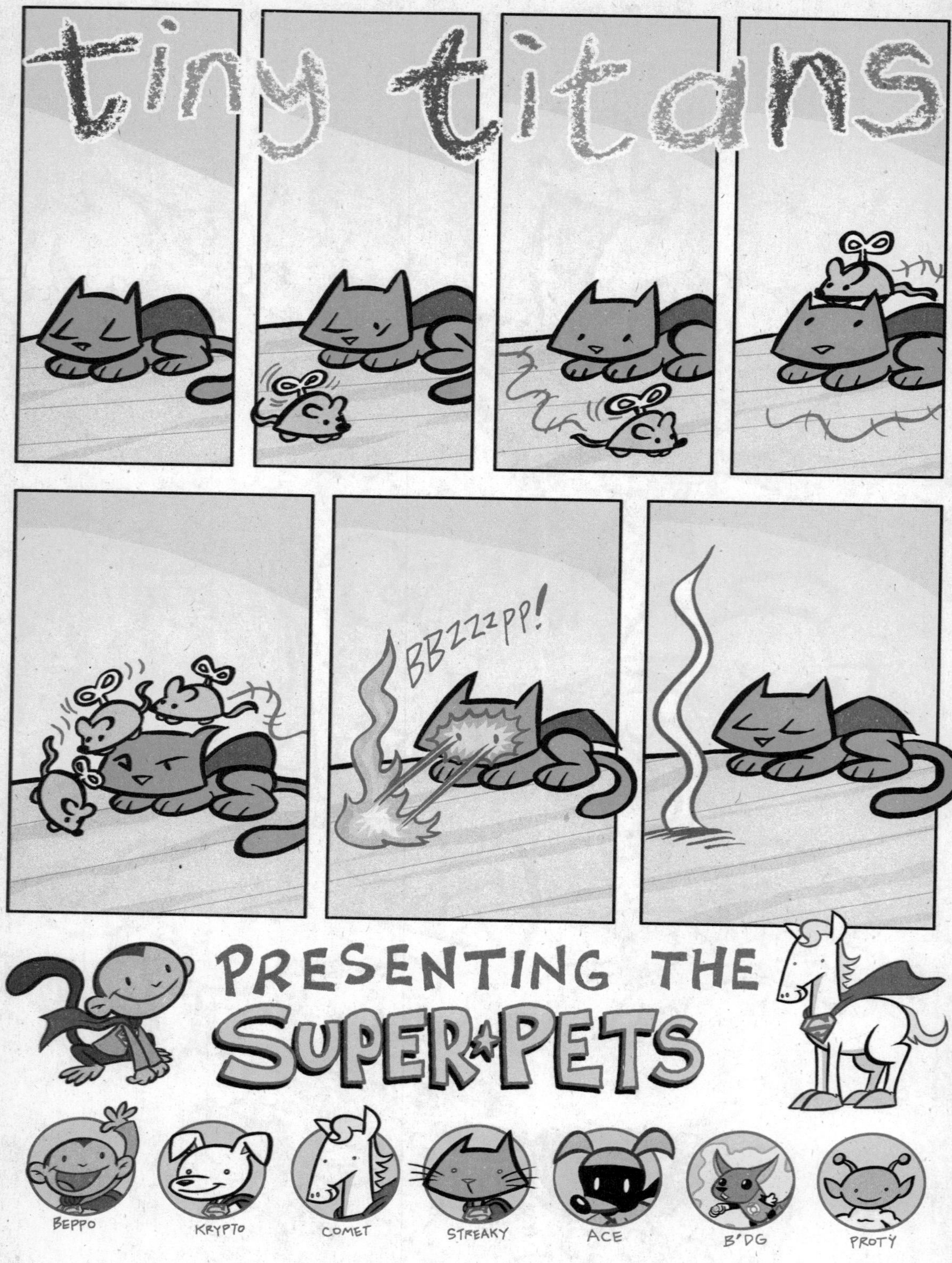
tiny titans
BBZZZzpp!
PRESENTING THE
SUPER*PETS
BEPPO
KRYPTO
COMET
STREAKY
ACE
B'DG
PROTY

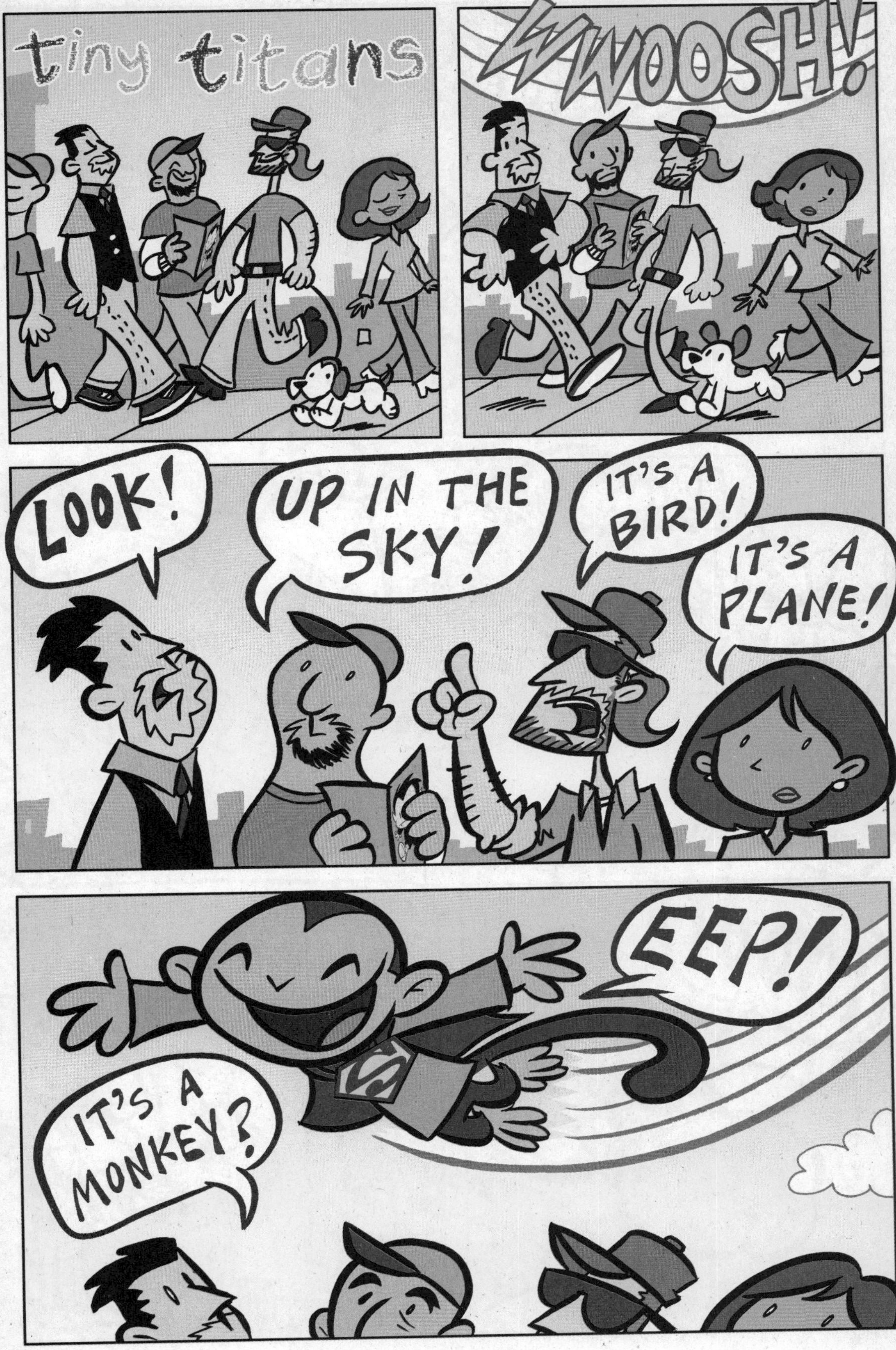
tiny titans
WWOOSH!
LOOK!
UP IN THE SKY!
IT'S A BIRD!
IT'S A PLANE!
EEP!
IT'S A MONKEY?

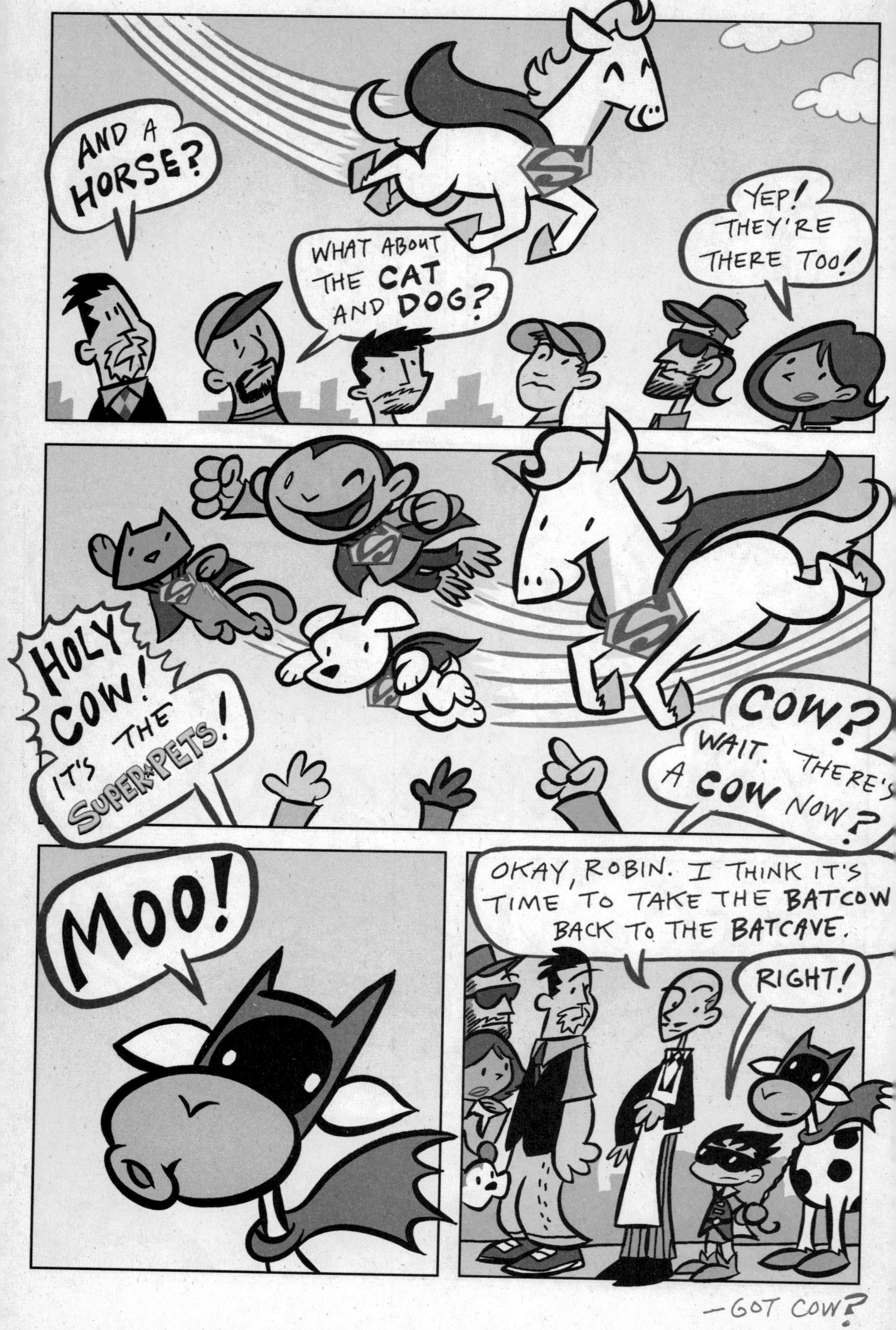
AND A HORSE?
WHAT ABOUT THE CAT AND DOG?
YEP! THEY'RE THERE TOO!
HOLY COW!
IT'S THE SUPER-PETS!
COW?
WAIT. THERE'S A COW NOW?
MOO!
OKAY, ROBIN. I THINK IT'S TIME TO TAKE THE BATCOW BACK TO THE BATCAVE.
RIGHT!
—GOT COW?

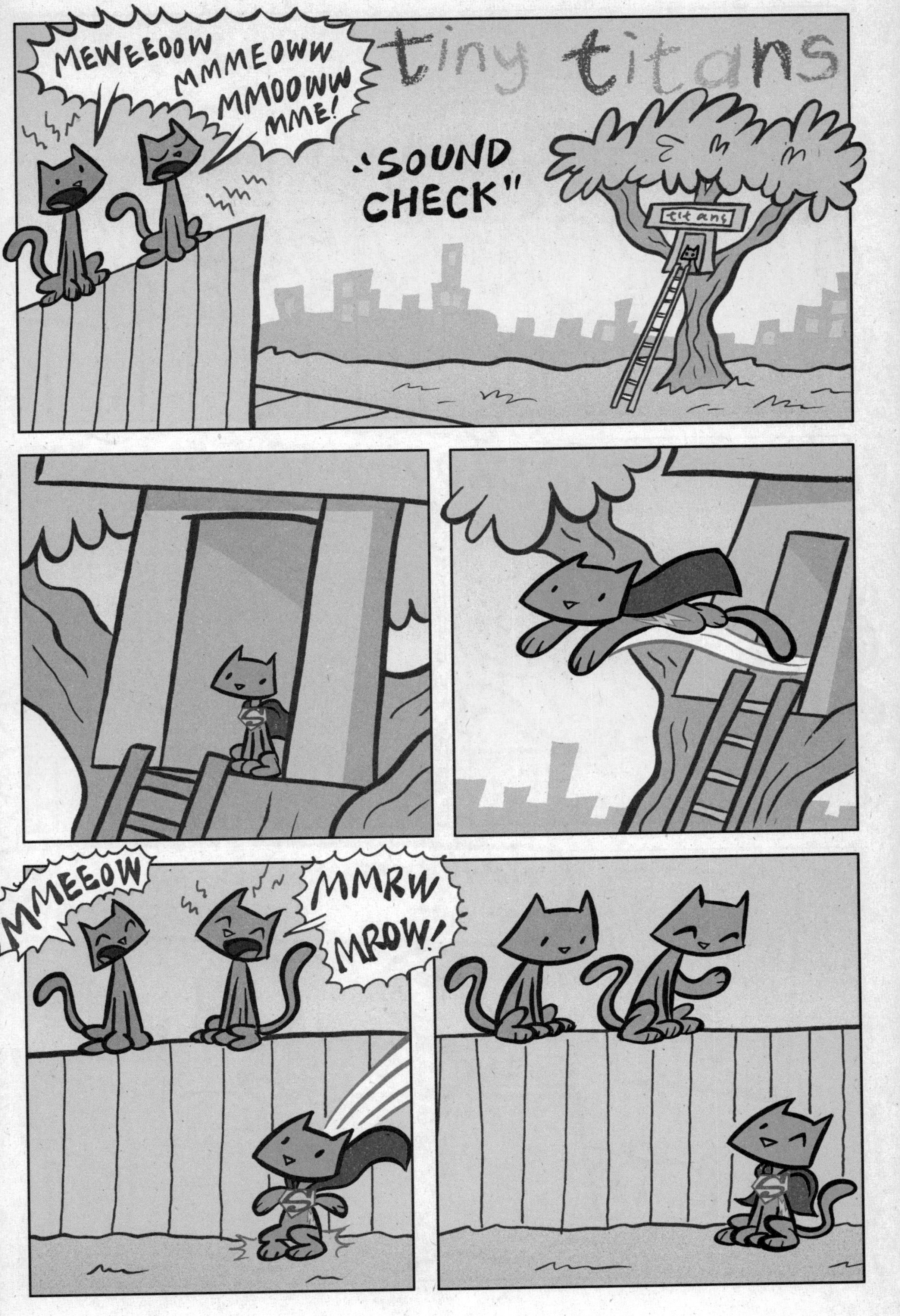
MEWEEOOW
MMMEOWW MMOOWW MME!
tiny titans
"SOUND CHECK"
titans
MMEEOW
MMRW MROW!

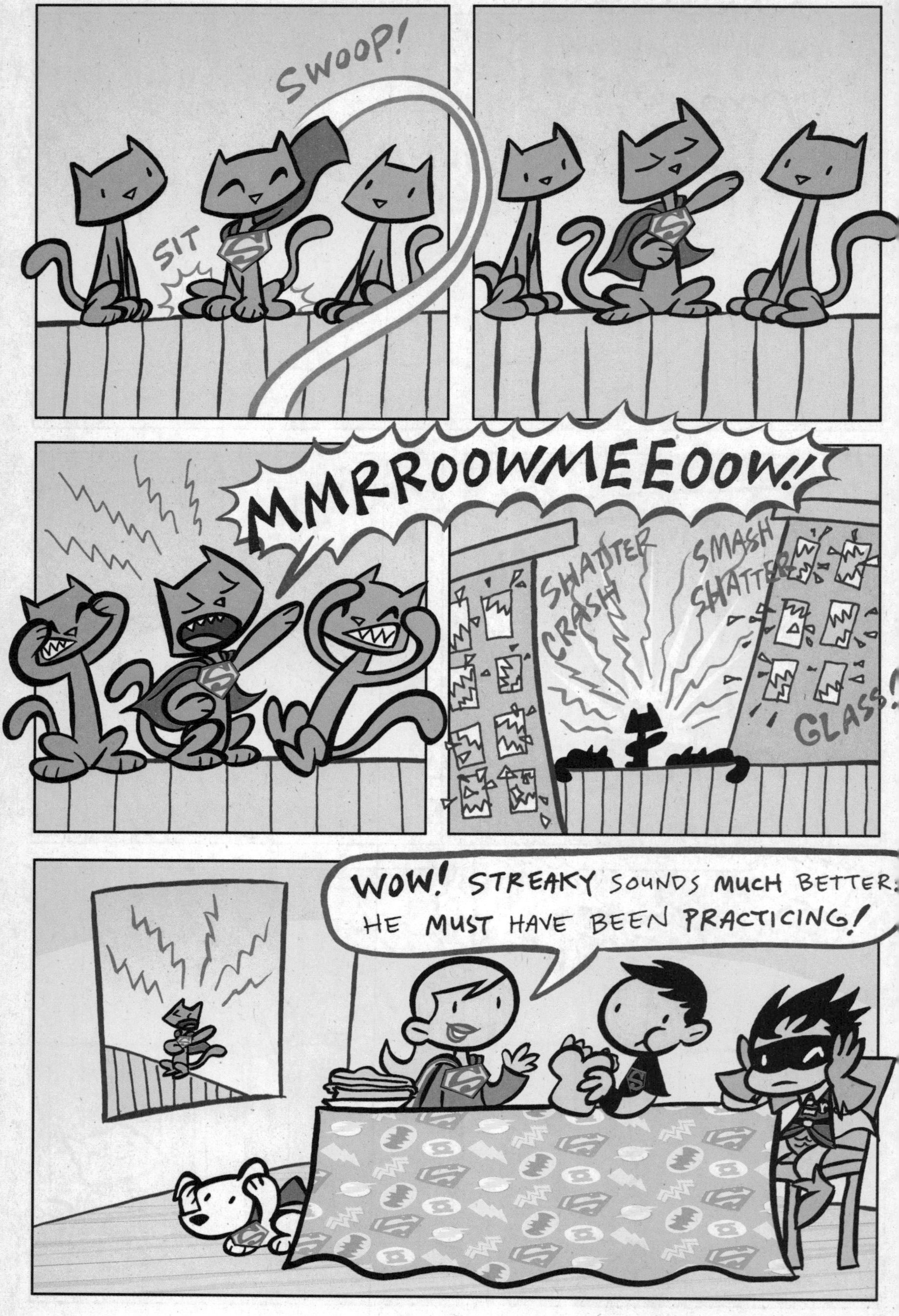
SWOOP!
SIT
MMRROOWMEEOOW!
SHATTER
CRASH
SMASH
SHATTER
GLASS!
WOW! STREAKY SOUNDS MUCH BETTER:
HE MUST HAVE BEEN PRACTICING!

—TUNE A TUNA.

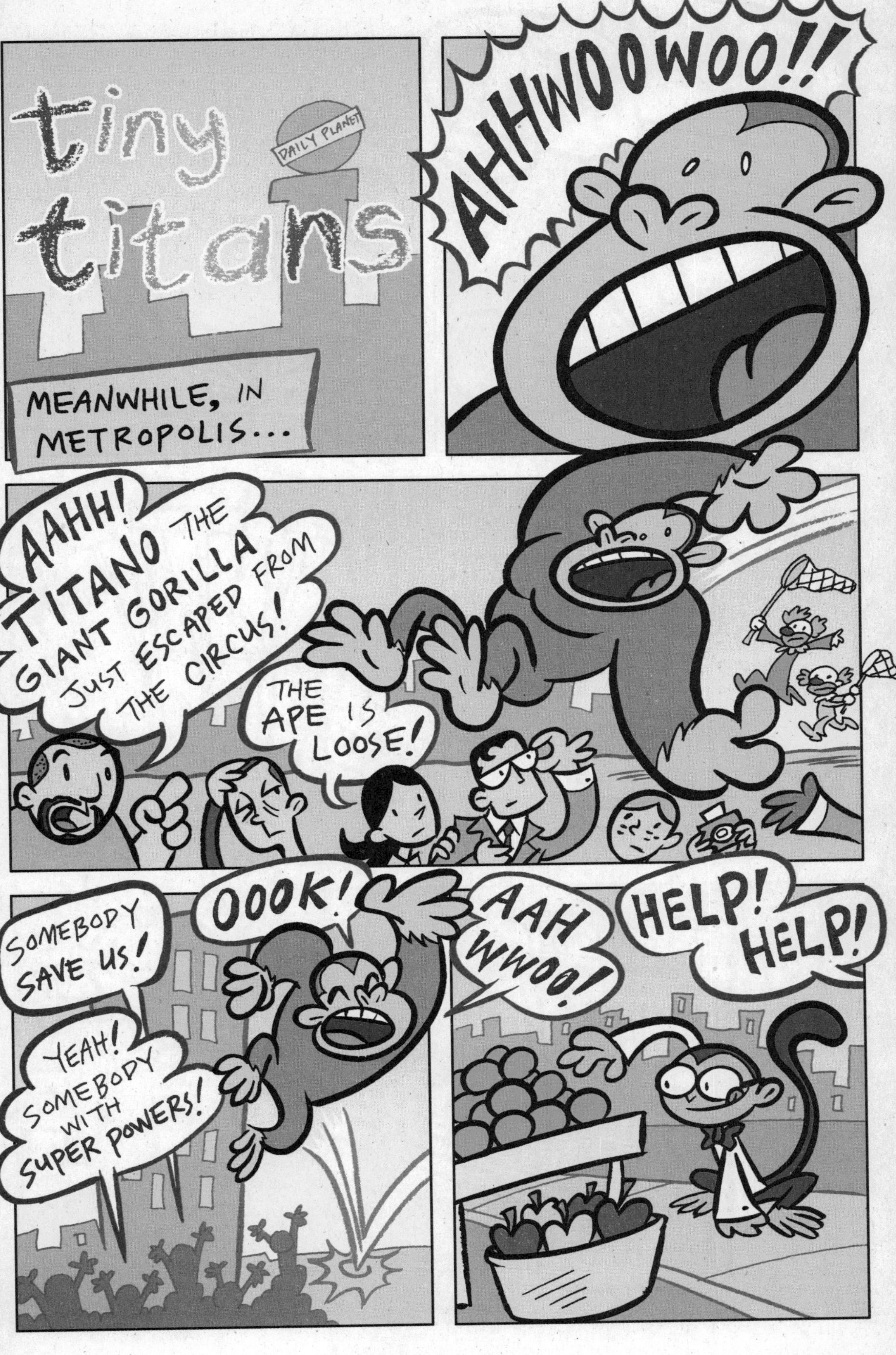
tiny titans
DAILY PLANET
MEANWHILE, IN METROPOLIS...
AHHWOOWOO!!
AAHH! TITANO THE GIANT GORILLA JUST ESCAPED FROM THE CIRCUS!
THE APE IS LOOSE!
SOMEBODY SAVE US!
OOOK!
YEAH! SOMEBODY WITH SUPER POWERS!
AAH WWOO!
HELP! HELP!

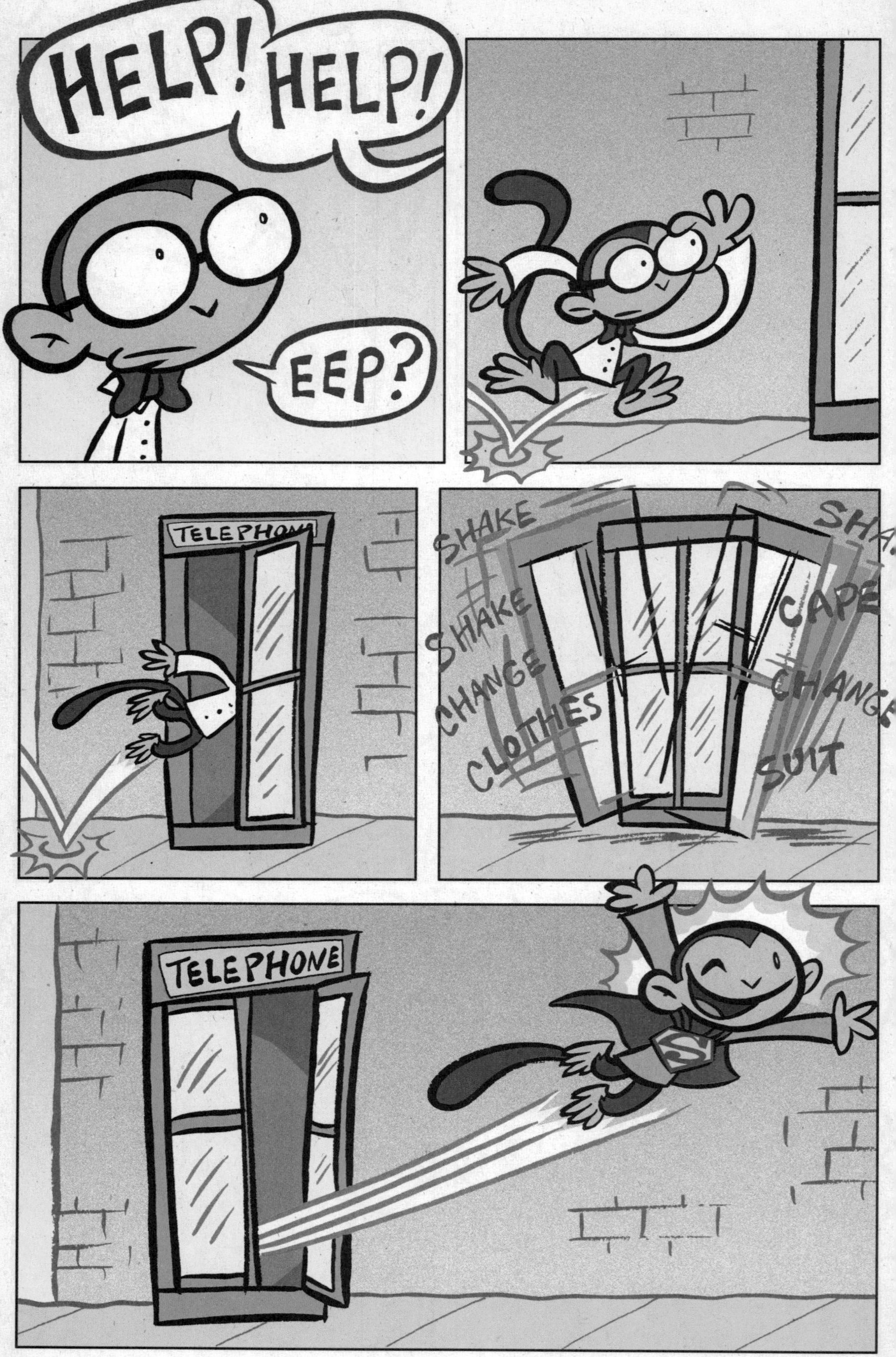
HELP! HELP!
EEP?
TELEPHONE
SHAKE
SHAKE
CHANGE
CLOTHES
CAPE
CHANGE
SUIT
TELEPHONE

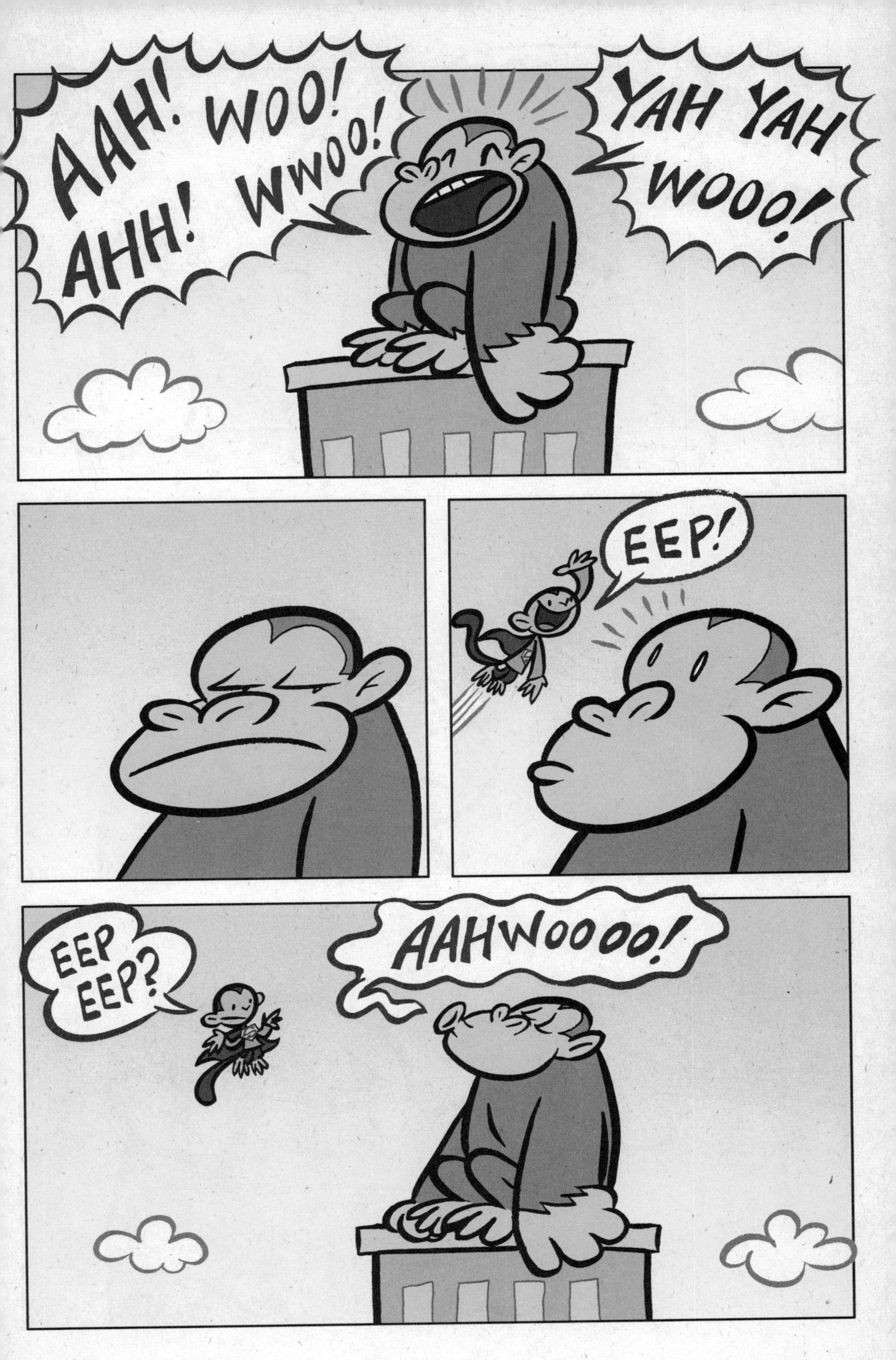
AAH! WOO! AHH! WWOO!
YAH YAH WOOO!
EEP!
EEP EEP?
AAHWOOOO!

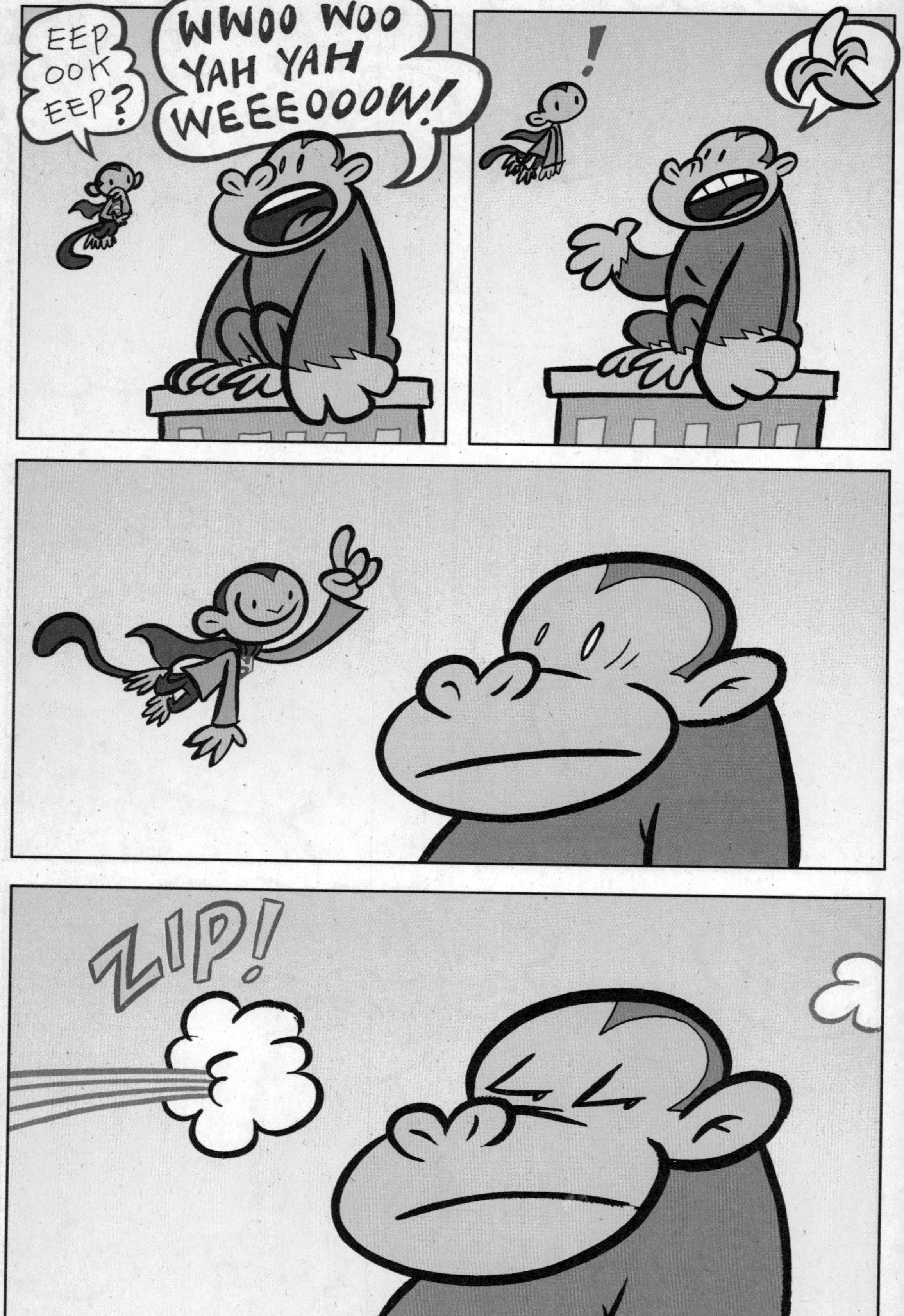
EEP OOK EEP?
WWOO WOO YAH YAH WEEEOOOW!
!
ZIP!

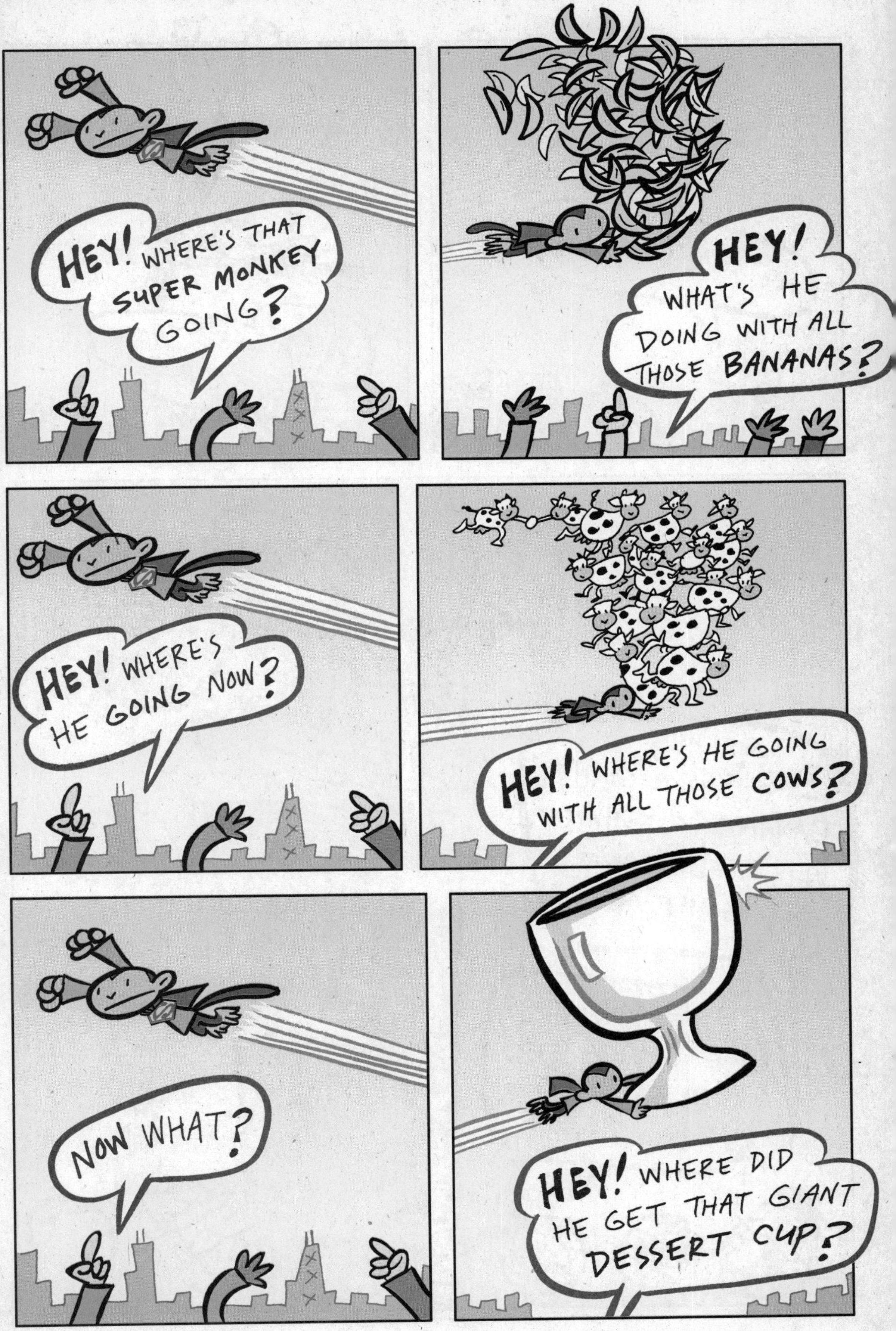
HEY! WHERE'S THAT SUPER MONKEY GOING?
HEY! WHAT'S HE DOING WITH ALL THOSE BANANAS?
HEY! WHERE'S HE GOING NOW?
HEY! WHERE'S HE GOING WITH ALL THOSE COWS?
NOW WHAT?
HEY! WHERE DID HE GET THAT GIANT DESSERT CUP?

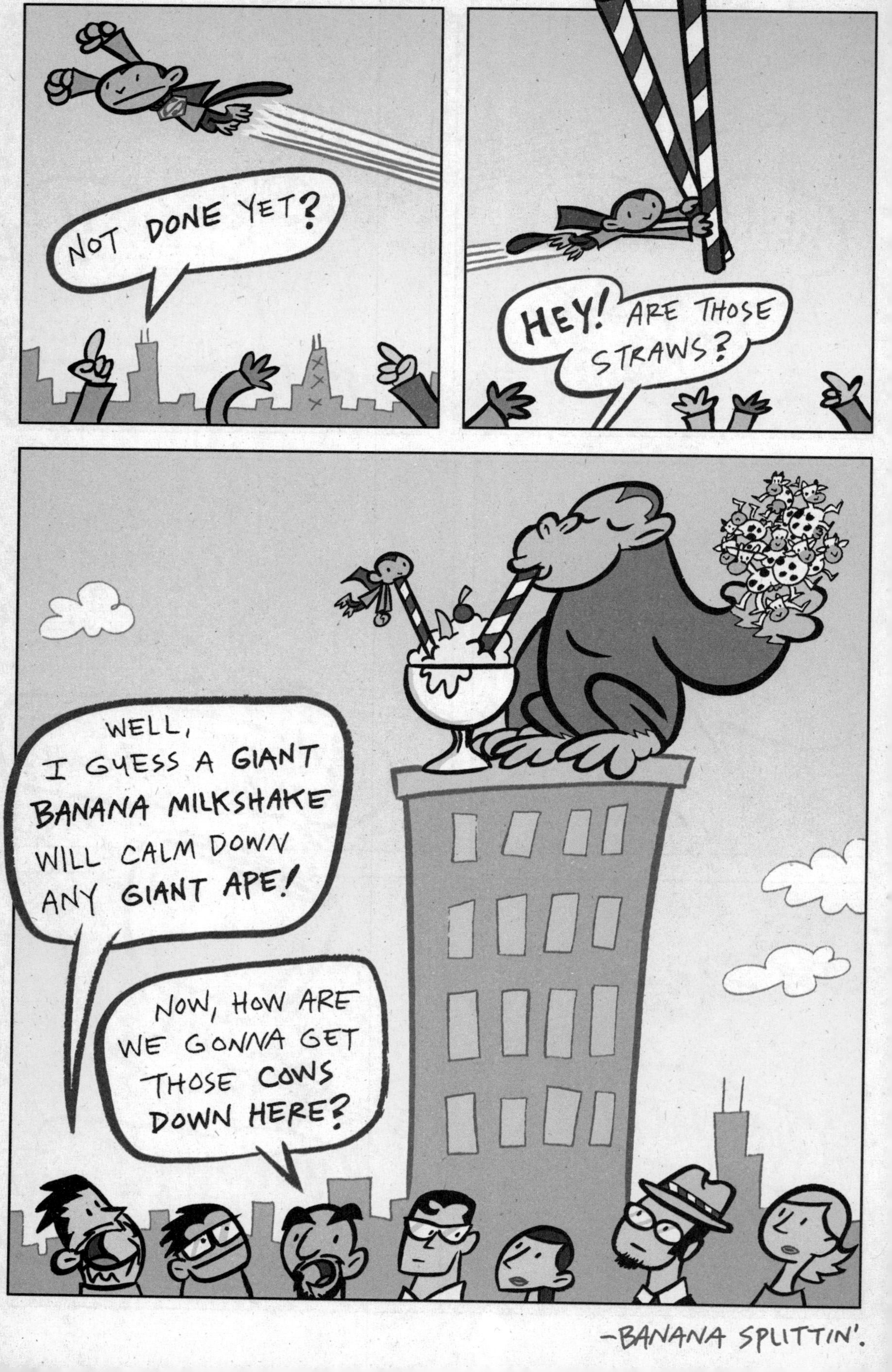
NOT DONE YET?
HEY! ARE THOSE STRAWS?
WELL, I GUESS A GIANT BANANA MILKSHAKE WILL CALM DOWN ANY GIANT APE!
NOW, HOW ARE WE GONNA GET THOSE COWS DOWN HERE?

—BANANA SPLITTIN'.

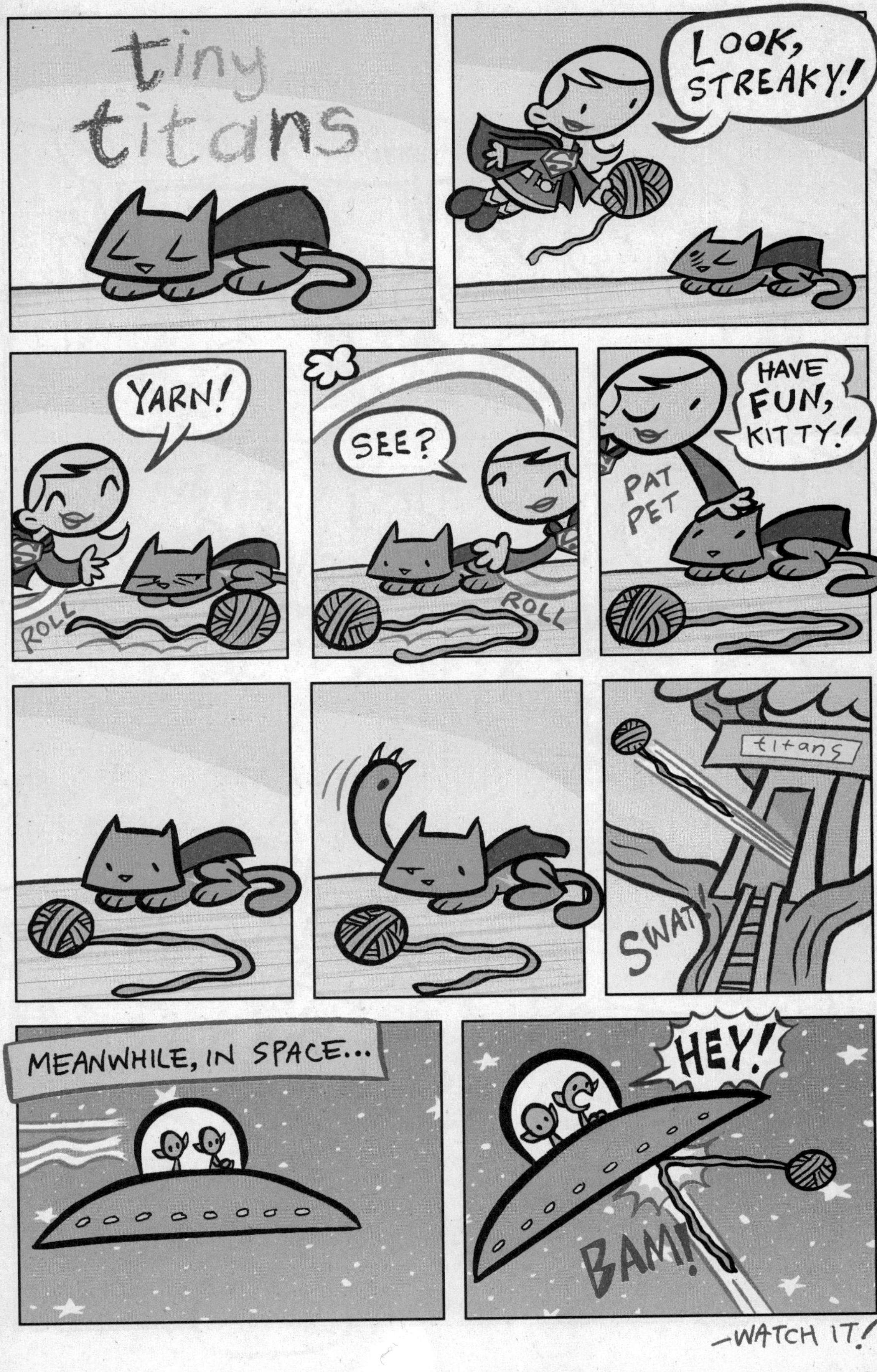
tiny titans
LOOK, STREAKY!
YARN!
ROLL
SEE?
ROLL
HAVE FUN, KITTY!
PAT PET
titans
SWAT!
MEANWHILE, IN SPACE...
HEY!
BAM!
-WATCH IT!

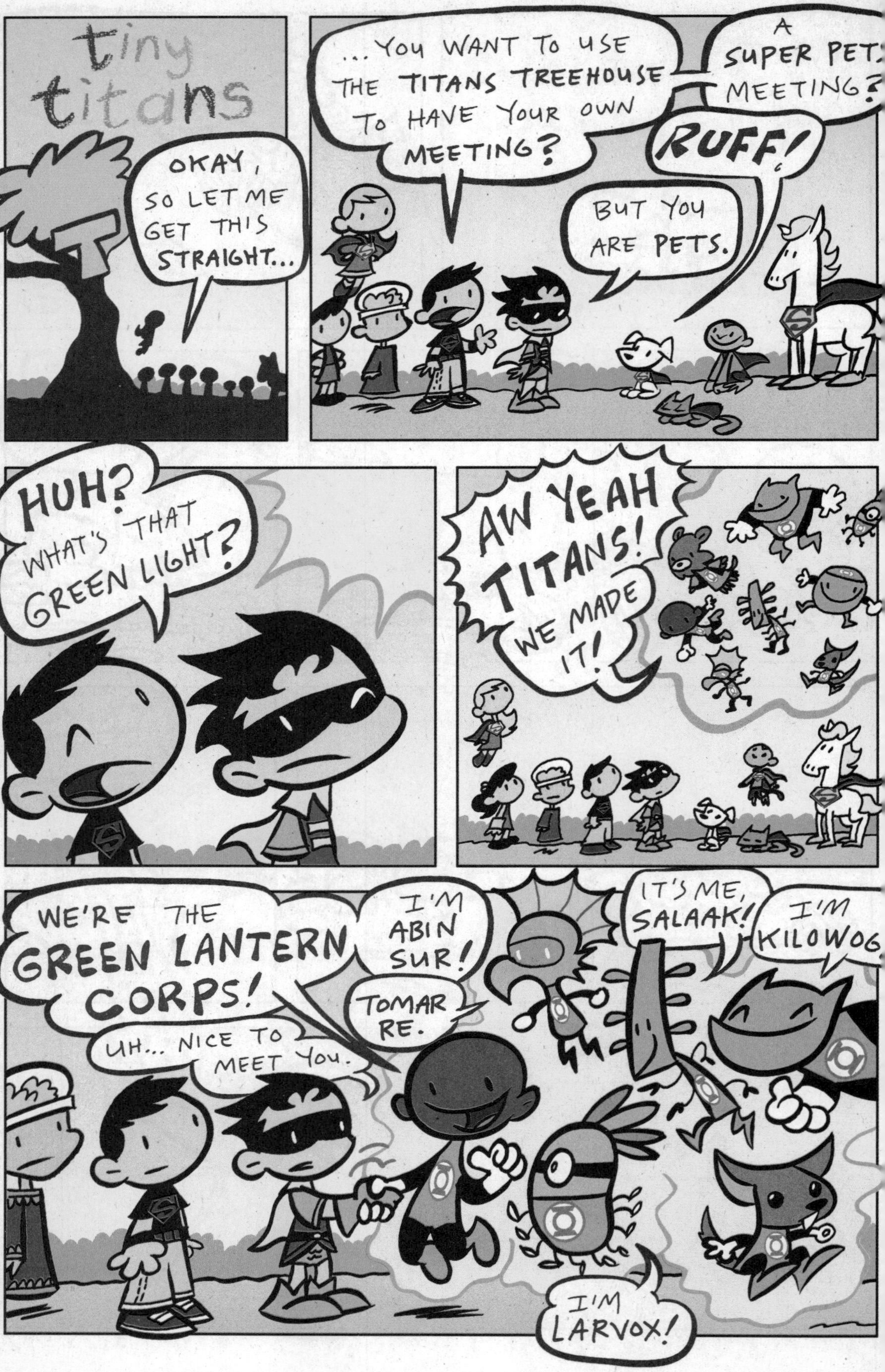
tiny titans
OKAY, SO LET ME GET THIS STRAIGHT...
...YOU WANT TO USE THE TITANS TREEHOUSE TO HAVE YOUR OWN MEETING?
A SUPER PET MEETING?
RUFF!
BUT YOU ARE PETS.
HUH? WHAT'S THAT GREEN LIGHT?
AW YEAH TITANS!
WE MADE IT!
WE'RE THE GREEN LANTERN CORPS!
I'M ABIN SUR!
TOMAR RE.
IT'S ME, SALAAK!
I'M KILOWOG
UH... NICE TO MEET YOU.
I'M LARVOX!

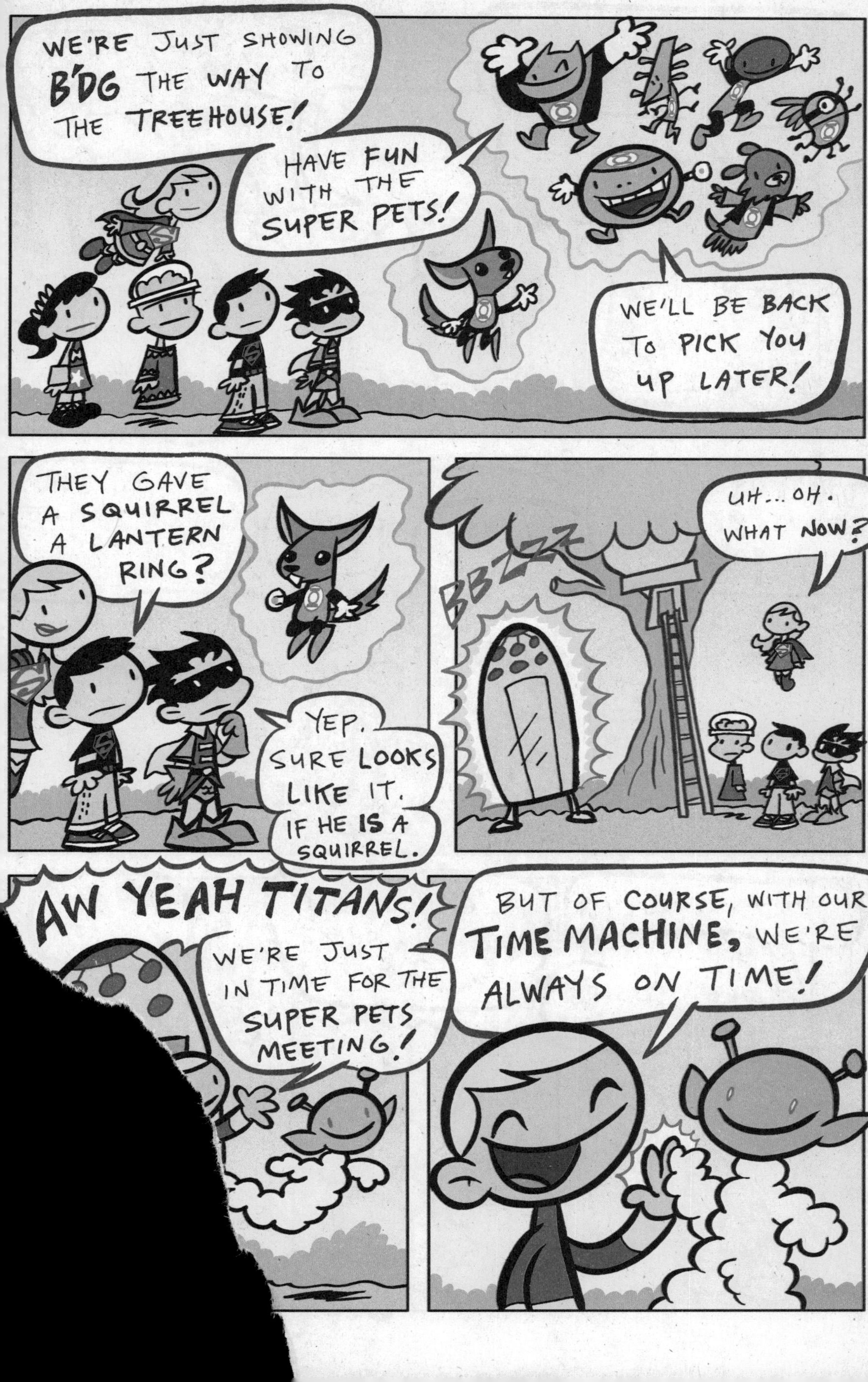

WE'RE JUST SHOWING B'DG THE WAY TO THE TREEHOUSE!
HAVE FUN WITH THE SUPER PETS!
WE'LL BE BACK TO PICK YOU UP LATER!
THEY GAVE A SQUIRREL A LANTERN RING?
YEP. SURE LOOKS LIKE IT. IF HE IS A SQUIRREL.
BBZZZZ
UH... OH. WHAT NOW?
AW YEAH TITANS!
WE'RE JUST IN TIME FOR THE SUPER PETS MEETING!
BUT OF COURSE, WITH OUR TIME MACHINE, WE'RE ALWAYS ON TIME!

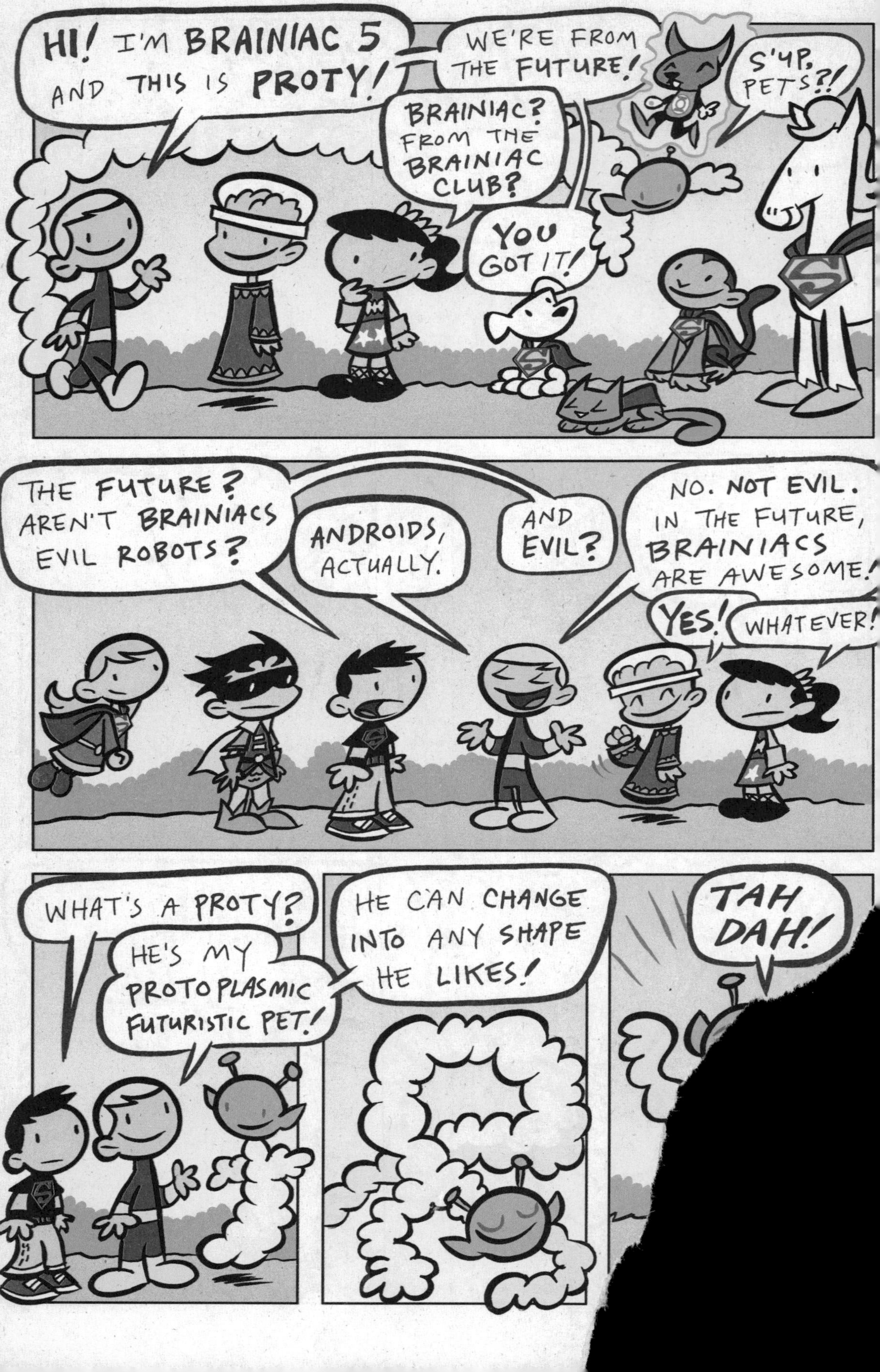

HI! I'M BRAINIAC 5 AND THIS IS PROTY!
WE'RE FROM THE FUTURE!
S'UP, PETS?!
BRAINIAC? FROM THE BRAINIAC CLUB?
YOU GOT IT!
THE FUTURE? AREN'T BRAINIACS EVIL ROBOTS?
ANDROIDS, ACTUALLY.
AND EVIL?
NO. NOT EVIL. IN THE FUTURE, BRAINIACS ARE AWESOME!
YES!
WHATEVER!
WHAT'S A PROTY?
HE'S MY PROTOPLASMIC FUTURISTIC PET!
HE CAN CHANGE INTO ANY SHAPE HE LIKES!
TAH DAH!

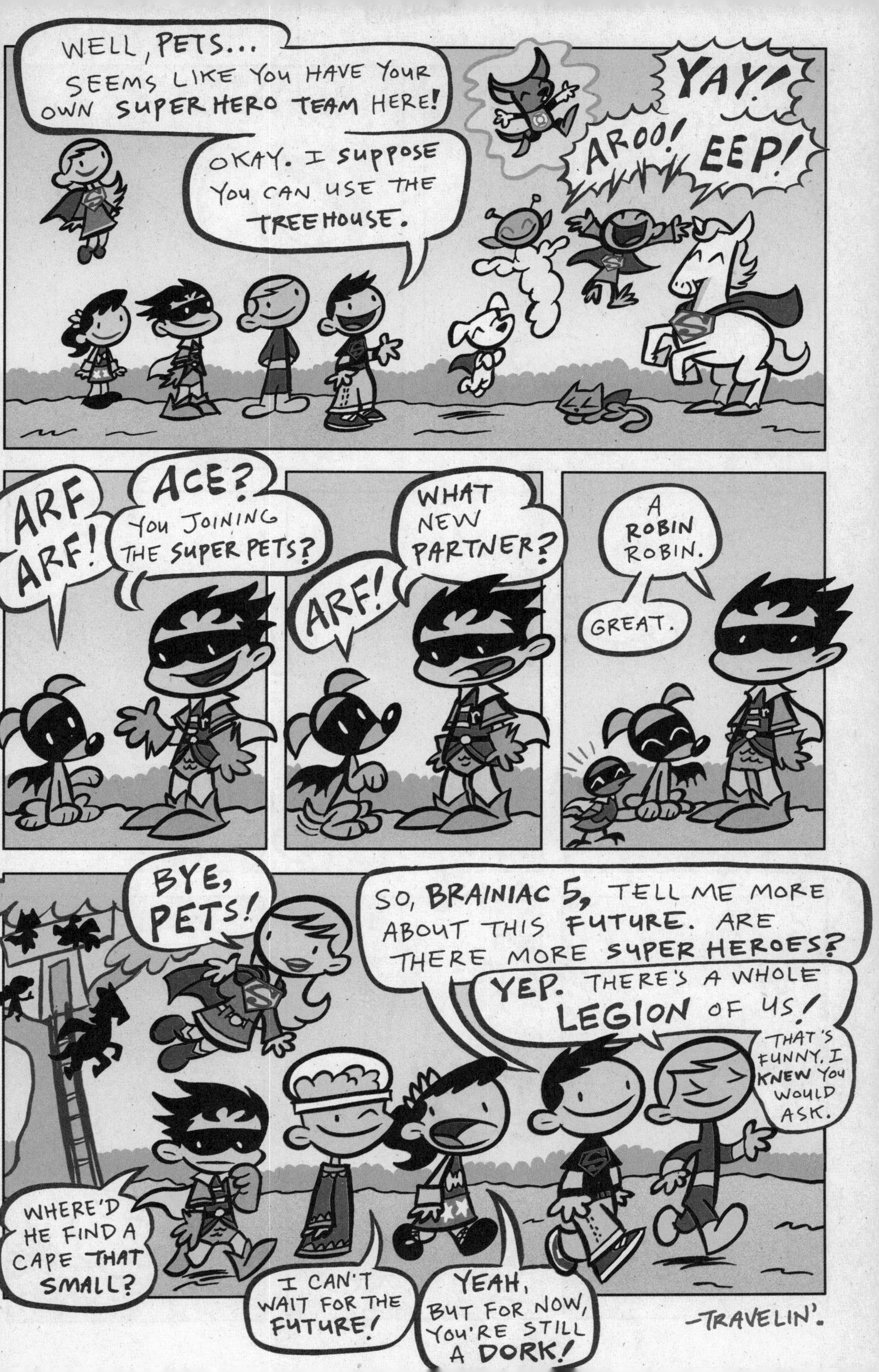
WELL, PETS... SEEMS LIKE YOU HAVE YOUR OWN SUPER HERO TEAM HERE!
OKAY. I SUPPOSE YOU CAN USE THE TREEHOUSE.
YAY!
AROO!
EEP!
ARF ARF!
ACE? YOU JOINING THE SUPER PETS?
ARF!
WHAT NEW PARTNER?
A ROBIN ROBIN.
GREAT.
BYE, PETS!
SO, BRAINIAC 5, TELL ME MORE ABOUT THIS FUTURE. ARE THERE MORE SUPER HEROES?
YEP. THERE'S A WHOLE LEGION OF US!
THAT'S FUNNY. I KNEW YOU WOULD ASK.
WHERE'D HE FIND A CAPE THAT SMALL?
I CAN'T WAIT FOR THE FUTURE!
YEAH, BUT FOR NOW, YOU'RE STILL A DORK!
-TRAVELIN'.

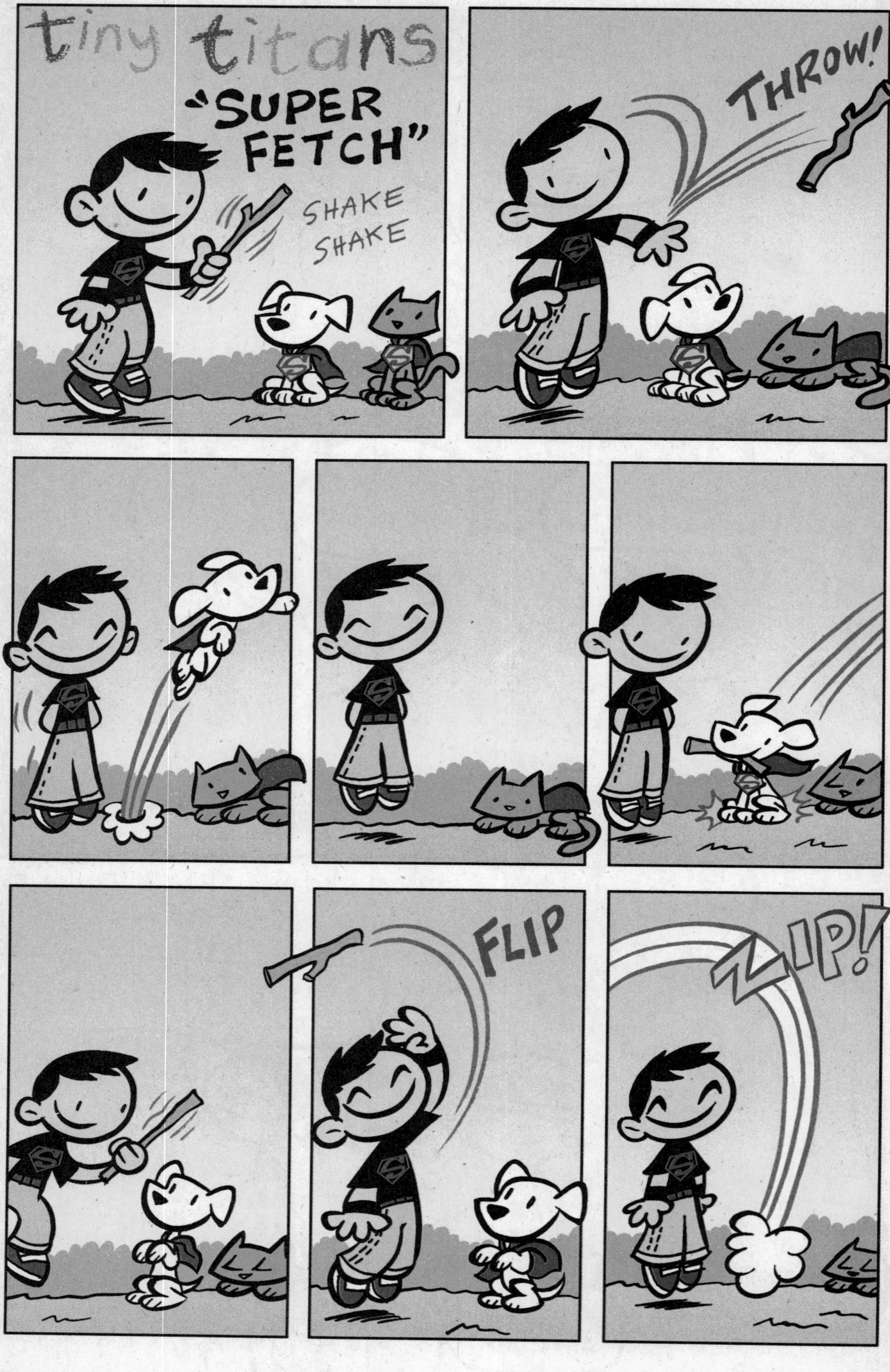
tiny titans
"SUPER FETCH"
SHAKE SHAKE
THROW!
FLIP
ZIP!

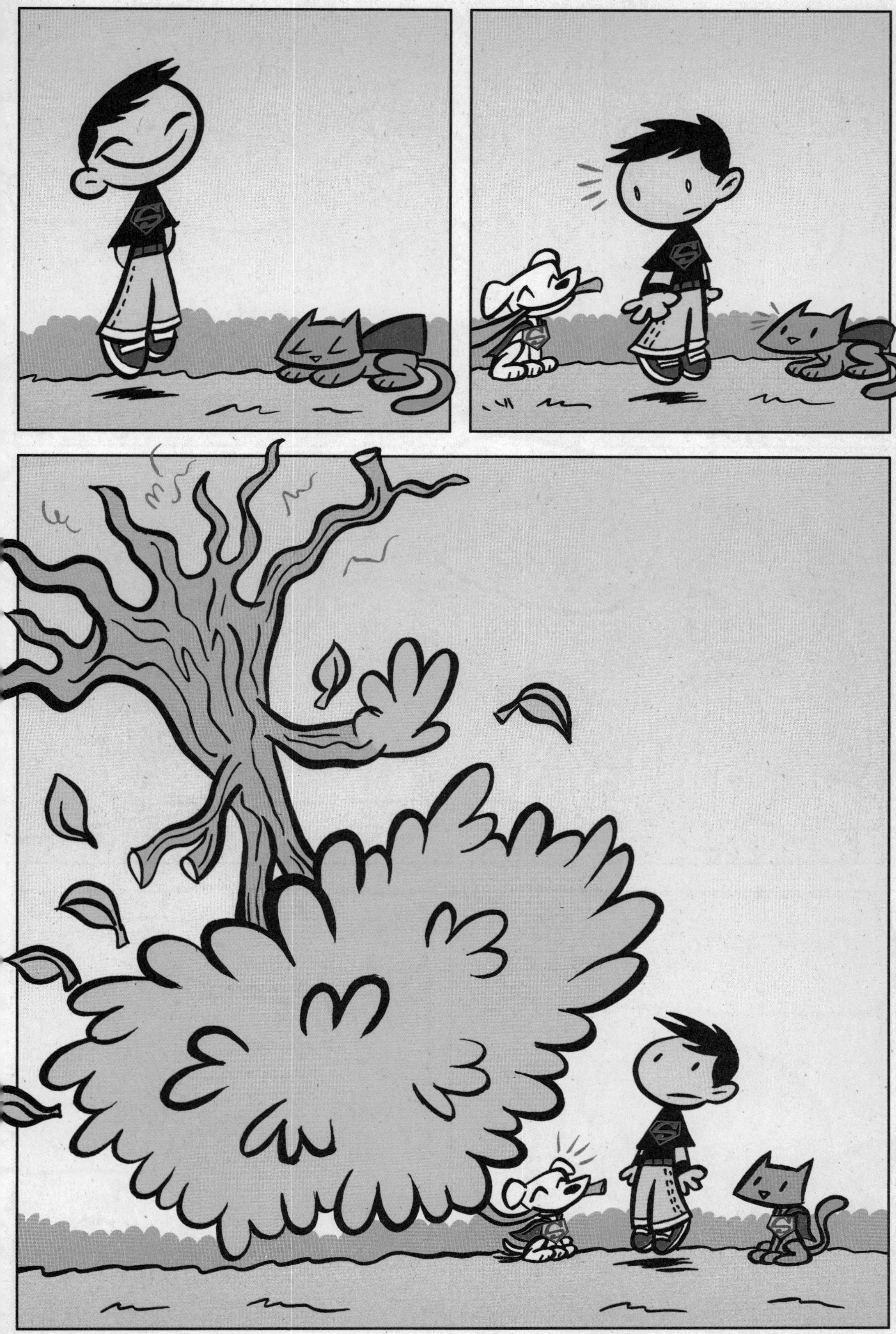

—BARK!

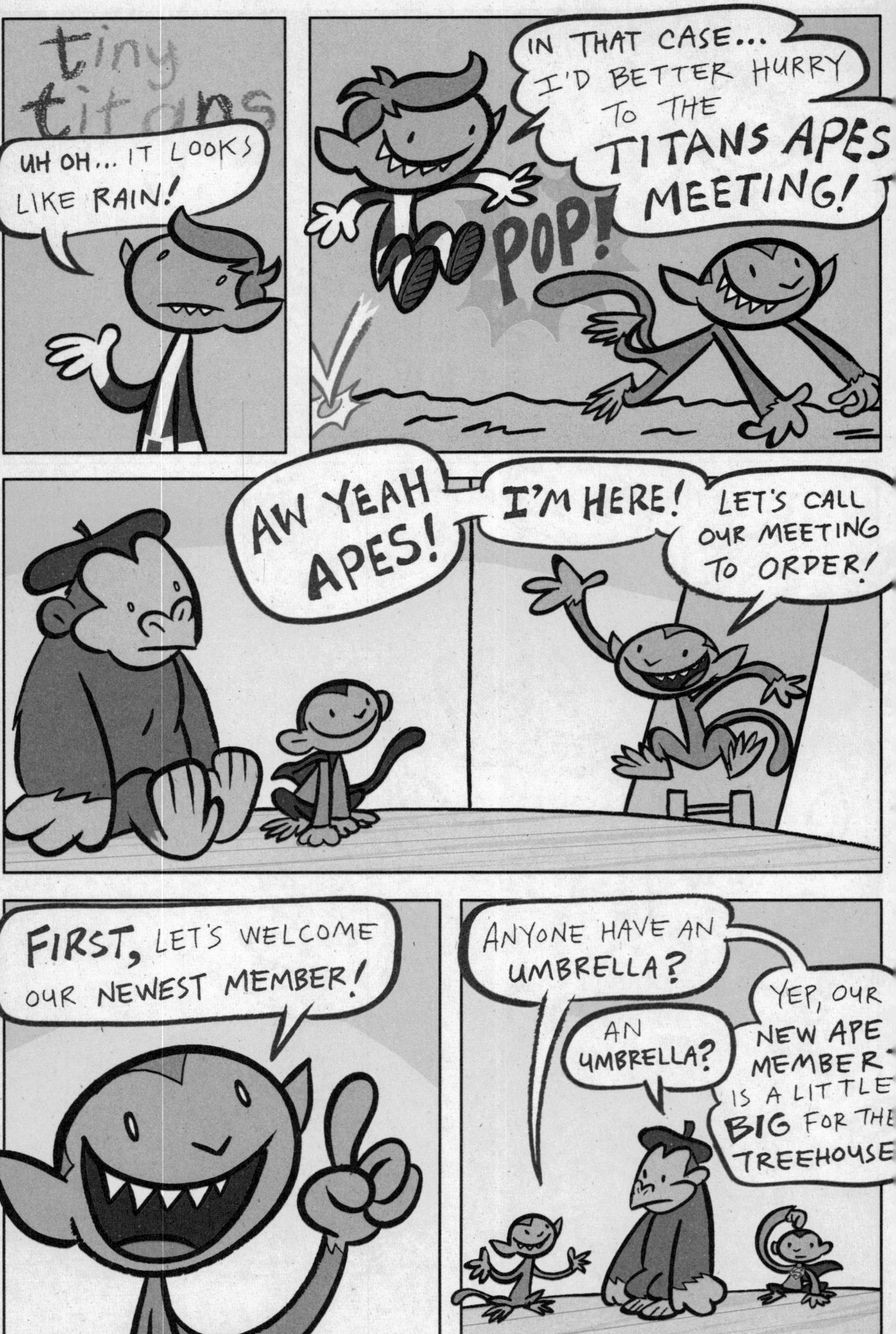
tiny titans
UH OH... IT LOOKS LIKE RAIN!
IN THAT CASE... I'D BETTER HURRY TO THE TITANS APES MEETING!
POP!
AW YEAH APES!
I'M HERE!
LET'S CALL OUR MEETING TO ORDER!
FIRST, LET'S WELCOME OUR NEWEST MEMBER!
ANYONE HAVE AN UMBRELLA?
AN UMBRELLA?
YEP, OUR NEW APE MEMBER IS A LITTLE BIG FOR THE TREEHOUSE

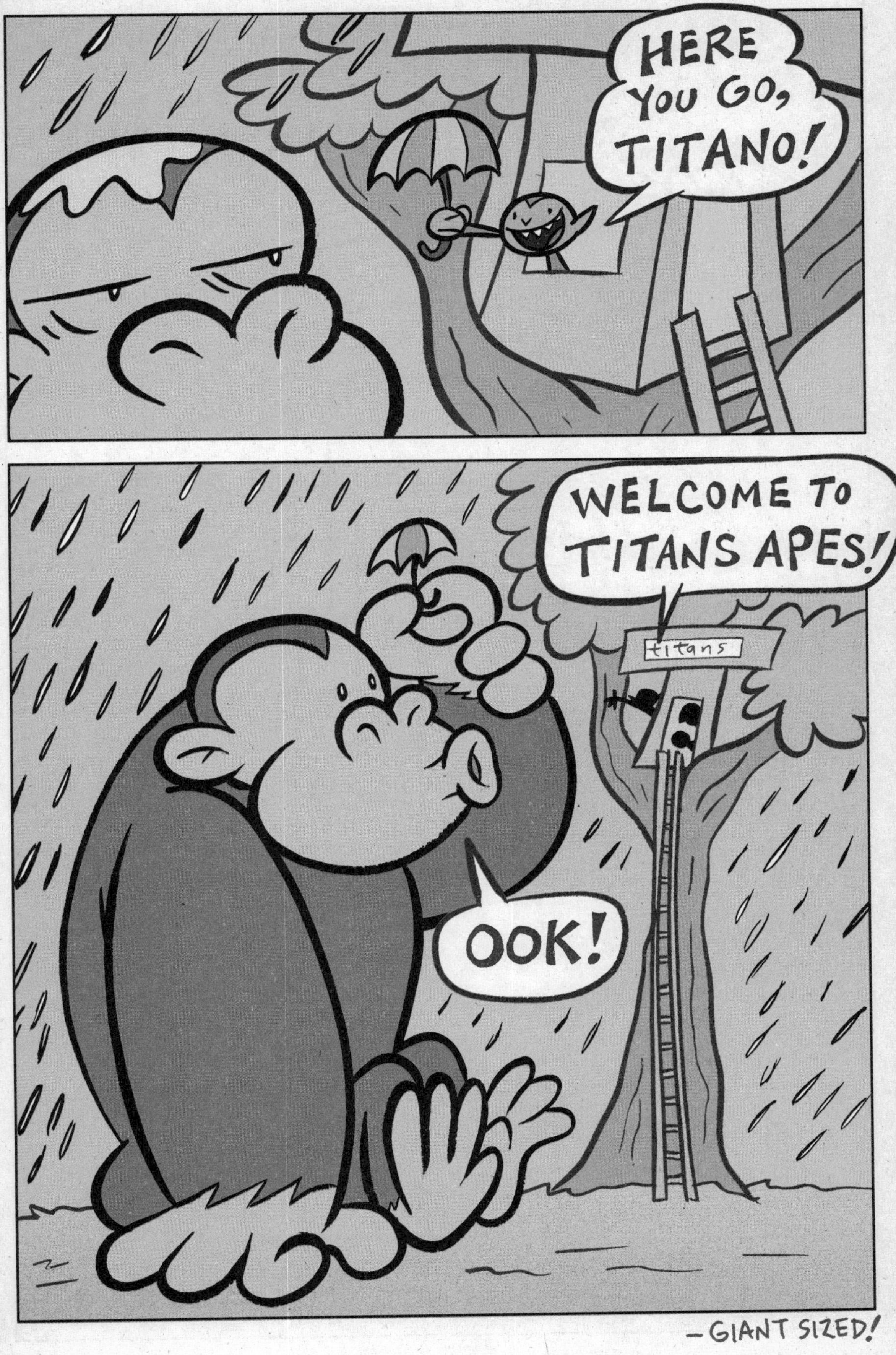
HERE YOU GO, TITANO!
WELCOME TO TITANS APES!
titans
OOK!
—GIANT SIZED!

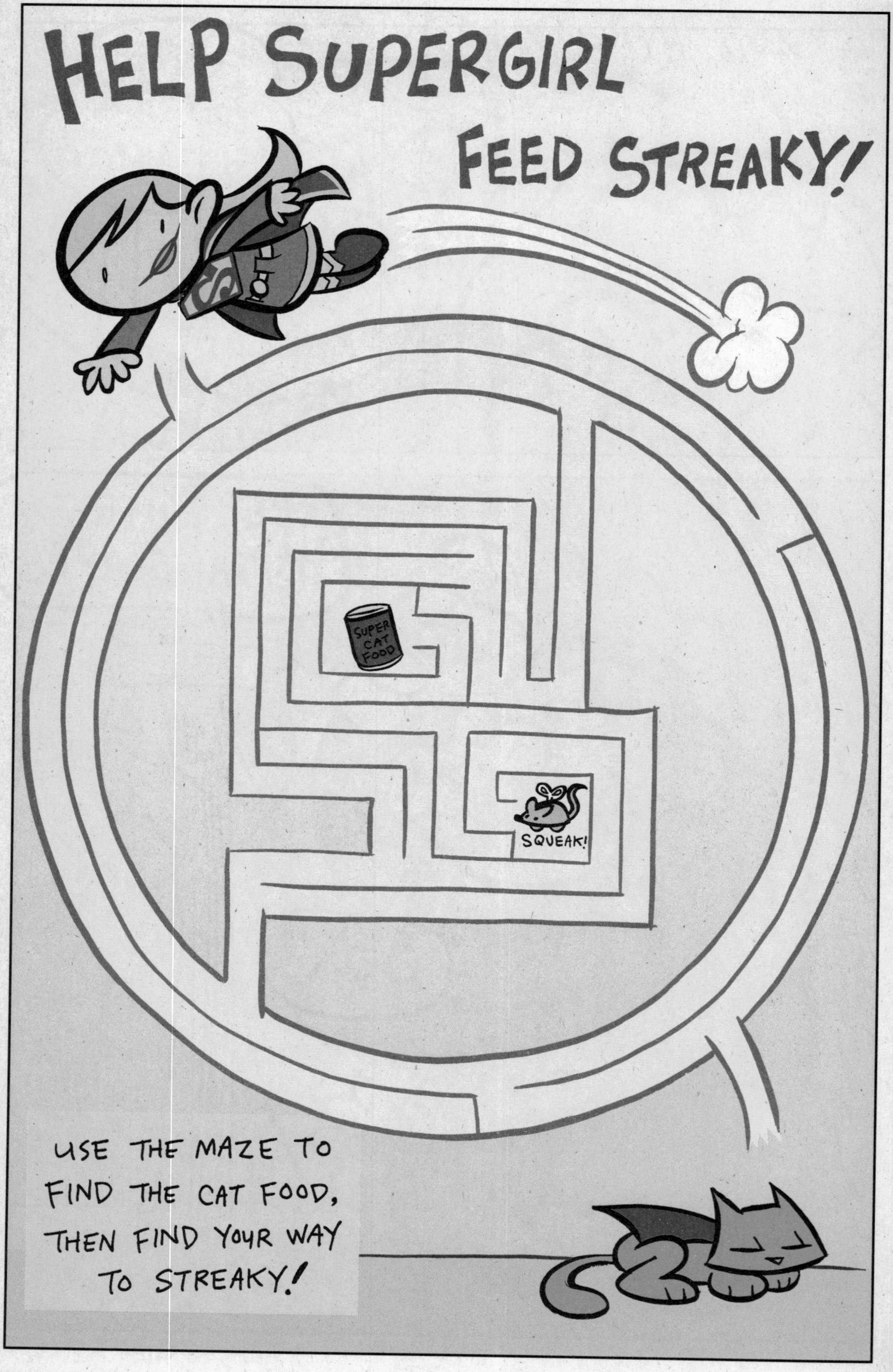
HELP SUPERGIRL FEED STREAKY!
SUPER CAT FOOD
SQUEAK!
USE THE MAZE TO FIND THE CAT FOOD, THEN FIND YOUR WAY TO STREAKY!

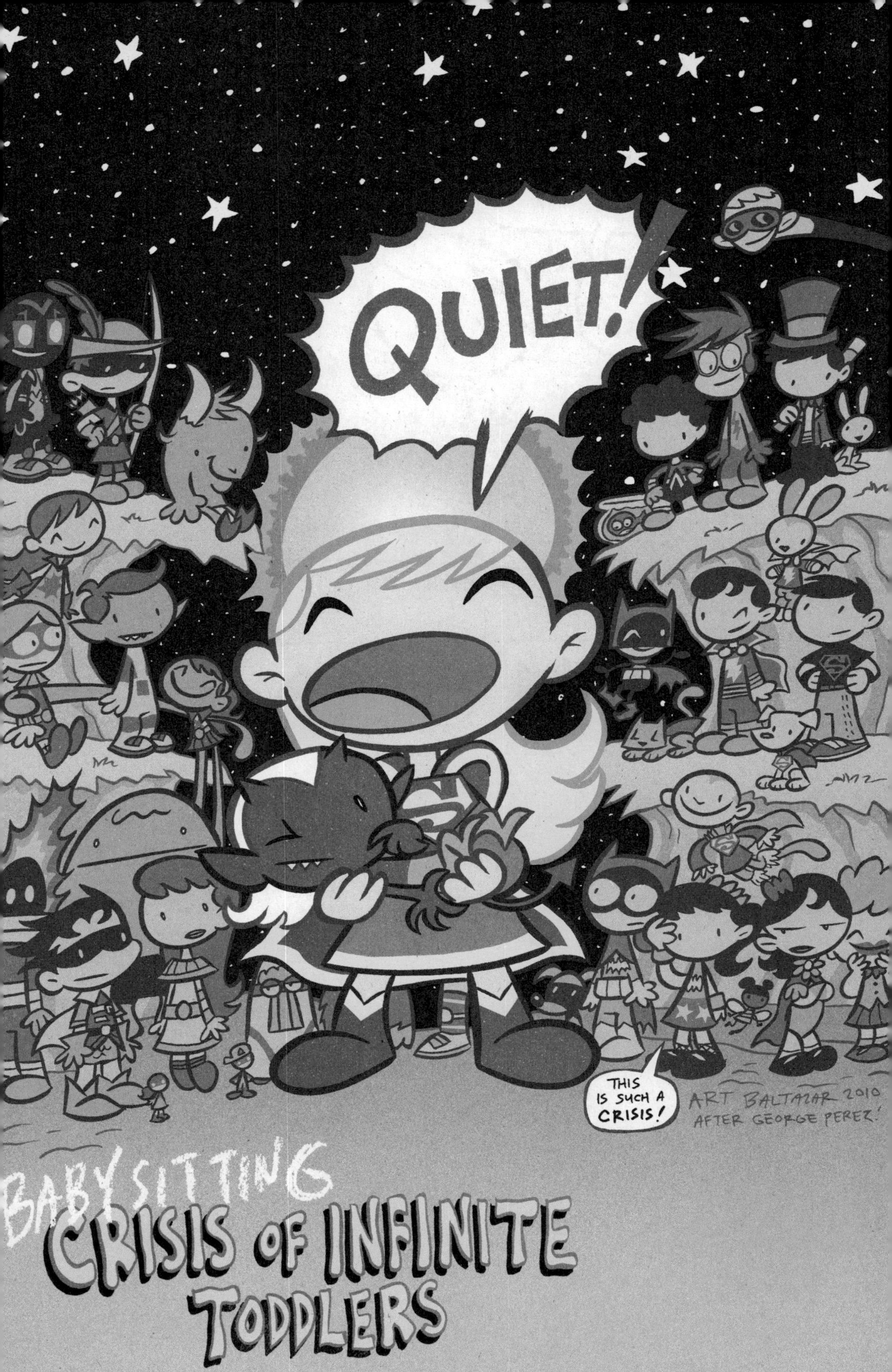
QUIET!
THIS IS SUCH A CRISIS!
ART BALTAZAR 2010
AFTER GEORGE PEREZ!

BABYSITTING CRISIS OF INFINITE TODDLERS

tiny titans

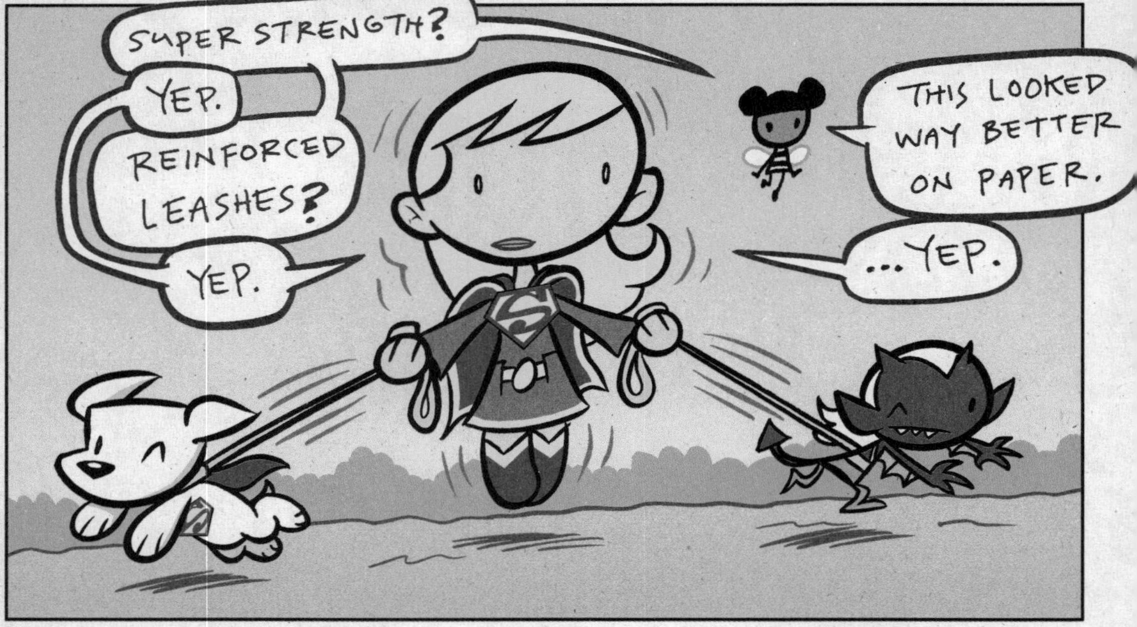
SUPER STRENGTH?
YEP.
REINFORCED LEASHES?
YEP.
THIS LOOKED WAY BETTER ON PAPER.
...YEP.

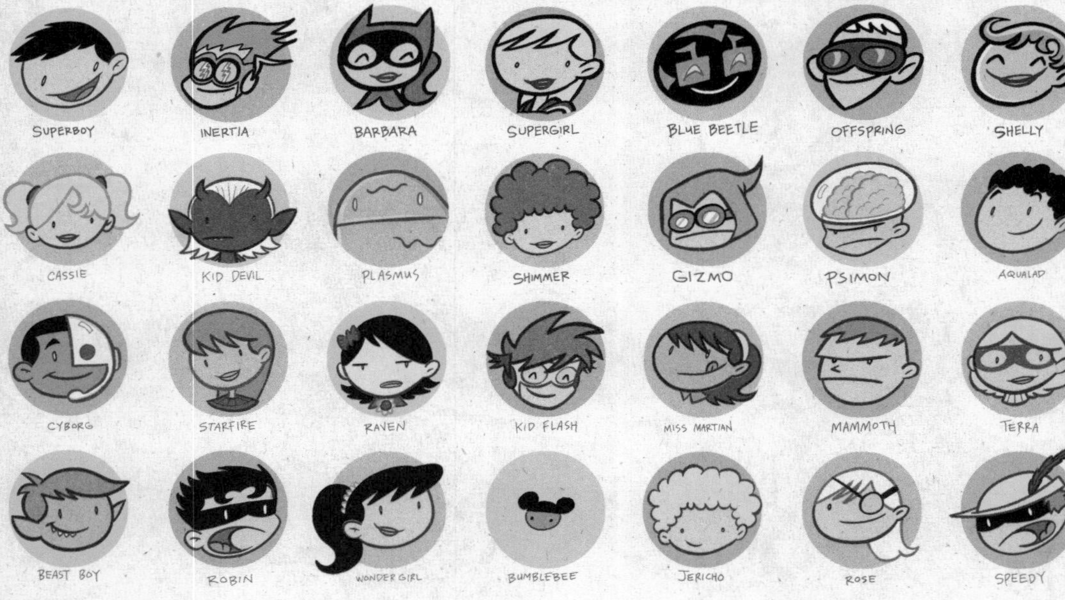
SUPERBOY
INERTIA
BARBARA
SUPERGIRL
BLUE BEETLE
OFFSPRING
SHELLY
CASSIE
KID DEVIL
PLASMUS
SHIMMER
GIZMO
PSIMON
AQUALAD
CYBORG
STARFIRE
RAVEN
KID FLASH
MISS MARTIAN
MAMMOTH
TERRA
BEAST BOY
ROBIN
WONDER GIRL
BUMBLEBEE
JERICHO
ROSE
SPEEDY

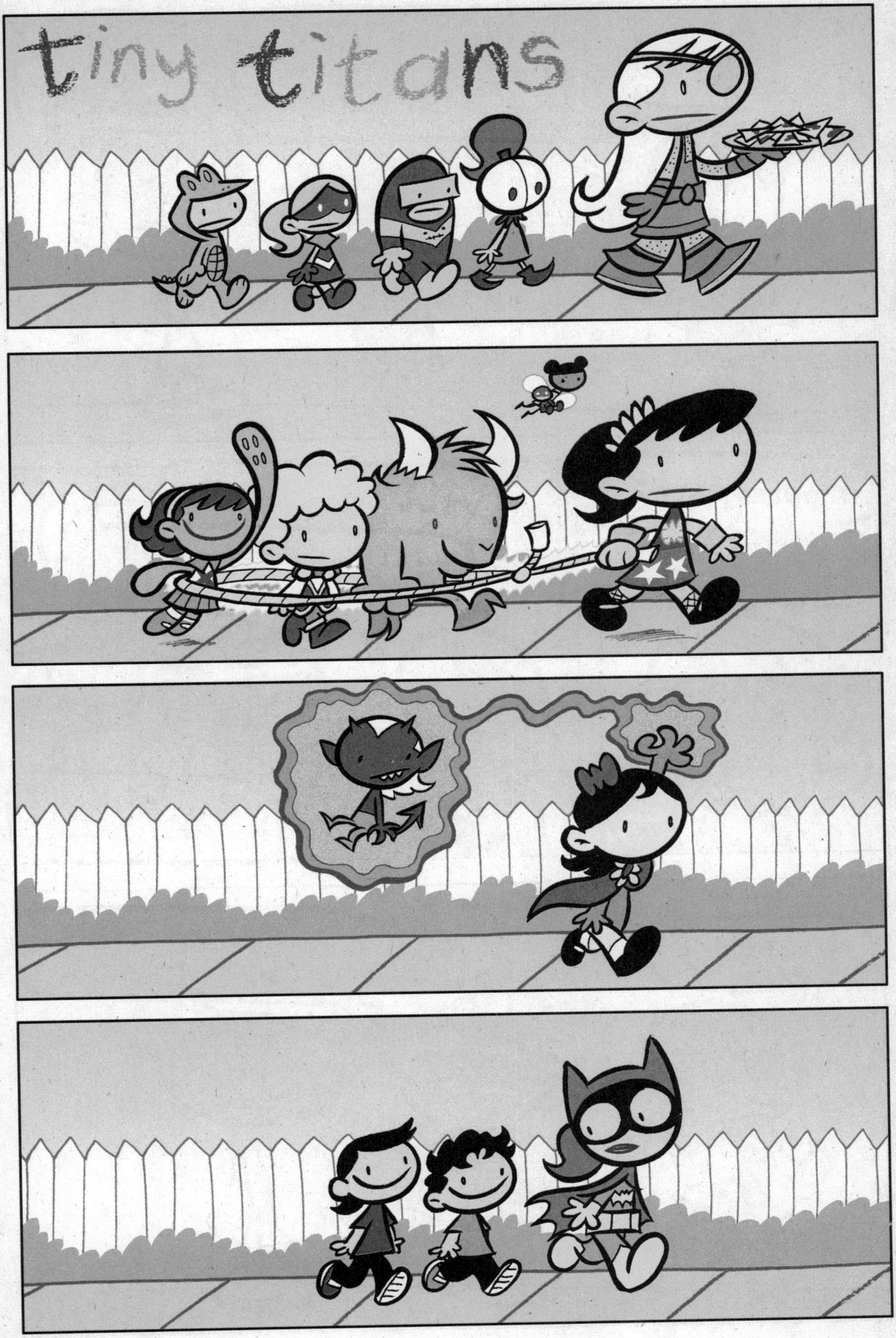
tiny titans

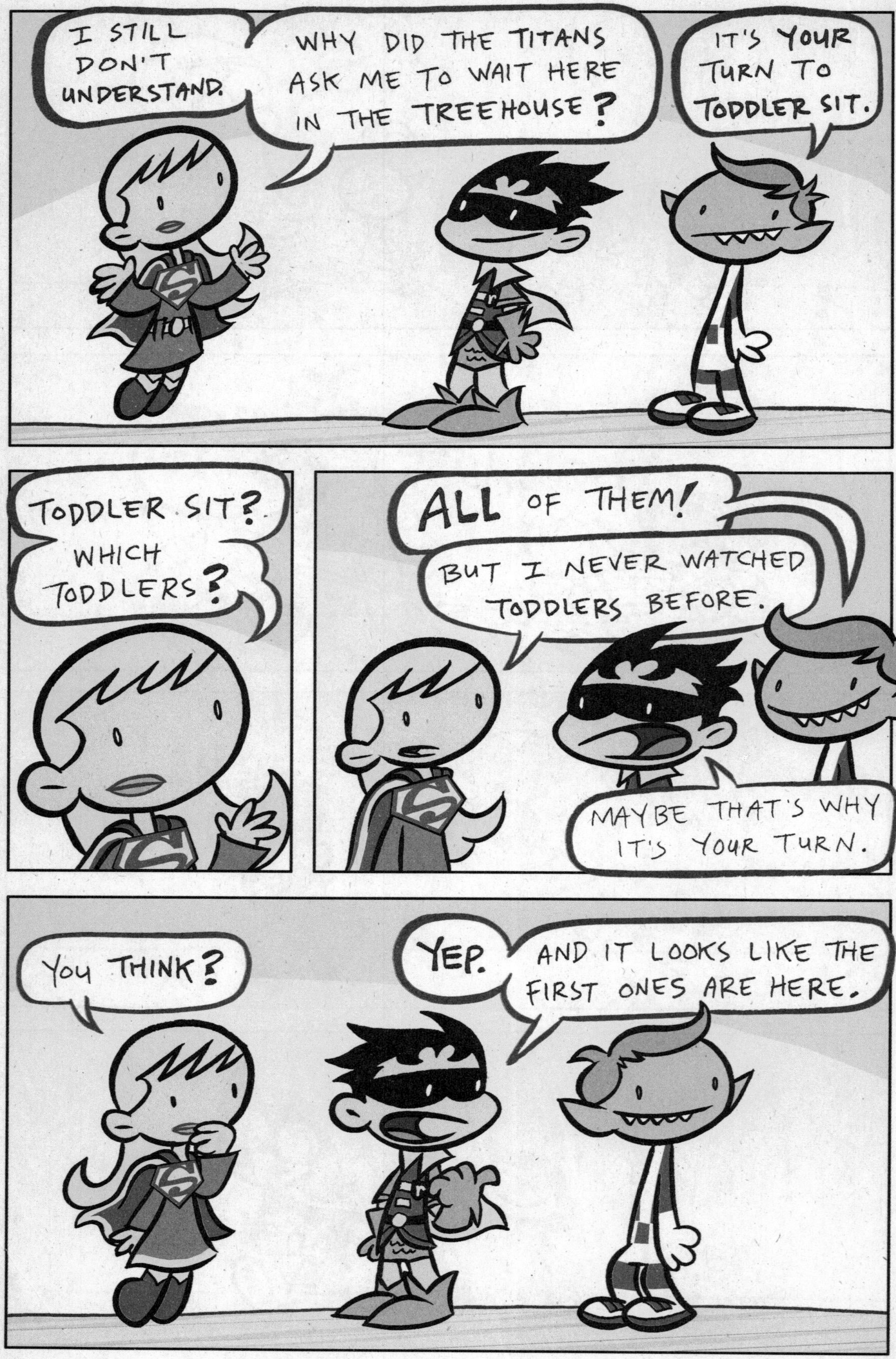
I STILL DON'T UNDERSTAND.
WHY DID THE TITANS ASK ME TO WAIT HERE IN THE TREEHOUSE?
IT'S YOUR TURN TO TODDLER SIT.
TODDLER SIT? WHICH TODDLERS?
ALL OF THEM!
BUT I NEVER WATCHED TODDLERS BEFORE.
MAYBE THAT'S WHY IT'S YOUR TURN.
YOU THINK?
YEP.
AND IT LOOKS LIKE THE FIRST ONES ARE HERE.

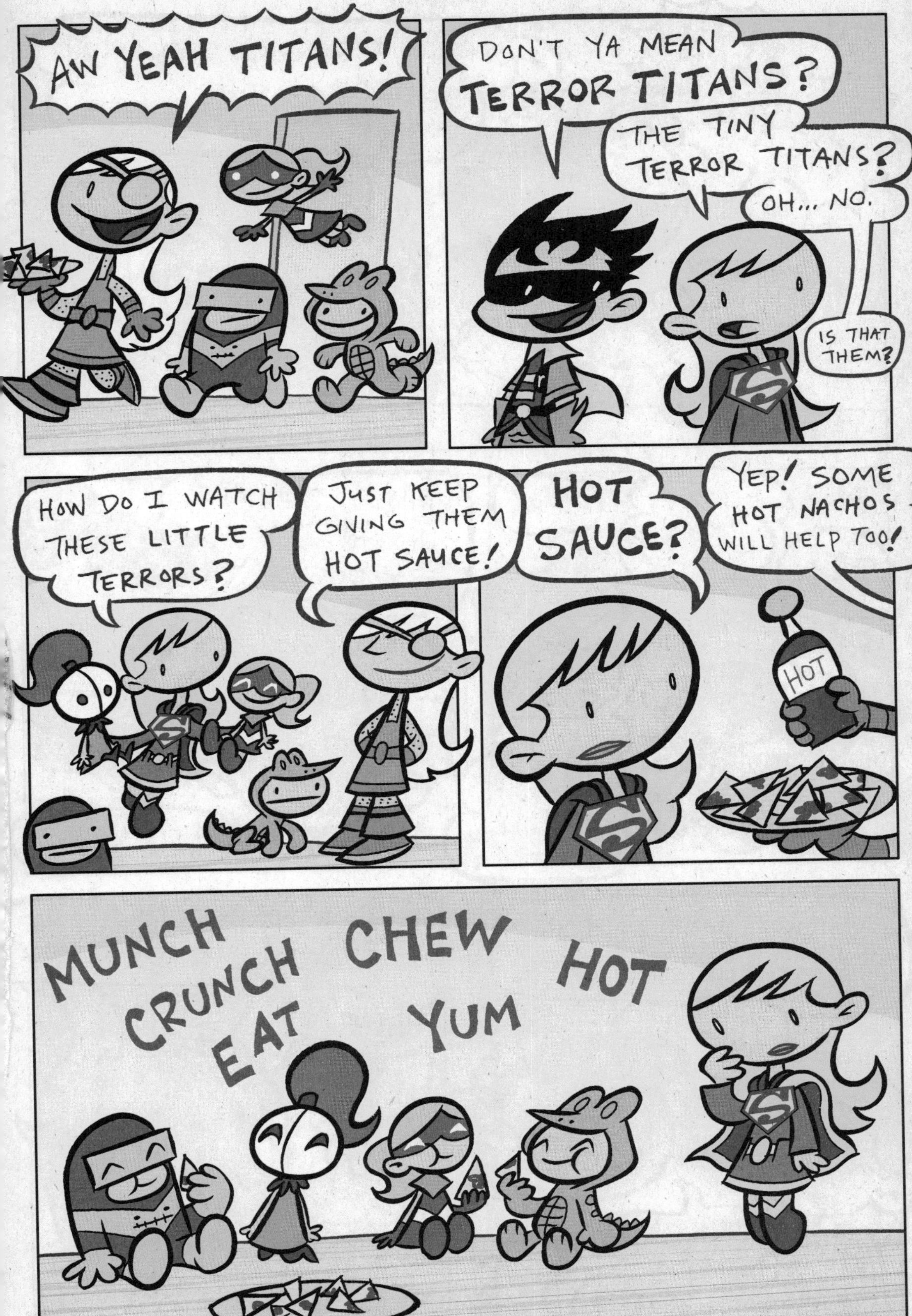
AW YEAH TITANS!
DON'T YA MEAN TERROR TITANS?
THE TINY TERROR TITANS?
OH... NO.
IS THAT THEM?
HOT
HOW DO I WATCH THESE LITTLE TERRORS?
JUST KEEP GIVING THEM HOT SAUCE!
HOT SAUCE?
YEP! SOME HOT NACHOS WILL HELP TOO!
HOT
MUNCH
CRUNCH
EAT
CHEW
YUM
HOT

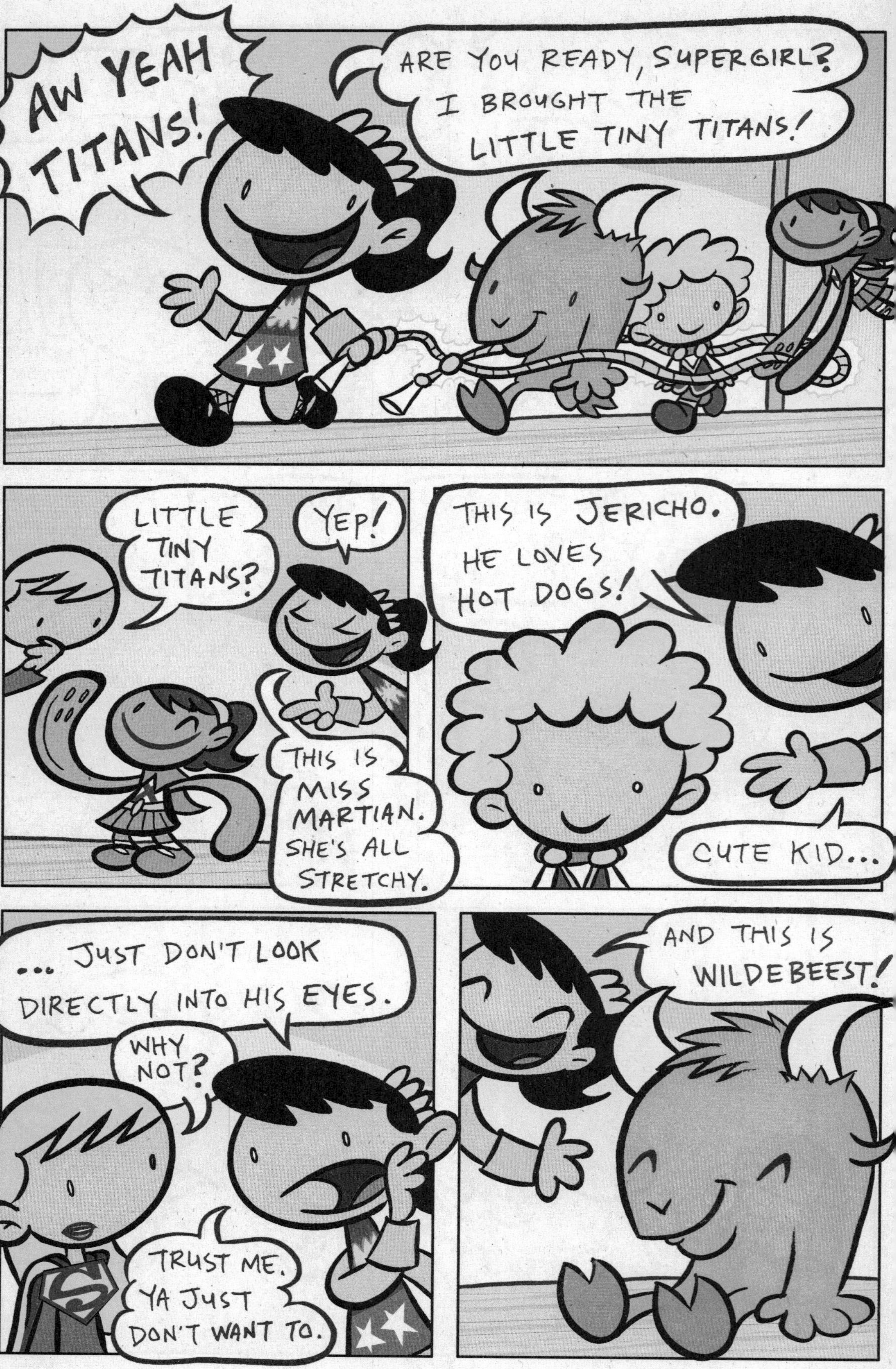
AW YEAH TITANS!
ARE YOU READY, SUPERGIRL? I BROUGHT THE LITTLE TINY TITANS!
LITTLE TINY TITANS?
YEP!
THIS IS MISS MARTIAN. SHE'S ALL STRETCHY.
THIS IS JERICHO. HE LOVES HOT DOGS!
CUTE KID...
... JUST DON'T LOOK DIRECTLY INTO HIS EYES.
WHY NOT?
TRUST ME. YA JUST DON'T WANT TO.
AND THIS IS WILDEBEEST!

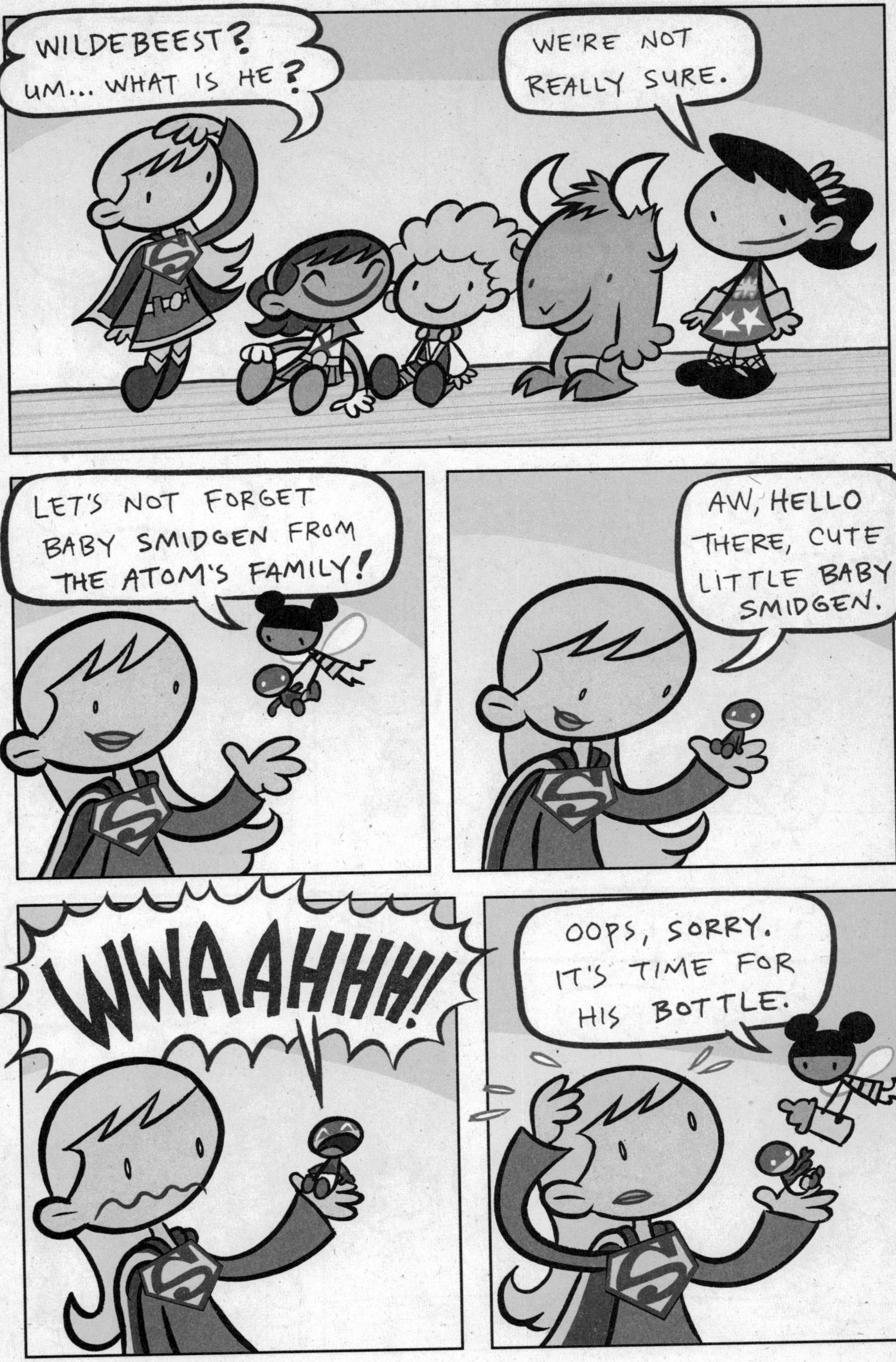
WILDEBEEST? UM... WHAT IS HE?
WE'RE NOT REALLY SURE.
LET'S NOT FORGET BABY SMIDGEN FROM THE ATOM'S FAMILY!
AW, HELLO THERE, CUTE LITTLE BABY SMIDGEN.
WWAAHHH!
OOPS, SORRY. IT'S TIME FOR HIS BOTTLE.

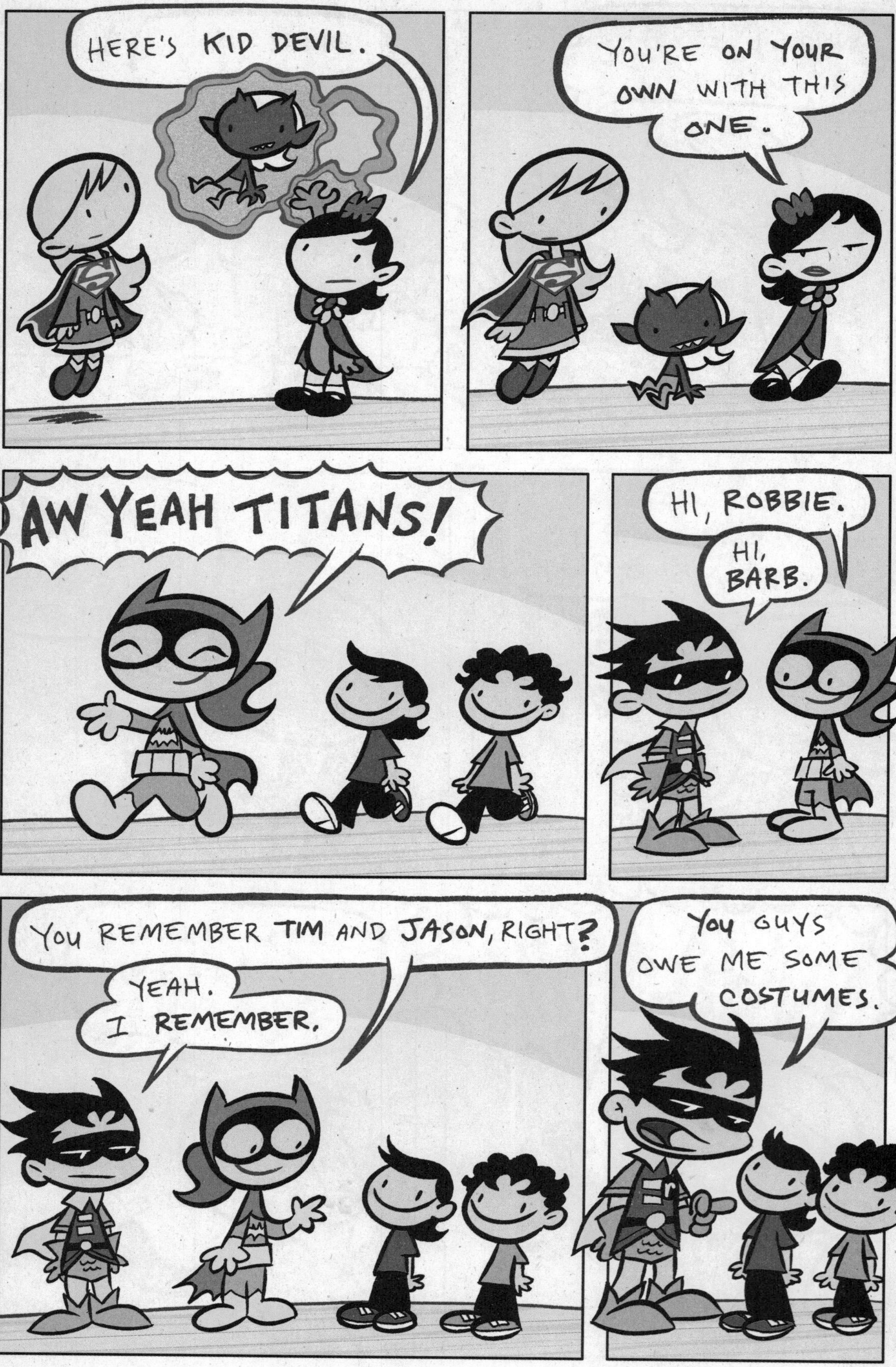
HERE'S KID DEVIL.
YOU'RE ON YOUR OWN WITH THIS ONE.
AW YEAH TITANS!
HI, ROBBIE.
HI, BARB.
YOU REMEMBER TIM AND JASON, RIGHT?
YEAH. I REMEMBER.
YOU GUYS OWE ME SOME COSTUMES.

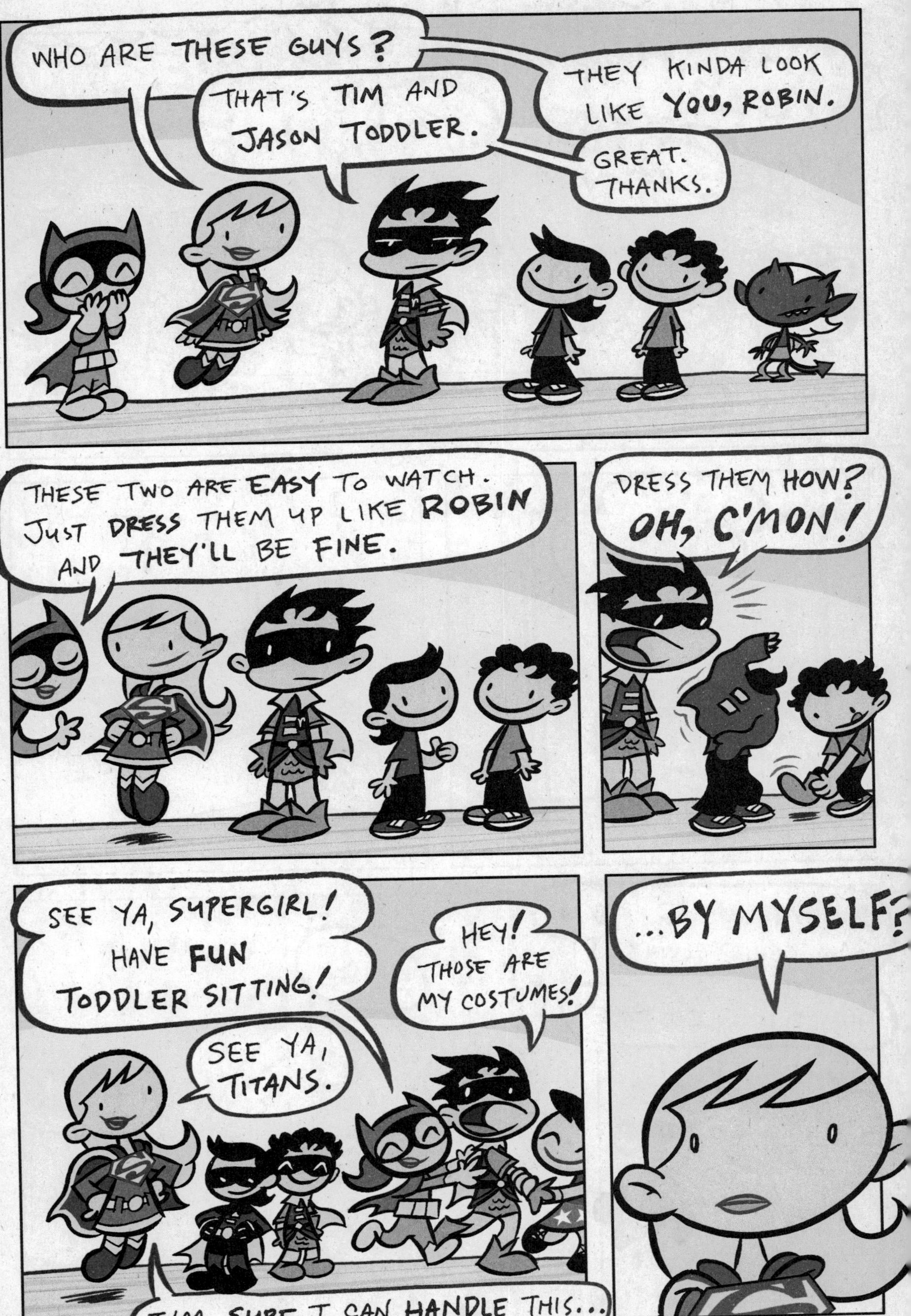
WHO ARE THESE GUYS?
THAT'S TIM AND JASON TODDLER.
THEY KINDA LOOK LIKE YOU, ROBIN.
GREAT. THANKS.
THESE TWO ARE EASY TO WATCH. JUST DRESS THEM UP LIKE ROBIN AND THEY'LL BE FINE.
DRESS THEM HOW? OH, C'MON!
SEE YA, SUPERGIRL! HAVE FUN TODDLER SITTING!
HEY! THOSE ARE MY COSTUMES!
SEE YA, TITANS.
I'M SURE I CAN HANDLE THIS...
...BY MYSELF?

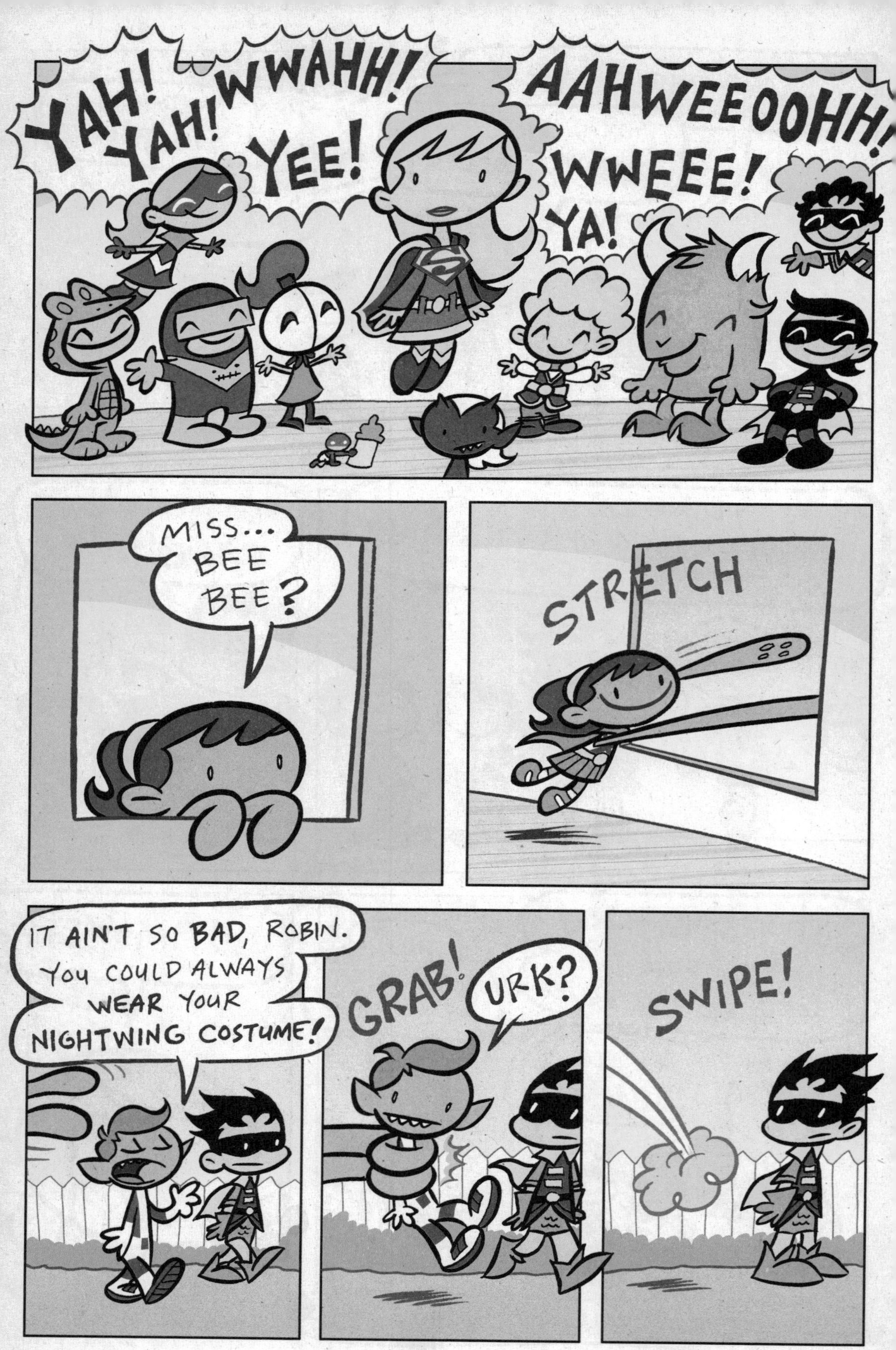
YAH! YAH!
WWAHH!
YEE!
AAHWEEOOHH!
WWEEE!
YA!
MISS... BEE BEE?
STRETCH
IT AIN'T SO BAD, ROBIN. YOU COULD ALWAYS WEAR YOUR NIGHTWING COSTUME!
GRAB!
URK?
SWIPE!

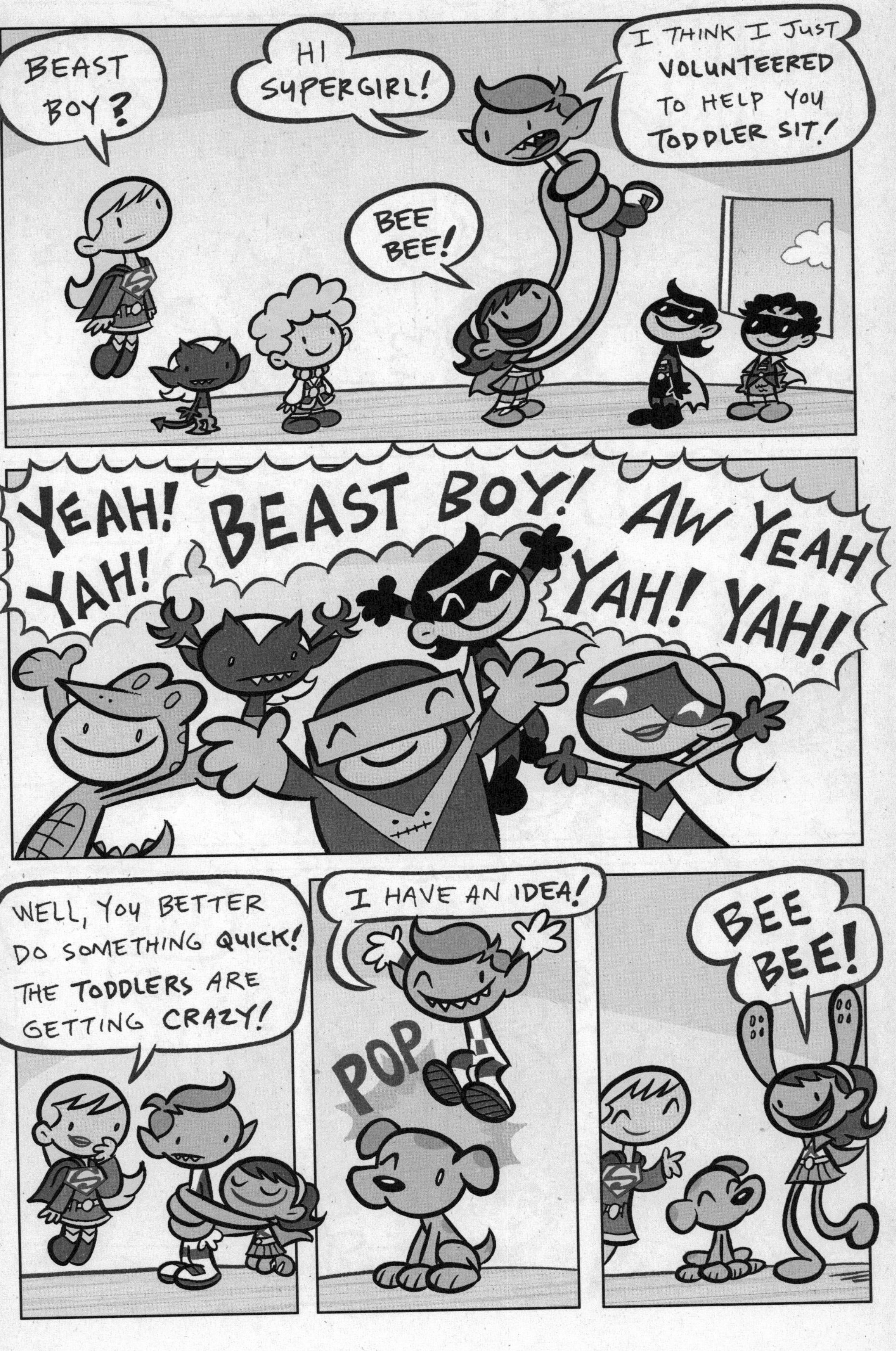
BEAST BOY?
HI SUPERGIRL!
I THINK I JUST VOLUNTEERED TO HELP YOU TODDLER SIT!
BEE BEE!
YEAH! YAH!
BEAST BOY!
AW YEAH YAH! YAH!
WELL, YOU BETTER DO SOMETHING QUICK! THE TODDLERS ARE GETTING CRAZY!
I HAVE AN IDEA!
POP
BEE BEE!

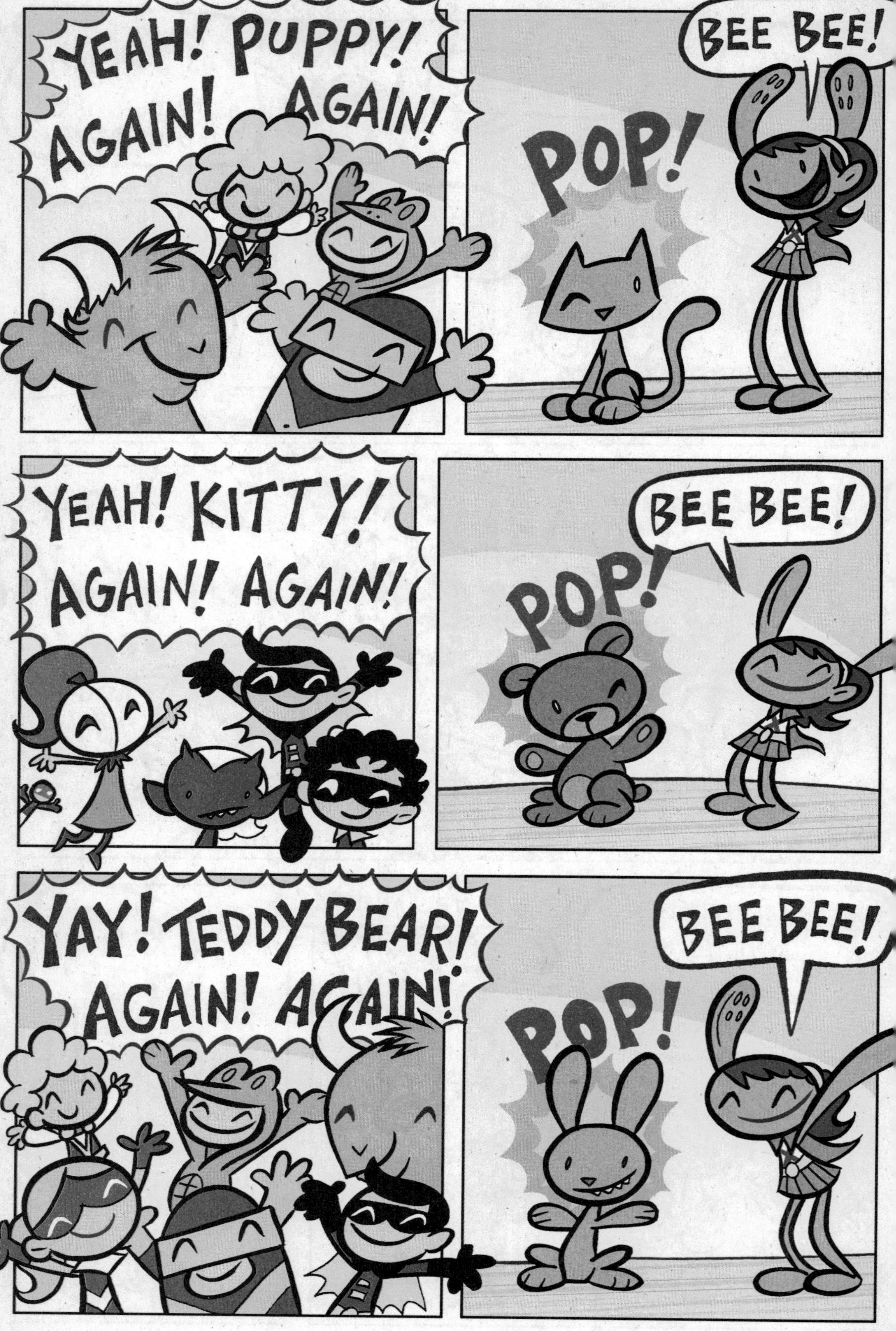
YEAH! PUPPY! AGAIN! AGAIN!
POP!
BEE BEE!
YEAH! KITTY! AGAIN! AGAIN!
POP!
BEE BEE!
YAY! TEDDY BEAR! AGAIN! AGAIN!
POP!
BEE BEE!

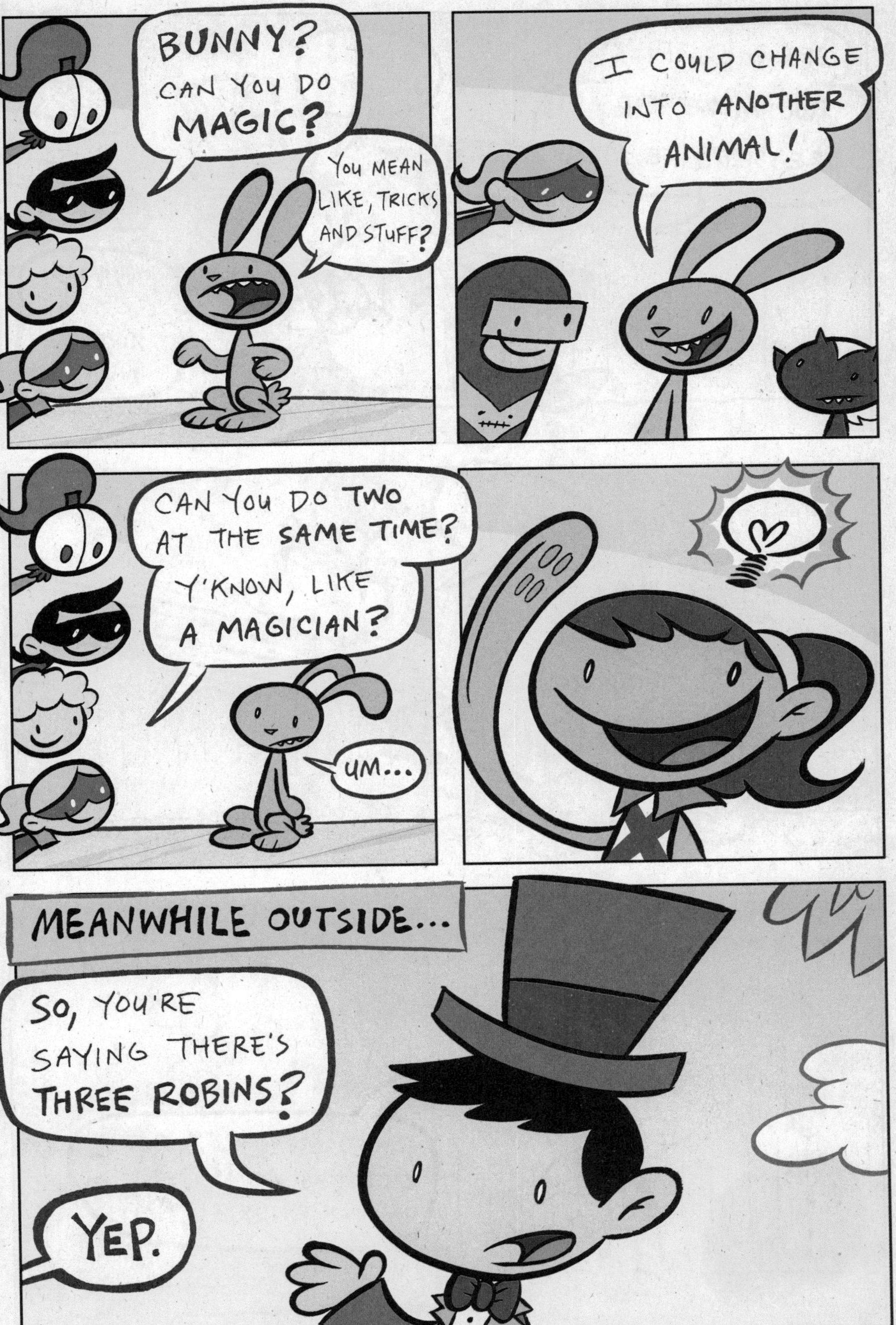
BUNNY? CAN YOU DO MAGIC?
YOU MEAN LIKE, TRICKS AND STUFF?
I COULD CHANGE INTO ANOTHER ANIMAL!
CAN YOU DO TWO AT THE SAME TIME?
Y'KNOW, LIKE A MAGICIAN?
UM...
MEANWHILE OUTSIDE...
SO, YOU'RE SAYING THERE'S THREE ROBINS?
YEP.

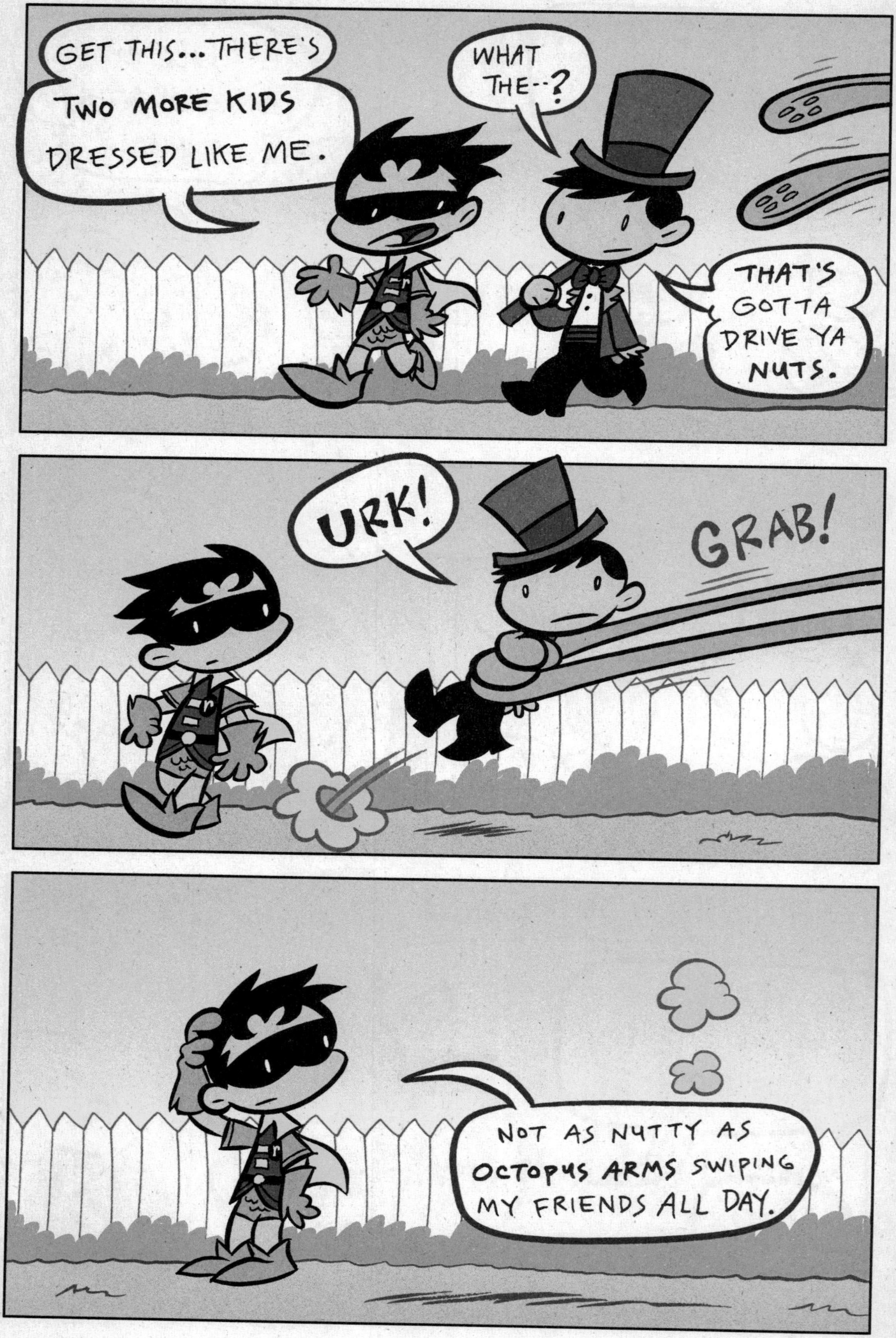
GET THIS... THERE'S TWO MORE KIDS DRESSED LIKE ME.
WHAT THE--?
THAT'S GOTTA DRIVE YA NUTS.
URK!
GRAB!
NOT AS NUTTY AS OCTOPUS ARMS SWIPING MY FRIENDS ALL DAY.

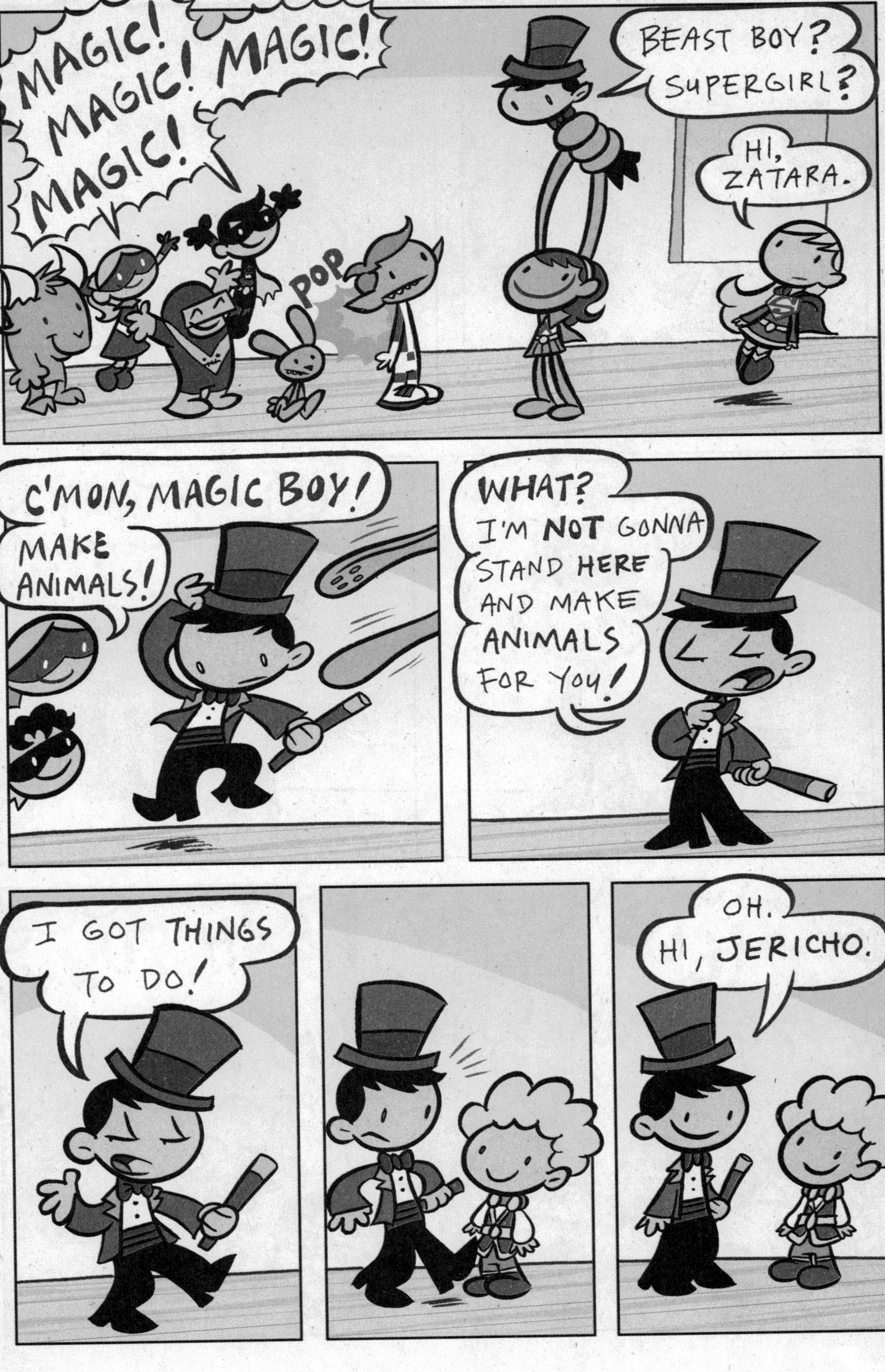
MAGIC! MAGIC! MAGIC! MAGIC!
POP
BEAST BOY? SUPERGIRL?
HI, ZATARA.
C'MON, MAGIC BOY!
MAKE ANIMALS!
WHAT? I'M **NOT** GONNA STAND **HERE** AND MAKE **ANIMALS** FOR YOU!
I GOT THINGS TO DO!
OH. HI, JERICHO.

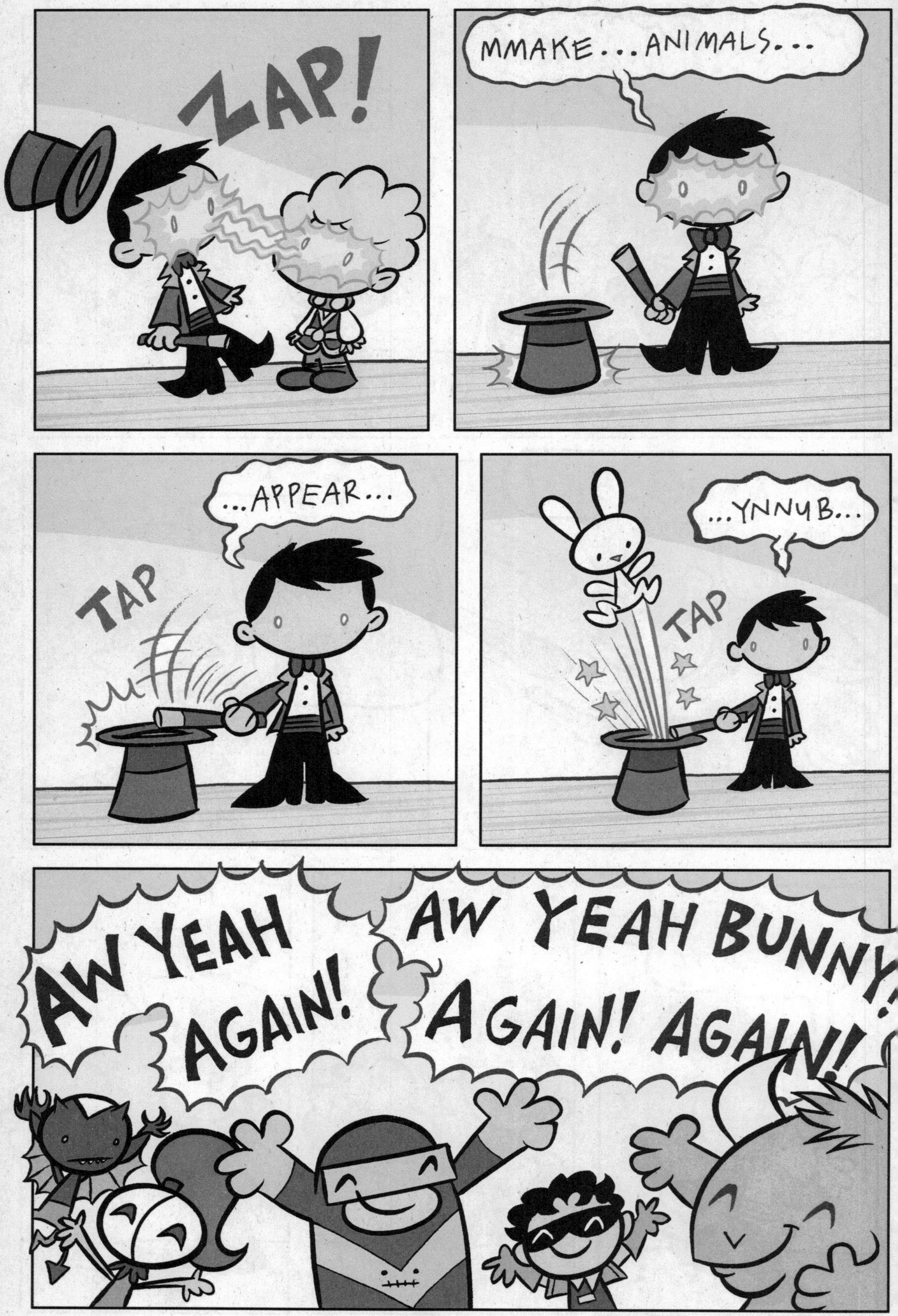
ZAP!
MMAKE...ANIMALS...
...APPEAR...
TAP
...YNNUB...
TAP
AW YEAH AGAIN!
AW YEAH BUNNY! AGAIN! AGAIN!

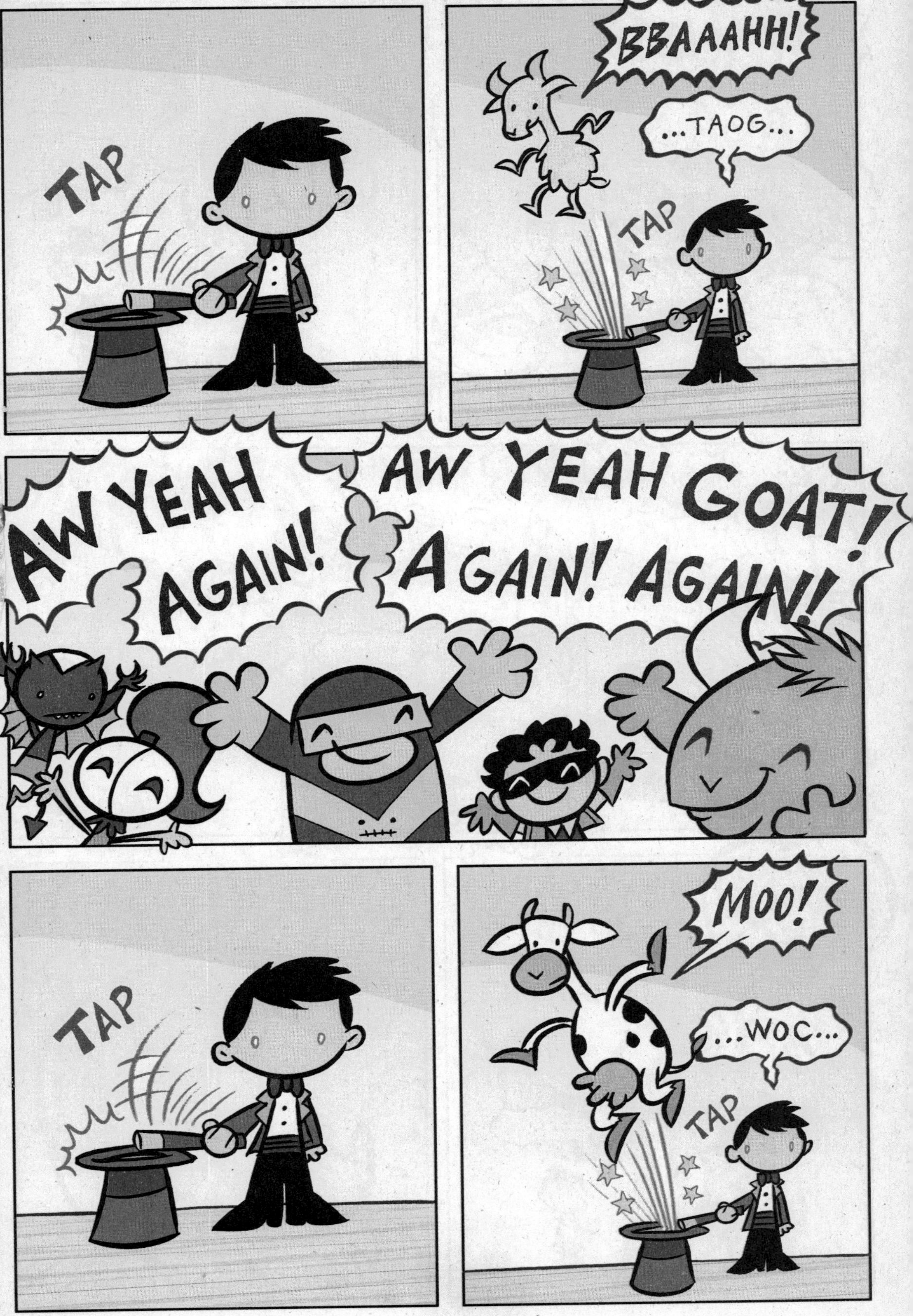
TAP
BBAAAHH!
...TAOG...
TAP
AW YEAH AGAIN!
AW YEAH GOAT! AGAIN! AGAIN!
TAP
MOO!
...WOC...
TAP

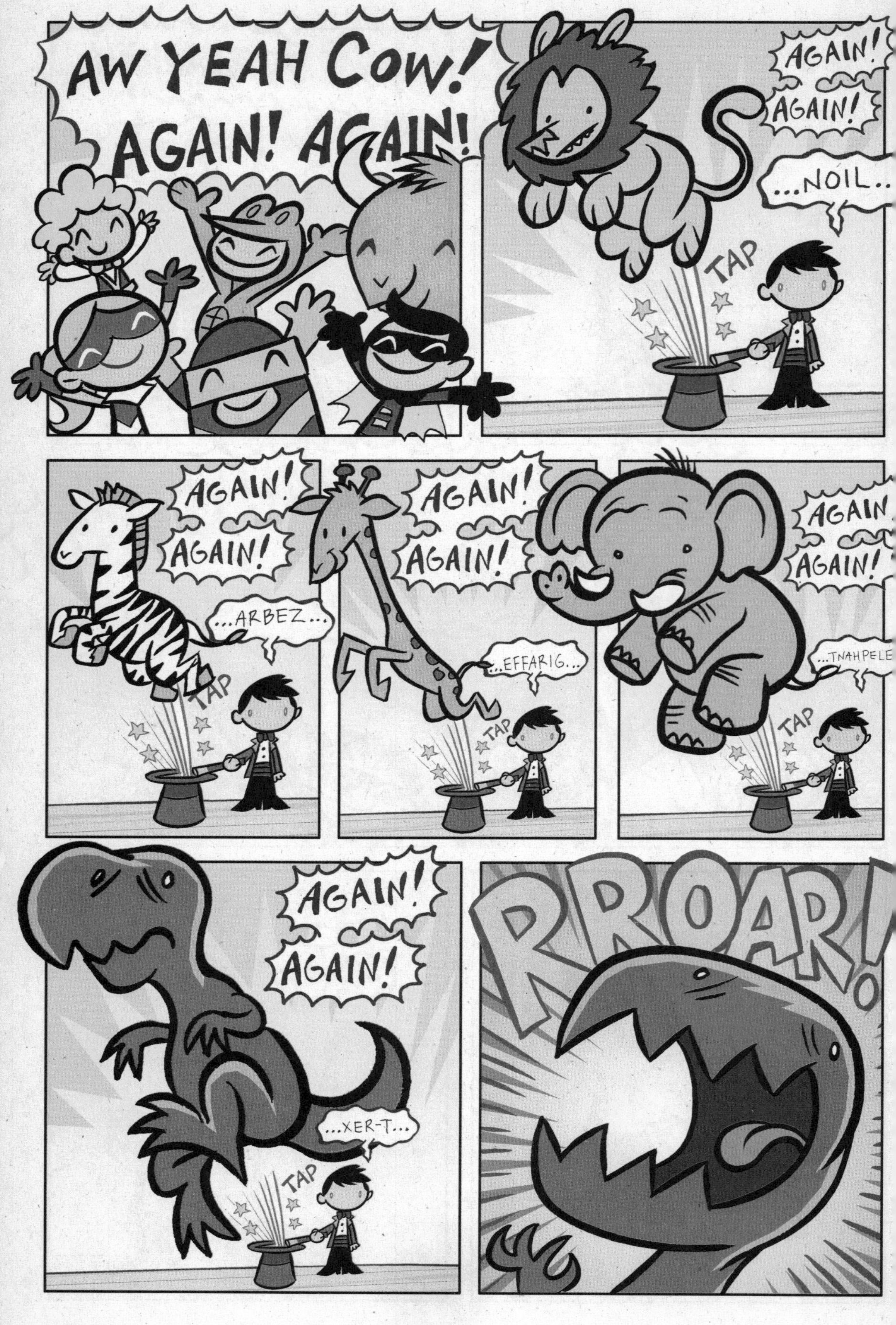
AW YEAH COW!
AGAIN! AGAIN!
AGAIN!
AGAIN!
...NOIL...
TAP
AGAIN!
AGAIN!
...ARBEZ...
TAP
AGAIN!
AGAIN!
...EFFARIG...
TAP
AGAIN
AGAIN!
...TNAHPELE
TAP
AGAIN!
AGAIN!
...XER-T...
TAP
RROAR!

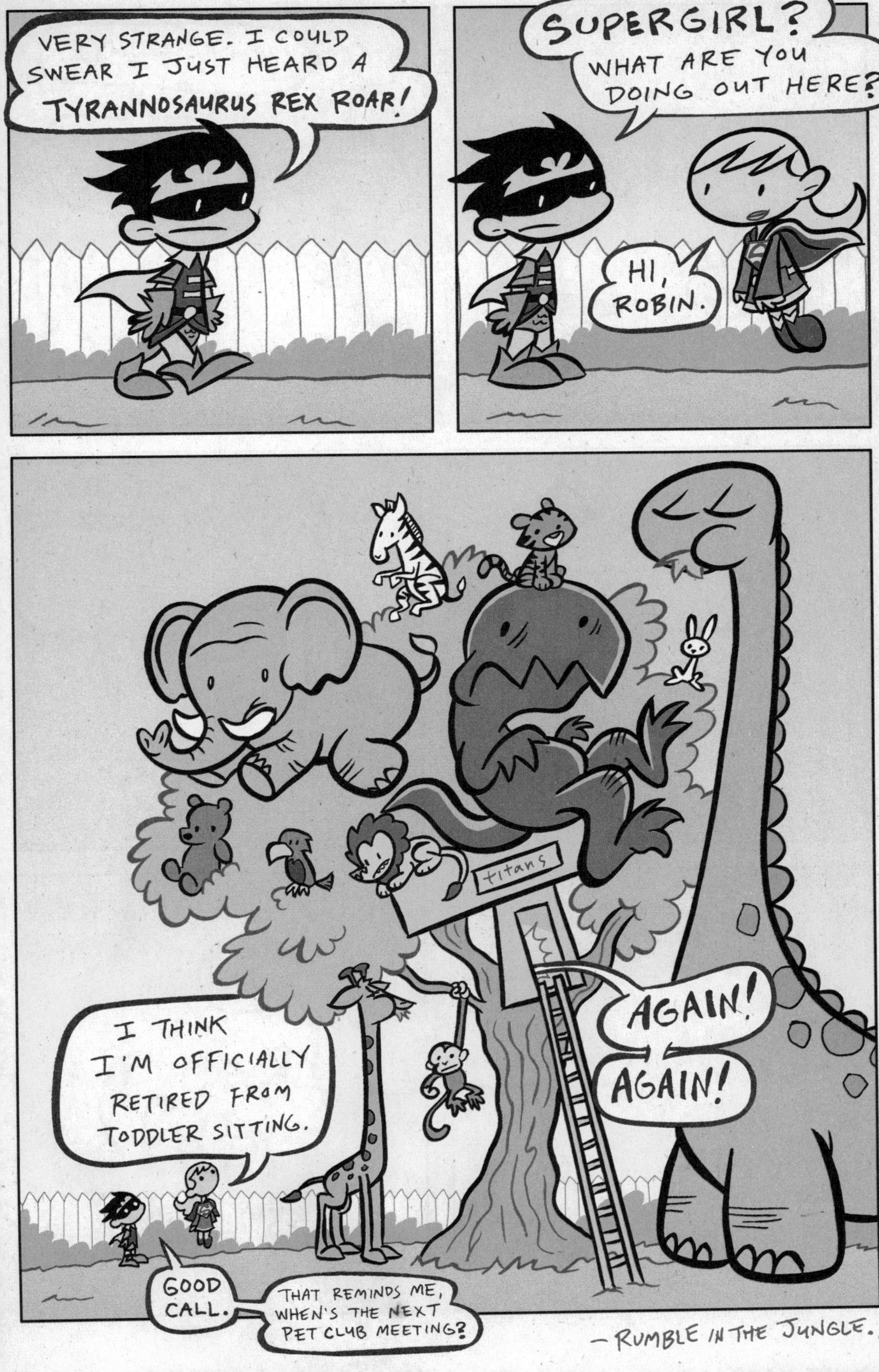
VERY STRANGE. I COULD SWEAR I JUST HEARD A TYRANNOSAURUS REX ROAR!
SUPERGIRL? WHAT ARE YOU DOING OUT HERE?
HI, ROBIN.
titans
AGAIN!
AGAIN!
I THINK I'M OFFICIALLY RETIRED FROM TODDLER SITTING.
GOOD CALL.
THAT REMINDS ME, WHEN'S THE NEXT PET CLUB MEETING?
— RUMBLE IN THE JUNGLE.

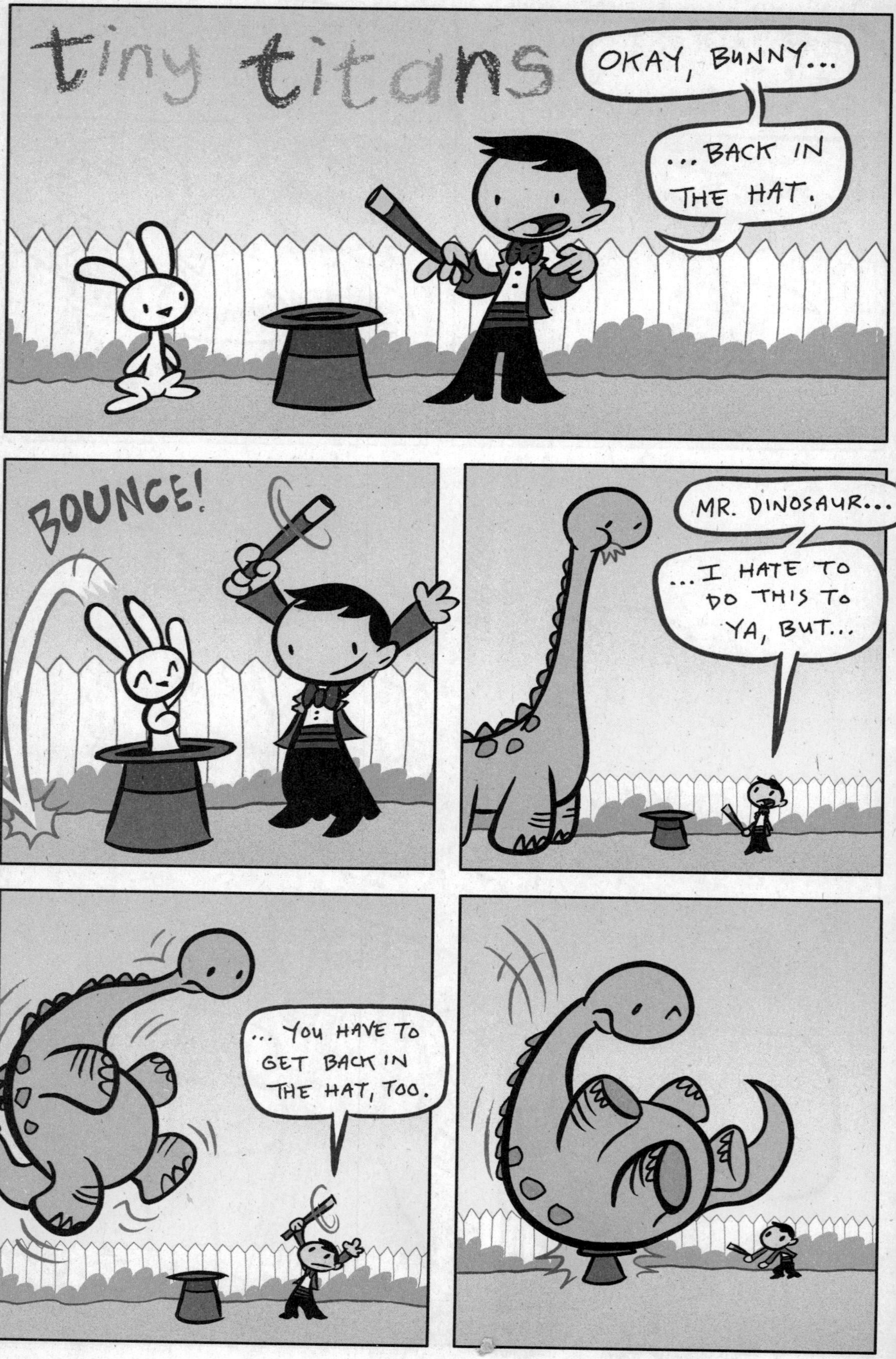
tiny titans
OKAY, BUNNY...
...BACK IN THE HAT.
BOUNCE!
MR. DINOSAUR...
...I HATE TO DO THIS TO YA, BUT...
...YOU HAVE TO GET BACK IN THE HAT, TOO.

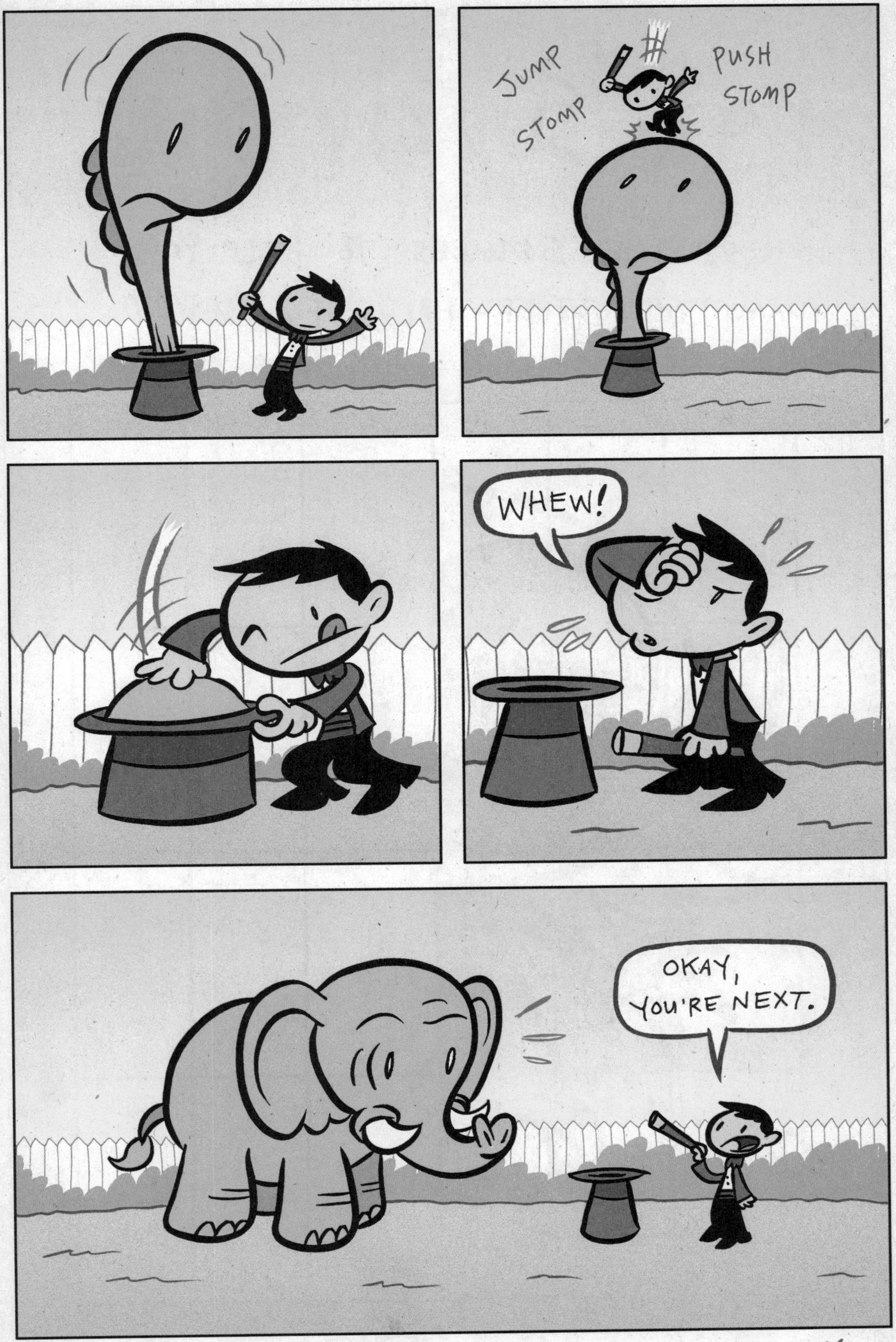
JUMP
STOMP
PUSH
STOMP
WHEW!
OKAY, YOU'RE NEXT.

-CAP IT!

let's draw!

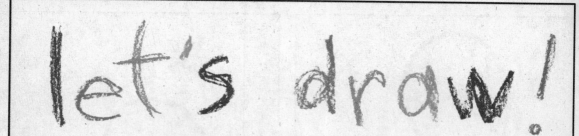

USE THE SQUARES TO HELP YOU
DRAW THE OTHER HALF OF KID DEVIL!

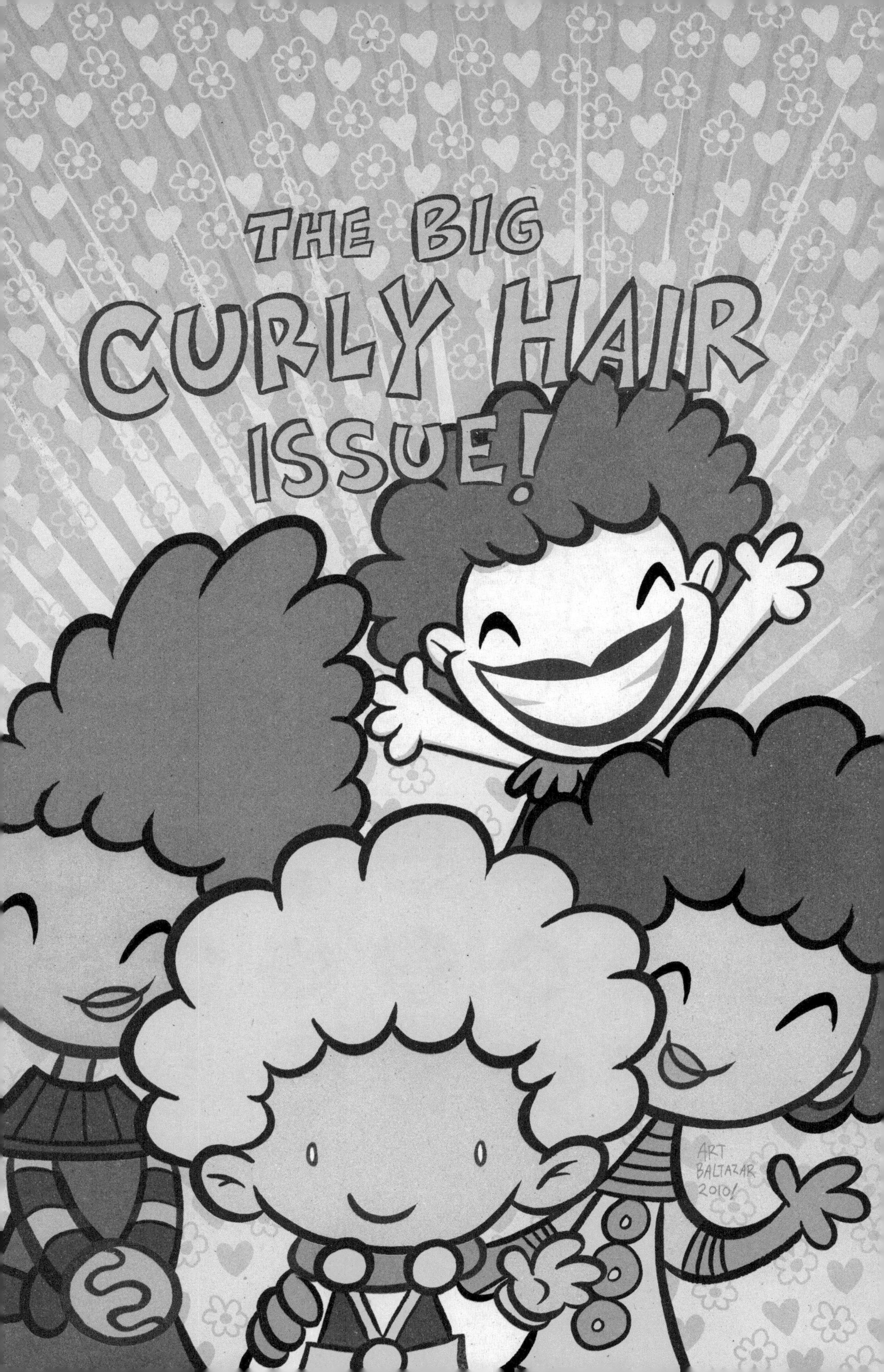
THE BIG
CURLY HAIR
ISSUE!
ART
BALTAZAR
2010!

tiny titans

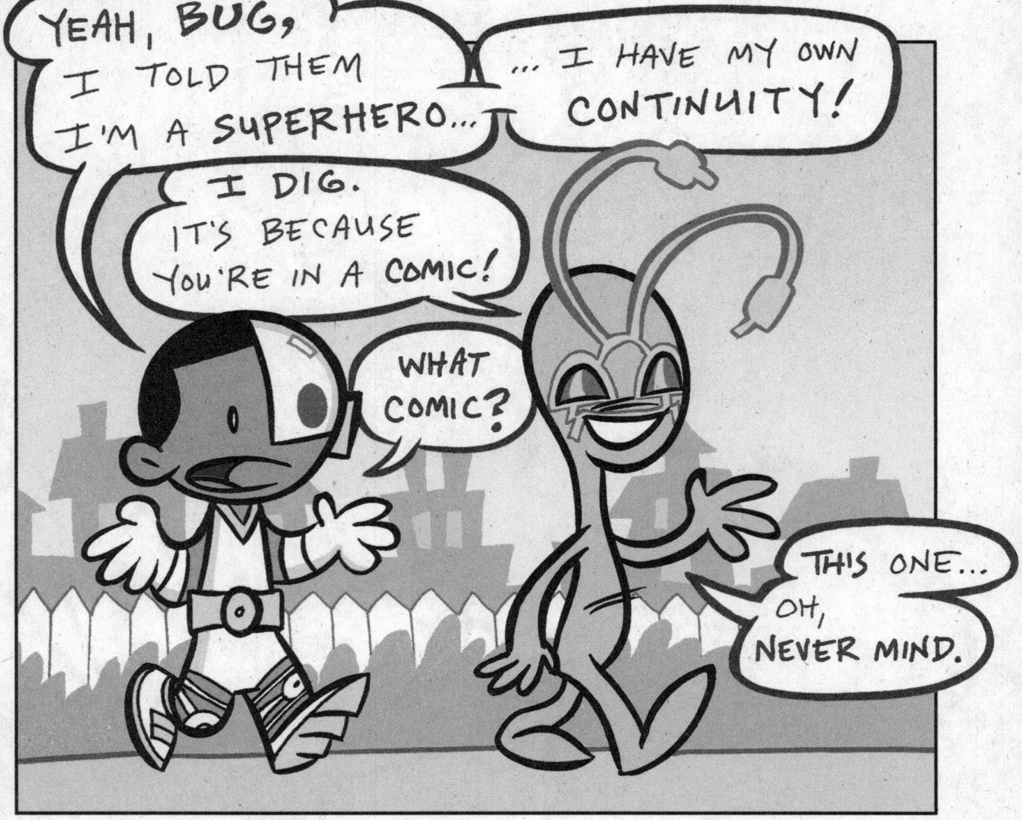
YEAH, BUG, I TOLD THEM I'M A SUPERHERO...
... I HAVE MY OWN CONTINUITY!
I DIG. IT'S BECAUSE YOU'RE IN A COMIC!
WHAT COMIC?
THIS ONE... OH, NEVER MIND.

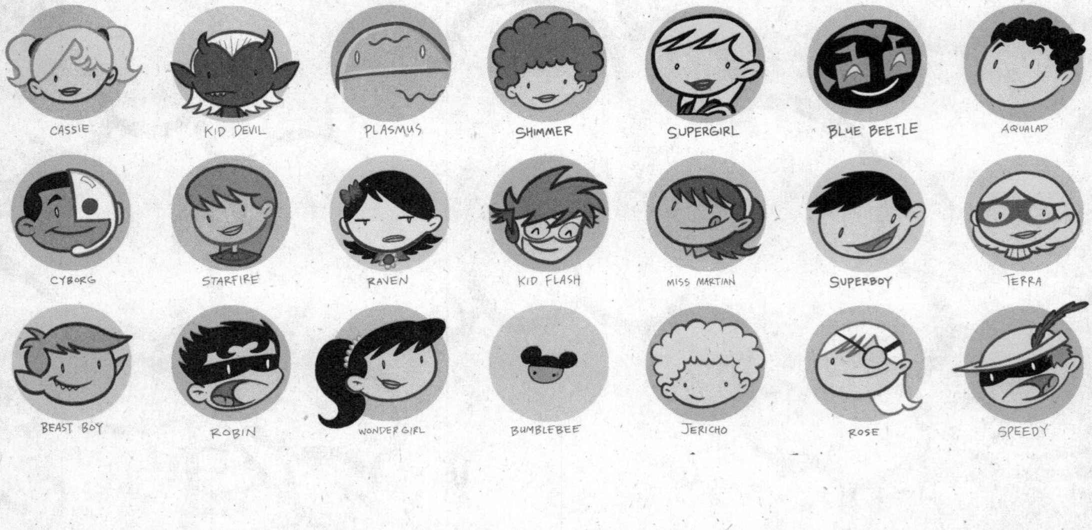
CASSIE
KID DEVIL
PLASMUS
SHIMMER
SUPERGIRL
BLUE BEETLE
AQUALAD
CYBORG
STARFIRE
RAVEN
KID FLASH
MISS MARTIAN
SUPERBOY
TERRA
BEAST BOY
ROBIN
WONDER GIRL
BUMBLEBEE
JERICHO
ROSE
SPEEDY

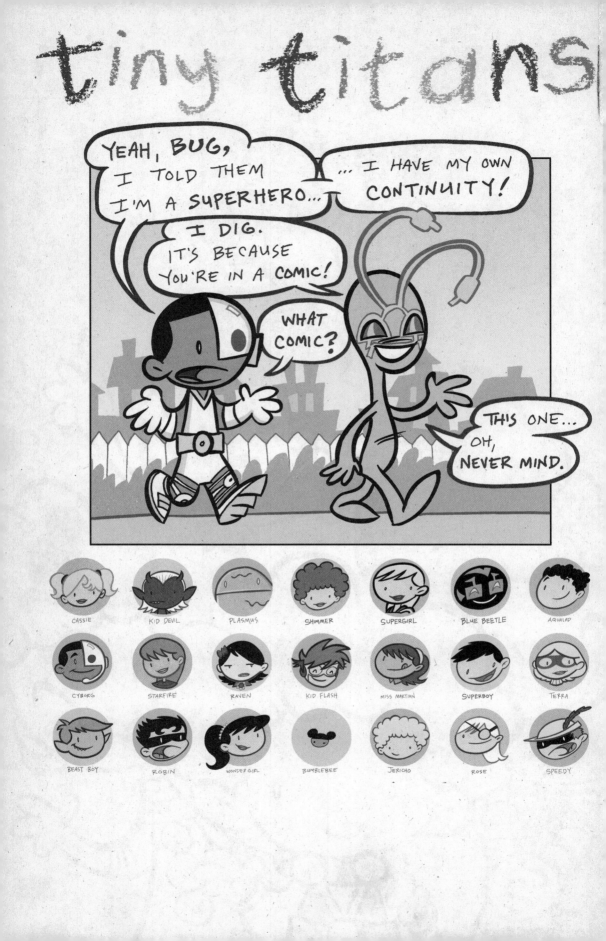

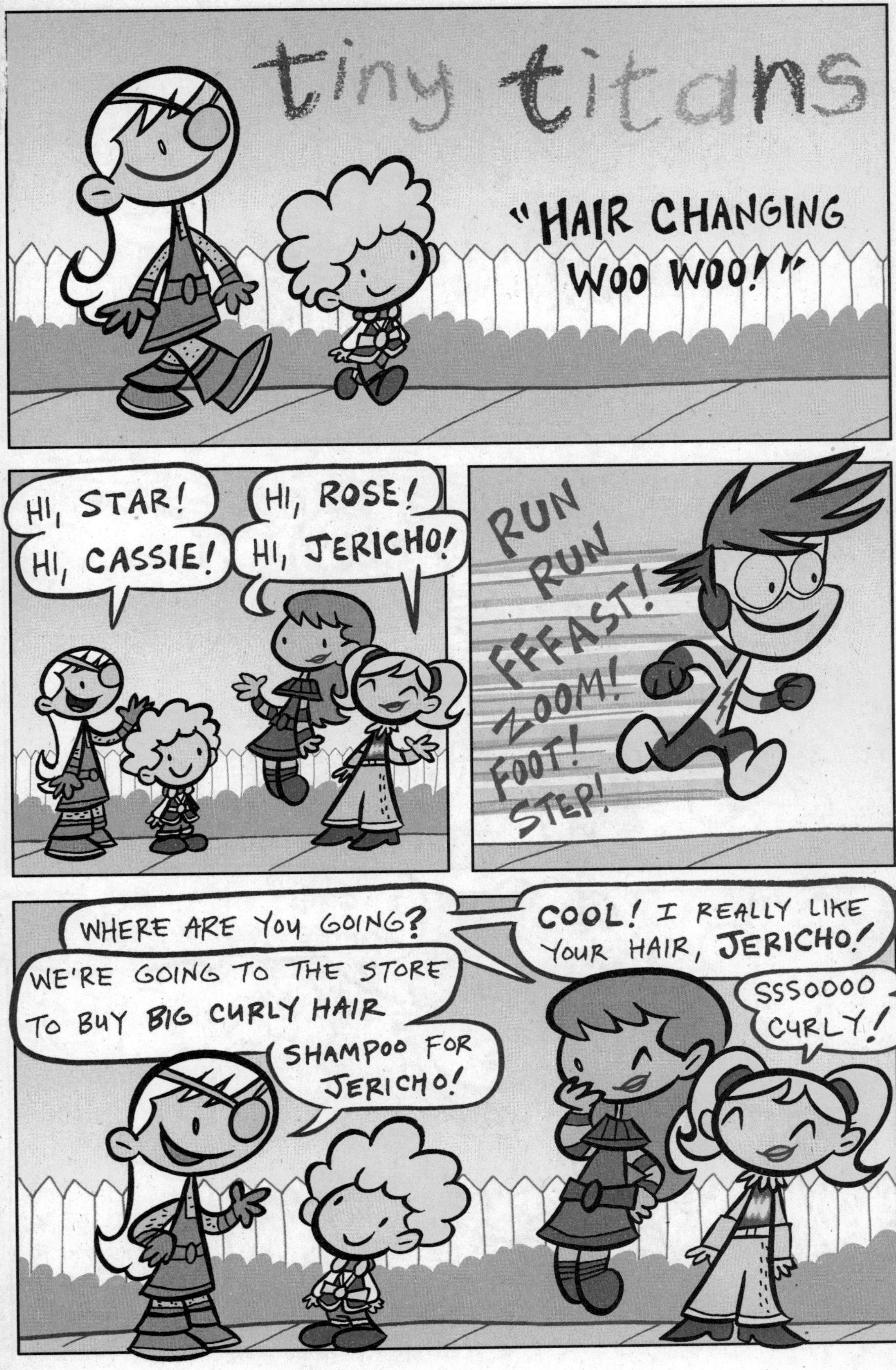
tiny titans
"HAIR CHANGING WOO WOO!"
HI, STAR! HI, CASSIE!
HI, ROSE! HI, JERICHO!
RUN RUN FFFAST! ZOOM! FOOT! STEP!
WHERE ARE YOU GOING?
COOL! I REALLY LIKE YOUR HAIR, JERICHO!
WE'RE GOING TO THE STORE TO BUY BIG CURLY HAIR
SHAMPOO FOR JERICHO!
SSSOOOO CURLY!

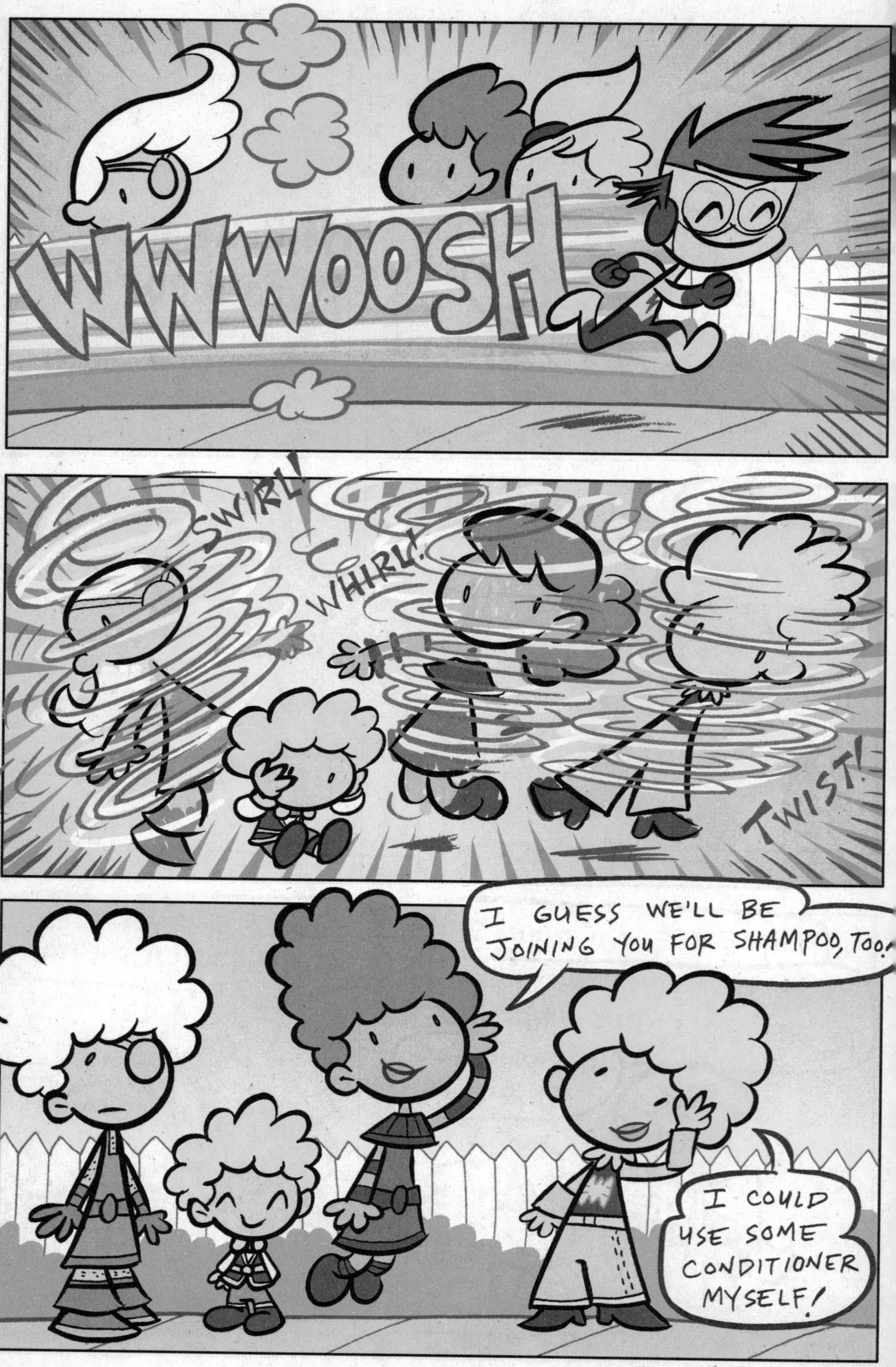
WWWOOSH
SWIRL!
WHIRL!
TWIST!
I GUESS WE'LL BE JOINING YOU FOR SHAMPOO, TOO!
I COULD USE SOME CONDITIONER MYSELF!

—HAIR TODAY!

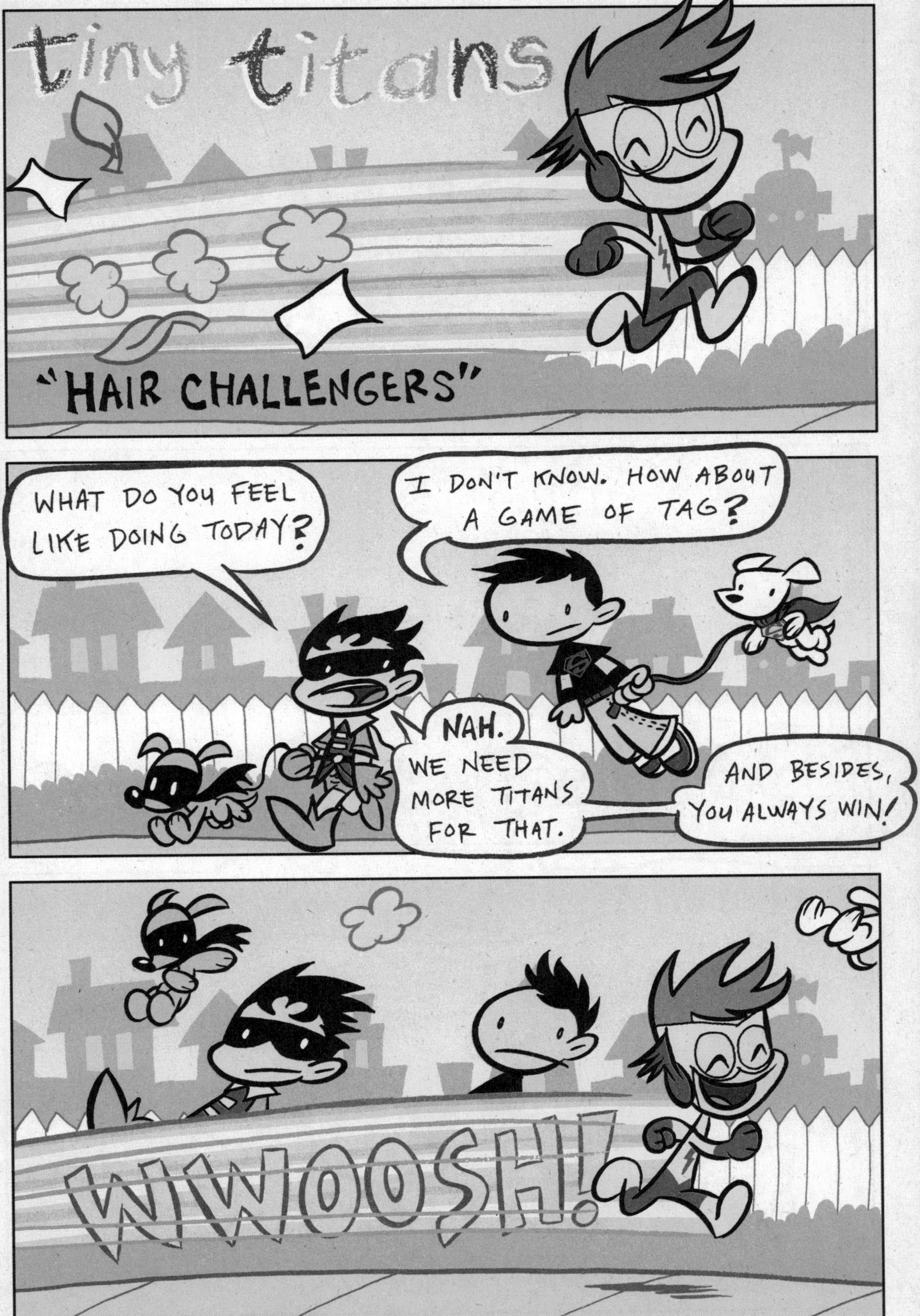
tiny titans
"HAIR CHALLENGERS"
WHAT DO YOU FEEL LIKE DOING TODAY?
I DON'T KNOW. HOW ABOUT A GAME OF TAG?
NAH. WE NEED MORE TITANS FOR THAT.
AND BESIDES, YOU ALWAYS WIN!
WWOOSH!

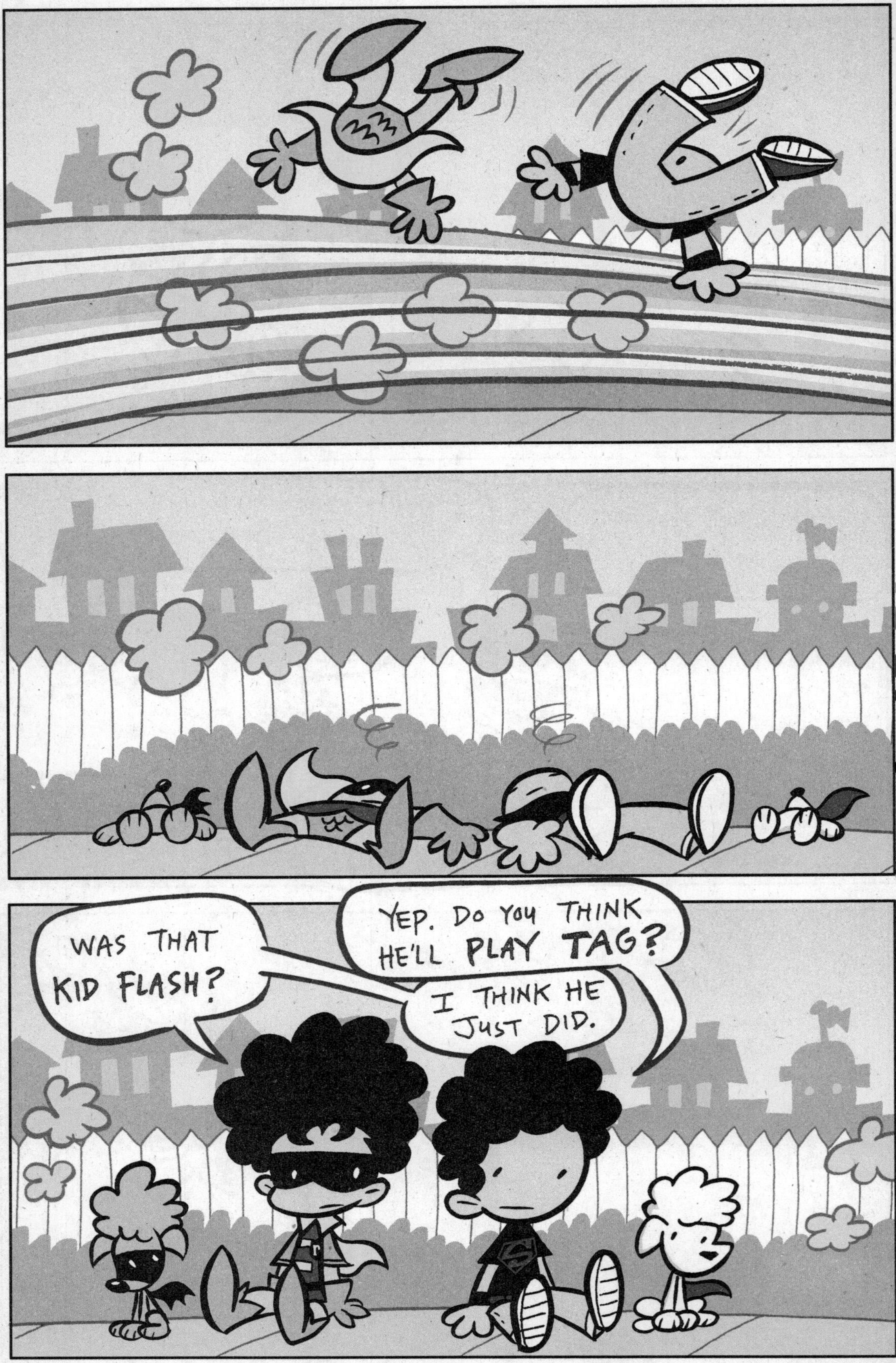
WAS THAT KID FLASH?
YEP. DO YOU THINK HE'LL PLAY TAG?
I THINK HE JUST DID.

-YOU'RE IT!

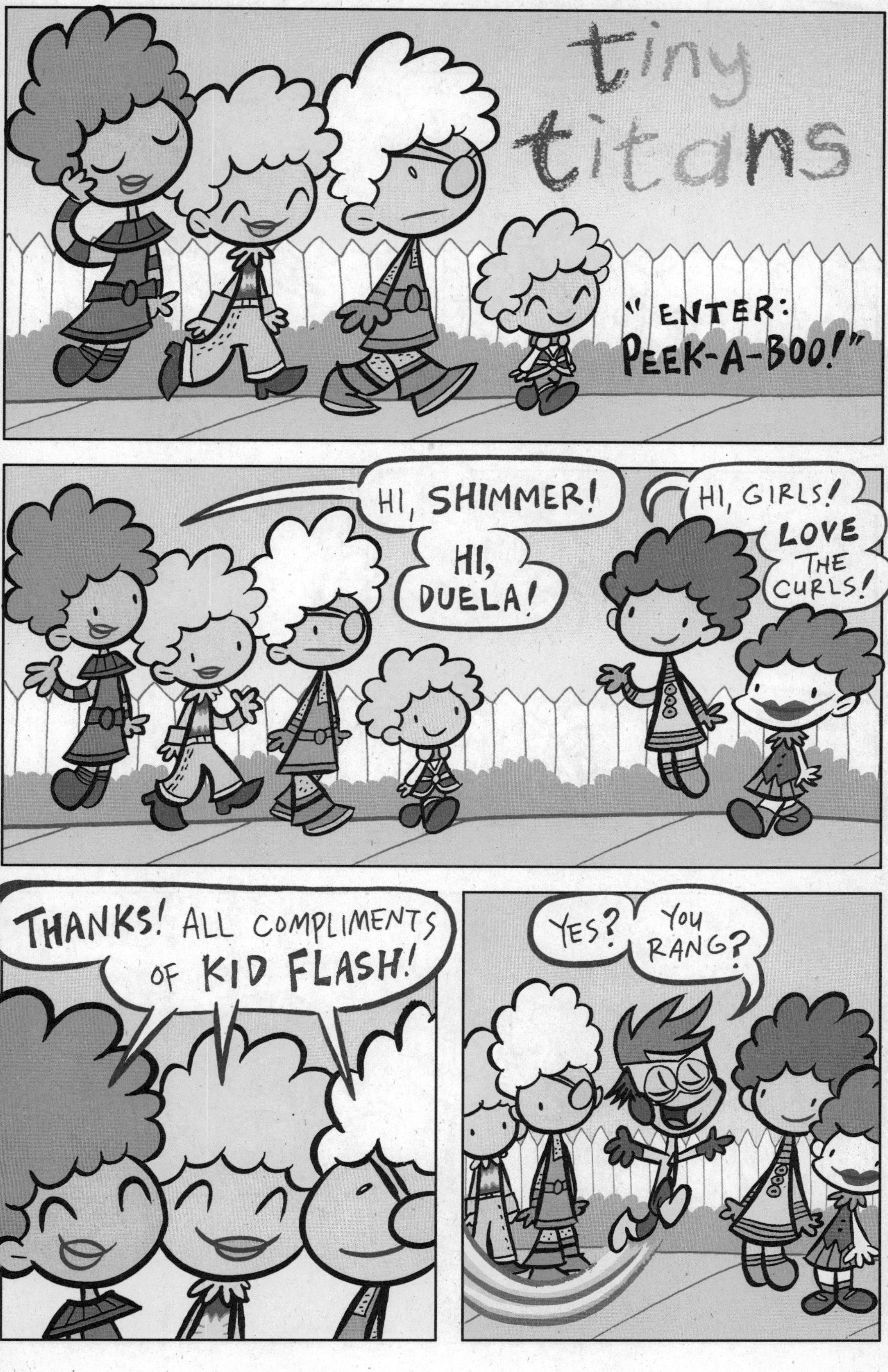
tiny titans
"ENTER: PEEK-A-BOO!"
HI, SHIMMER!
HI, DUELA!
HI, GIRLS!
LOVE THE CURLS!
THANKS! ALL COMPLIMENTS OF KID FLASH!
YES?
YOU RANG?

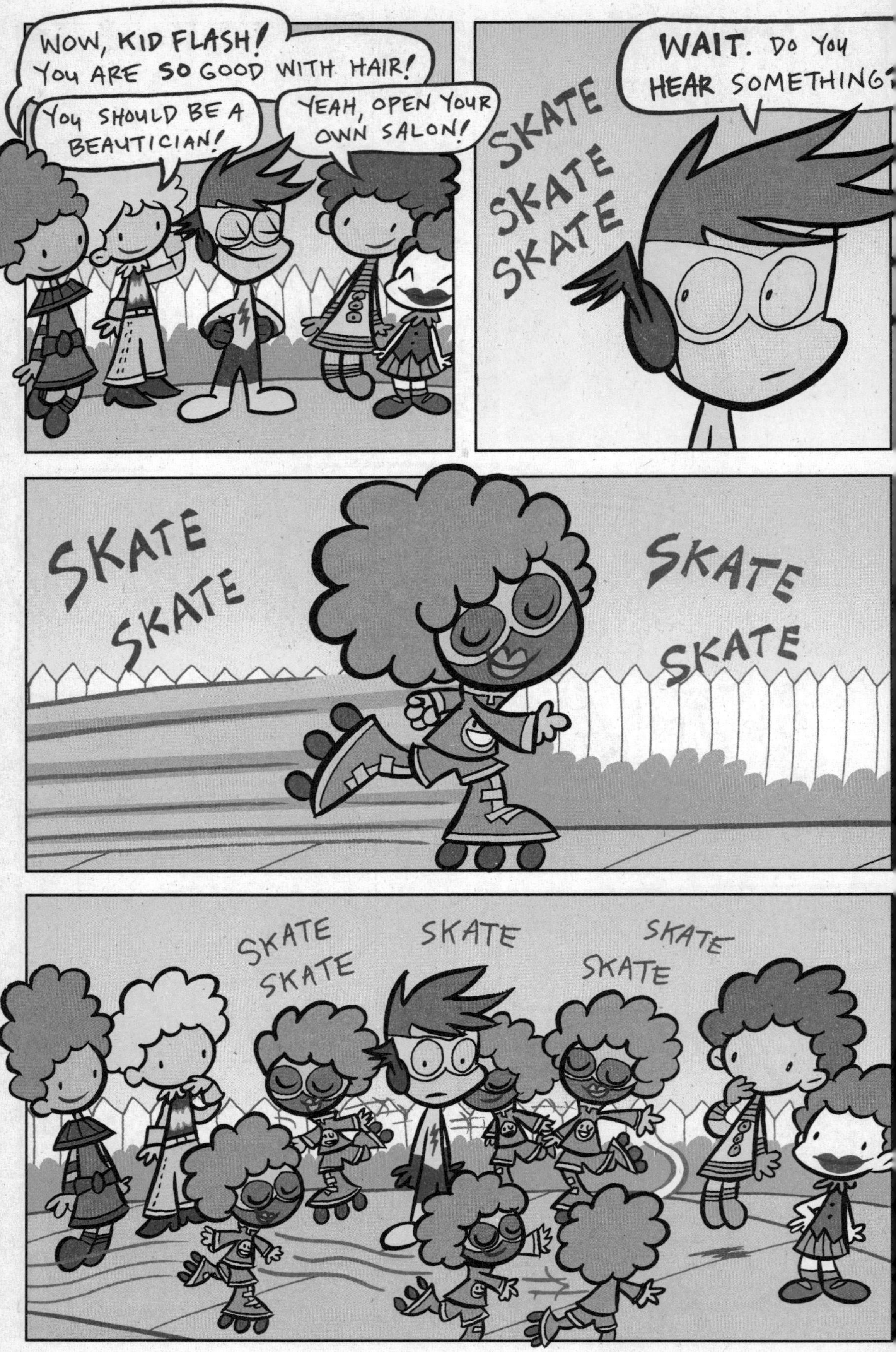
WOW, KID FLASH! You ARE SO GOOD WITH HAIR!
You SHOULD BE A BEAUTICIAN!
YEAH, OPEN YOUR OWN SALON!
WAIT. DO YOU HEAR SOMETHING?
SKATE SKATE SKATE
SKATE SKATE
SKATE SKATE
SKATE SKATE
SKATE
SKATE SKATE

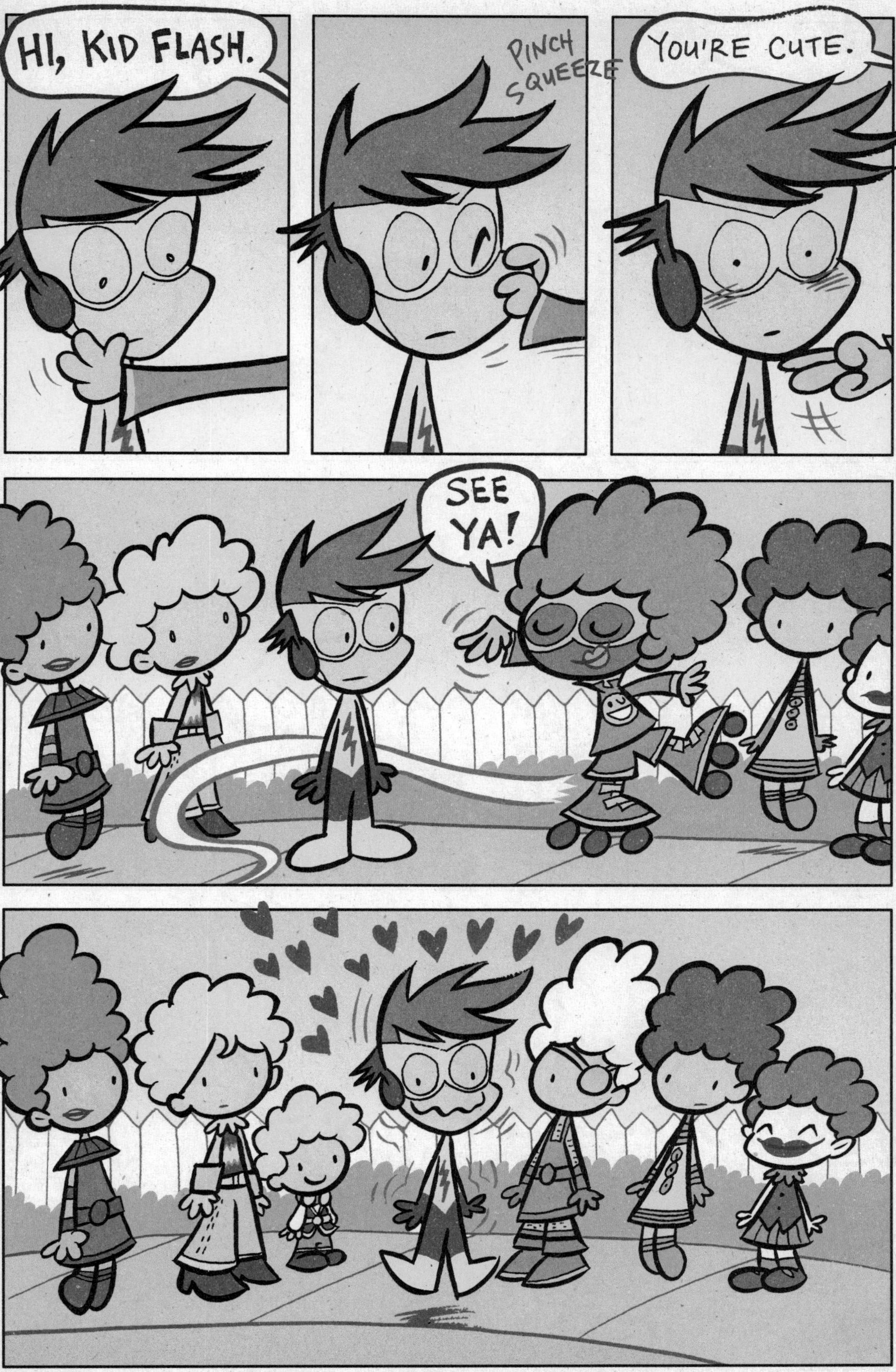
HI, KID FLASH.
PINCH
SQUEEZE
YOU'RE CUTE.
SEE YA!

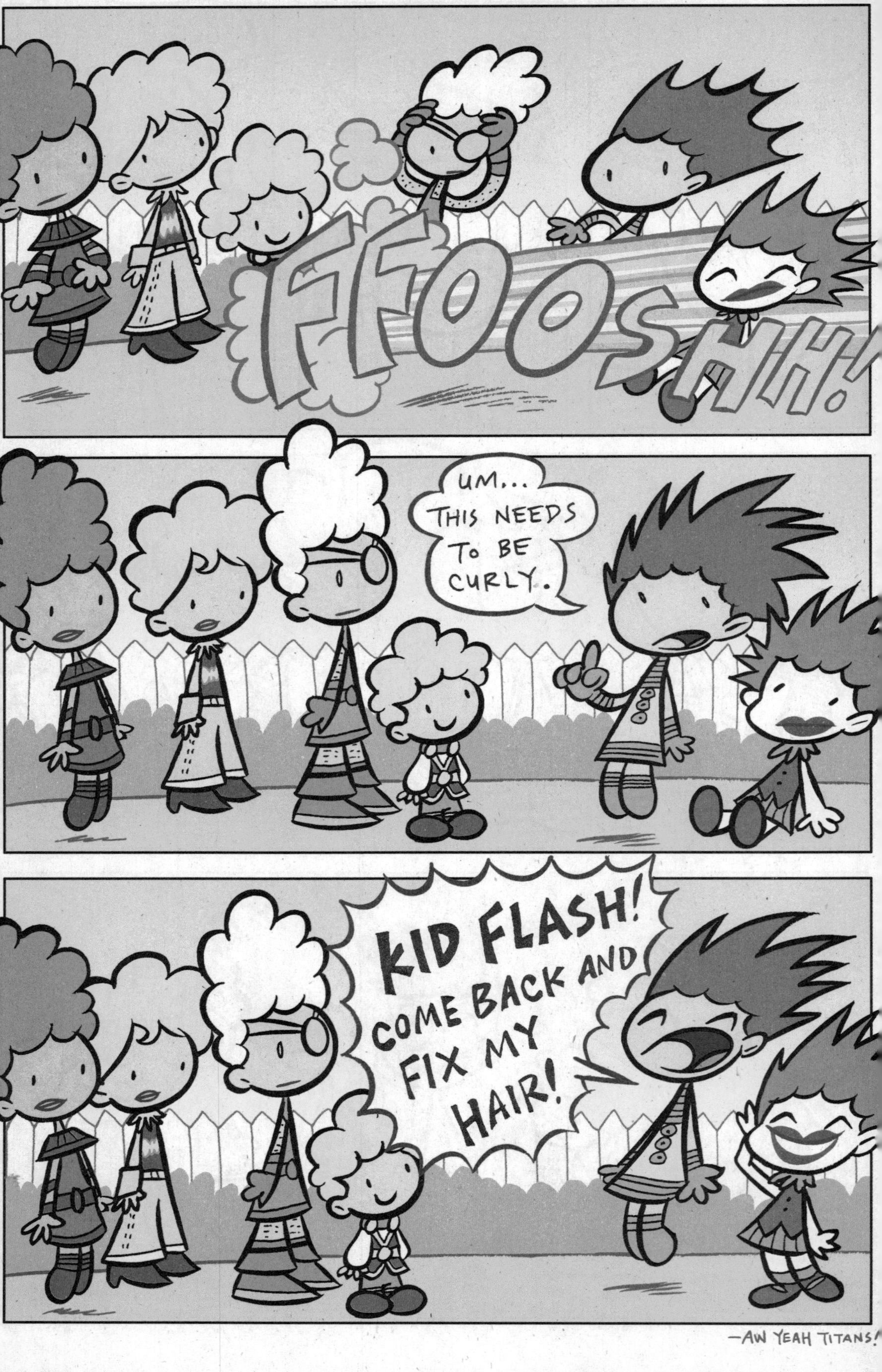
FFOOSHH!
UM... THIS NEEDS TO BE CURLY.
KID FLASH! COME BACK AND FIX MY HAIR!

—AW YEAH TITANS!

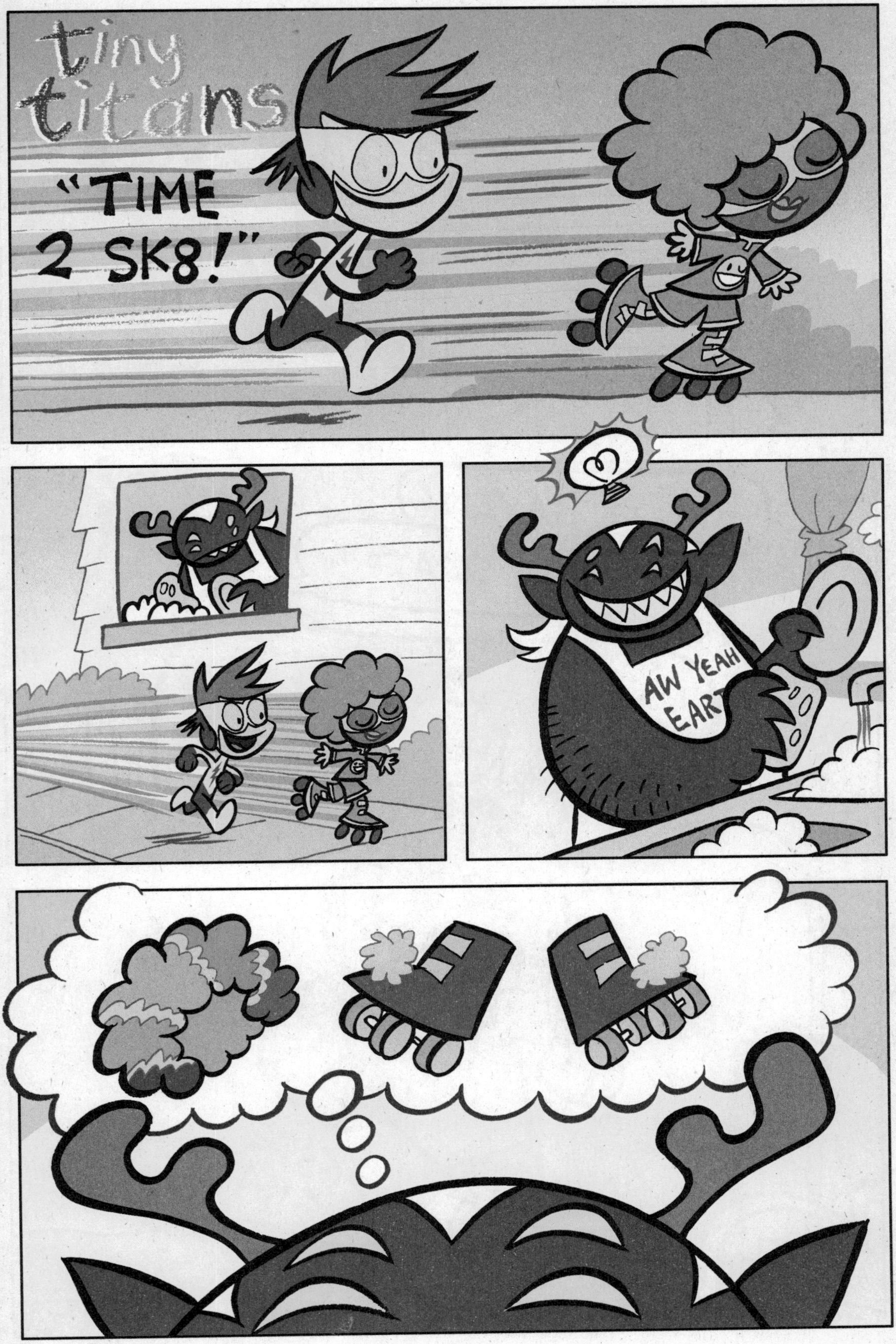

tiny titans
"TIME 2 SK8!"
AW YEAH EART

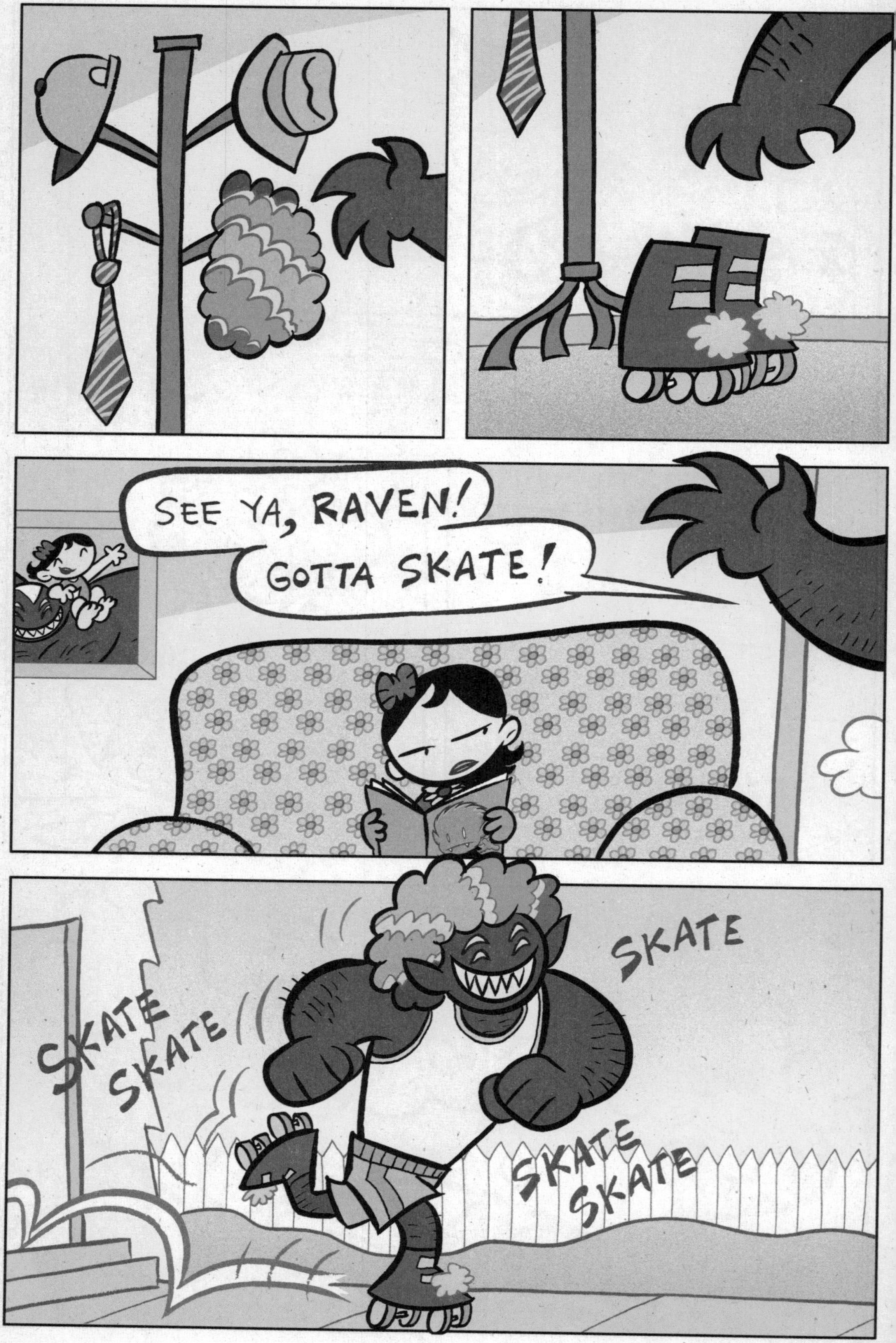
SEE YA, RAVEN!
GOTTA SKATE!
SKATE
SKATE SKATE
SKATE SKATE

-LET'S BOOGIE!

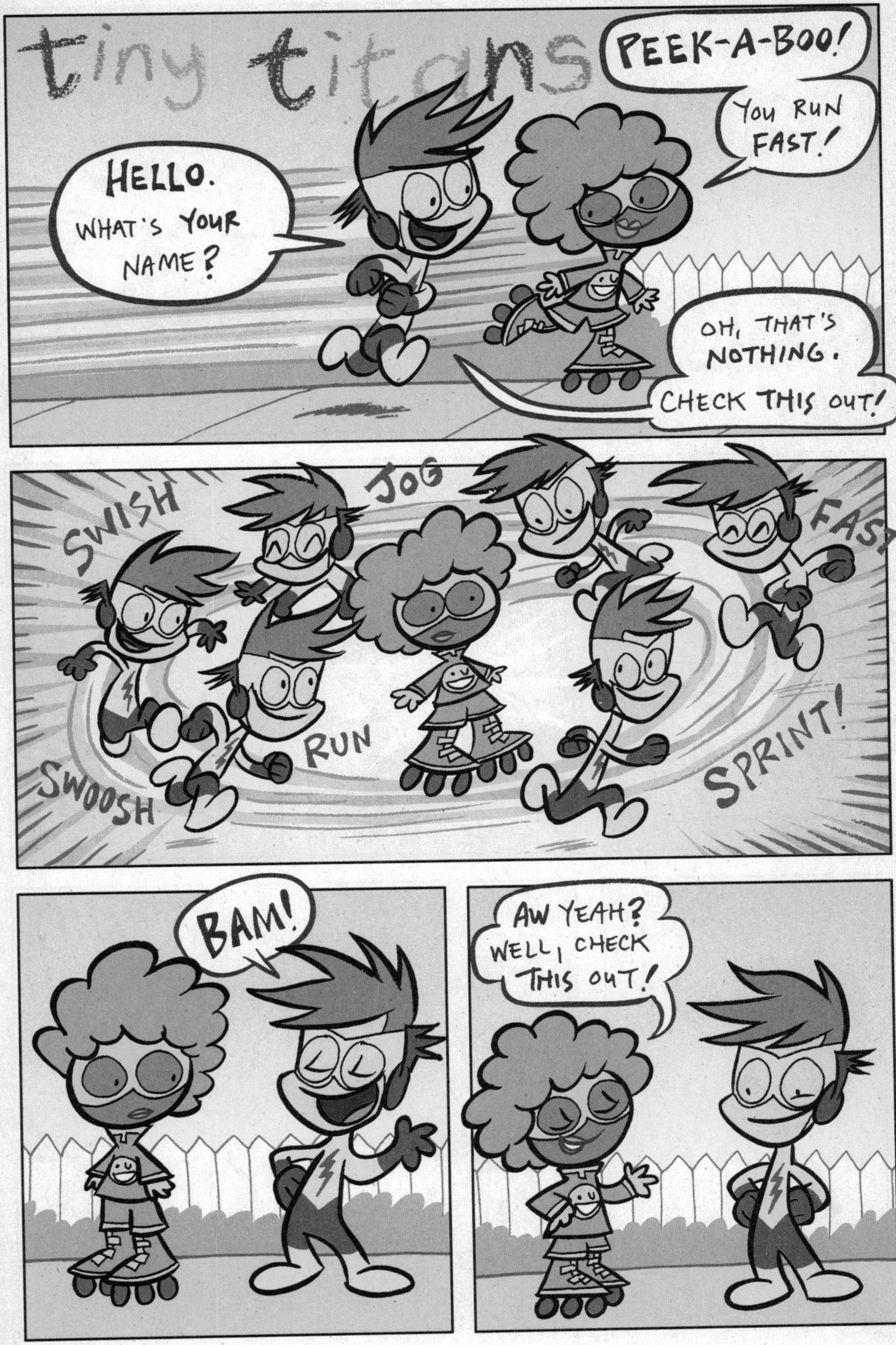
tiny titans
PEEK-A-BOO!
YOU RUN FAST!
HELLO. WHAT'S YOUR NAME?
OH, THAT'S NOTHING.
CHECK THIS OUT!
SWISH
JOG
FAST
RUN
SWOOSH
SPRINT!
BAM!
AW YEAH? WELL, CHECK THIS OUT!

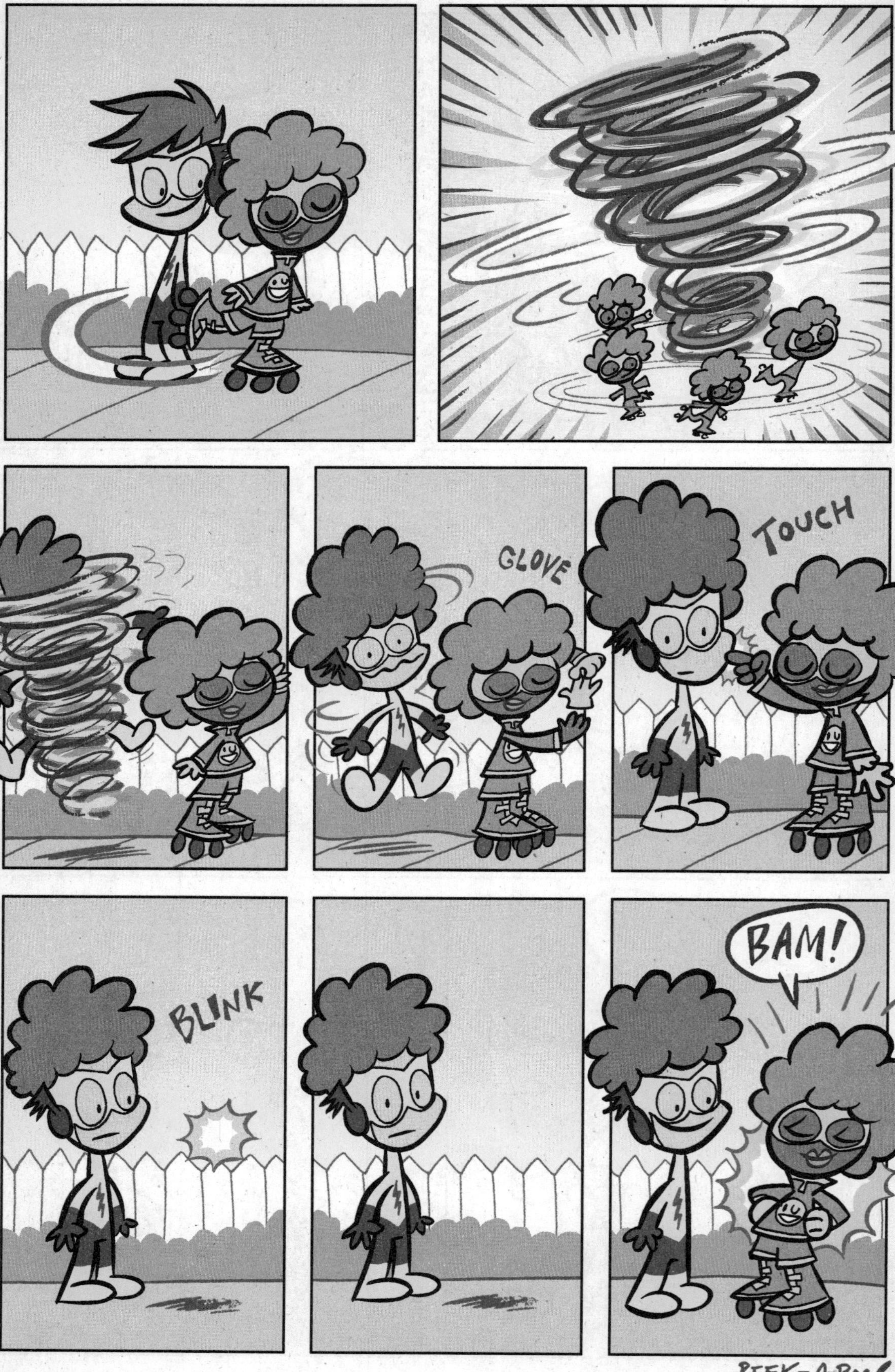
GLOVE
TOUCH
BLINK
BAM!

—PEEK-A-BOO!

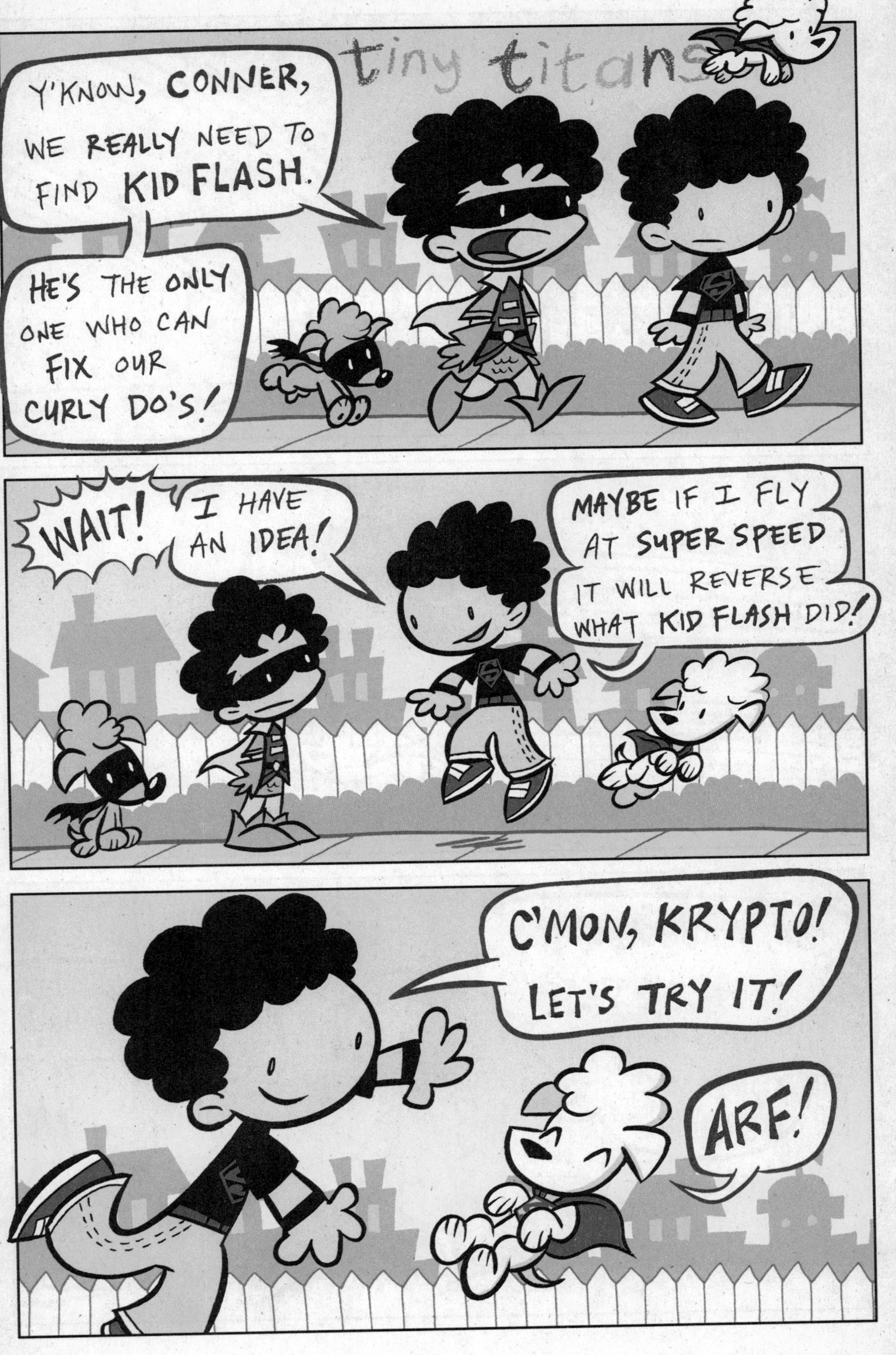
tiny titans
Y'KNOW, CONNER, WE REALLY NEED TO FIND KID FLASH.
HE'S THE ONLY ONE WHO CAN FIX OUR CURLY DO'S!
WAIT!
I HAVE AN IDEA!
MAYBE IF I FLY AT SUPER SPEED IT WILL REVERSE WHAT KID FLASH DID!
C'MON, KRYPTO! LET'S TRY IT!
ARF!

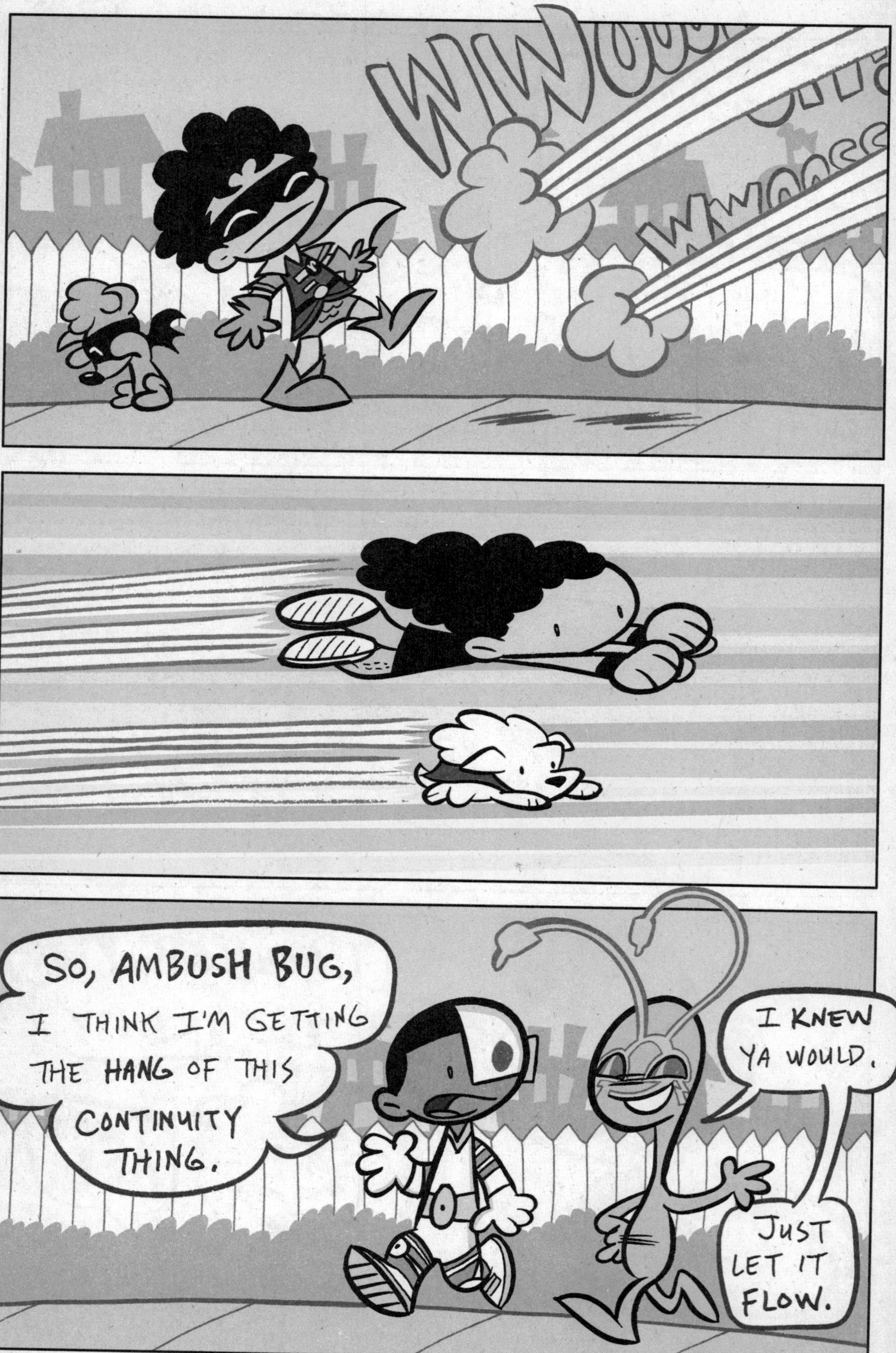
SO, AMBUSH BUG, I THINK I'M GETTING THE HANG OF THIS CONTINUITY THING.
I KNEW YA WOULD.
JUST LET IT FLOW.

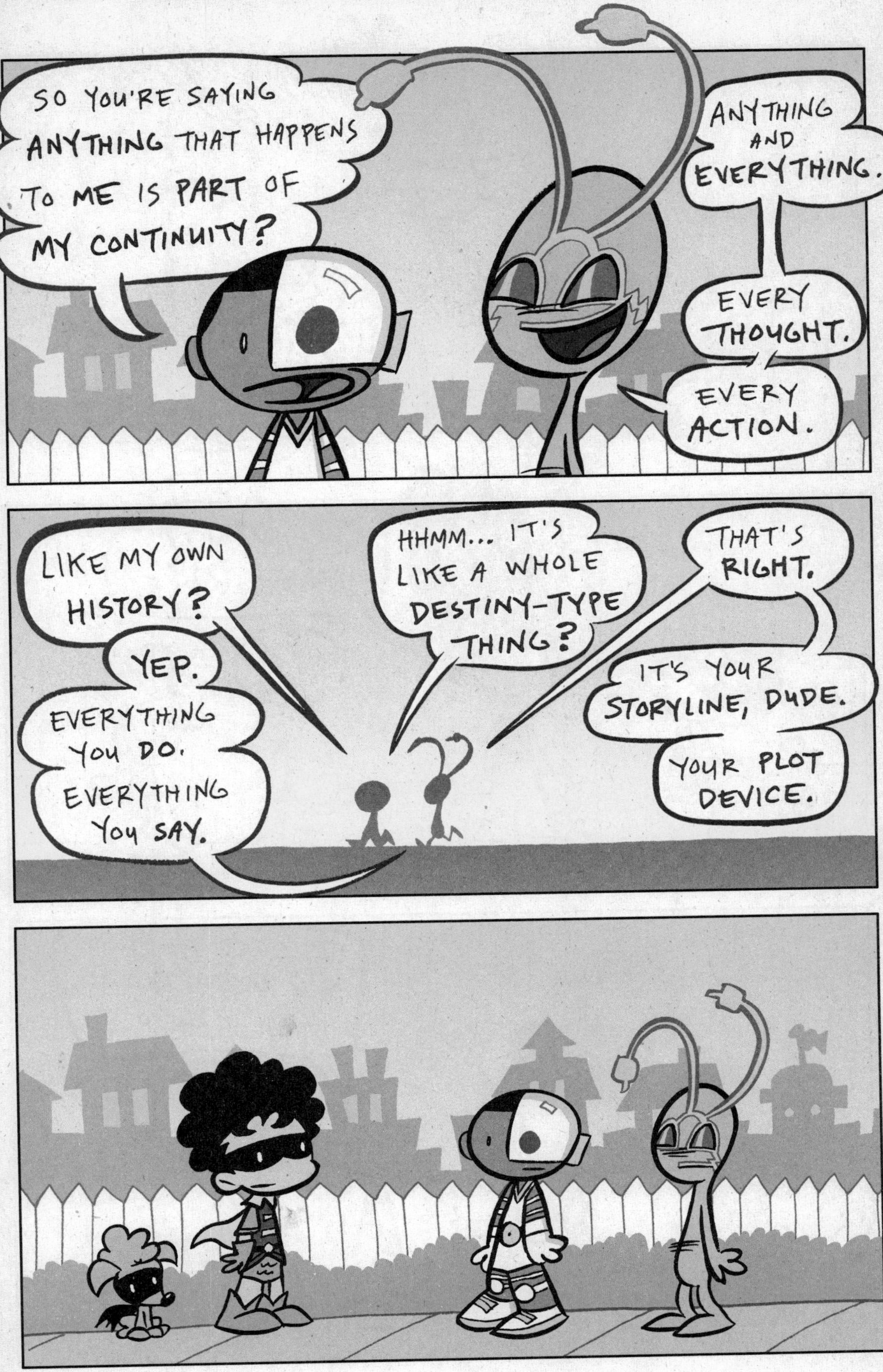
SO YOU'RE SAYING ANYTHING THAT HAPPENS TO ME IS PART OF MY CONTINUITY?
ANYTHING AND EVERYTHING.
EVERY THOUGHT.
EVERY ACTION.
LIKE MY OWN HISTORY?
YEP.
EVERYTHING YOU DO. EVERYTHING YOU SAY.
HHMM... IT'S LIKE A WHOLE DESTINY-TYPE THING?
THAT'S RIGHT.
IT'S YOUR STORYLINE, DUDE.
YOUR PLOT DEVICE.

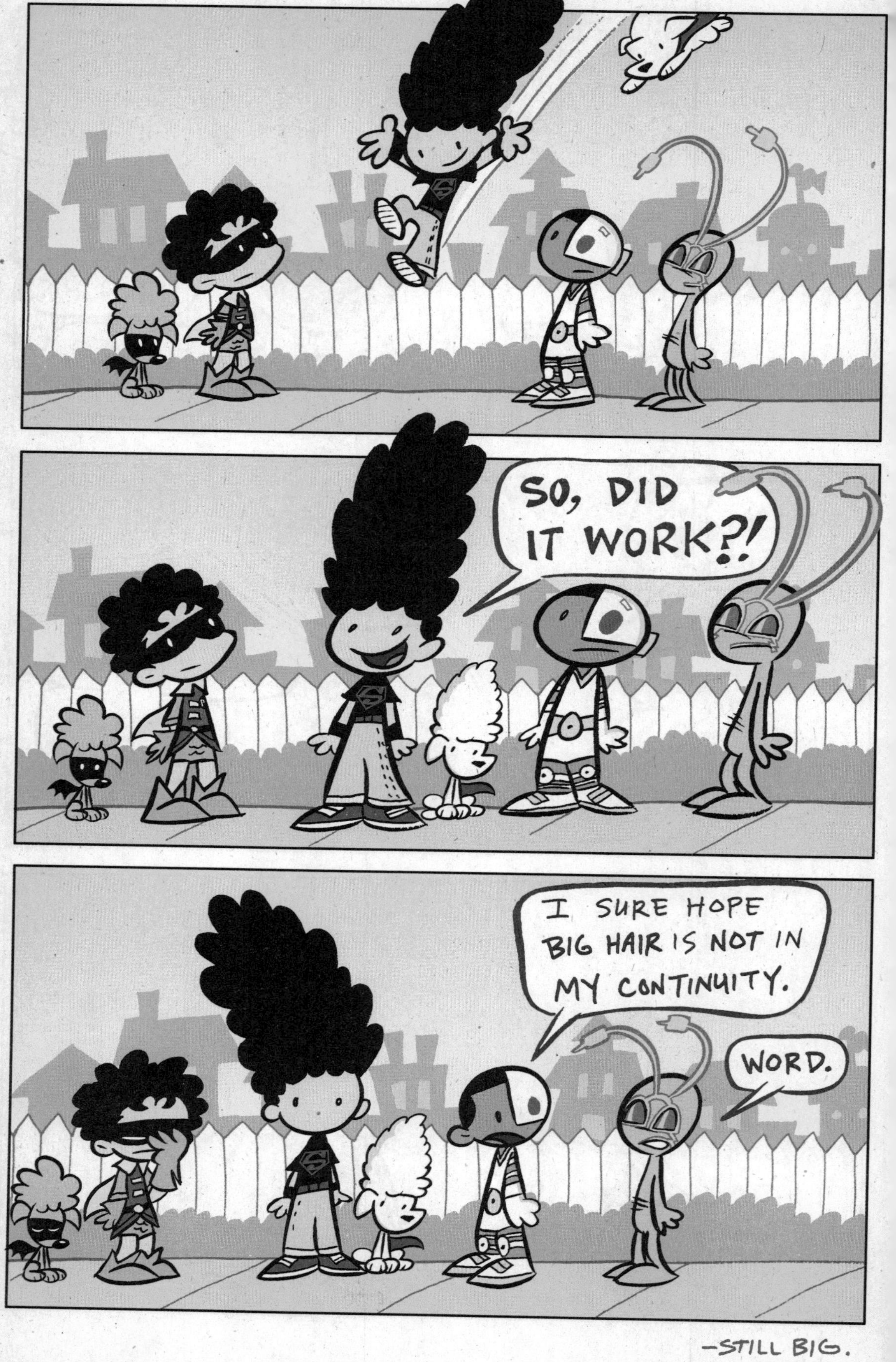
SO, DID IT WORK?!
I SURE HOPE BIG HAIR IS NOT IN MY CONTINUITY.
WORD.

—STILL BIG.

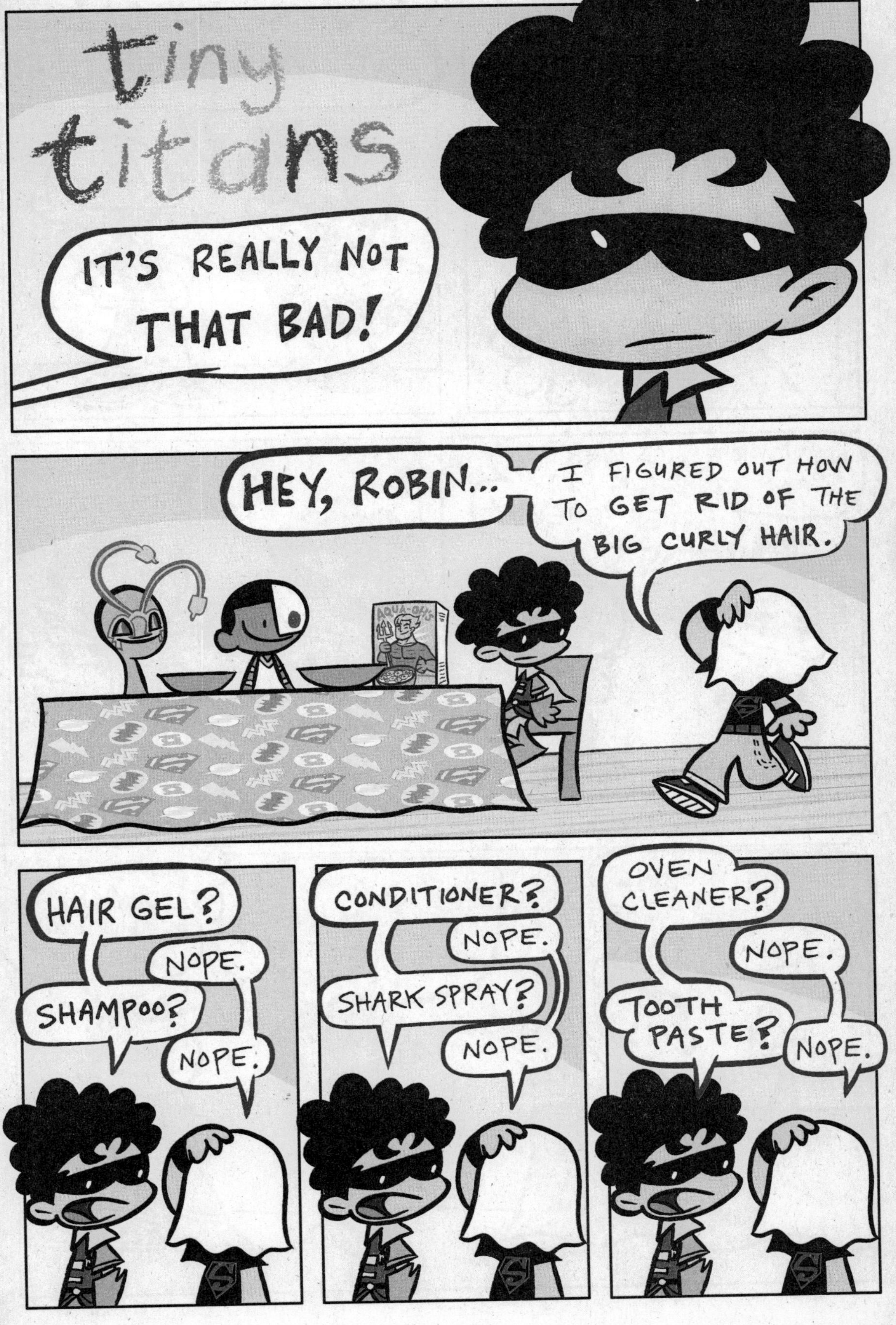
tiny titans
IT'S REALLY NOT THAT BAD!
HEY, ROBIN...
I FIGURED OUT HOW TO GET RID OF THE BIG CURLY HAIR.
AQUA-OH'S
HAIR GEL?
NOPE.
SHAMPOO?
NOPE.
CONDITIONER?
NOPE.
SHARK SPRAY?
NOPE.
OVEN CLEANER?
NOPE.
TOOTH PASTE?
NOPE.

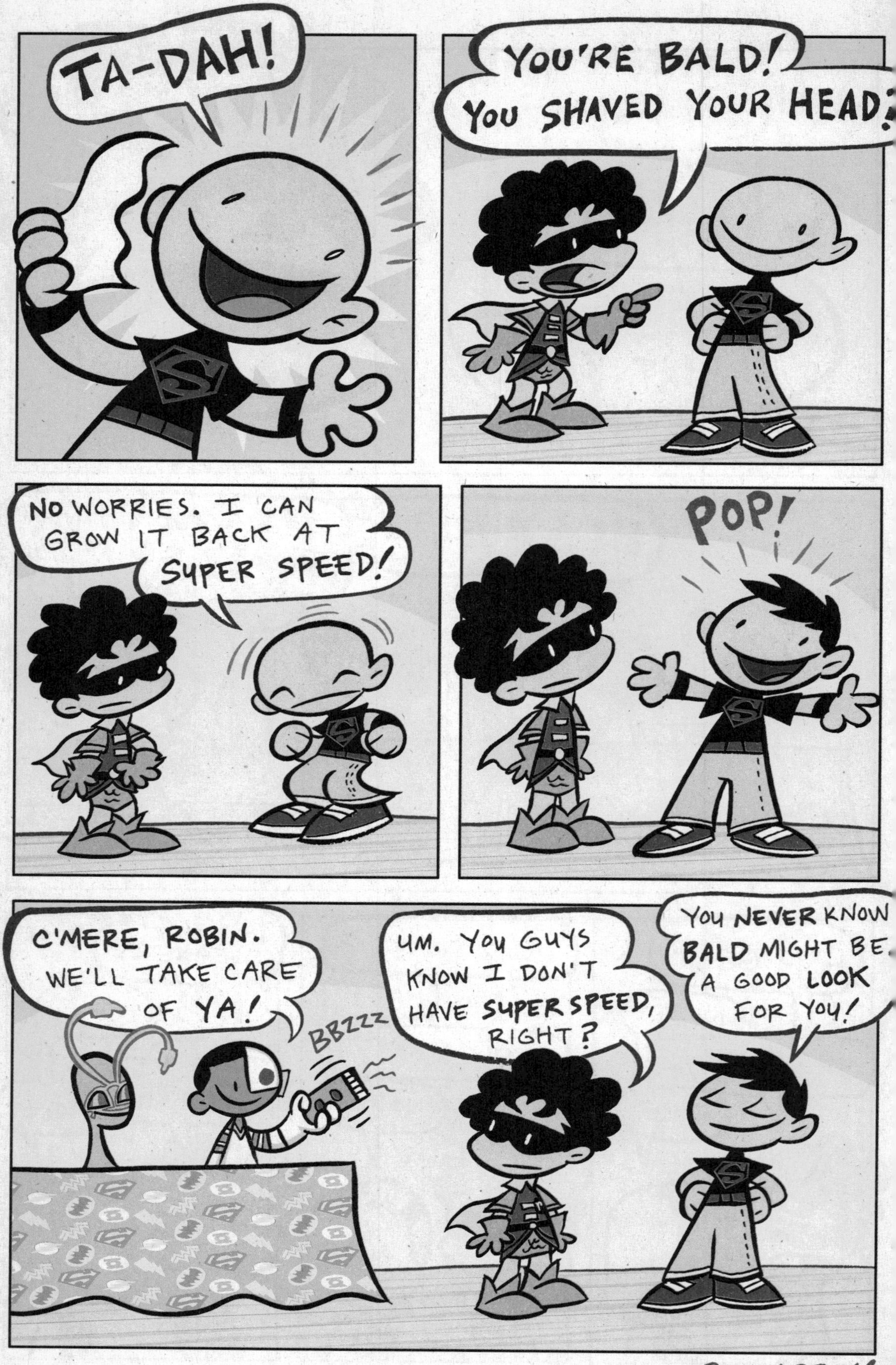
TA-DAH!
YOU'RE BALD! YOU SHAVED YOUR HEAD?
NO WORRIES. I CAN GROW IT BACK AT SUPER SPEED!
POP!
C'MERE, ROBIN. WE'LL TAKE CARE OF YA!
BBZZZ
UM. YOU GUYS KNOW I DON'T HAVE SUPER SPEED, RIGHT?
YOU NEVER KNOW BALD MIGHT BE A GOOD LOOK FOR YOU!

—BUZZWORTHY!

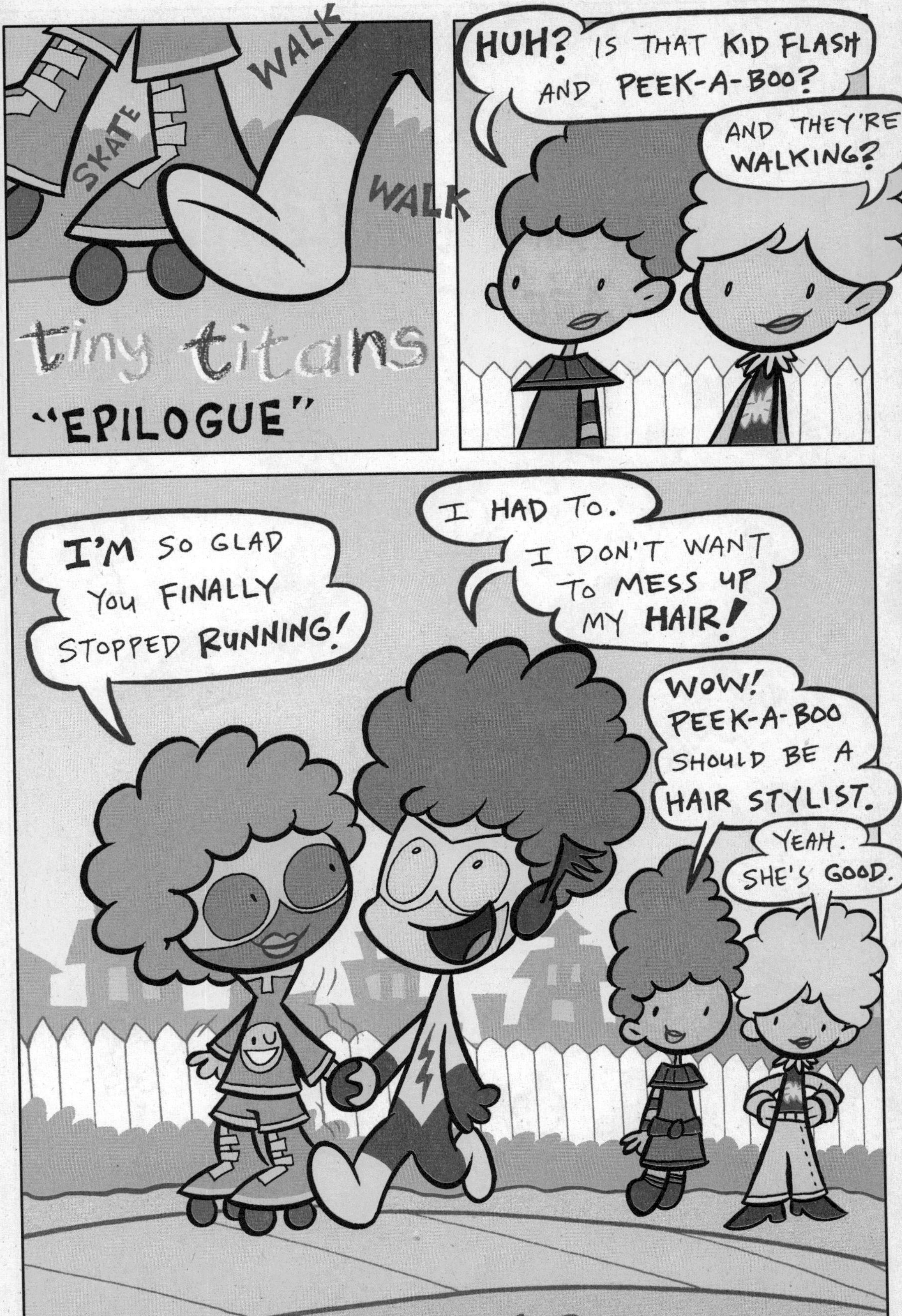
WALK
SKATE
WALK
tiny titans
"EPILOGUE"
HUH? IS THAT KID FLASH AND PEEK-A-BOO?
AND THEY'RE WALKING?
I'M SO GLAD YOU FINALLY STOPPED RUNNING!
I HAD TO.
I DON'T WANT TO MESS UP MY HAIR!
WOW! PEEK-A-BOO SHOULD BE A HAIR STYLIST.
YEAH. SHE'S GOOD.

—HOT ROLLIN'.

time to count!

HOW MANY BUMBLEBEES ARE THERE?

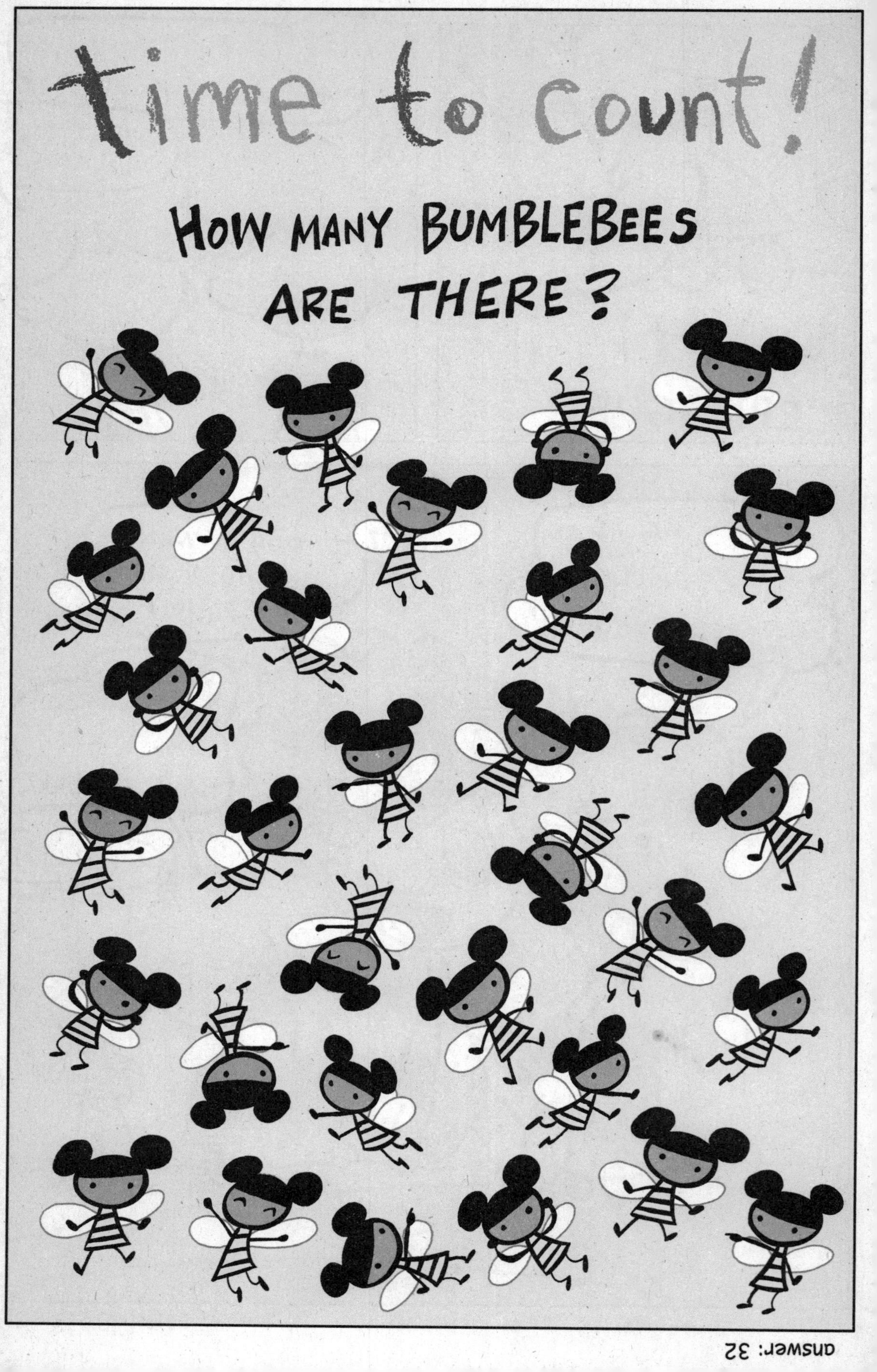

answer: 32

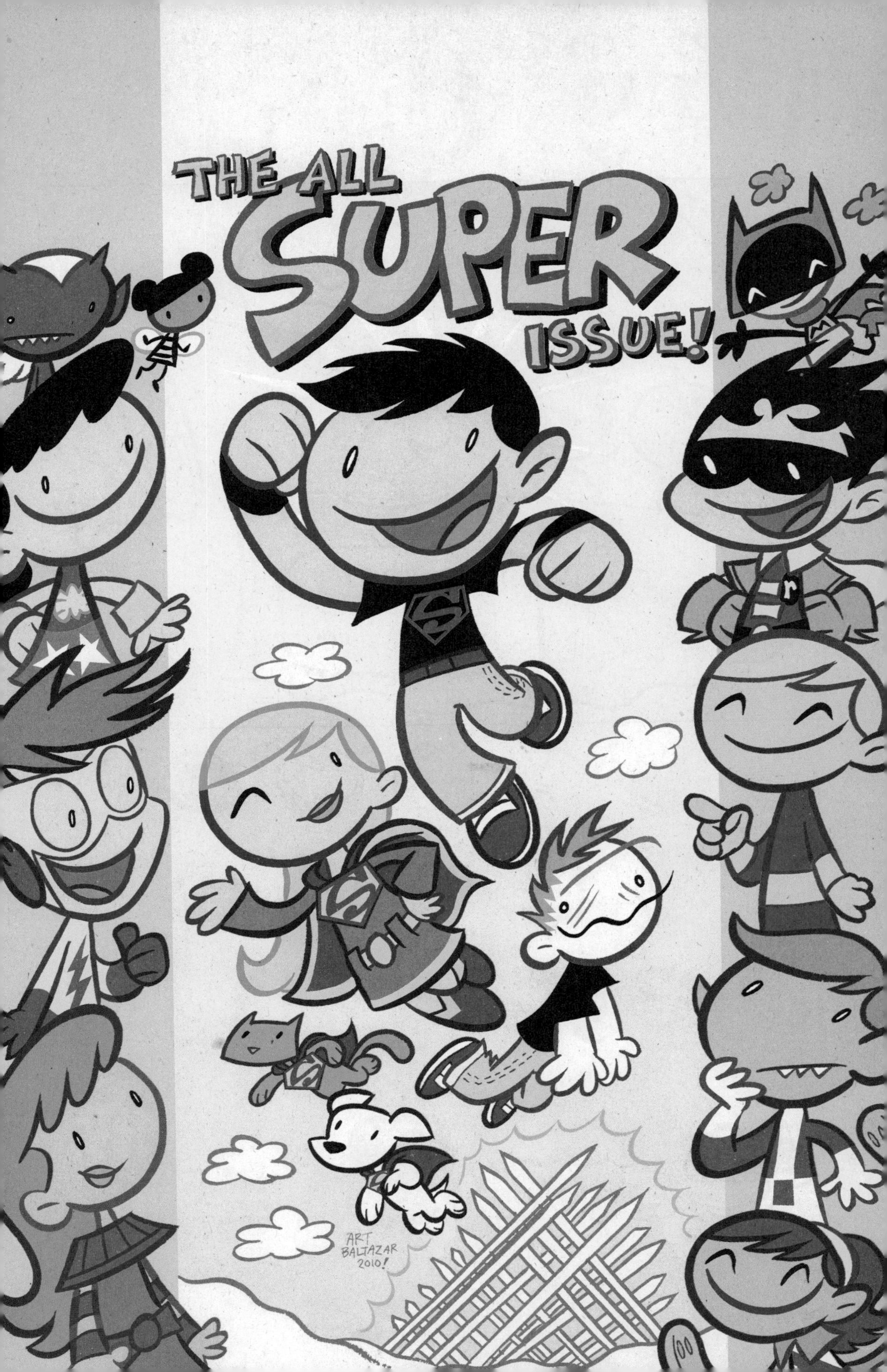
THE ALL SUPER ISSUE!
ART BALTAZAR 2010!

tiny titans

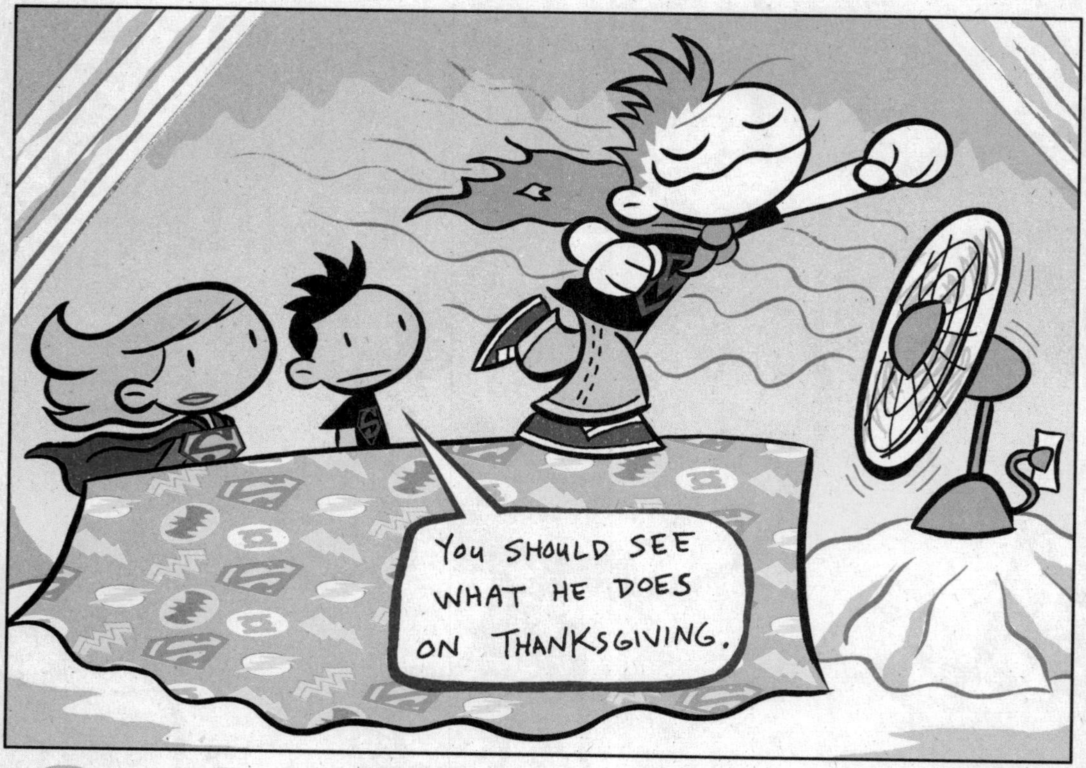
You SHOULD SEE WHAT HE DOES ON THANKSGIVING.

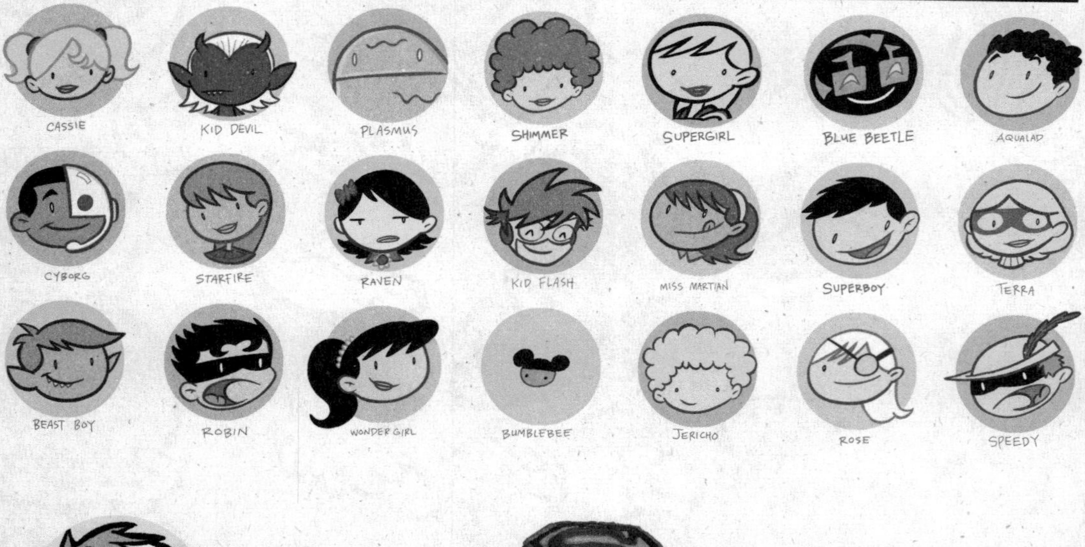
CASSIE
KID DEVIL
PLASMUS
SHIMMER
SUPERGIRL
BLUE BEETLE
AQUALAD
CYBORG
STARFIRE
RAVEN
KID FLASH
MISS MARTIAN
SUPERBOY
TERRA
BEAST BOY
ROBIN
WONDER GIRL
BUMBLEBEE
JERICHO
ROSE
SPEEDY

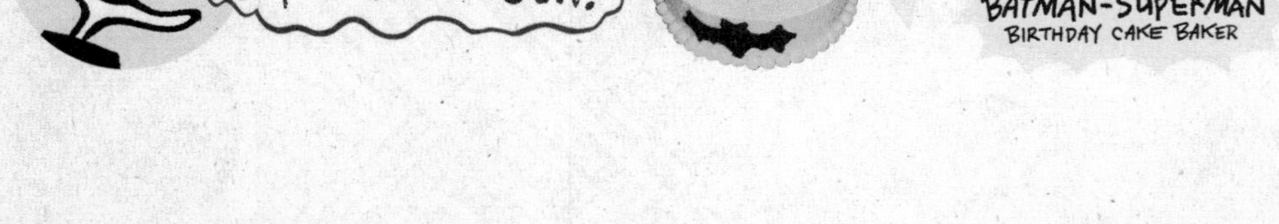
MMMUUHHGGN.
ART'S COUSIN
LAUREN SCIALABBA,
BATMAN-SUPERMAN
BIRTHDAY CAKE BAKER

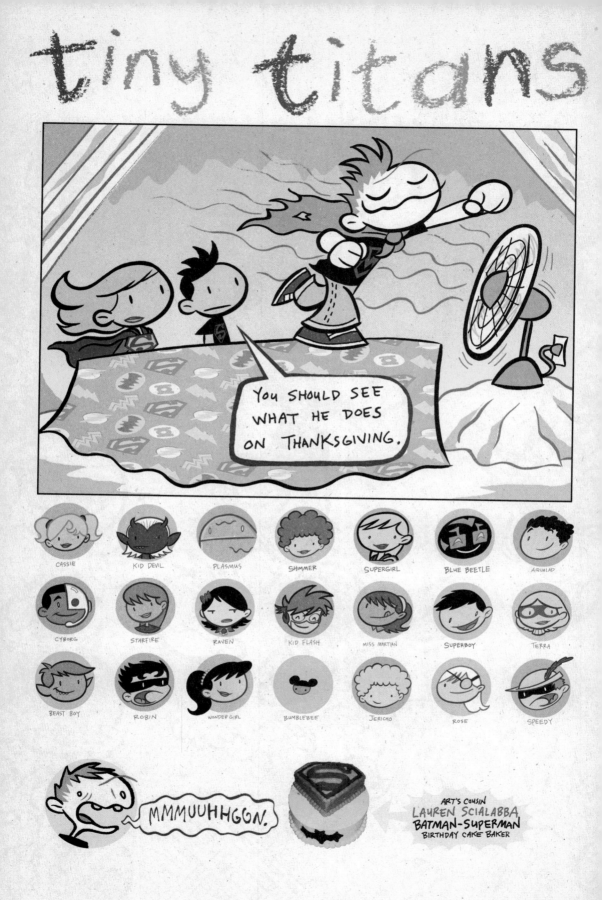

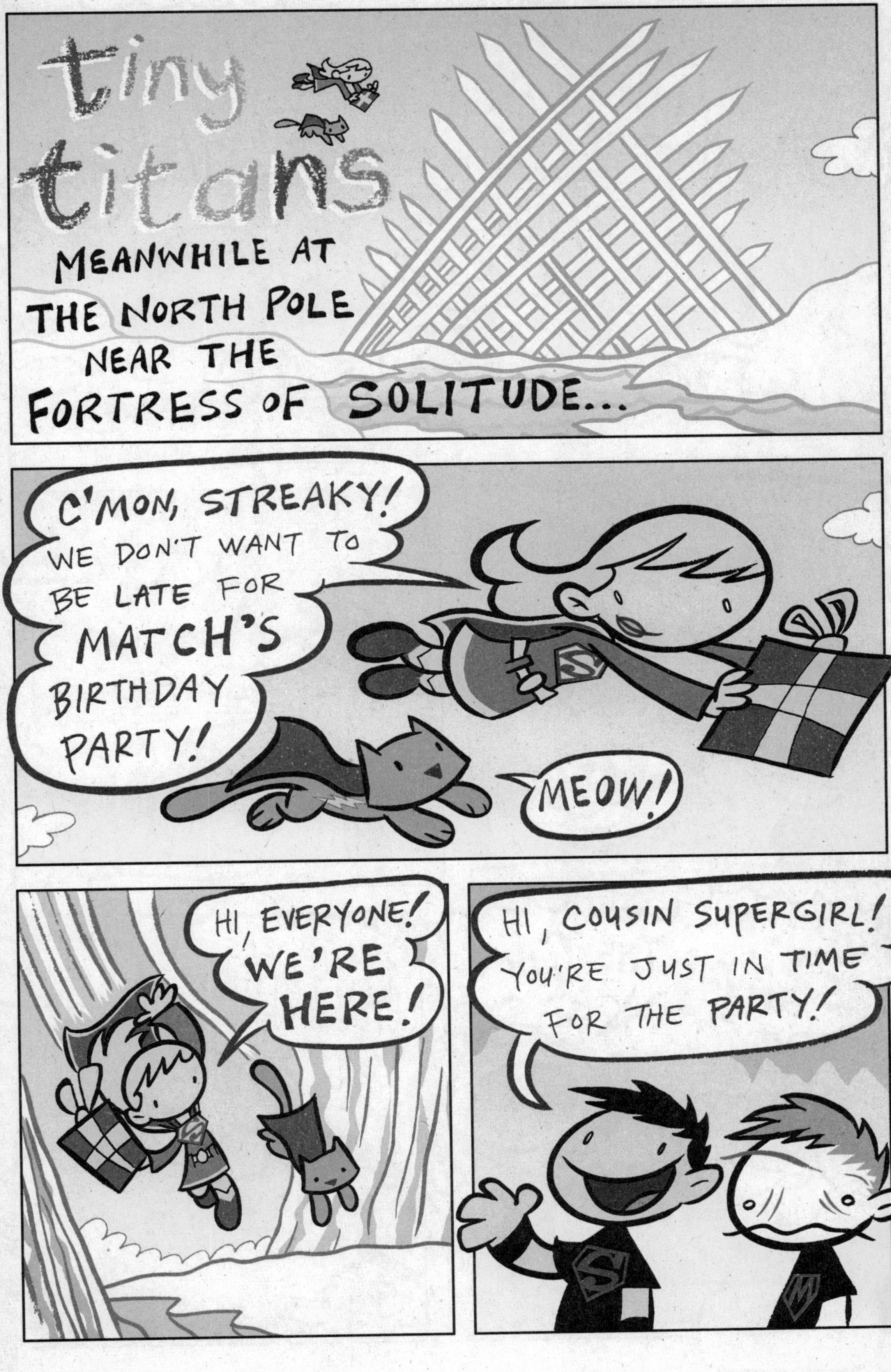
tiny titans
MEANWHILE AT THE NORTH POLE NEAR THE FORTRESS OF SOLITUDE...
C'MON, STREAKY! WE DON'T WANT TO BE LATE FOR MATCH'S BIRTHDAY PARTY!
MEOW!
HI, EVERYONE! WE'RE HERE!
HI, COUSIN SUPERGIRL! YOU'RE JUST IN TIME FOR THE PARTY!

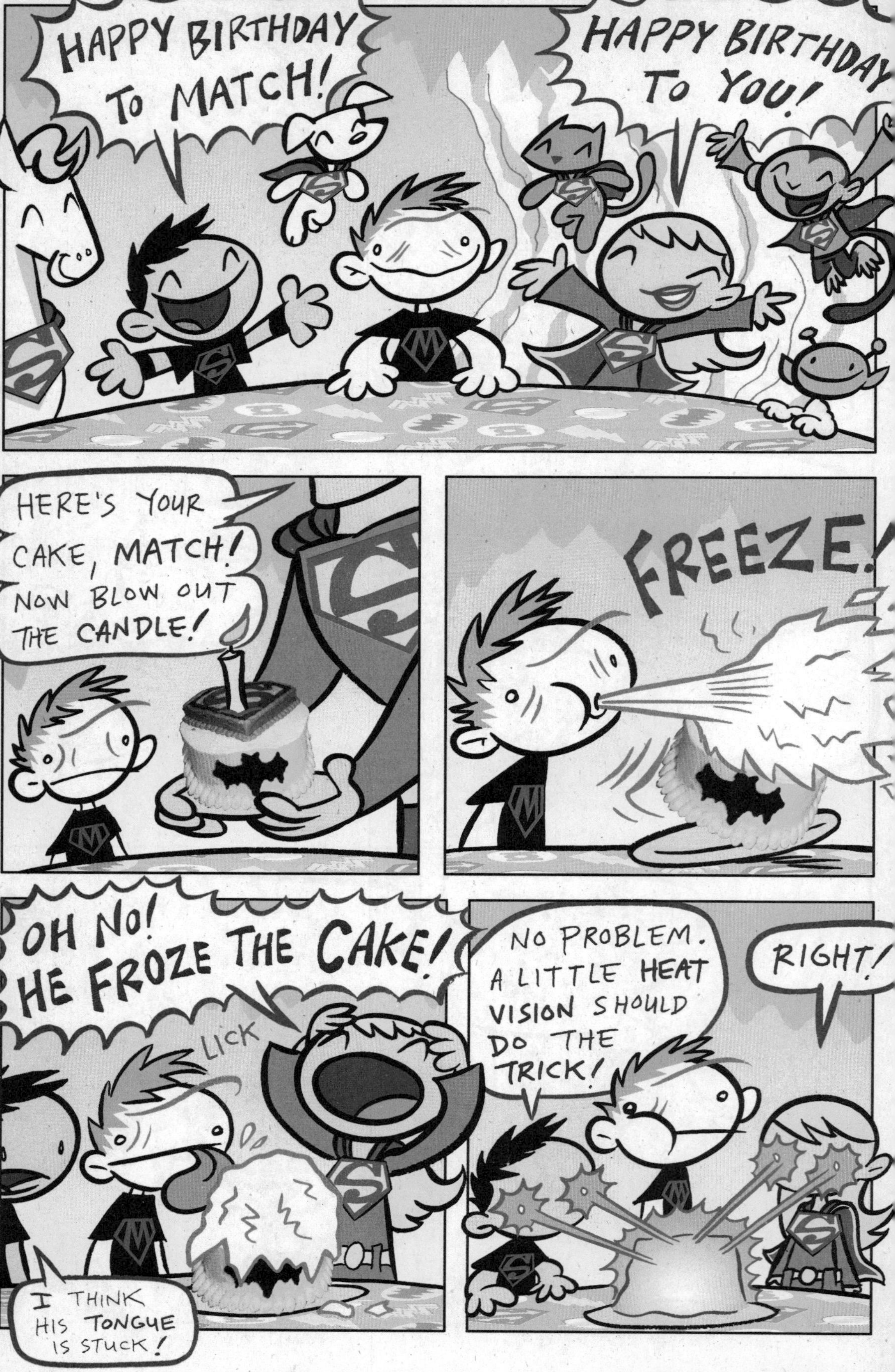
HAPPY BIRTHDAY TO MATCH!
HAPPY BIRTHDAY TO YOU!
HERE'S YOUR CAKE, MATCH! NOW BLOW OUT THE CANDLE!
FREEZE!
OH NO! HE FROZE THE CAKE!
LICK
I THINK HIS TONGUE IS STUCK!
NO PROBLEM. A LITTLE HEAT VISION SHOULD DO THE TRICK!
RIGHT!

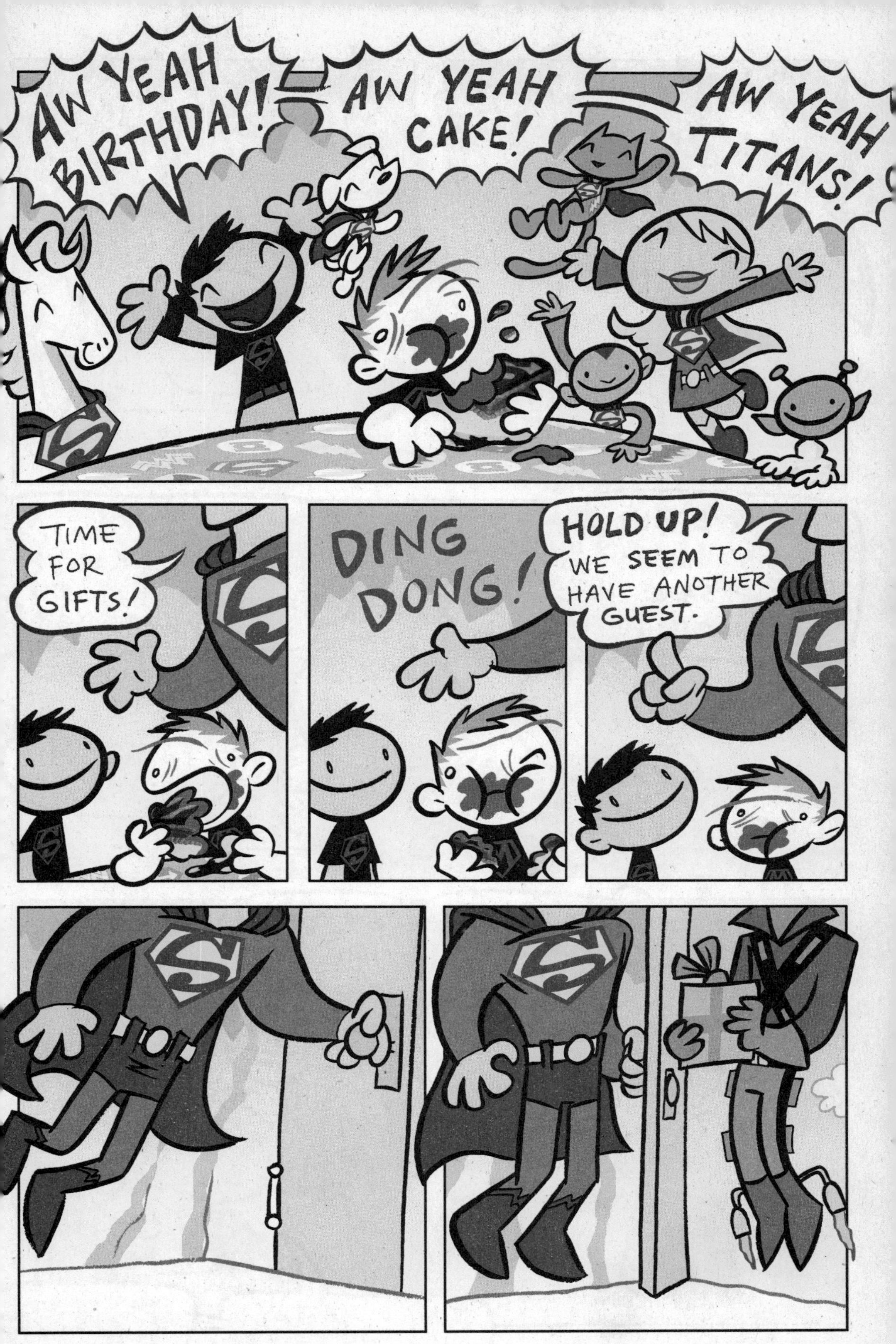
AW YEAH BIRTHDAY!
AW YEAH CAKE!
AW YEAH TITANS!
TIME FOR GIFTS!
DING DONG!
HOLD UP! WE SEEM TO HAVE ANOTHER GUEST.

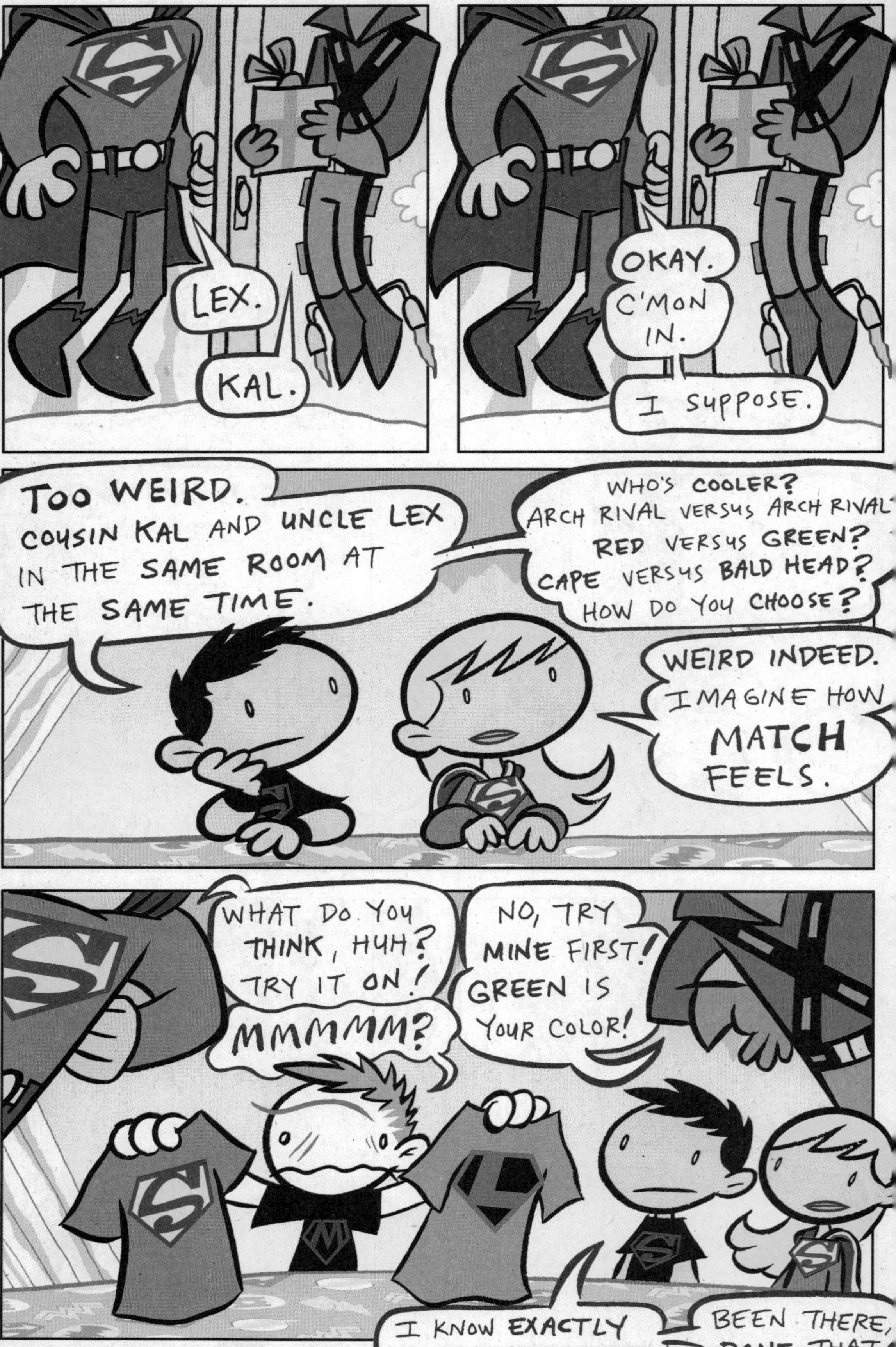
LEX.
KAL.
OKAY. C'MON IN.
I SUPPOSE.
TOO WEIRD. COUSIN KAL AND UNCLE LEX IN THE SAME ROOM AT THE SAME TIME.
WHO'S COOLER? ARCH RIVAL VERSUS ARCH RIVAL? RED VERSUS GREEN? CAPE VERSUS BALD HEAD? HOW DO YOU CHOOSE?
WEIRD INDEED. IMAGINE HOW MATCH FEELS.
WHAT DO YOU THINK, HUH? TRY IT ON!
MMMMM?
NO, TRY MINE FIRST! GREEN IS YOUR COLOR!
I KNOW EXACTLY HOW HE FEELS.
BEEN THERE, DONE THAT!

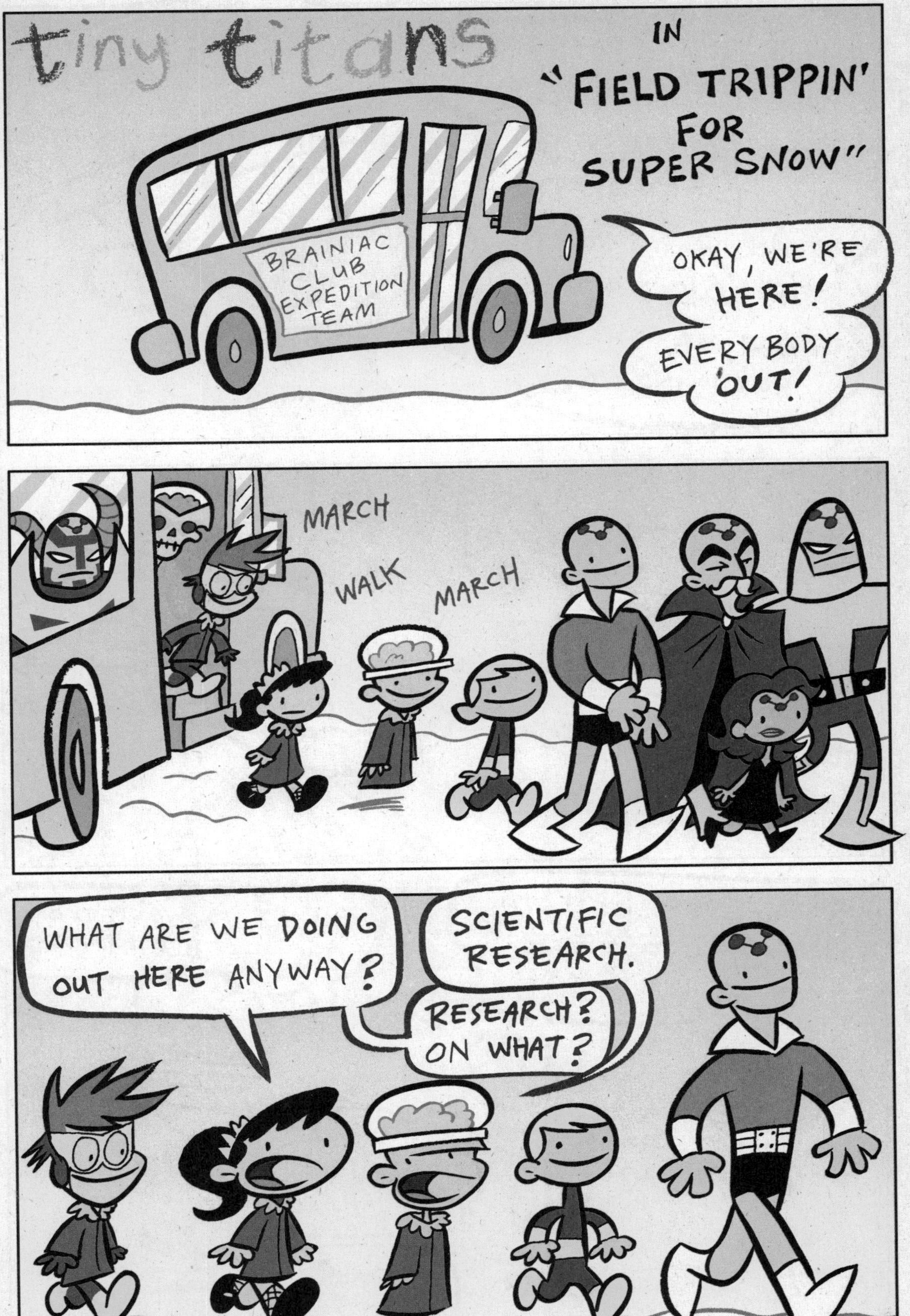

tiny titans
IN
"FIELD TRIPPIN' FOR SUPER SNOW"
BRAINIAC CLUB EXPEDITION TEAM
OKAY, WE'RE HERE!
EVERY BODY OUT!
MARCH
WALK
MARCH
WHAT ARE WE DOING OUT HERE ANYWAY?
SCIENTIFIC RESEARCH.
RESEARCH? ON WHAT?

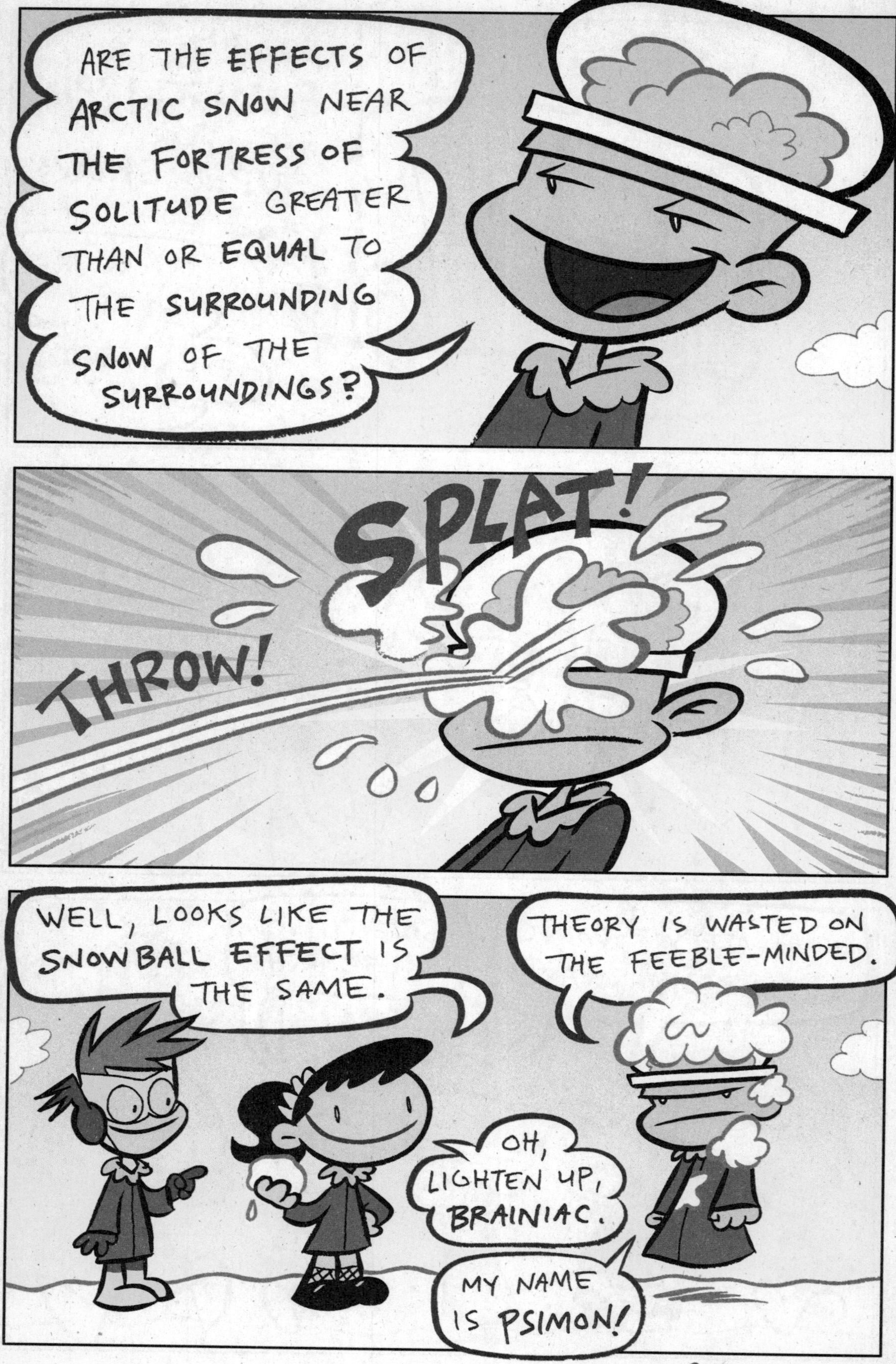
ARE THE EFFECTS OF ARCTIC SNOW NEAR THE FORTRESS OF SOLITUDE GREATER THAN OR EQUAL TO THE SURROUNDING SNOW OF THE SURROUNDINGS?
SPLAT!
THROW!
WELL, LOOKS LIKE THE SNOWBALL EFFECT IS THE SAME.
THEORY IS WASTED ON THE FEEBLE-MINDED.
OH, LIGHTEN UP, BRAINIAC.
MY NAME IS PSIMON!
– SUPER SNOW.

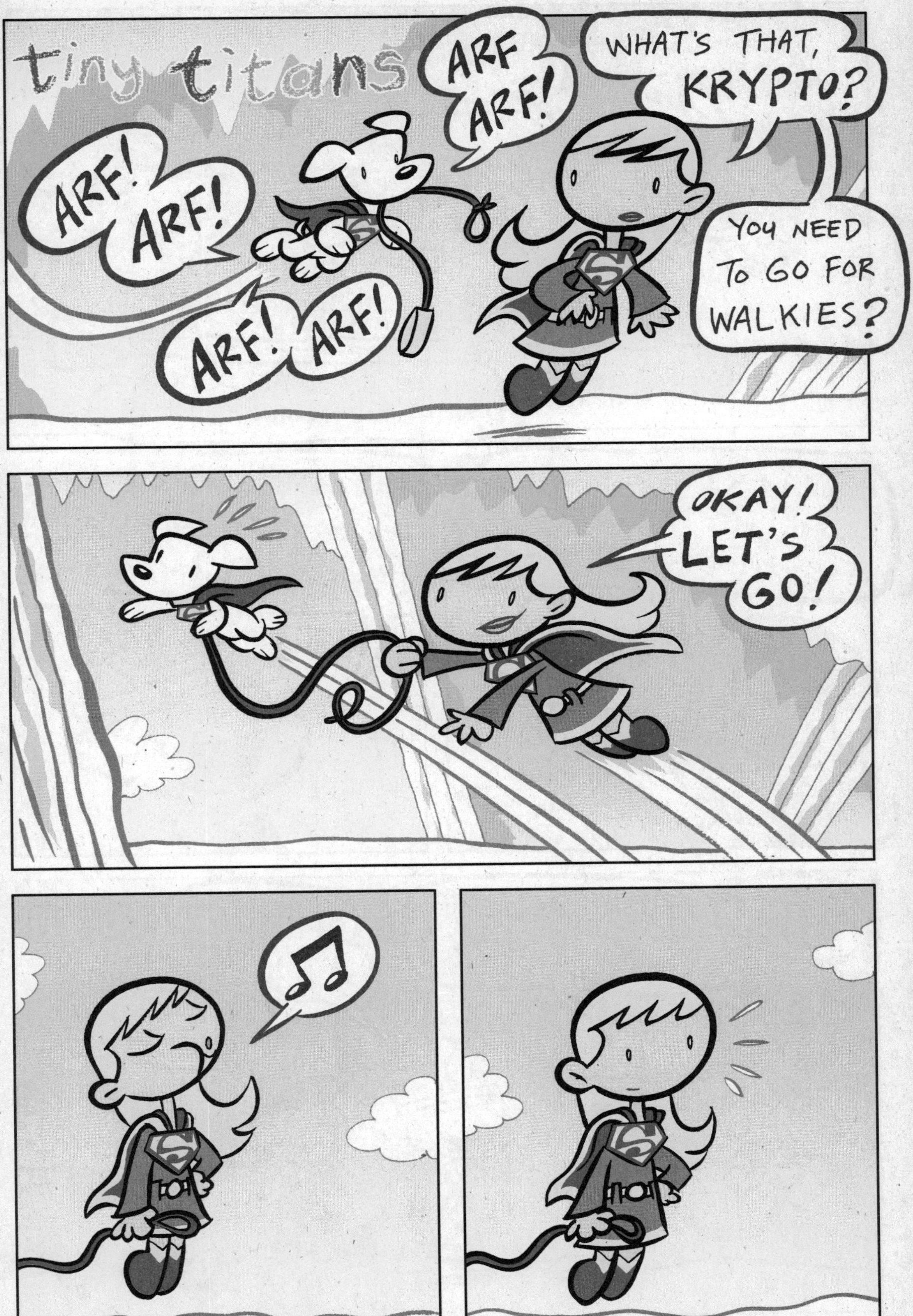
tiny titans
ARF! ARF!
ARF! ARF!
ARF ARF!
WHAT'S THAT, KRYPTO?
YOU NEED TO GO FOR WALKIES?
OKAY! LET'S GO!

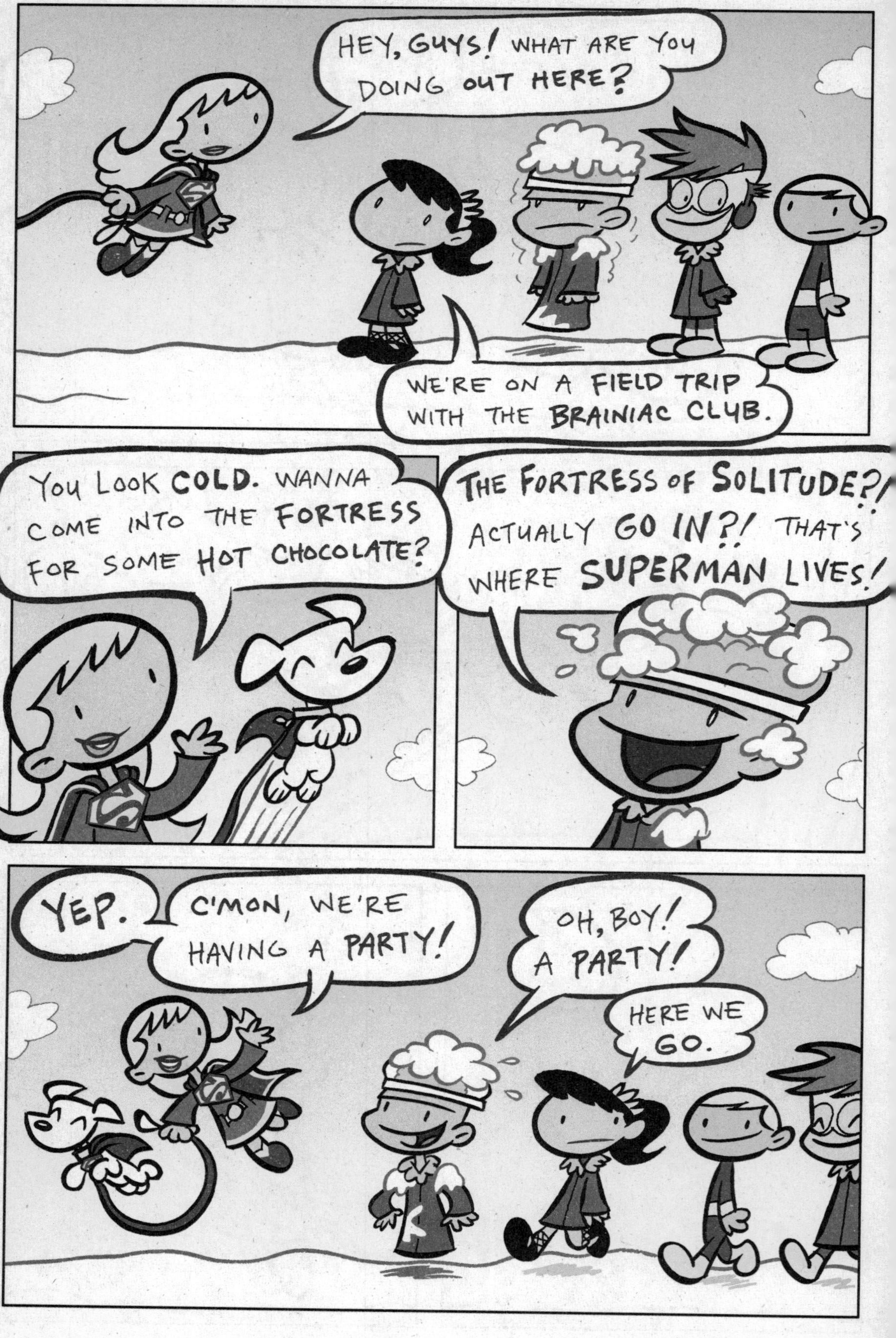

HEY, GUYS! WHAT ARE YOU DOING OUT HERE?
WE'RE ON A FIELD TRIP WITH THE BRAINIAC CLUB.
YOU LOOK COLD. WANNA COME INTO THE FORTRESS FOR SOME HOT CHOCOLATE?
THE FORTRESS OF SOLITUDE?! ACTUALLY GO IN?! THAT'S WHERE SUPERMAN LIVES!
YEP.
C'MON, WE'RE HAVING A PARTY!
OH, BOY! A PARTY!
HERE WE GO.

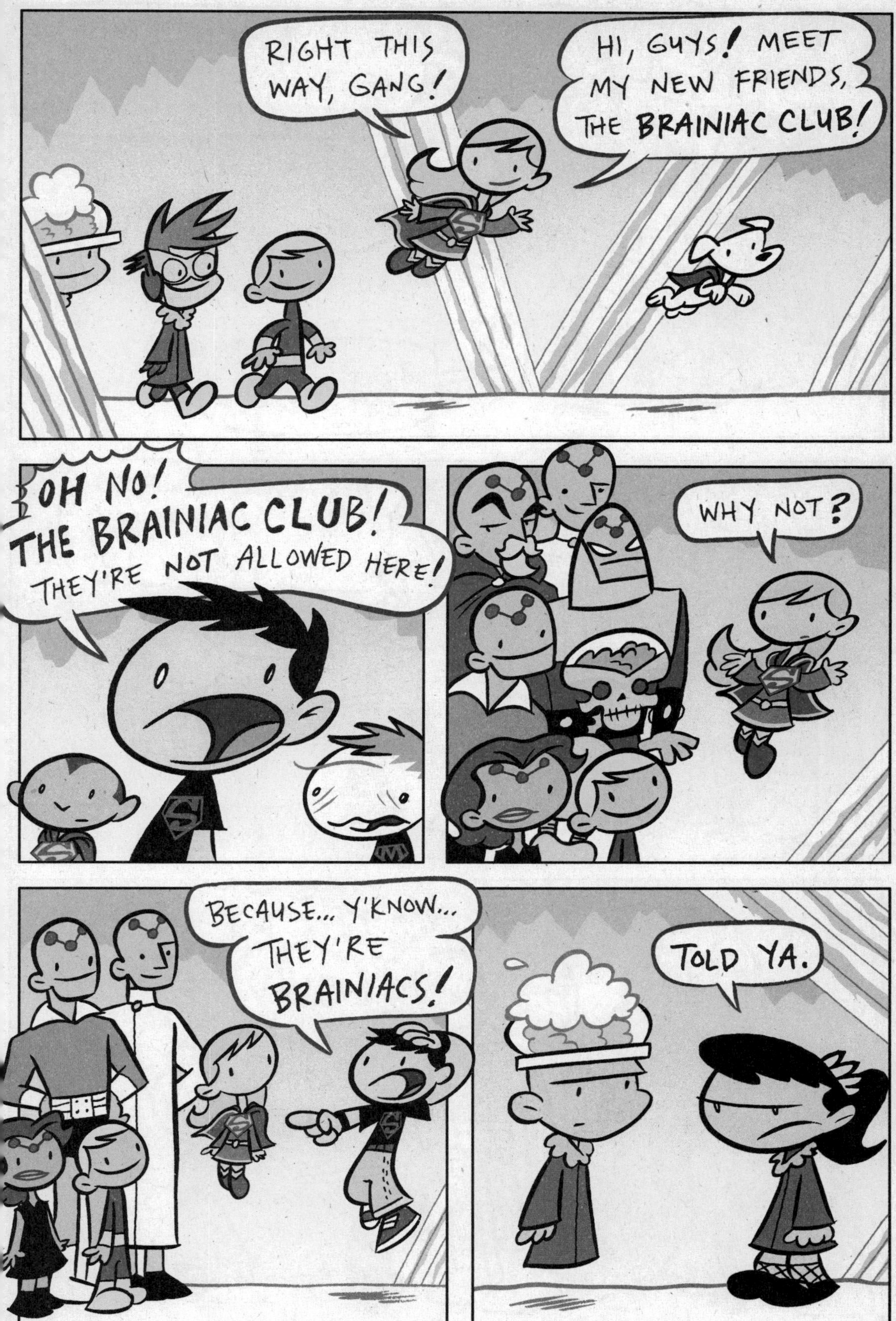
RIGHT THIS WAY, GANG!
HI, GUYS! MEET MY NEW FRIENDS, THE BRAINIAC CLUB!
OH NO! THE BRAINIAC CLUB! THEY'RE NOT ALLOWED HERE!
WHY NOT?
BECAUSE... Y'KNOW... THEY'RE BRAINIACS!
TOLD YA.

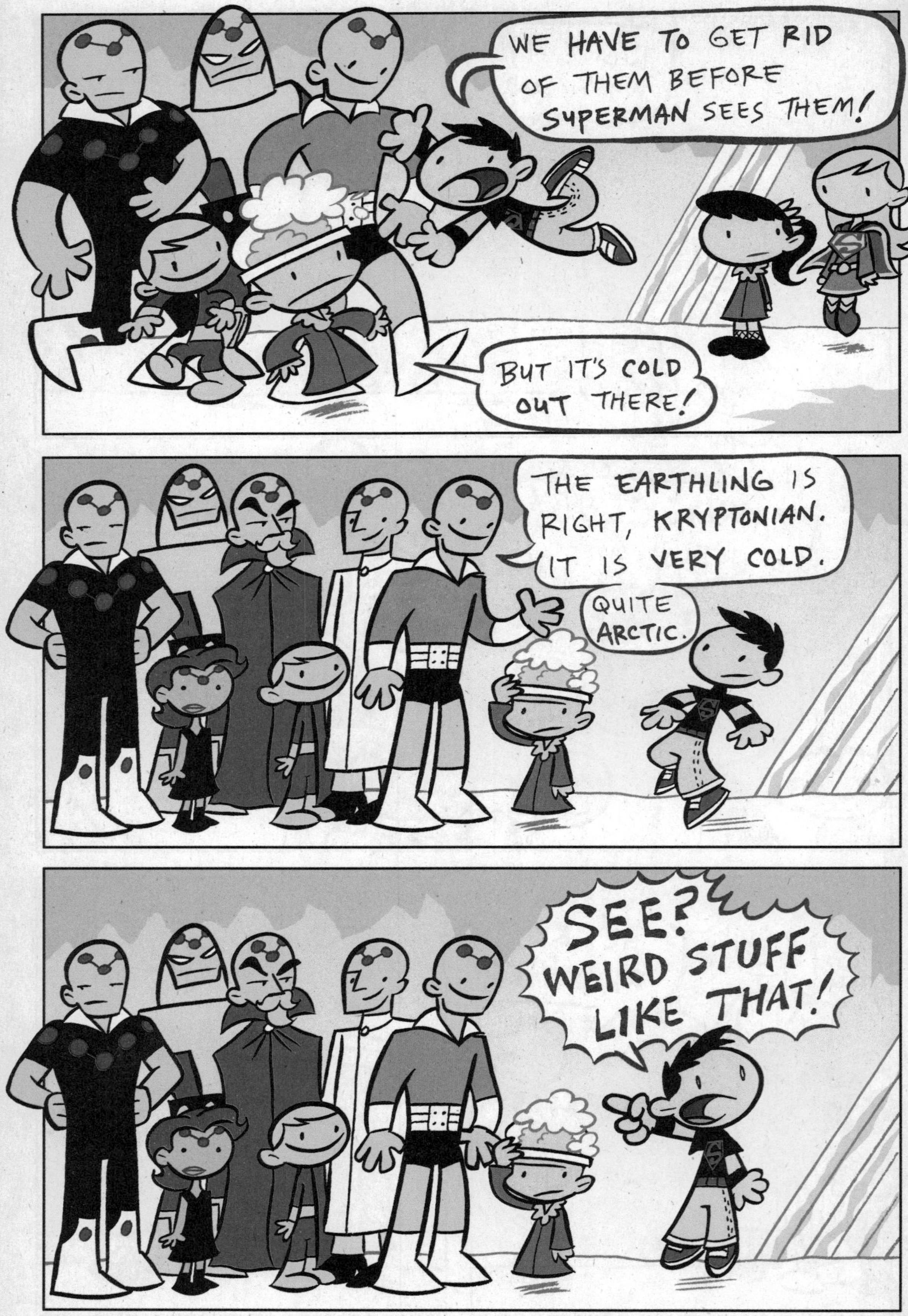
WE HAVE TO GET RID OF THEM BEFORE SUPERMAN SEES THEM!
BUT IT'S COLD OUT THERE!
THE EARTHLING IS RIGHT, KRYPTONIAN. IT IS VERY COLD.
QUITE ARCTIC.
SEE? WEIRD STUFF LIKE THAT!

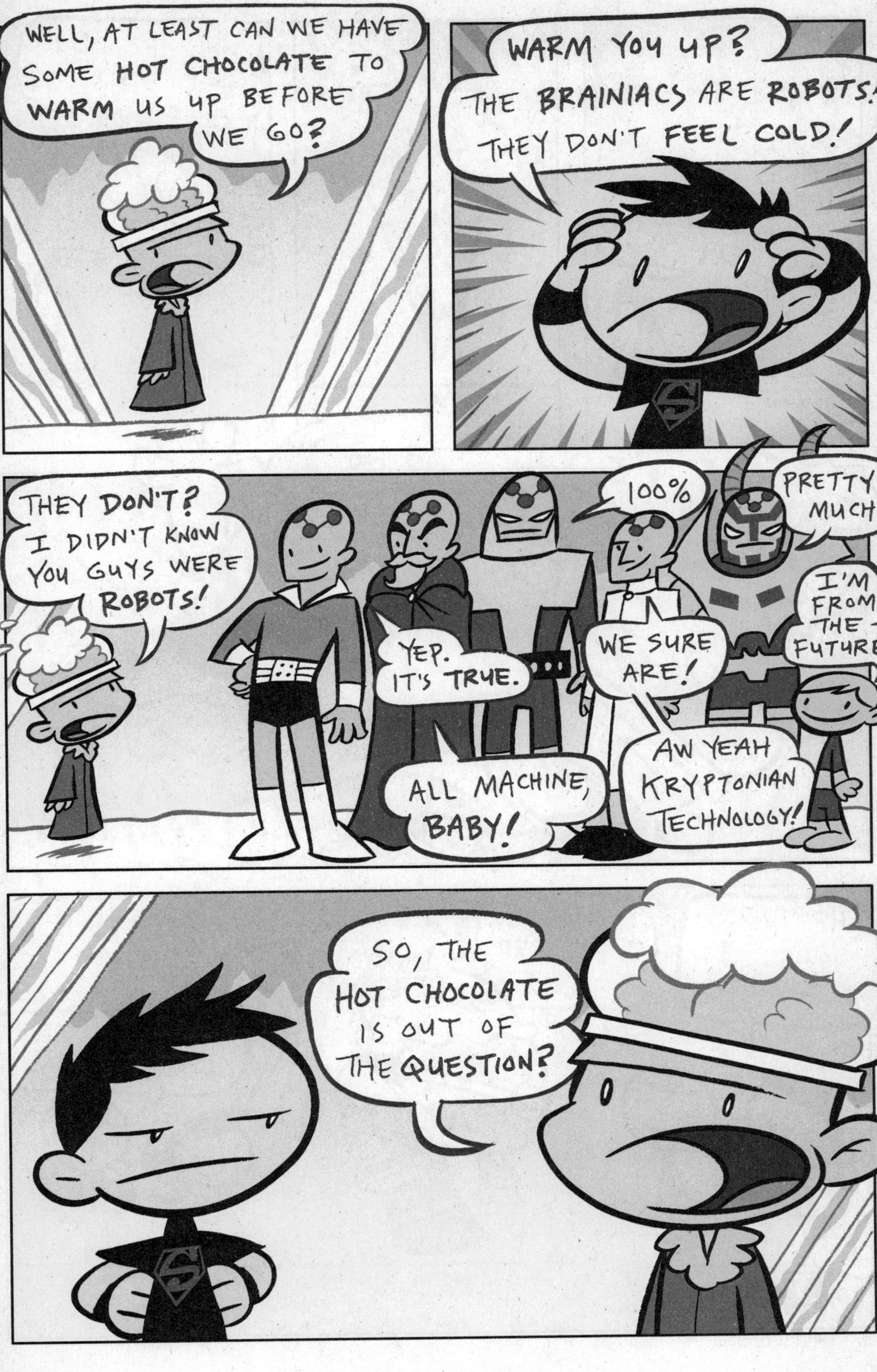
WELL, AT LEAST CAN WE HAVE SOME HOT CHOCOLATE TO WARM US UP BEFORE WE GO?
WARM YOU UP? THE BRAINIACS ARE ROBOTS! THEY DON'T FEEL COLD!
THEY DON'T? I DIDN'T KNOW YOU GUYS WERE ROBOTS!
YEP. IT'S TRUE.
ALL MACHINE, BABY!
100%
WE SURE ARE!
AW YEAH KRYPTONIAN TECHNOLOGY!
PRETTY MUCH.
I'M FROM THE FUTURE.
SO, THE HOT CHOCOLATE IS OUT OF THE QUESTION?

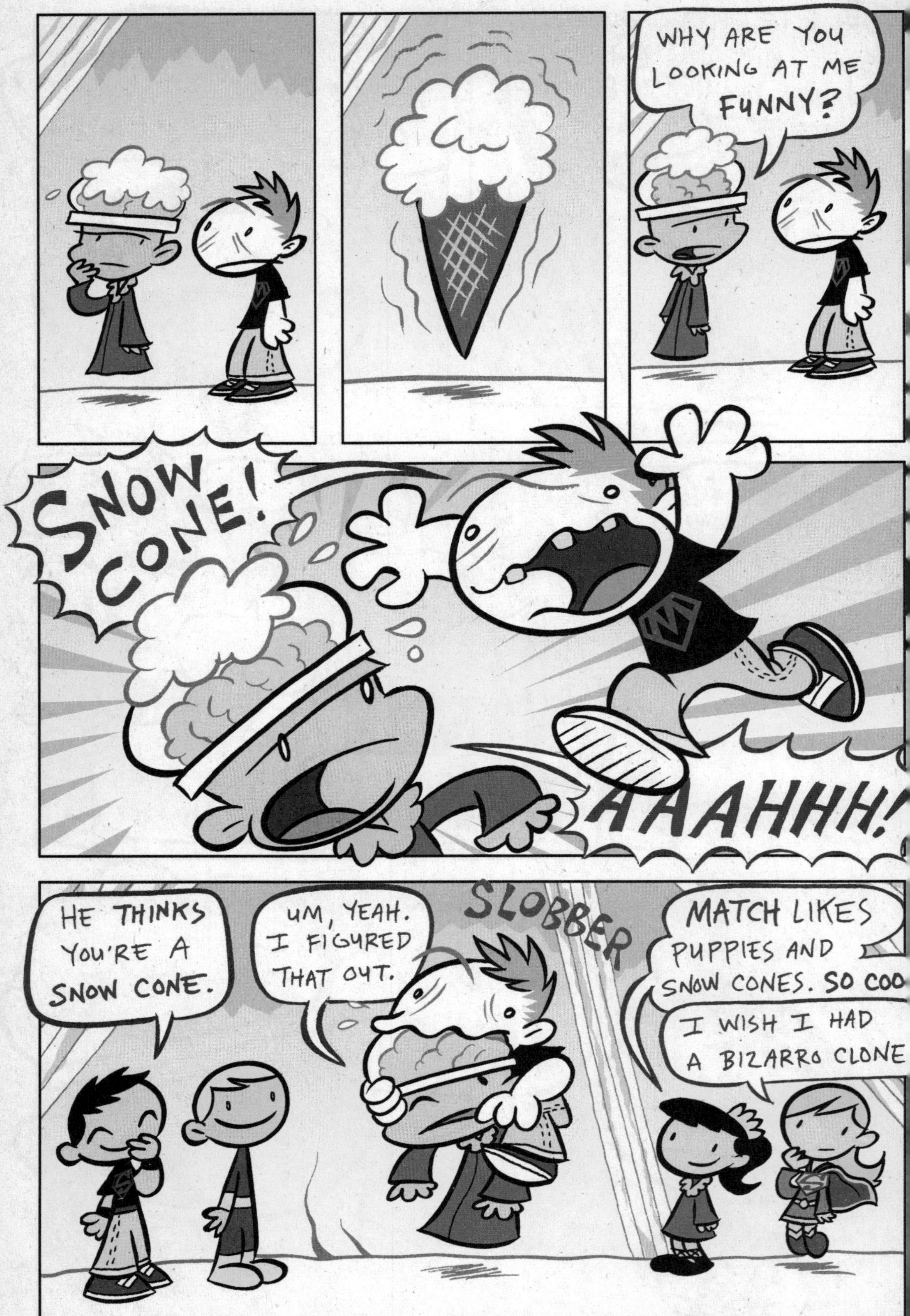

WHY ARE YOU LOOKING AT ME FUNNY?
SNOW CONE!
AAAAHHH!
HE THINKS YOU'RE A SNOW CONE.
UM, YEAH. I FIGURED THAT OUT.
SLOBBER
MATCH LIKES PUPPIES AND SNOW CONES. SO COO
I WISH I HAD A BIZARRO CLONE

—REFRESHING!

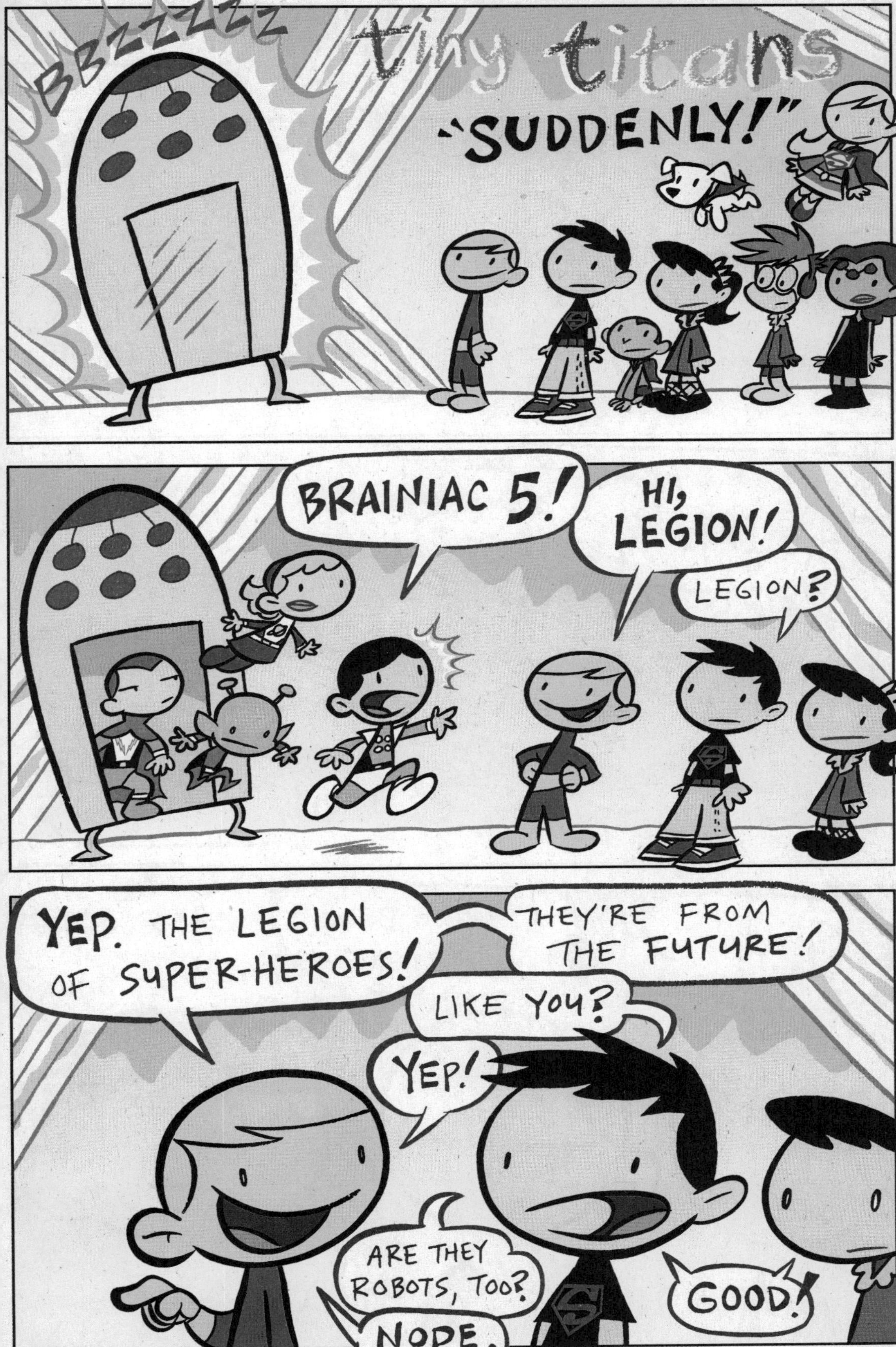
BBZZZZZZZ
tiny titans
"SUDDENLY!"
BRAINIAC 5!
HI, LEGION!
LEGION?
YEP. THE LEGION OF SUPER-HEROES!
THEY'RE FROM THE FUTURE!
LIKE YOU?
YEP!
ARE THEY ROBOTS, TOO?
NOPE.
GOOD!

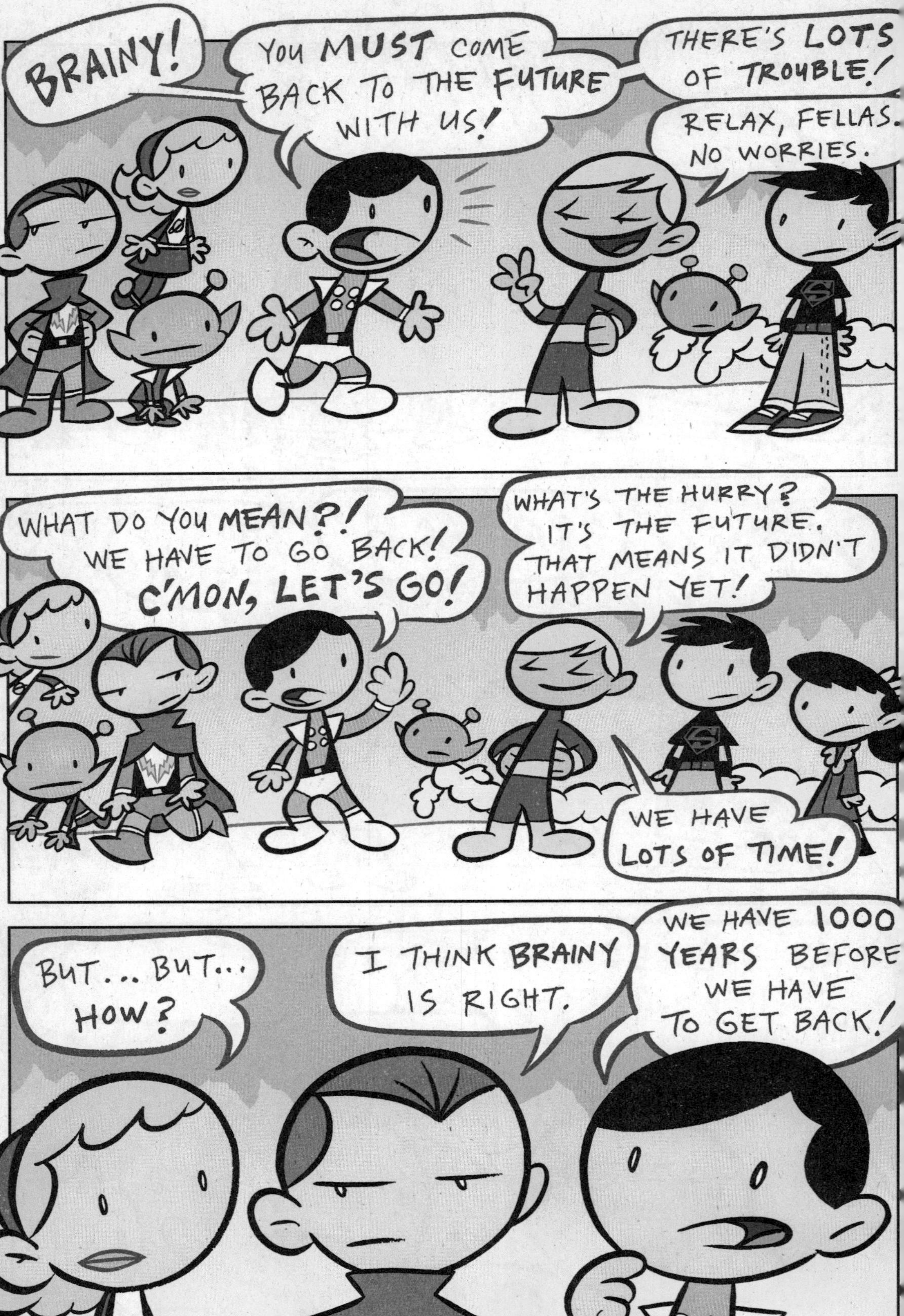
BRAINY!
YOU MUST COME BACK TO THE FUTURE WITH US!
THERE'S LOTS OF TROUBLE!
RELAX, FELLAS. NO WORRIES.
WHAT DO YOU MEAN?! WE HAVE TO GO BACK! C'MON, LET'S GO!
WHAT'S THE HURRY? IT'S THE FUTURE. THAT MEANS IT DIDN'T HAPPEN YET!
WE HAVE LOTS OF TIME!
BUT... BUT... HOW?
I THINK BRAINY IS RIGHT.
WE HAVE 1000 YEARS BEFORE WE HAVE TO GET BACK!

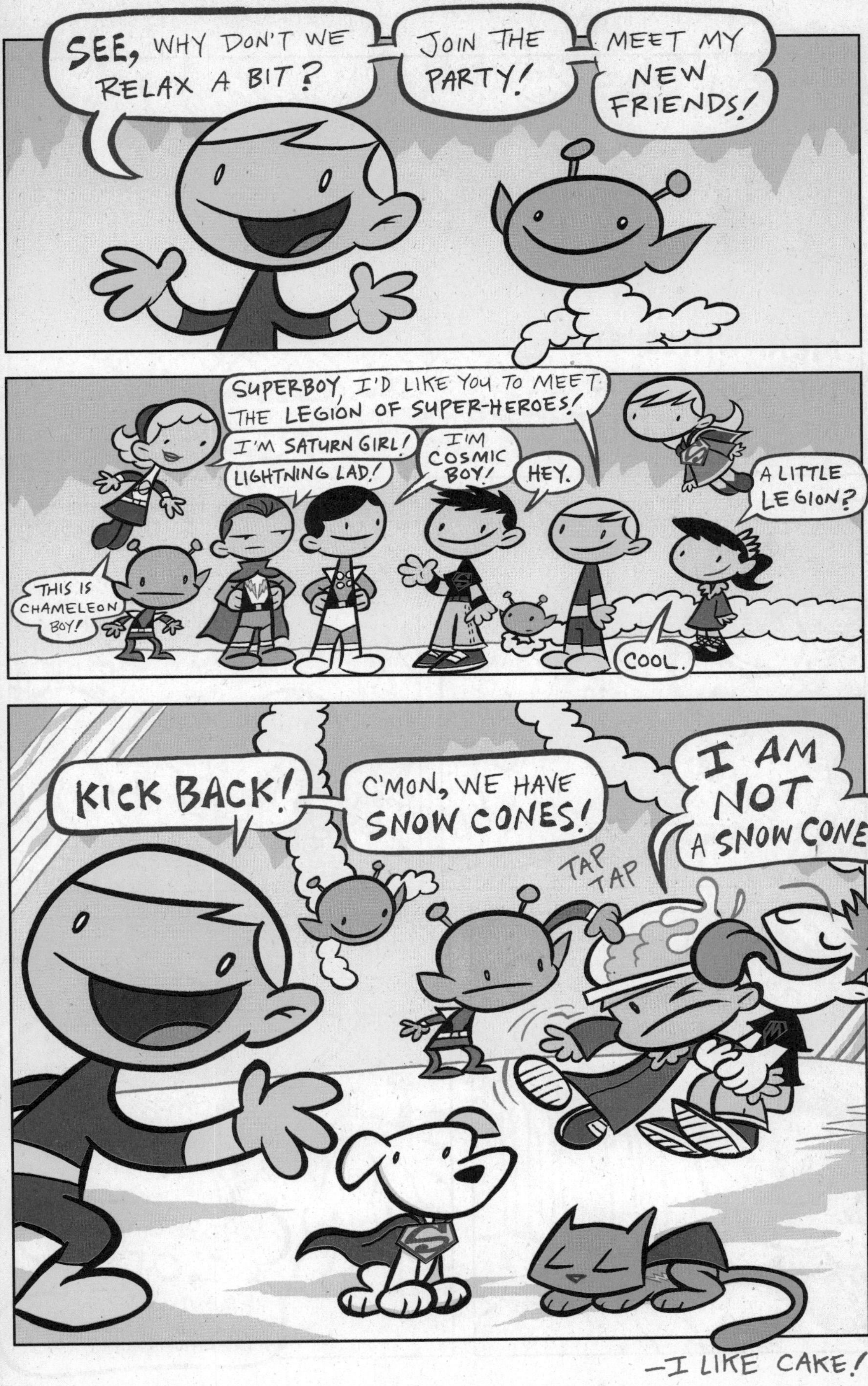
SEE, WHY DON'T WE RELAX A BIT?
JOIN THE PARTY!
MEET MY NEW FRIENDS!
SUPERBOY, I'D LIKE YOU TO MEET THE LEGION OF SUPER-HEROES!
I'M SATURN GIRL!
LIGHTNING LAD!
I'M COSMIC BOY!
HEY.
A LITTLE LEGION?
THIS IS CHAMELEON BOY!
COOL.
KICK BACK!
C'MON, WE HAVE SNOW CONES!
I AM NOT A SNOW CONE!
TAP TAP

—I LIKE CAKE!

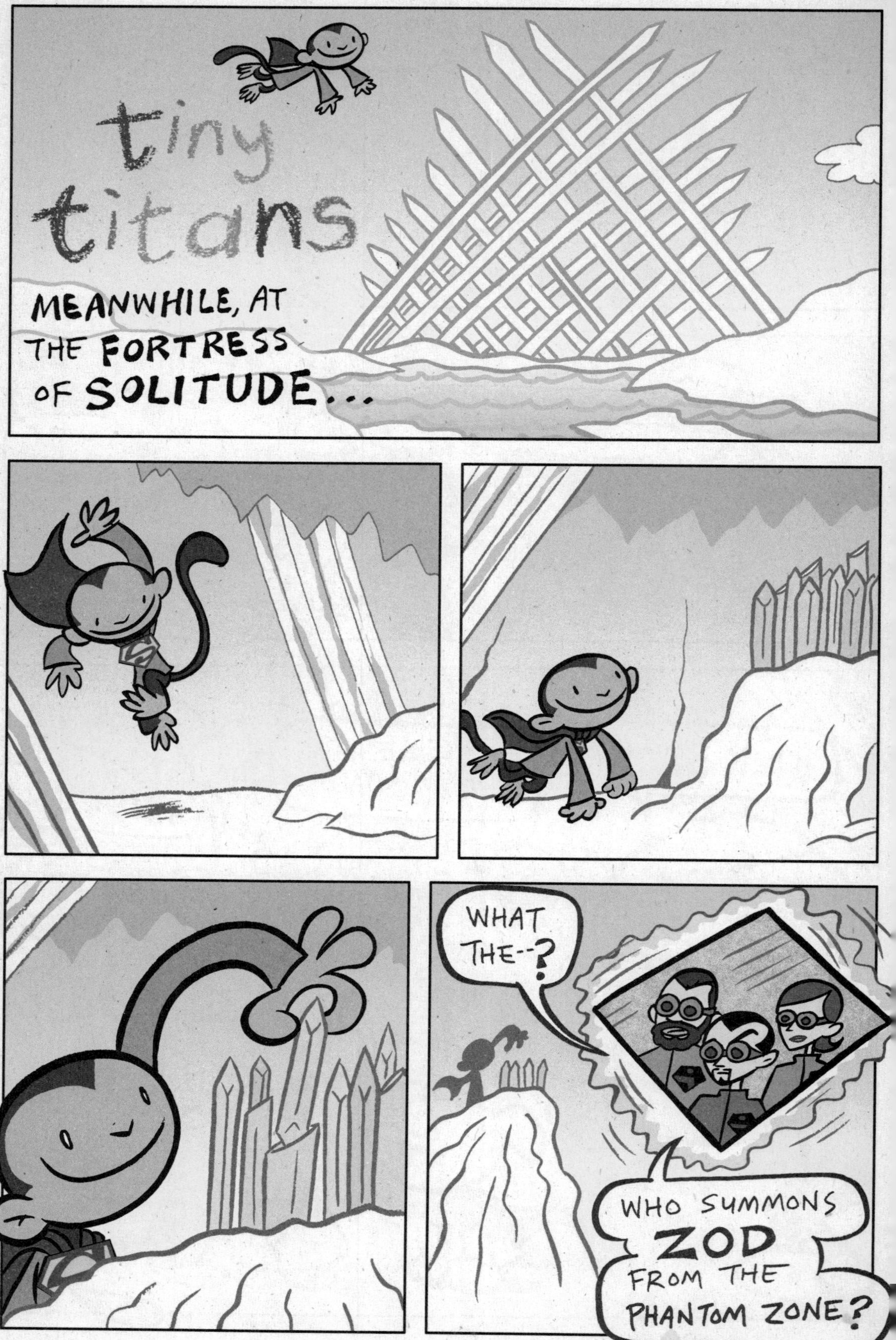
tiny titans
MEANWHILE, AT THE FORTRESS OF SOLITUDE...
WHAT THE--?
WHO SUMMONS ZOD FROM THE PHANTOM ZONE?

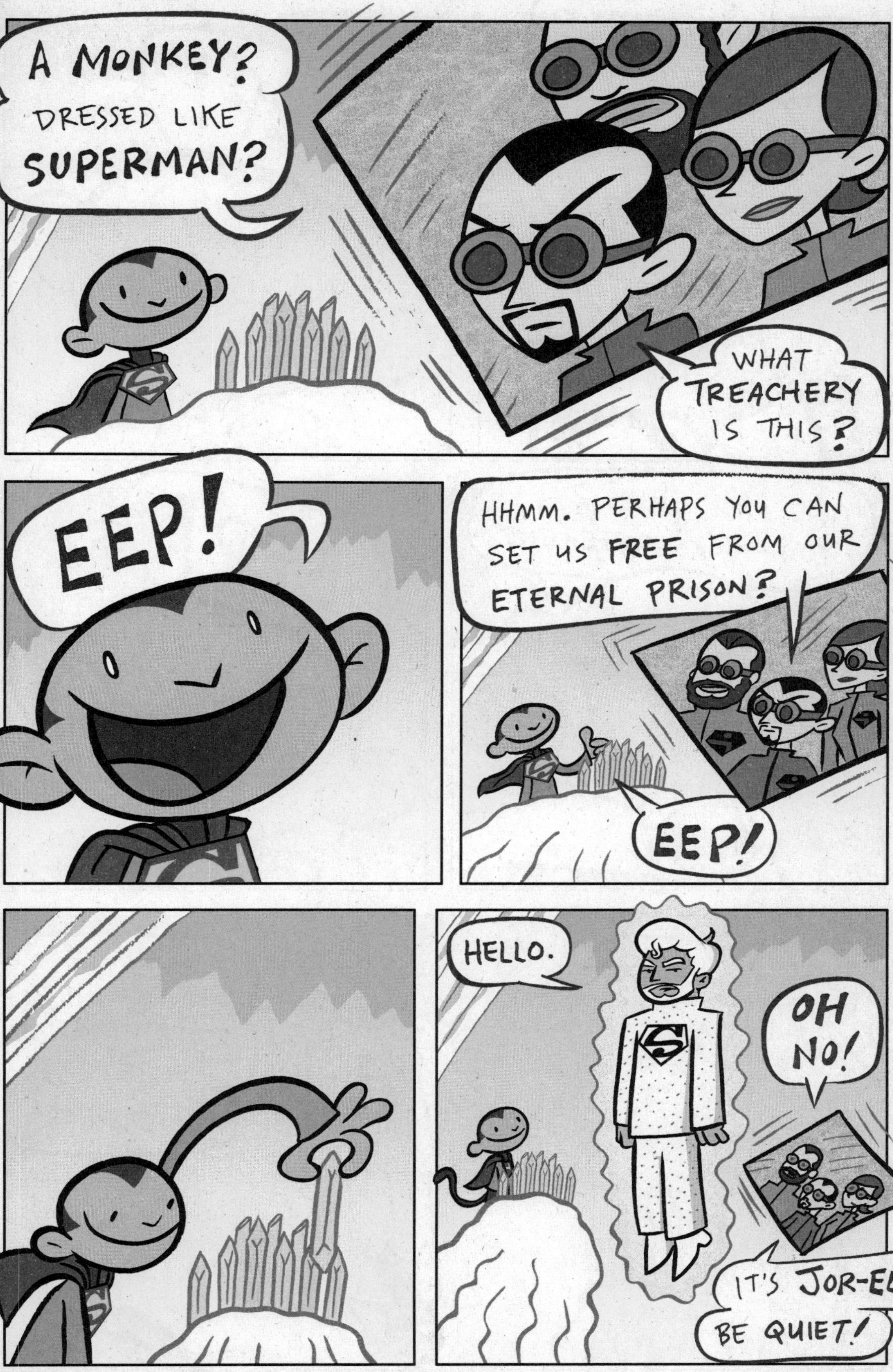

A MONKEY? DRESSED LIKE SUPERMAN?
WHAT TREACHERY IS THIS?
EEP!
HHMM. PERHAPS YOU CAN SET US FREE FROM OUR ETERNAL PRISON?
EEP!
HELLO.
OH NO!
IT'S JOR-EL! BE QUIET!

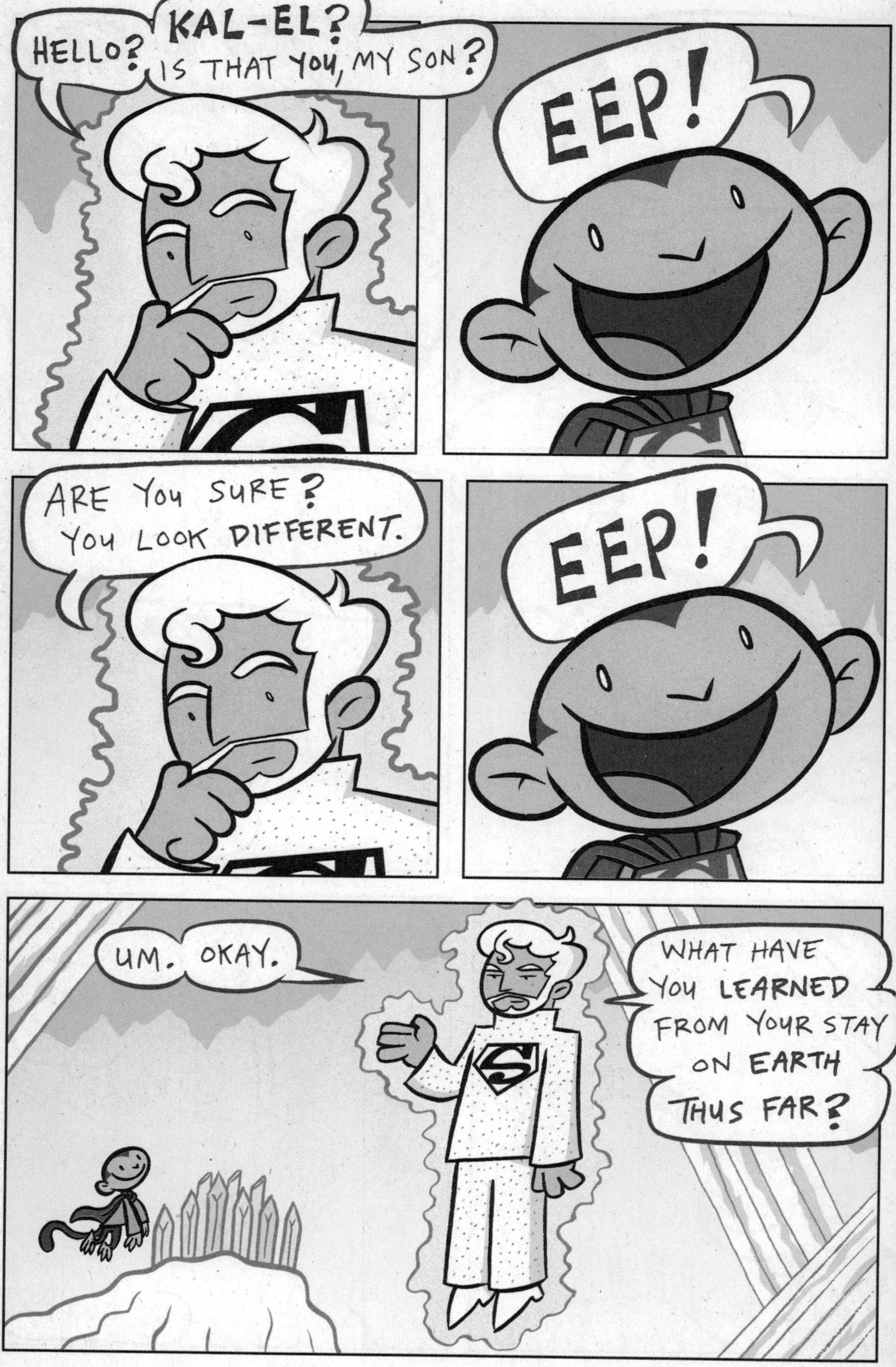
HELLO?
KAL-EL? IS THAT YOU, MY SON?
EEP!
ARE YOU SURE? YOU LOOK DIFFERENT.
EEP!
UM. OKAY.
WHAT HAVE YOU LEARNED FROM YOUR STAY ON EARTH THUS FAR?

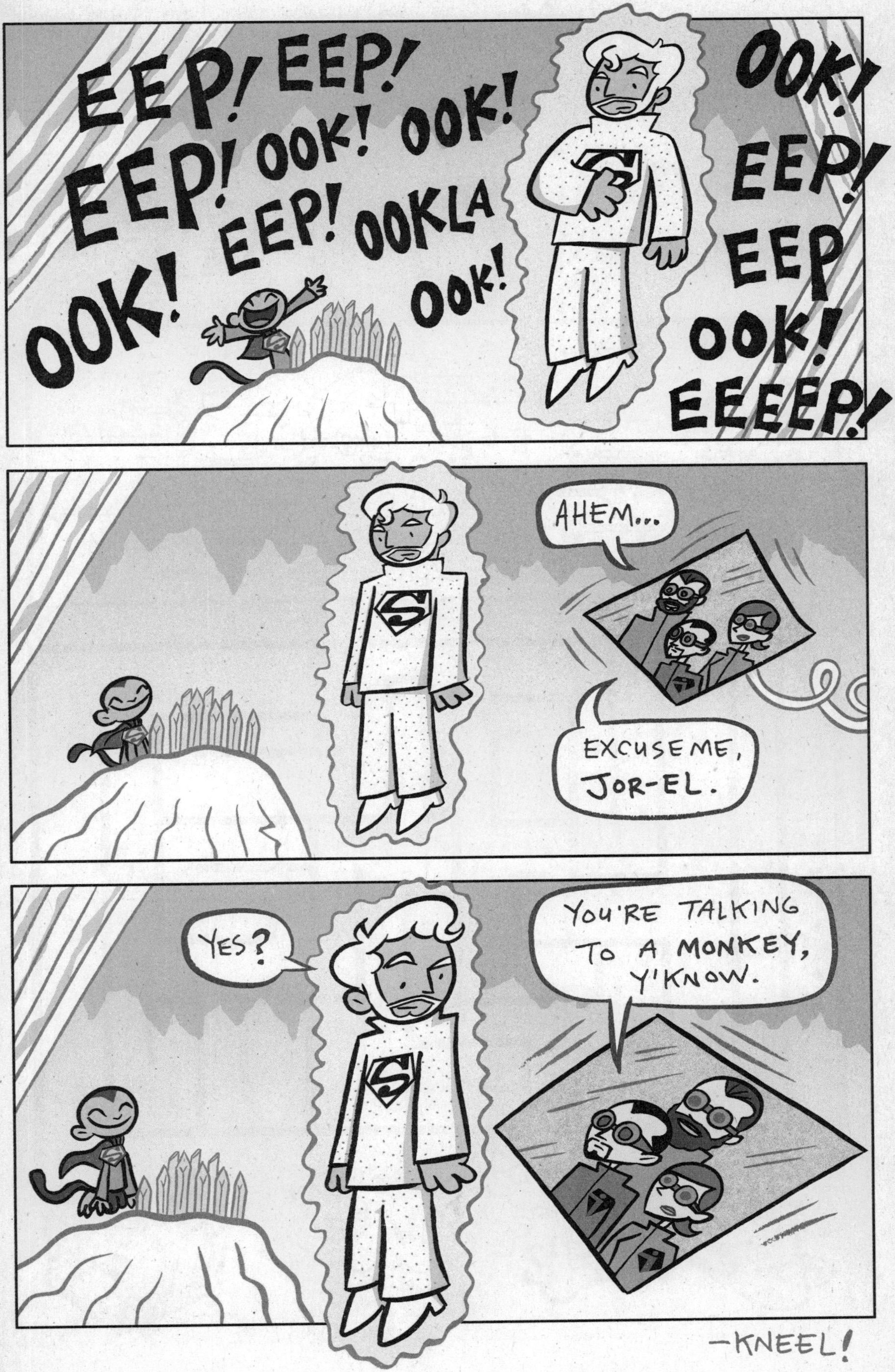
EEP! EEP!
EEP! OOK! OOK!
OOK! EEP! OOKLA
OOK!
OOK!
EEP!
EEP
OOK!
EEEEP!
AHEM...
EXCUSE ME, JOR-EL.
YES?
YOU'RE TALKING TO A MONKEY, Y'KNOW.

—KNEEL!

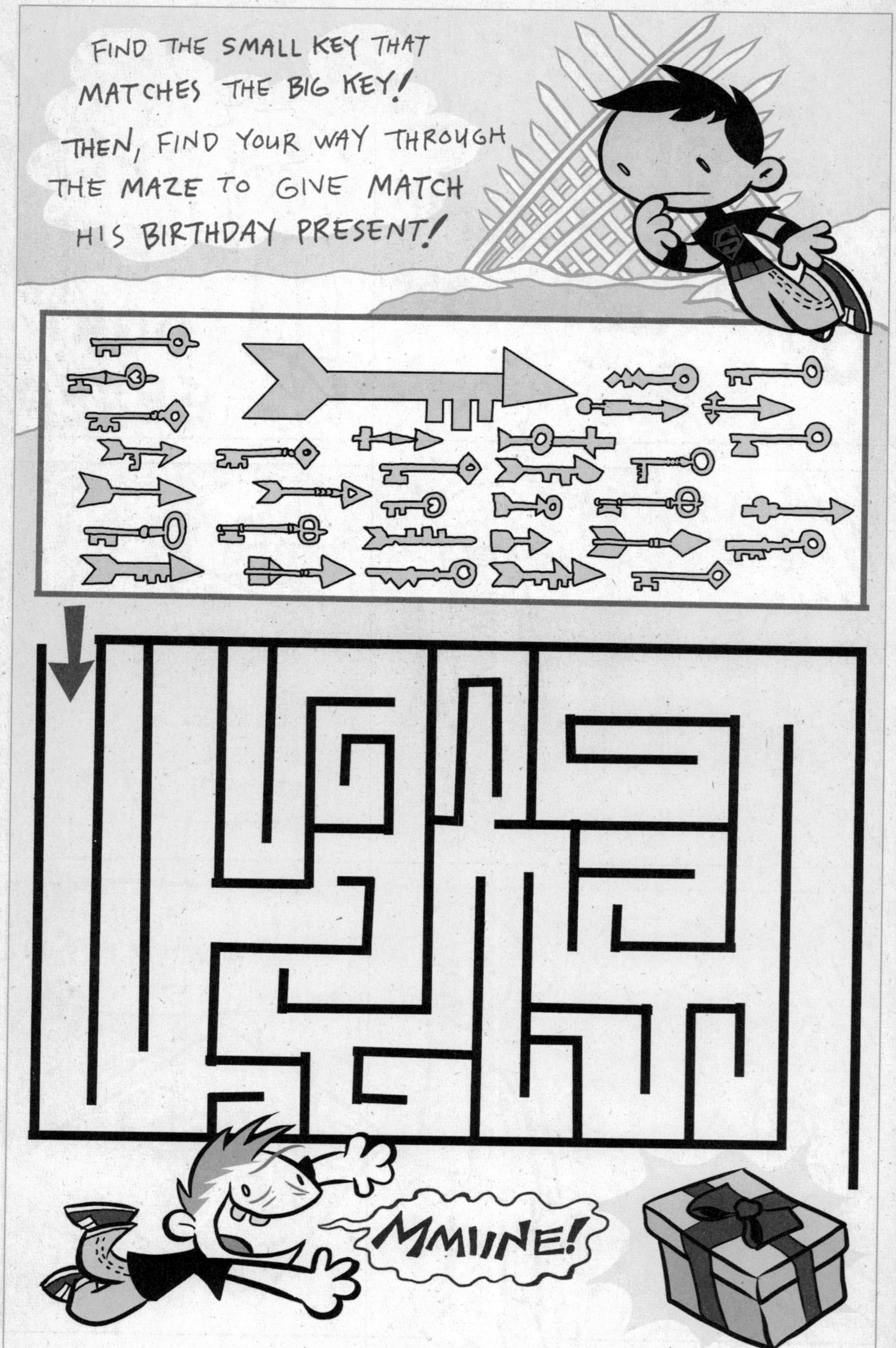
FIND THE SMALL KEY THAT MATCHES THE BIG KEY! THEN, FIND YOUR WAY THROUGH THE MAZE TO GIVE MATCH HIS BIRTHDAY PRESENT!
MMIINE!

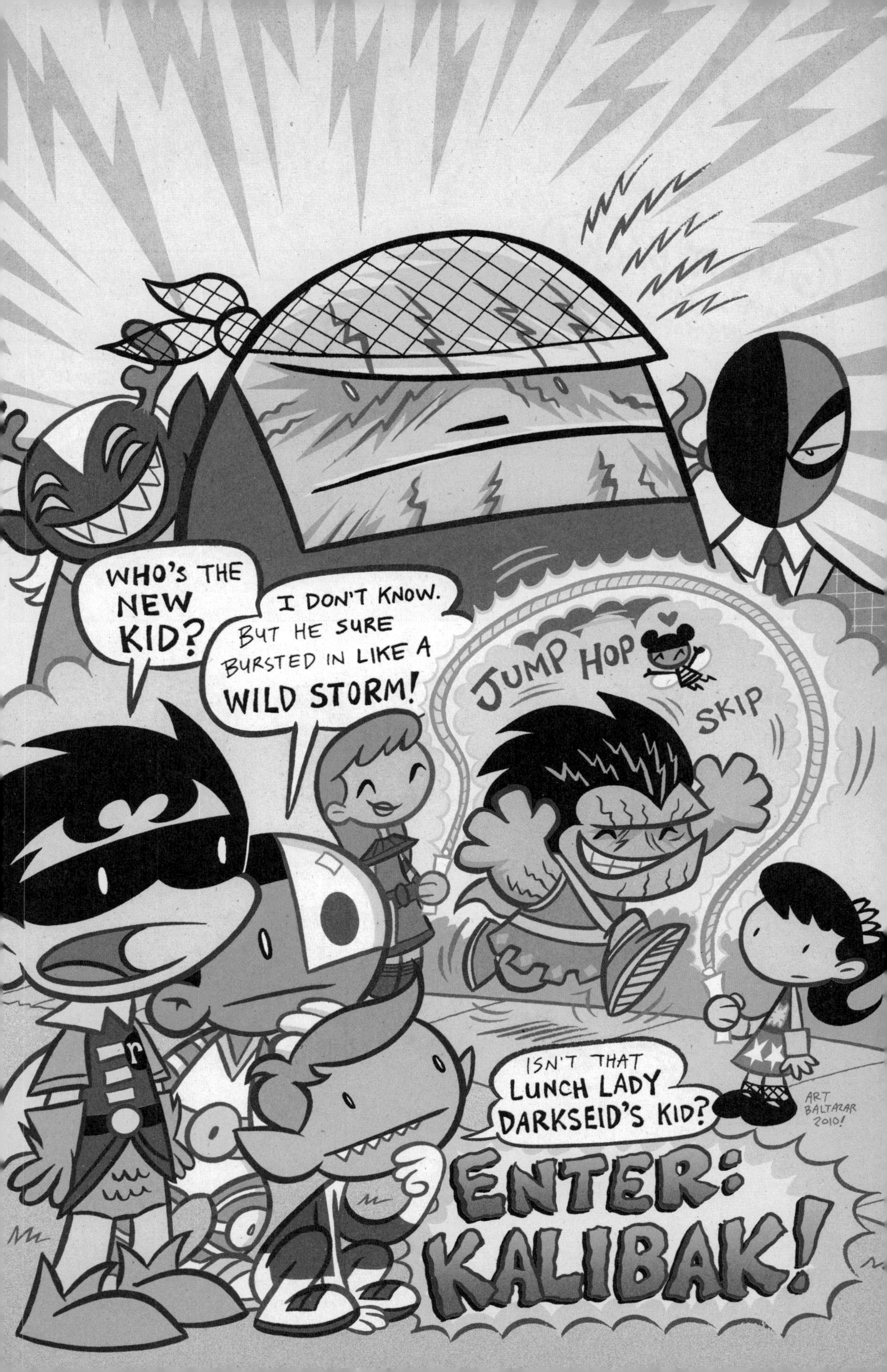
WHO'S THE NEW KID?
I DON'T KNOW. BUT HE SURE BURSTED IN LIKE A WILD STORM!
JUMP HOP SKIP
ISN'T THAT LUNCH LADY DARKSEID'S KID?
ART BALTAZAR 2010!
ENTER: KALIBAK!

tiny titans

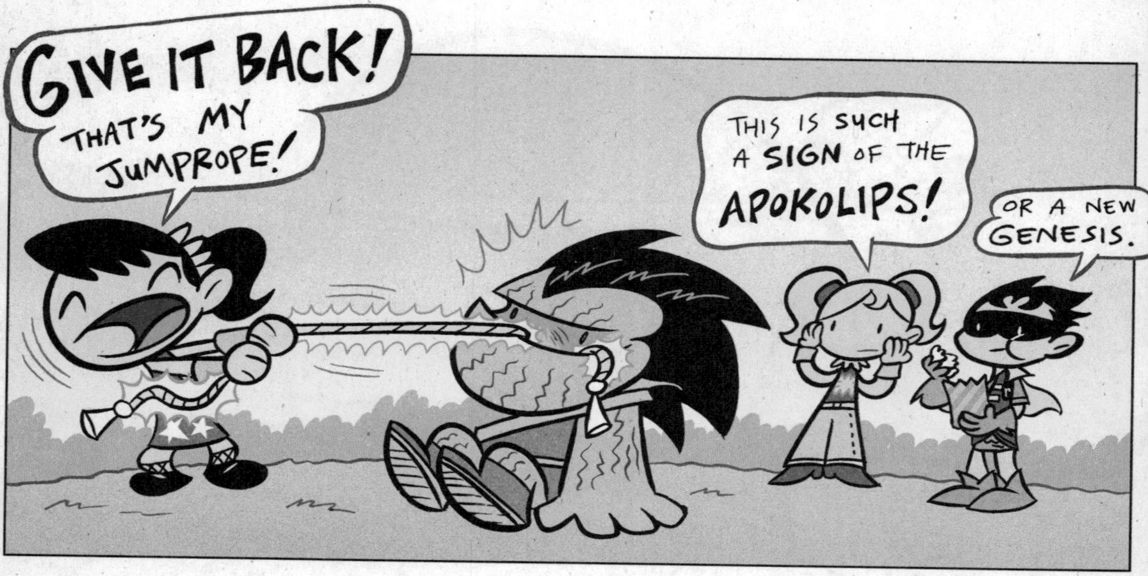
GIVE IT BACK! THAT'S MY JUMPROPE!
THIS IS SUCH A SIGN OF THE APOKOLIPS!
OR A NEW GENESIS.

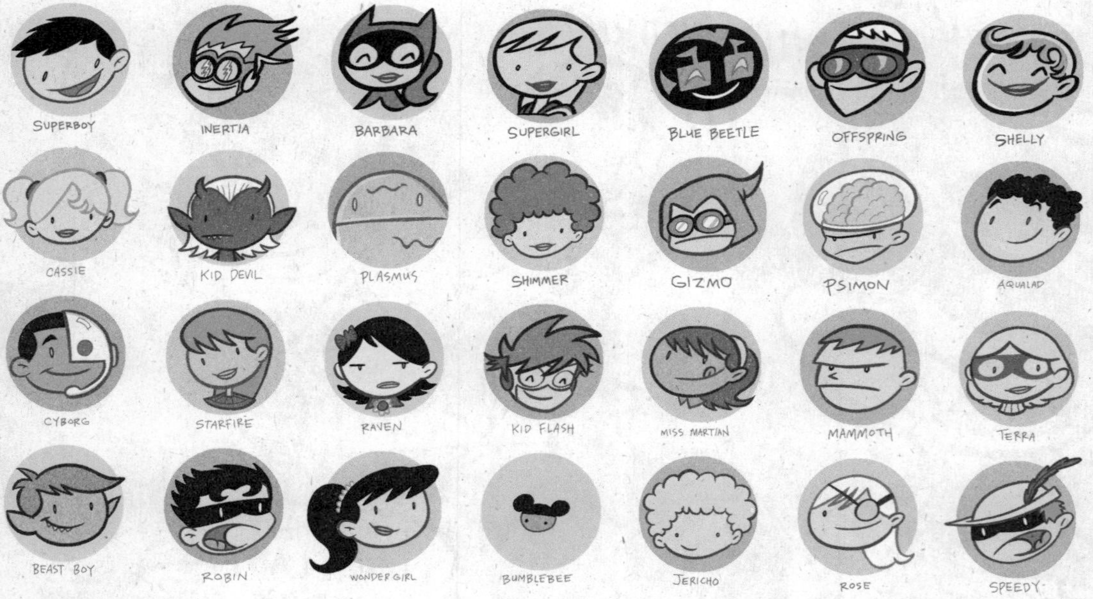
SUPERBOY
INERTIA
BARBARA
SUPERGIRL
BLUE BEETLE
OFFSPRING
SHELLY
CASSIE
KID DEVIL
PLASMUS
SHIMMER
GIZMO
PSIMON
AQUALAD
CYBORG
STARFIRE
RAVEN
KID FLASH
MISS MARTIAN
MAMMOTH
TERRA
BEAST BOY
ROBIN
WONDER GIRL
BUMBLEBEE
JERICHO
ROSE
SPEEDY

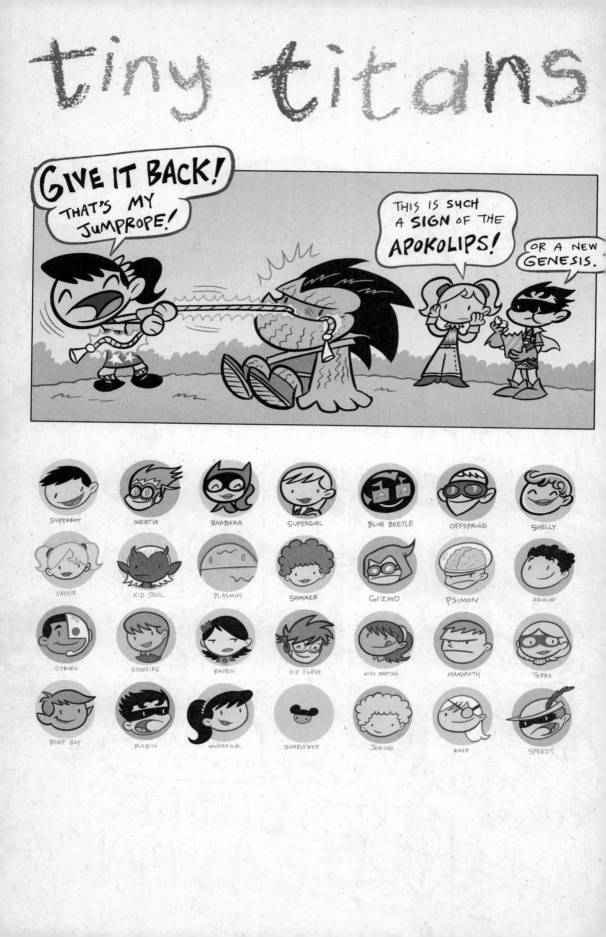

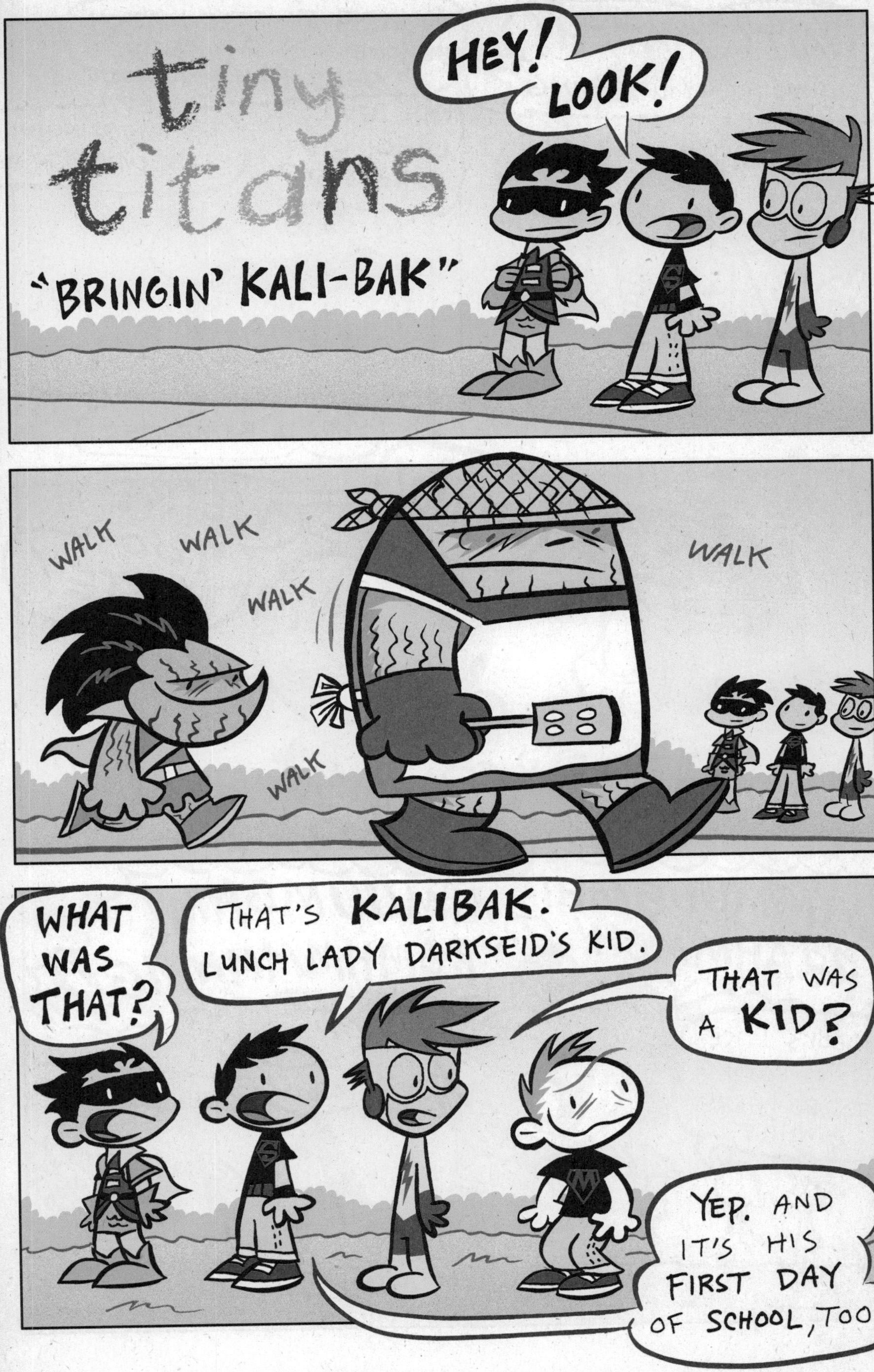
tiny titans
"BRINGIN' KALI-BAK"
HEY! LOOK!
WALK
WALK
WALK
WALK
WALK
WHAT WAS THAT?
THAT'S KALIBAK. LUNCH LADY DARKSEID'S KID.
THAT WAS A KID?
YEP. AND IT'S HIS FIRST DAY OF SCHOOL, TOO.

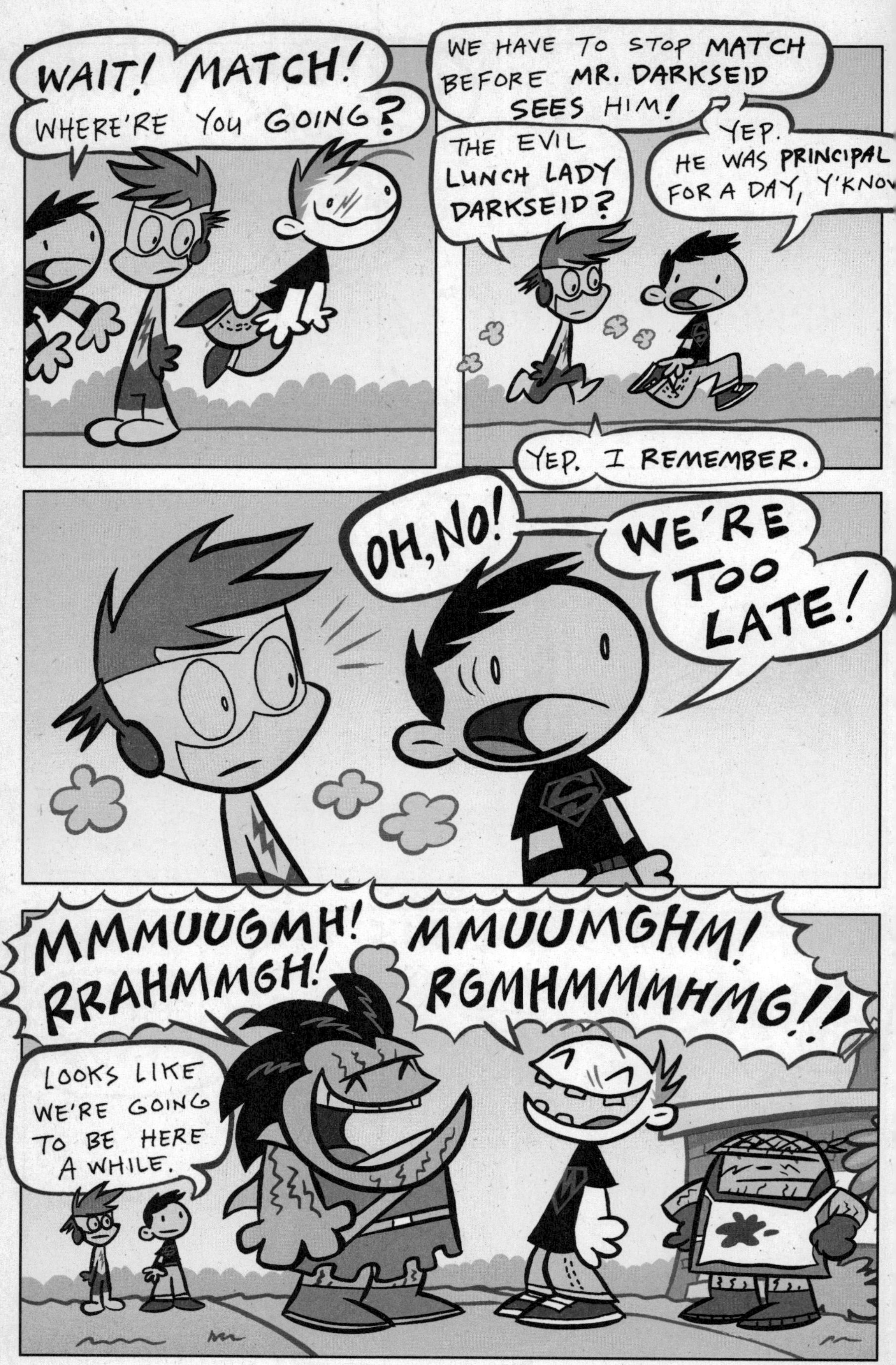
WAIT! MATCH! WHERE'RE YOU GOING?
WE HAVE TO STOP MATCH BEFORE MR. DARKSEID SEES HIM!
THE EVIL LUNCH LADY DARKSEID?
YEP. HE WAS PRINCIPAL FOR A DAY, Y'KNOW
YEP. I REMEMBER.
OH, NO!
WE'RE TOO LATE!
MMMUUGMH! RRAHMMGH!
MMUUMGHM! RGMHMMMHMG!!
LOOKS LIKE WE'RE GOING TO BE HERE A WHILE.

—MINDLESS.

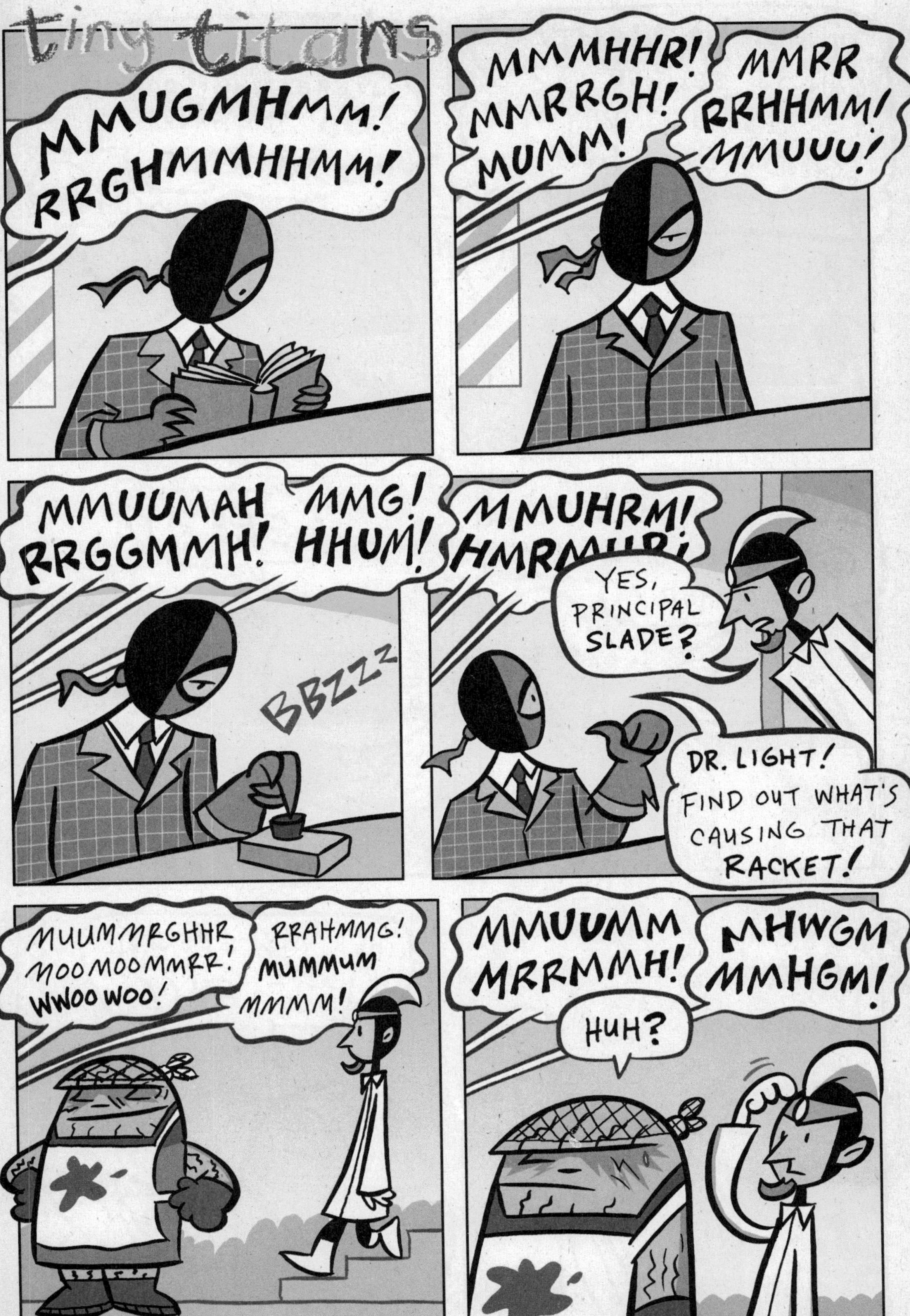
tiny titans
MMUGMHMM! RRGHMMHHMM!
MMMHHR! MMRRGH! MUMM!
MMRR RRHHMM! MMUUU!
MMUUMAH RRGGMMH!
MMG! HHUM!
BBZZZ
MMUHRM!
YES, PRINCIPAL SLADE?
DR. LIGHT! FIND OUT WHAT'S CAUSING THAT RACKET!
MUUMMRGHHR MOOMOOMMRR! WWOO WOO!
RRAHMMG! MUMMUM MMMM!
MMUUMM MRRMMH!
MHWGM MMHGM!
HUH?

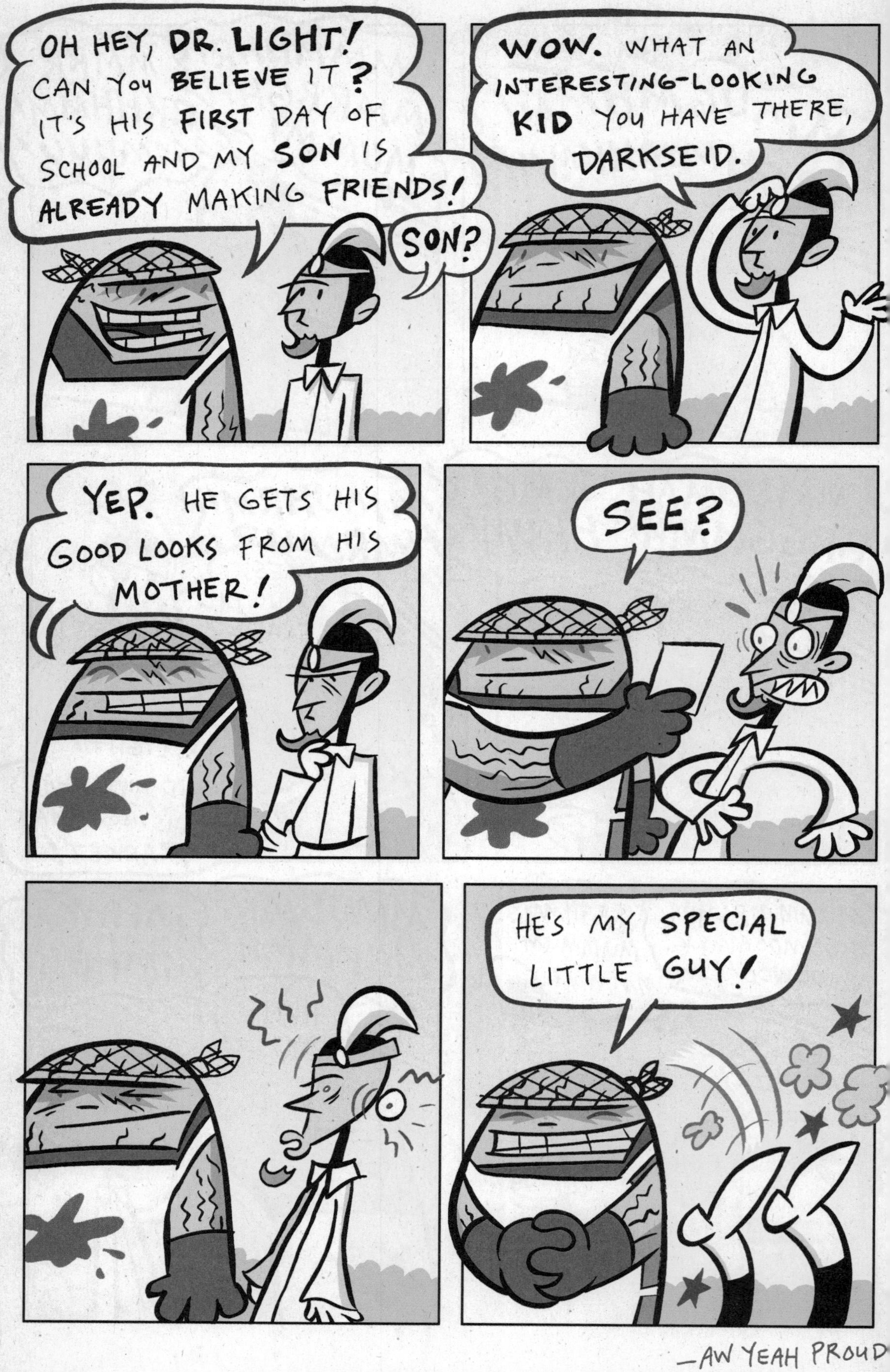
OH HEY, DR. LIGHT! CAN YOU BELIEVE IT? IT'S HIS FIRST DAY OF SCHOOL AND MY SON IS ALREADY MAKING FRIENDS!
SON?
WOW. WHAT AN INTERESTING-LOOKING KID YOU HAVE THERE, DARKSEID.
YEP. HE GETS HIS GOOD LOOKS FROM HIS MOTHER!
SEE?
HE'S MY SPECIAL LITTLE GUY!

—AW YEAH PROUD

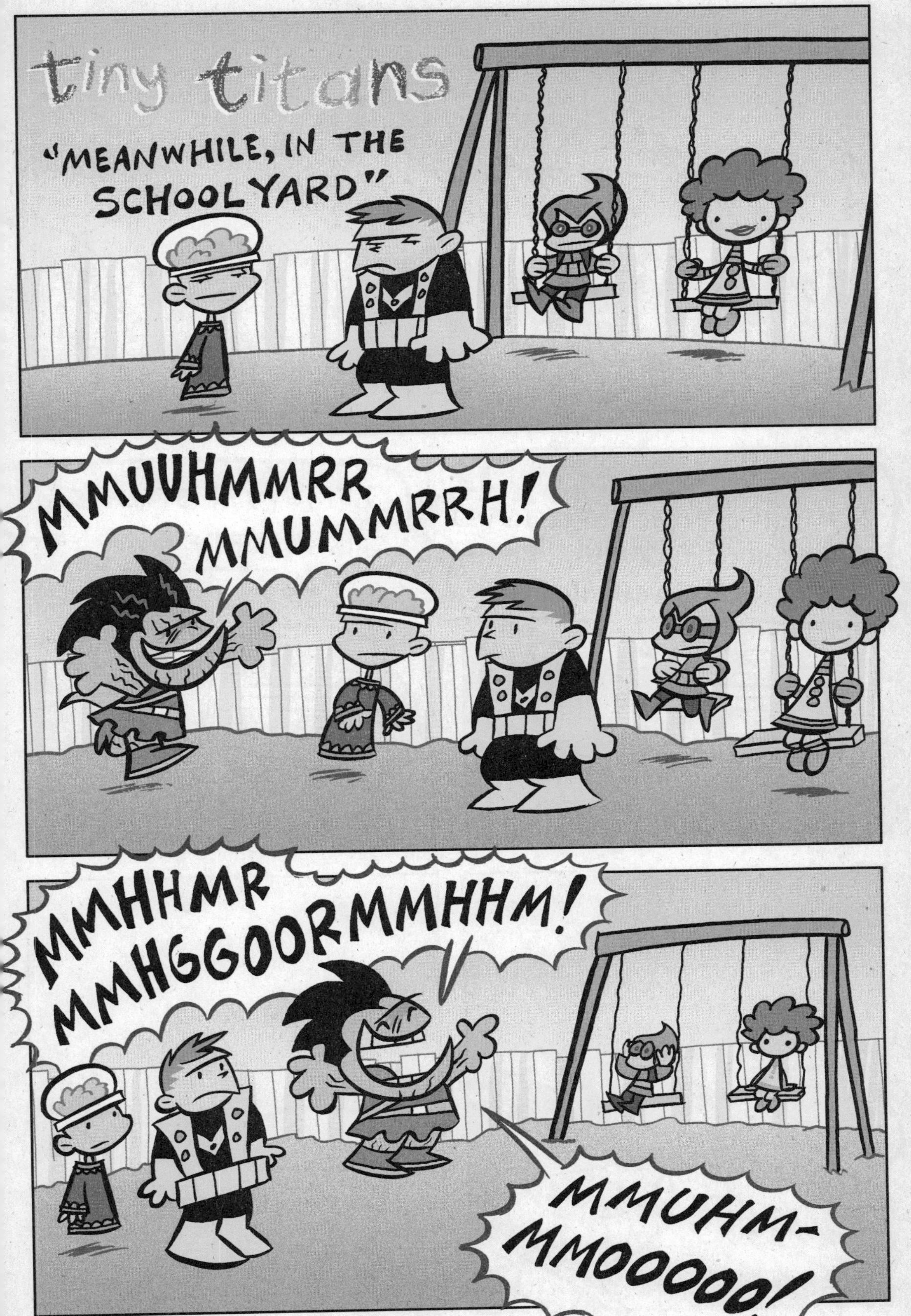
tiny titans
"MEANWHILE, IN THE SCHOOLYARD"
MMUUHMMRR MMUMMRRH!
MMHHMR MMHGGOORMMHHM!
MMUHM-MMOOOOO!

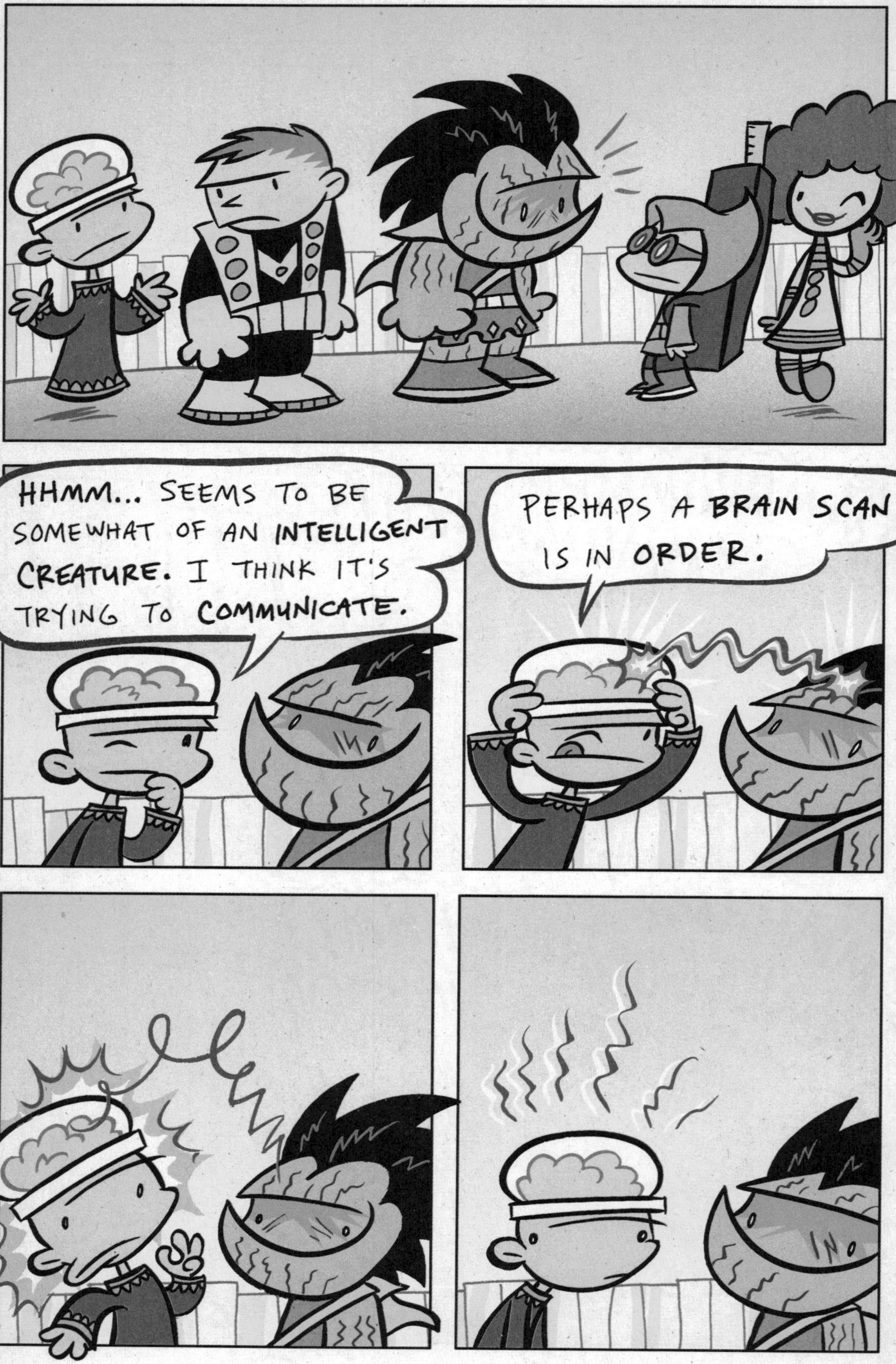
HHMM... SEEMS TO BE SOMEWHAT OF AN INTELLIGENT CREATURE. I THINK IT'S TRYING TO COMMUNICATE.
PERHAPS A BRAIN SCAN IS IN ORDER.

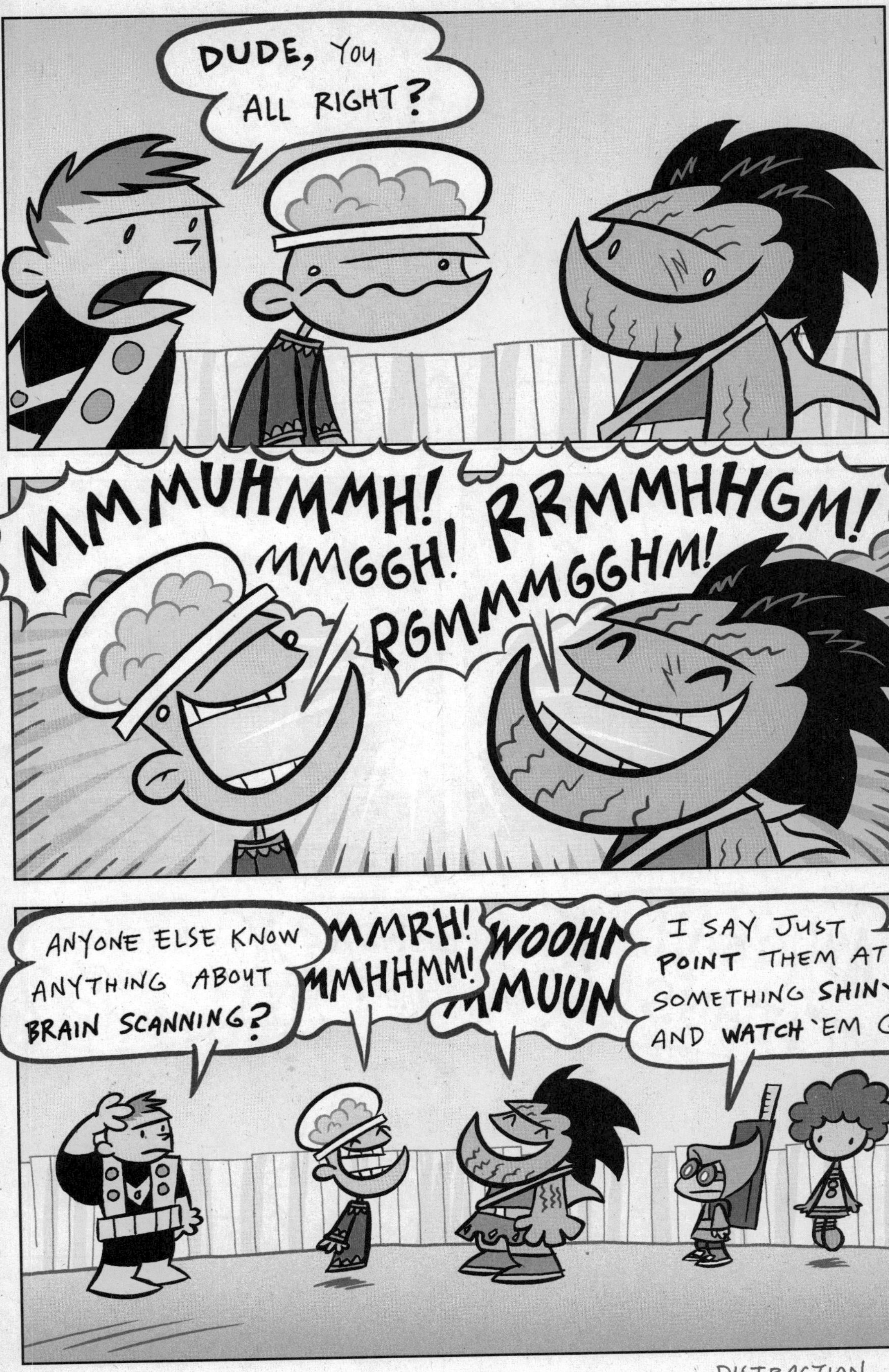
DUDE, YOU ALL RIGHT?
MMMUHMMH! MMGGH! RRMMHHGM! RGMMMGGHM!
ANYONE ELSE KNOW ANYTHING ABOUT BRAIN SCANNING?
MMRH! MMHHMM!
WOOH MUUN
I SAY JUST POINT THEM AT SOMETHING SHINY AND WATCH 'EM GO!

-DISTRACTION.

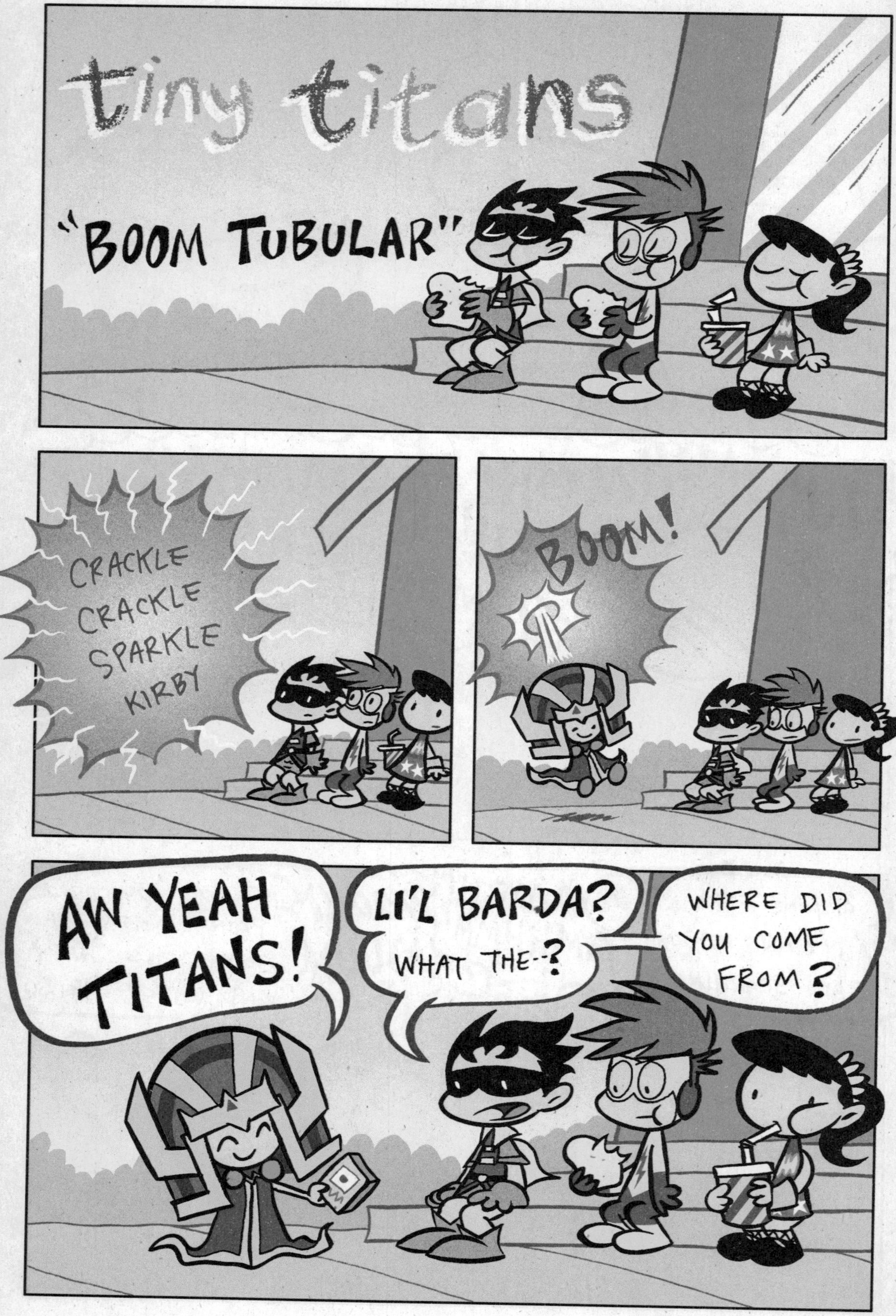
tiny titans
"BOOM TUBULAR"
CRACKLE CRACKLE SPARKLE KIRBY
BOOM!
AW YEAH TITANS!
LI'L BARDA? WHAT THE--?
WHERE DID YOU COME FROM?

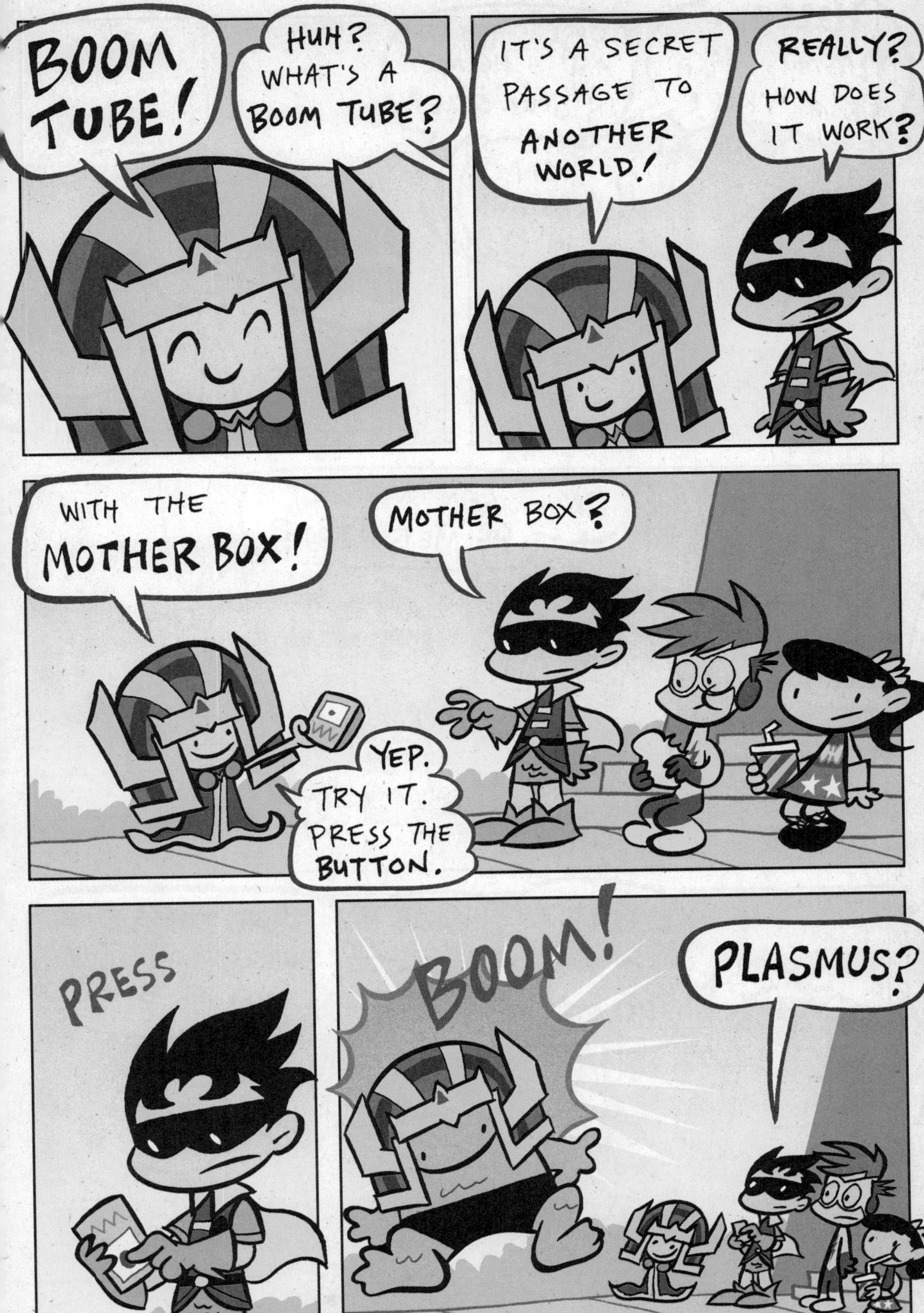
BOOM TUBE!
HUH? WHAT'S A BOOM TUBE?
IT'S A SECRET PASSAGE TO ANOTHER WORLD!
REALLY? HOW DOES IT WORK?
WITH THE MOTHER BOX!
MOTHER BOX?
YEP. TRY IT. PRESS THE BUTTON.
PRESS
BOOM!
PLASMUS?

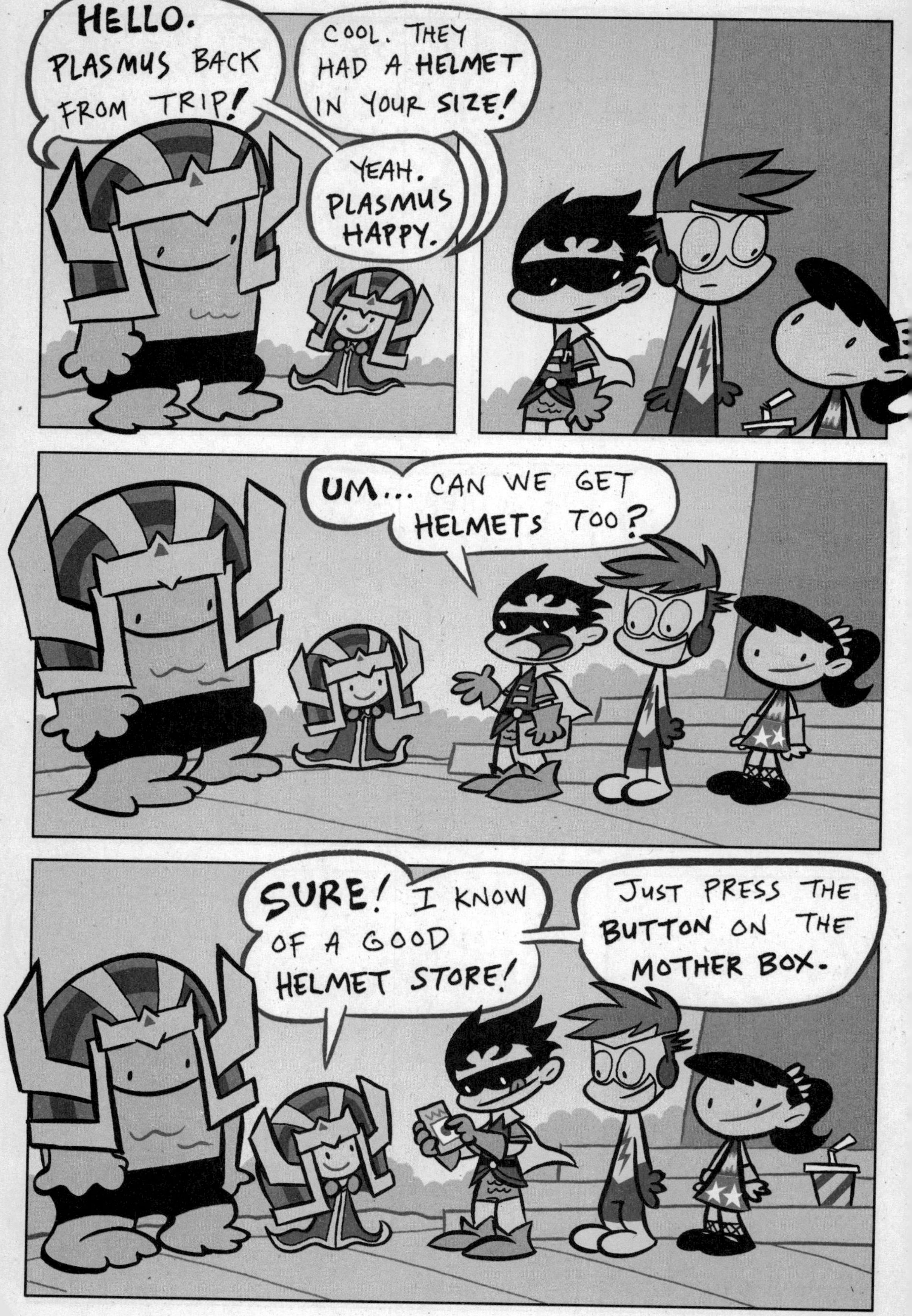
HELLO. PLASMUS BACK FROM TRIP!
COOL. THEY HAD A HELMET IN YOUR SIZE!
YEAH. PLASMUS HAPPY.
UM... CAN WE GET HELMETS TOO?
SURE! I KNOW OF A GOOD HELMET STORE!
JUST PRESS THE BUTTON ON THE MOTHER BOX.

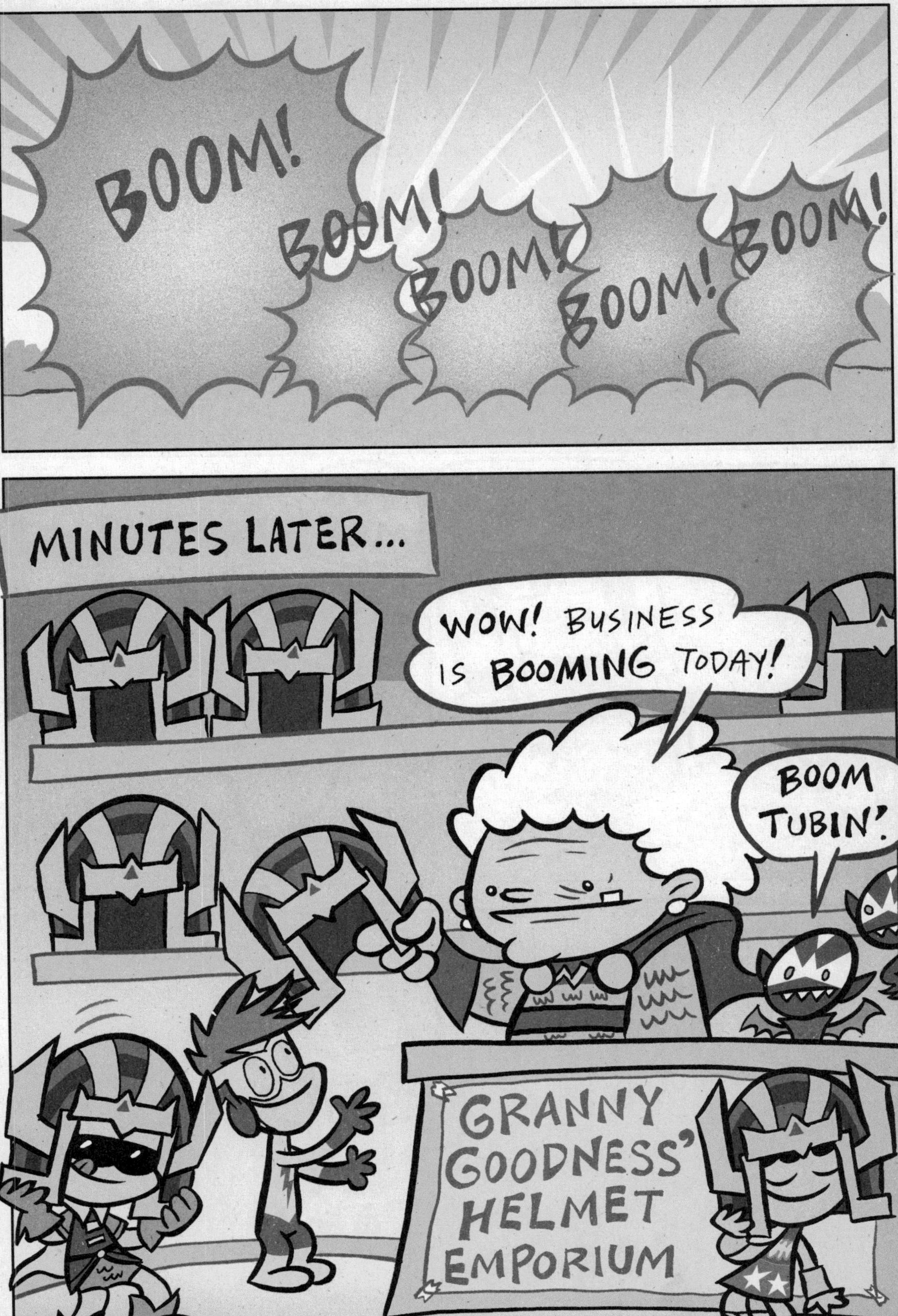
BOOM!
BOOM!
BOOM!
BOOM!
BOOM!
MINUTES LATER...
WOW! BUSINESS IS BOOMING TODAY!
BOOM TUBIN'.
GRANNY GOODNESS' HELMET EMPORIUM

—PERFECT

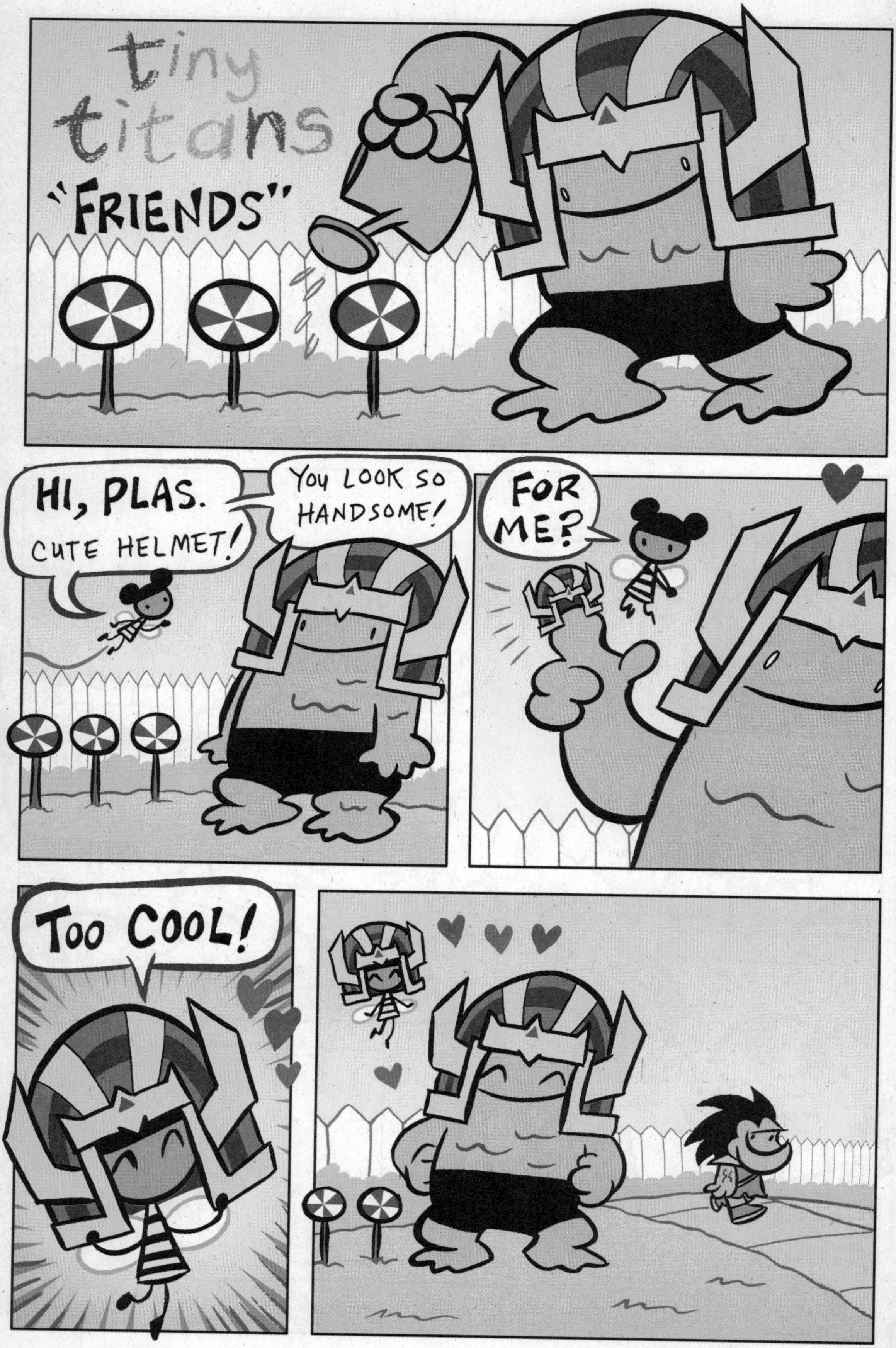
tiny titans
"FRIENDS"
HI, PLAS. CUTE HELMET!
YOU LOOK SO HANDSOME!
FOR ME?
TOO COOL!

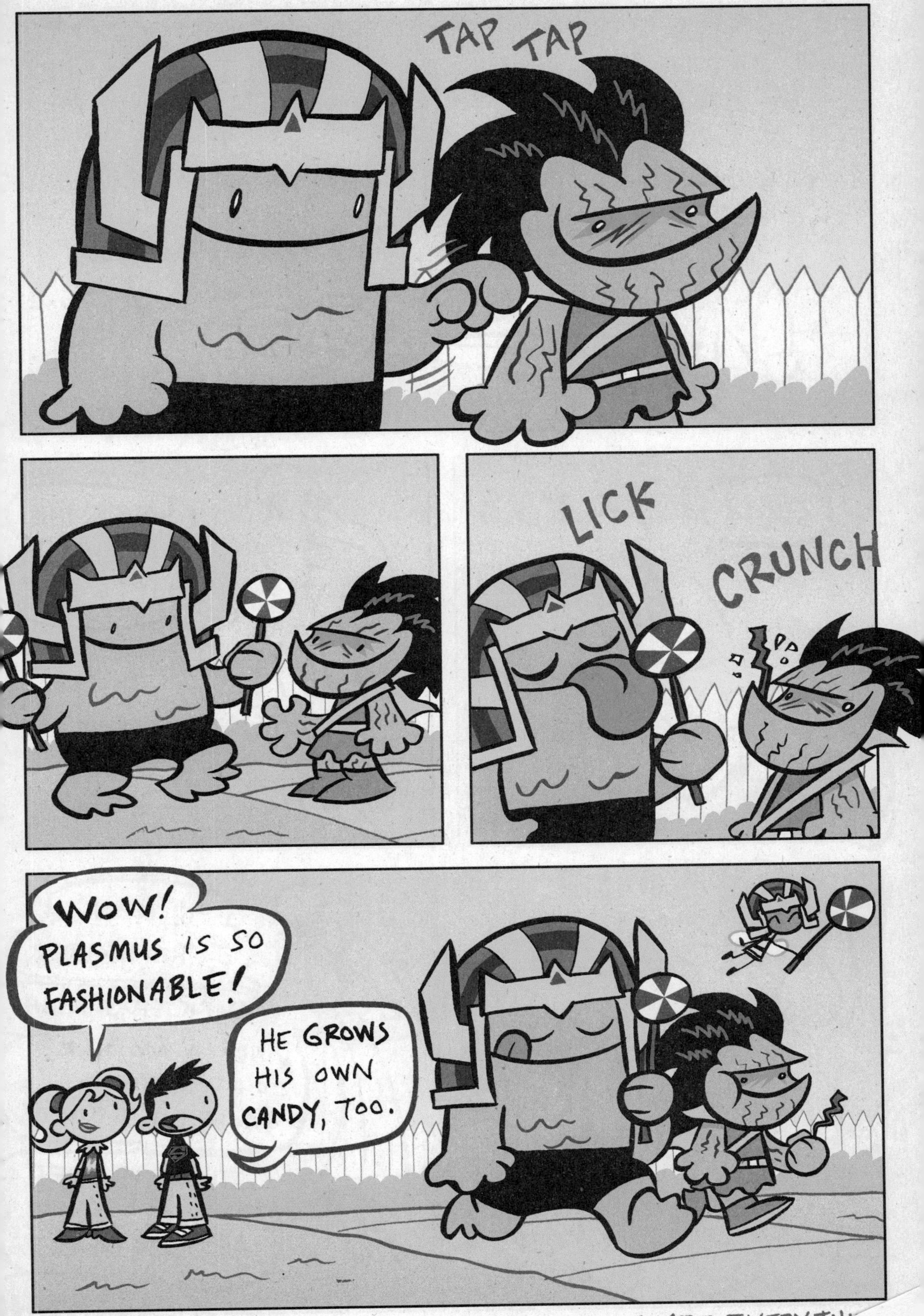
TAP TAP
LICK
CRUNCH
WOW! PLASMUS IS SO FASHIONABLE!
HE GROWS HIS OWN CANDY, TOO.

—SHARE EVERYTHI

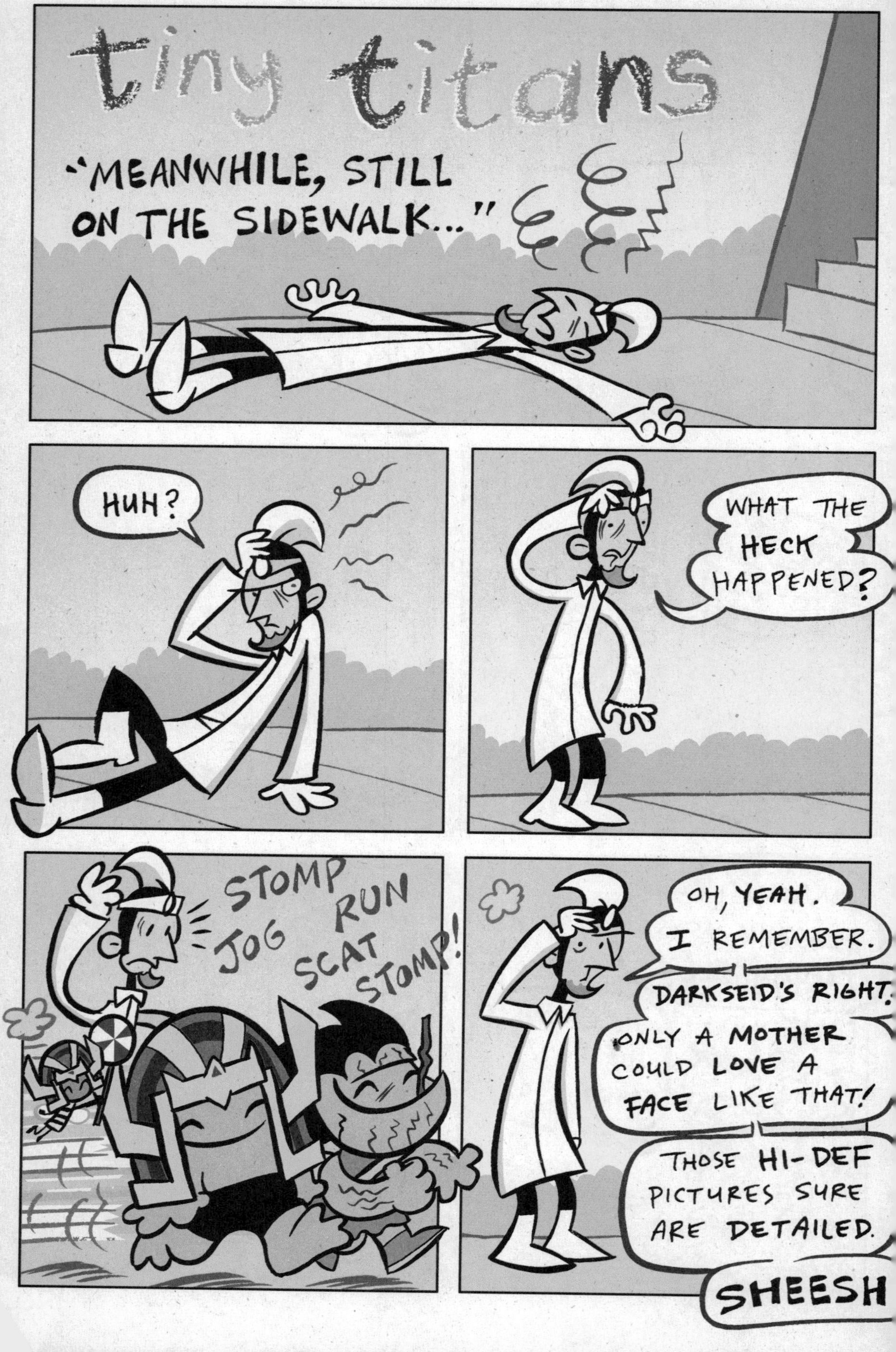
tiny titans
"MEANWHILE, STILL ON THE SIDEWALK..."
HUH?
WHAT THE HECK HAPPENED?
STOMP
RUN
JOG
SCAT
STOMP!
OH, YEAH. I REMEMBER.
DARKSEID'S RIGHT.
ONLY A MOTHER COULD LOVE A FACE LIKE THAT!
THOSE HI-DEF PICTURES SURE ARE DETAILED.
SHEESH

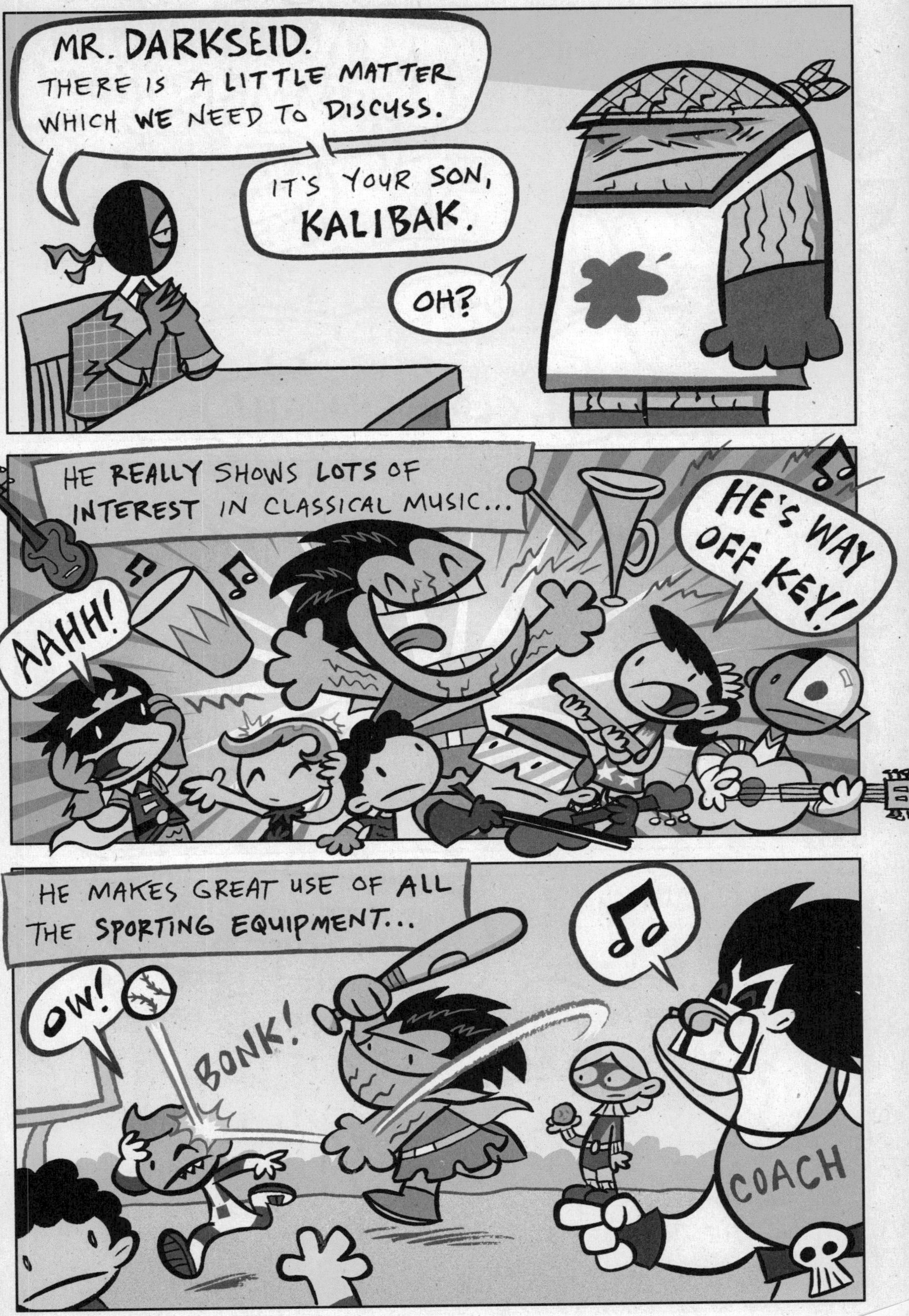
MR. DARKSEID.
THERE IS A LITTLE MATTER WHICH WE NEED TO DISCUSS.
IT'S YOUR SON, KALIBAK.
OH?
HE REALLY SHOWS LOTS OF INTEREST IN CLASSICAL MUSIC...
AAHH!
HE'S WAY OFF KEY!
HE MAKES GREAT USE OF ALL THE SPORTING EQUIPMENT...
OW!
BONK!
COACH

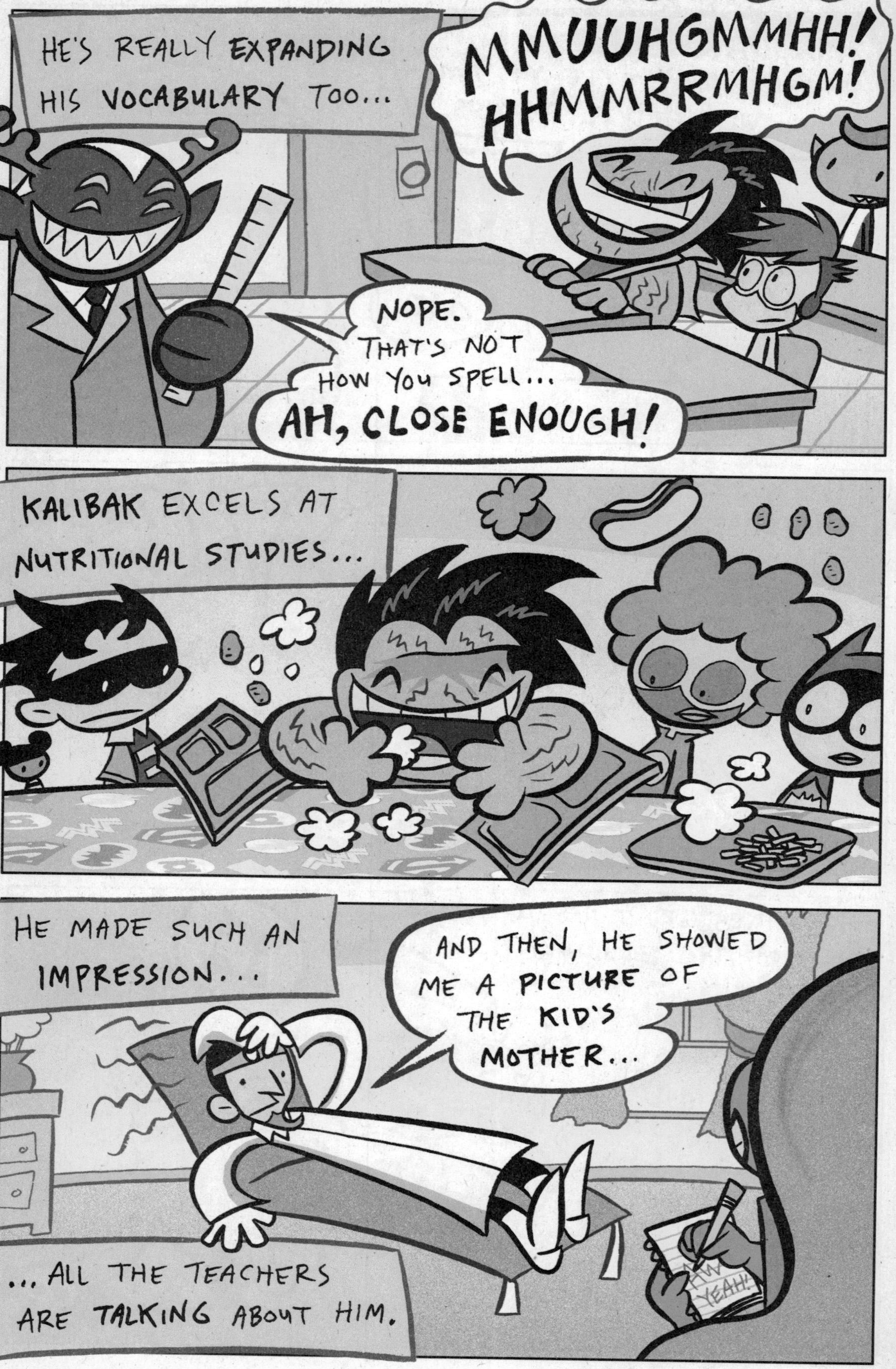
HE'S REALLY EXPANDING HIS VOCABULARY TOO...
MMUUHGMMHH! HHMMRRMHGM!
NOPE. THAT'S NOT HOW YOU SPELL... AH, CLOSE ENOUGH!
KALIBAK EXCELS AT NUTRITIONAL STUDIES...
HE MADE SUCH AN IMPRESSION...
AND THEN, HE SHOWED ME A PICTURE OF THE KID'S MOTHER...
AW YEAH!
...ALL THE TEACHERS ARE TALKING ABOUT HIM.

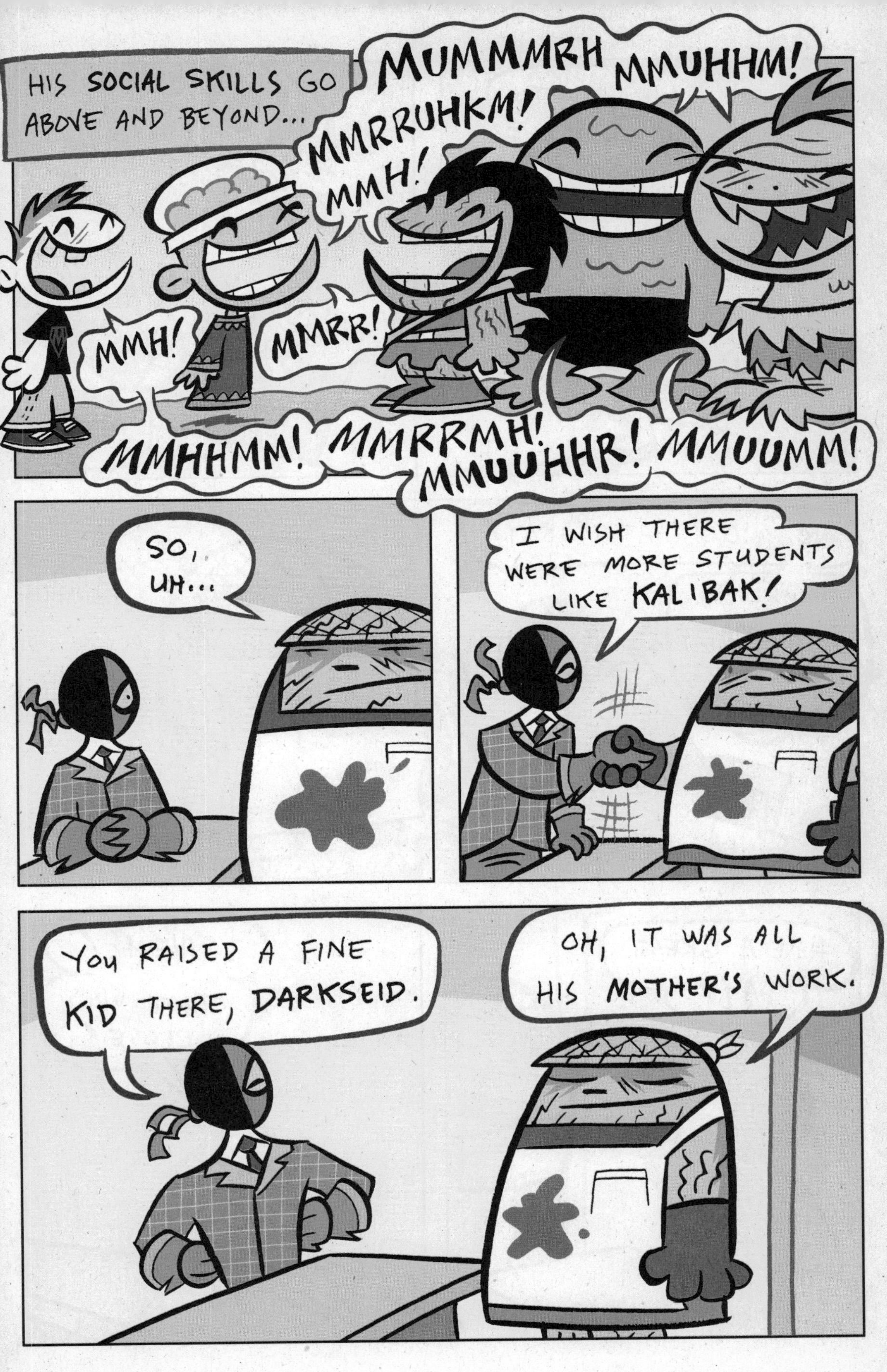
HIS SOCIAL SKILLS GO ABOVE AND BEYOND...
MUMMMRH MMUHHM!
MMRRUHKM! MMH!
MMH!
MMRR!
MMHHMM! MMRRMH! MMUUHHR! MMUUMM!
SO, UH...
I WISH THERE WERE MORE STUDENTS LIKE KALIBAK!
YOU RAISED A FINE KID THERE, DARKSEID.
OH, IT WAS ALL HIS MOTHER'S WORK.

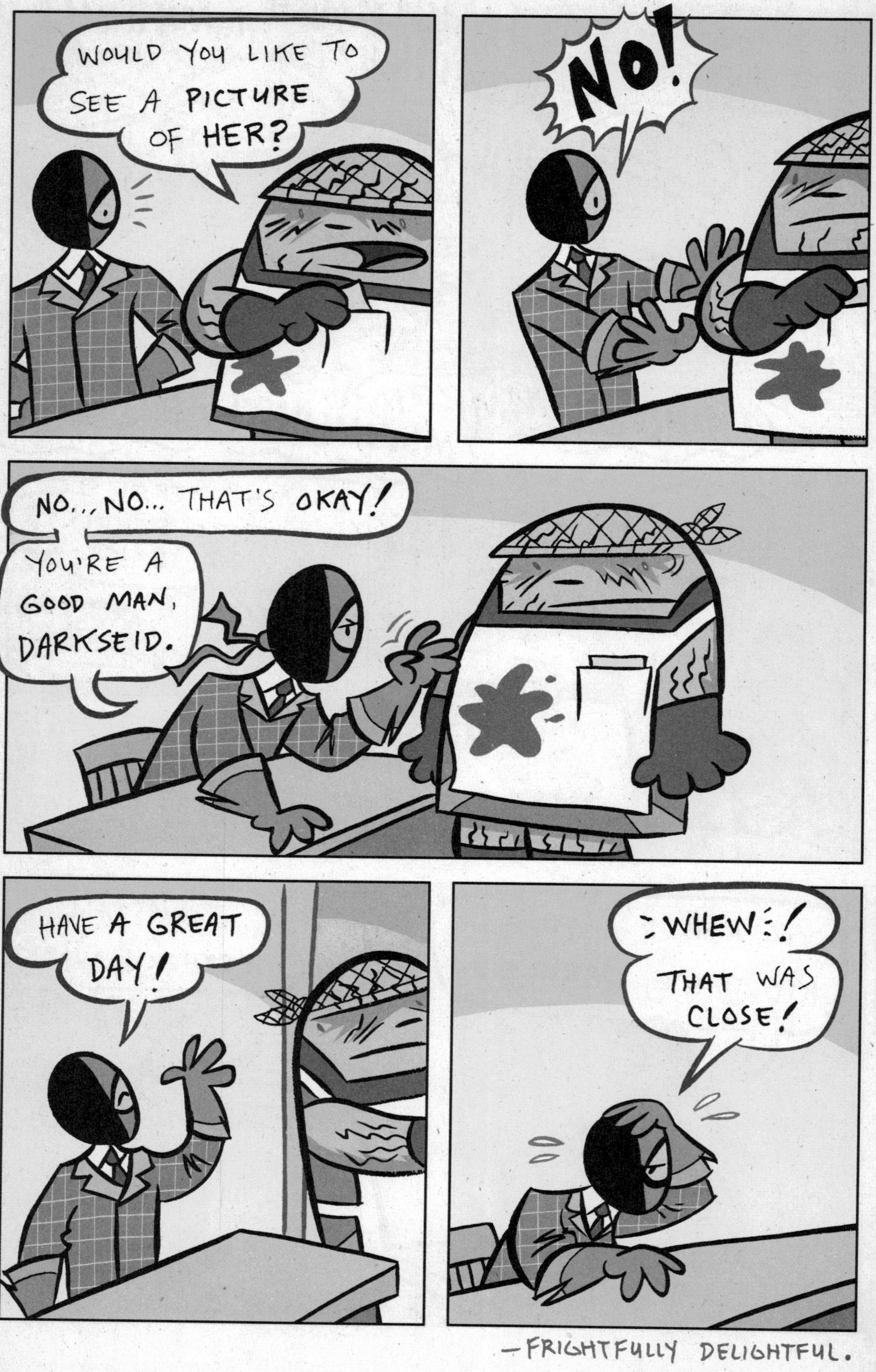
WOULD YOU LIKE TO SEE A PICTURE OF HER?
NO!
NO..., NO... THAT'S OKAY!
YOU'RE A GOOD MAN, DARKSEID.
HAVE A GREAT DAY!
WHEW!
THAT WAS CLOSE!

—FRIGHTFULLY DELIGHTFUL.

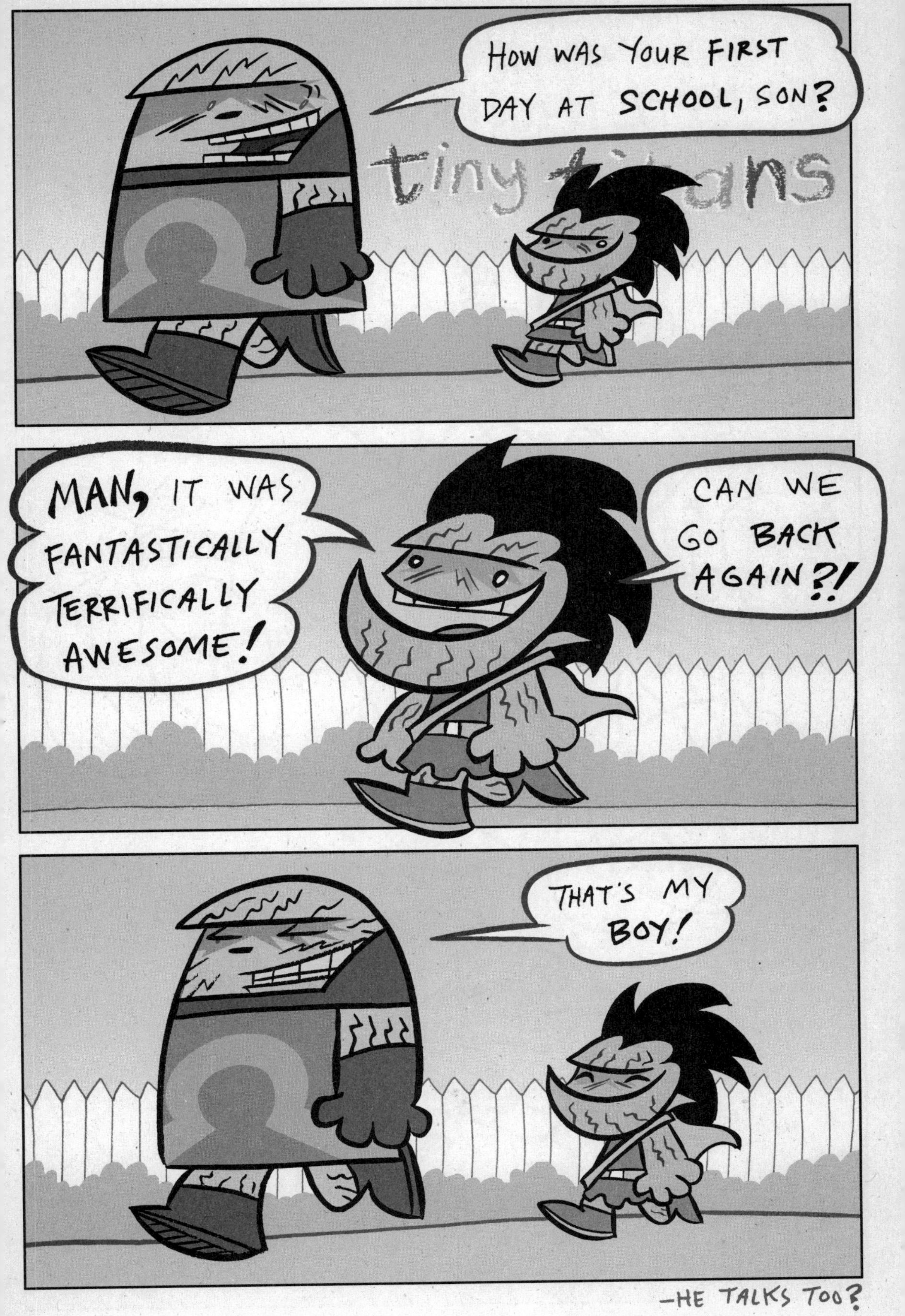
HOW WAS YOUR FIRST DAY AT SCHOOL, SON?
MAN, IT WAS FANTASTICALLY TERRIFICALLY AWESOME!
CAN WE GO BACK AGAIN?!
THAT'S MY BOY!

—HE TALKS TOO?

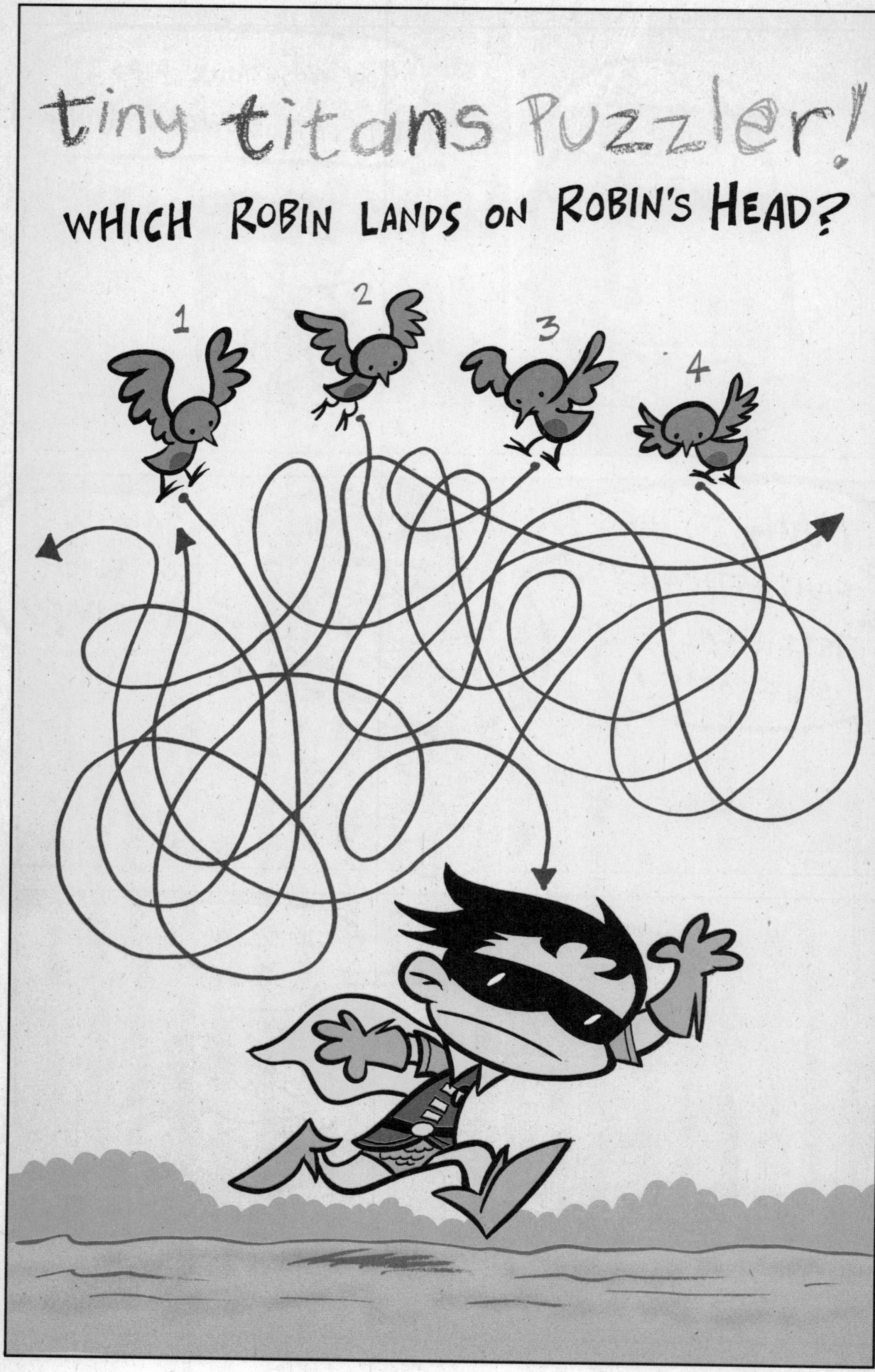
tiny titans Puzzler!
WHICH ROBIN LANDS ON ROBIN'S HEAD?
1
2
3
4

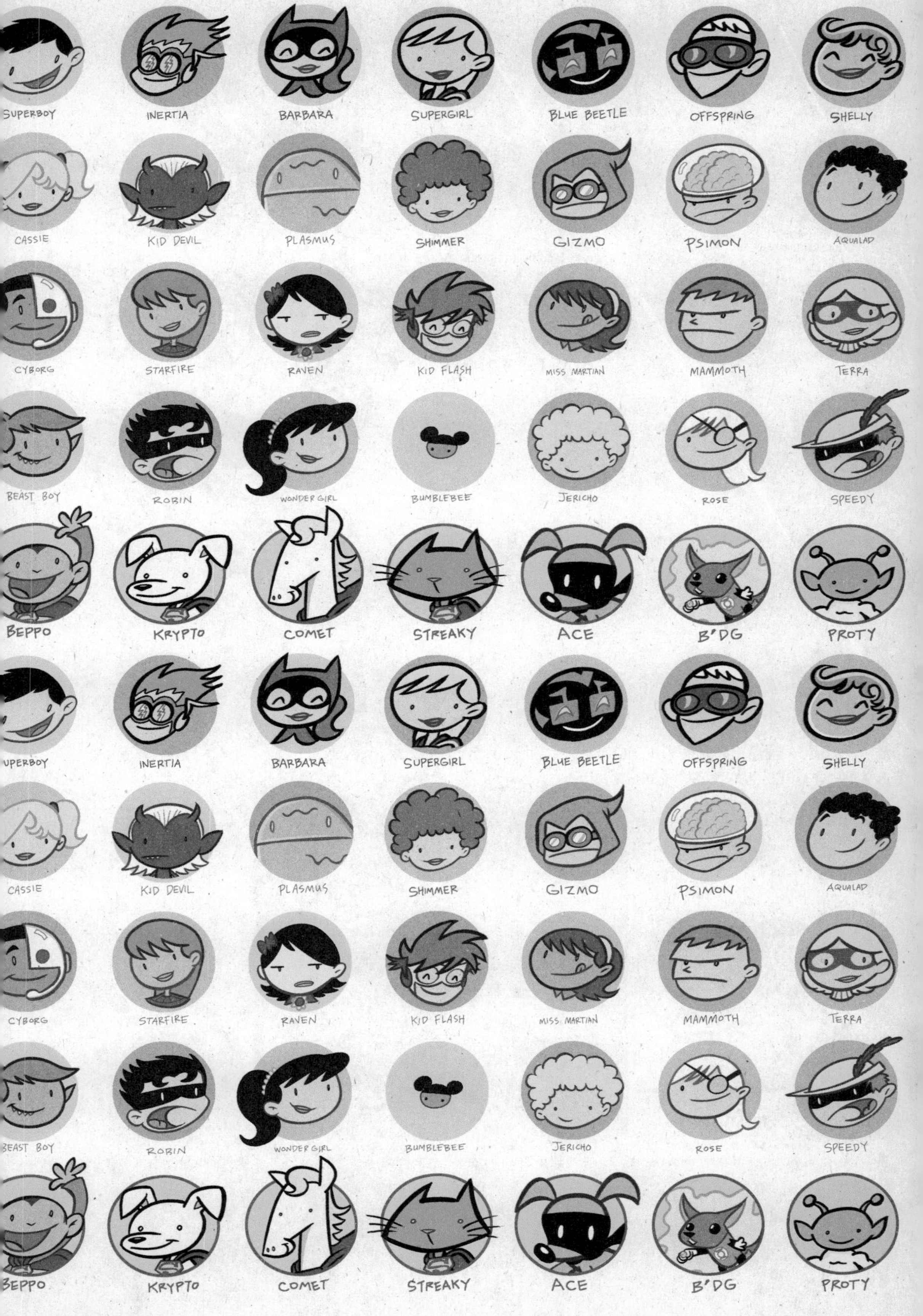
SUPERBOY
INERTIA
BARBARA
SUPERGIRL
BLUE BEETLE
OFFSPRING
SHELLY
CASSIE
KID DEVIL
PLASMUS
SHIMMER
GIZMO
PSIMON
AQUALAD
CYBORG
STARFIRE
RAVEN
KID FLASH
MISS MARTIAN
MAMMOTH
TERRA
BEAST BOY
ROBIN
WONDER GIRL
BUMBLEBEE
JERICHO
ROSE
SPEEDY
BEPPO
KRYPTO
COMET
STREAKY
ACE
B'DG
PROTY
UPERBOY
INERTIA
BARBARA
SUPERGIRL
BLUE BEETLE
OFFSPRING
SHELLY
CASSIE
KID DEVIL
PLASMUS
SHIMMER
GIZMO
PSIMON
AQUALAD
CYBORG
STARFIRE
RAVEN
KID FLASH
MISS MARTIAN
MAMMOTH
TERRA
EAST BOY
ROBIN
WONDER GIRL
BUMBLEBEE
JERICHO
ROSE
SPEEDY
EPPO
KRYPTO
COMET
STREAKY
ACE
B'DG
PROTY

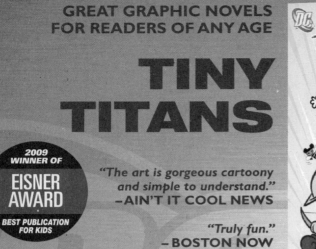